I JUST
HITCHED IN
from THE COAST

The Ed McClanahan Reader

I JUST

HITCHED

IN from

THE COAST

Edited by Tom Marksbury

COUNTERPOINT

BERKELEY

The author wishes especially to acknowledge his friend and colleague
Tom Marksbury for his invaluable help in selecting and editing the
contents of this book.

Portions of this book previously appeared, some in different form, in *Ace
Weekly, Open 24 Hours, Place Magazine, Stanford Short Stories 1964, Pine
Mountain Sand and Gravel, Esquire, Playboy, Kentucky Monthly, Louisville
Magazine, New Madrid Review, The Last Supplement to the Whole Earth
Catalog, Wild Duck Review, The Journal of Kentucky Studies, Conjunctions*,
and *Spit in the Ocean #7*. "Fondelle" was originally published in 2002 in a
hand-set, letterpress edition by Larkspur Press of Monterey, Kentucky. A
number of the stories in this collection also appeared in *O the Clear Moment*
(Counterpoint, 2008), *My Vita, If You Will* (Counterpoint, 1998), *A Congress
of Wonders* (Counterpoint, 1996) and *Famous People I Have Known* (Farrar,
Straus and Giroux, 1985; reprinted by Gnomon Press in 1997, and by the
University Press of Kentucky in 2003).

Library of Congress Cataloging-in-Publication Data is available.
ISBN: 978-1-58243-758-3

Cover design by Debbie Berne
Interior design by David Bullen
Printed in the United States of America

COUNTERPOINT
2560 Ninth Street, Suite 318
Berkeley, CA 94710
www.counterpointpress.com

for Hildeka, keeper of the light

CONTENTS

"If any part of the following mixture of truth and fiction strikes the reader as unconvincing, he has my permission to disregard it. I would be content to stick to the facts if there were any."

William Maxwell

I JUST HITCHED IN from THE COAST

FONDELLE
or: THE WHORE WITH A HEART OF GOLD

"But I was one and twenty,
no use to talk to me."
Housman

In 1954, the summer before my senior year in college (at Miami University—the one in Ohio, alas), my dad, a small-time Maysville, Kentucky, businessman with pretty good contacts amongst the lower political life-forms that grace our benighted state, somehow gathered up all his chits at once and used them to prevail upon our congressman, one Rep. Bates, to arrange a summertime job for me on a road crew in Yosemite National Park, at the other end of the world in California. Although I'd gone to Europe on a student tour the previous summer, this would be, literally, the first time I'd been west of Paducah.

What a summer! I lived in a tent cabin (a tent with a wooden frame and floor) beneath the great ponderosa pines and Douglas firs of Yosemite Valley, within sight of the majesty of El Capitan and within earshot of the roar of Bridal Veil Falls. I earned the amazing sum of two dollars and seventy-five cents an hour—that would've covered, say, a carton of smokes, three beers, and maybe a Twinkie or two—mostly for feeding a cement mixer. (I still remember the recipe: eighteen shovels gravel, nine shovels sand, one ninety-four-pound bag Portland cement, two buckets water; mix four additional minutes; pour; repeat; repeat; repeat . . . a magic elixir; it made me both strong and rich that summer.) From my post by the cement mixer, while we were building a curb around the Government Center, I once saw

Hailie Selassie, the emperor of Ethiopia, who was touring the park with the Secretary of the Interior. My crew chief caught me gawking and threatened to transfer my sorry ass to the garbage detail.

And is anybody else old enough to remember that ancient photo in the sixth-grade geography books of the 2,000-year-old giant sequoia with the tunnel through its trunk, and a 1940 Buick convertible passing through with room to spare? Well, that summer I helped build a low stone wall right up to the mouth of that tunnel. I thought I'd left my mark upon the ages; my wall, I figured, would last at least as long as the tree, maybe another thousand years or so. But the tree came down in a terrible windstorm in 1969, and my little wall came down with it. There's probably a lesson in there somewhere on the subject of mortality—but I don't want to think about it.

During my junior year back at Miami, I had somehow contrived to get myself romantically entangled with a young lady I'll call Betsy, from up Youngstown way. She was a sweet, pretty little thing, was my Betsy, but something of a clinging vine; indeed, I must admit that it was her unprecedented enthusiasm for my physical person that had beguiled me in the first place. On the Miami campus, we'd been as inseparable as an oyster and its shell—and by the end of spring semester the oyster had begun to feel ever so slightly claustrophobic. Nonetheless, before we tore our symbiotic selves asunder for the coming summer, Betsy and I had declared ourselves "engaged to be engaged" and had received congratulations from several other bivalvular couples in our social set.

So even in Yosemite, a continent away from Youngstown, I was . . . committed. Shrouded in the mist of Bridal Veil Falls, I dutifully posted Betsy's hand-tinted glamour photo above my bunk in the tent and endeavored to compose myself for a looming eternity of wedded bliss.

However, it is written (which I know because I wrote it myself), we must never presume upon the cosmos. For example, consider this: When I arrived in the employees' village in Yosemite Valley to claim my place in tent cabin no. 6, I discovered that the previous occupant of my bunk had left on the floor beneath it a stack of dog-eared twenty-five-cent paperback westerns and Rex Stout mysteries. But among them, improbably enough, was a first novel by a very fine writer named Bernard Malamud—a sexy, adult tale called *The Natural* about, of all things, major league baseball.

The Natural was unlike anything I'd ever read—a very far remove indeed from the John R. Tunis sports novels of my adolescence—and I read it over and over that summer, and even allowed myself to imagine that someday I too might write such a book. But how could I have known then that only four years later, when I landed my first teaching job as a freshman comp instructor at a college in Oregon, Bernard Malamud would be one of my new colleagues and would soon become my friend as well? Or that, after only twenty-five more years, I would publish—you guessed it—my own sexy, adult (well, sort of adult) first novel, which would be called, not altogether coincidentally, *The Natural Man*, and would be about, of all things, high school basketball.

Speaking of colleagues, my fellow inmates in our little tent cabin ensquatment were an eclectic lot. There were probably thirty-five or forty of us, all male of course, living four to a tent; we ate our meals in common in a central mess hall with long, narrow tables like in boot camp or a prison, so we got to know each other pretty quickly. Perhaps as many as a third of us were college students, mostly from San Francisco and the Bay Area; the rest were relatively grizzled older guys, a raggedy-assed assortment of road-weary drifters and unskilled day laborers and farmhands up from the Central Valley between harvest seasons.

Although we all made the same egalitarian two dollars and seventy-five cents an hour, there was a sort of pecking order among us, based on job description: My outfit, the road crew, was the elite because we sometimes got to ride around in trucks up in the high country, looking for potholes, or even down in the Valley amongst the tourists, looking for girls. Next came the garbage crew, who also got to ride around in trucks, although they had to share the ride with stink and flies and maggots. After them came the guys who worked in the stables, tending to and cleaning up after the park rangers' horses (they got the stink and flies and maggots, but without the ride), and then the trail crew, who had to disappear into the wilderness for days at a time and always came back aflame with poison oak.

At the bottom was the idiot-stick crew, a handful of resuscitated winos whose intellects had perhaps been compromised by their lifestyle (they patrolled the park campgrounds wielding sawed-off broomsticks with a nail in the business end, spearing bits of flotsam cast off by the tourists). The most exalted member of the latter crew was a weird old bird named Mel, who had fashioned, out of a piece of redwood and two horseshoes, a handsome rack for his idiot stick and mounted it above his bunk, where it probably gave him more comfort than that tarted-up photo of Betsy was bringing me of late.

The thing is, you see, I was having much too good a time out there in California, and the affectionate Betsy had lately taken to looking down upon me with the merest hint of disapproval behind her painted smile. For my life that summer wasn't all potholes and cement mixers, no indeed—because the tourist campgrounds abounded with roving bevies of predatory teenage girls bored to tears after a few days of camping out with Mom and Dad and that pesky little brother and fairly spoiling for cool college guys to try their wiles upon.

Accordingly, almost every evening our little troop of cool college guys would hoof it over to Camp Curry to let our prepossessing selves be seen. Our rate of success was indifferent at best, yet enough of my evenings culminated in lip-locks on moonlit park benches that, after a month or so, Betsy was positively glowering. Her picture, thus enhanced, soon found its way back into the suitcase beneath my bunk and was replaced by a photo I'd clipped from that rascally new magazine *Playboy*, depicting Jayne Mansfield popping most gratifyingly out of her décolletage at some Hollywood dinner party, while Sophia Loren, seated next to her, looked on askance. I still wrote Betsy once a week, expressing my devotion, and hoped she didn't suspect that I missed the '51 Chevy Bel Air I'd left back home in Maysville a good deal more than I was missing her.

The reason I had flown to California, instead of driving the Bel Air, was that temporary employees weren't allowed to keep their cars inside the park, so I had assumed that I'd be better off without it—and besides, part of the romance of the whole enterprise was my plan to hitchhike home at the summer's end, one last hallelujah-I'm-a-bum adventure before the waiting tentacles of the vine-covered cottage embraced me.

But several of my new buddies, I found, had brought their cars anyhow and left them a few miles down the road in the little town of El Portal, just outside the western entrance to the park. Now and then, one of them would hitch out to El Portal and get his wheels, so we could buy beer and drive around the park and try to pick up girls. I was always included on these excursions, not because I was much help in the picking up of girls, but because (as the result of an embarrassing little anomaly in my educational history which we needn't go into here) I was a year older than most of my peers—old enough, that is, to buy the beer, strange, exotic West Coast brands, Burgermeister and Olympia and Acme, names so intoxicating that they made me tipsy just to ask for them in the liquor store. Back home, we favored a Cincinnati brew called Hudepohl, which we delighted in calling Pooty Hole. It would not have done to order a Pooty Hole in California.

One weekend four or five of my new friends and I (no girls) piled into somebody's car and went all the way to Reno, where I lost two weeks' pay at the blackjack table. Another weekend, a couple of pals from Oakland named Jay and Tom took me home with them; we went to San Francisco and rode the roller-coaster in Luna Park, and saw an Yma Sumac movie, and the next day we sailed under the Golden Gate Bridge in Jay's dad's boat, and I fell in love, ever so briefly, with Jay's exquisite older sister and—more permanently, say forever and ever—with San Francisco.

Among my buds from the garbage crew was a kid named Dave, a University of Texas student from Houston who had one of those cars in El Portal and would be driving home in late August. And Dave had a proposition for me: If I'd kick in for gas and help with the driving—and buy the beer—he'd take me all the way to Houston. Now despite my sketchy understanding of western geography, I had a pretty good idea of where Texas is located, but I had to look at a map to see where on Earth—where, that is, in Texas— Houston might be. And when I realized that it happens to be situated not all that far west of New Orleans, a port of call that would definitely add oodles of panache to my hitchhiking itinerary, I signed on then and there. We'd angle down through Nevada and Arizona and New Mexico to El Paso where, Dave proposed, we could cross the Rio Grande into Mexico—the clincher, if I'd needed one—for a little well-deserved R&R (Dave was a military brat) in the fleshpots of Juarez before we headed east for Houston, and the leading edge of the real world. Someday, I told myself, when I got around to launching my career as a celebrated freelance writer, I just might sit down before my Underwood in that vine-covered cottage, authorial pipe jutting from my authorial jaw, and write about this trip.

Over the course of the summer I'd managed to amass a tidy little fortune: more than three hundred bucks in cold cash. Before Dave and I left Yosemite, I pocketed fifty of it to cover travel expenses and stashed the rest in my suitcase, under Betsy's watchful eye, for the diamond engagement ring I'd promised to buy her in the fall.

Needless to say, I went back to the well a few times—more than a few—during the trip. By the time we got to Vegas, I had already discovered, in innumerable little wayside Nevada beer joints, the allure of nickel slot machines, which, nickel by nickel, depleted my capital most amazingly. In Vegas, not wanting to appear a piker, I moved on to the dime—and at last the quarter—slots, and before I knew it, I was dipping into my cash reserves again while Betsy scowled and gnashed her teeth. In El Paso, in preparation for that little foray south of the border, I was obliged to go mano-a-mano with her for another withdrawal, and (international travel having proved broadening but expensive) for yet another afterward. This time, half afraid that she might bite my hand, I snatched the cash like a starving man stealing cheese from a rat trap.

Two days later, around one o'clock on a blazing August afternoon, Dave deposited me on a sun-baked stretch of highway at the eastern city limits of Houston and left me sitting on my upended suitcase with my thumb out. At five-thirty I was still sitting there, gnawing on a Baby Ruth, my poor thumb worn to a mere nub of its former self, as the rush-hour traffic streamed past, heedless and indifferent, when a well-fed Pentecostal preacher and his wife in a tiny, decrepit Henry J took pity on me and offered me a ride to Beaumont, a whole seventy-five miles down the road. Gratefully, I climbed in. The backseat was as hard as a tombstone and as cramped as a French water closet, and the Henry J's top speed, flat out, was around thirty-five miles an hour, and the Reverend and Mrs. Quinton Hoakem, having discovered that I was a college student and surmised (quite correctly, as it happened) that I was therefore a godless sinner, grimly proselytized and sermonized me every foot of the way.

Threatening to pray assiduously for my safe passage, they dropped me off around eight-thirty in the evening on the eastern outskirts of Beaumont. Reverend Hoakem was obliged to get out of the car in order to free me from his backseat. I climbed out after him and found myself on a raised two-lane blacktop with a dismal-looking swamp on either side, near a road sign that cheerfully informed me that I was still two hundred and sixty-one miles from New Orleans. The landscape all around us, treeless but for blighted stobs, was relentlessly flat, relieved only by tiny factories on the distant horizon belching great oily clouds of toxic fumes. The air was sultry and stifling, mephitic with swamp gas, ominously unwholesome, and swarms of mosquitoes as big as horseflies were rising from the swamp, which no doubt teemed with gators and snakes.

"Boy!" I marveled aloud as Reverend Hoakem wedged himself back into the little car. "It sure is . . . *flat* around here!"

"My son," quoth the portly divine, looking up at me from his seat behind the wheel, "she's as flat as a plate of piss."

The Reverend hooked a U-turn, and the Henry J pottered back down the empty highway toward Beaumont into the setting sun. Glumly, I planted my suitcase on its end beside the road and sat down on it. Before the Hoakems were out of sight, I had joined them in prayer—though they were praying for my immortal soul, whereas I was just praying for a goddamn ride.

And lo, my prayers—though not the Hoakems'—were answered almost instantly. For I hadn't sat there more than three minutes when hurtling up the highway out of Beaumont came, praise His dear name, a car!

I leapt to my feet, thrust out my well-worn thumb, pasted a look of mingled hope, desperation, and old-college-try on my malleable young mug and, to my measureless delight, the car slowed, then skidded to a stop a few yards beyond me. And not just any car either; no dinky little four-horse Henry J this time, but an Olds 88 two-door hardtop, new as daybreak, cherry-red and white with whitewalls and fender-skirts and more chrome than a mobster's casket, and the windows opened all the way back to cool the ride, verily a cream puff, a heaven-sent dreamboat. As I grabbed my suitcase and hurried toward it, a balding, one-armed gent in a Hawaiian shirt stepped out on the passenger side.

"Hop in, Slick," he said amiably, holding the door open with the only hand he had, the right, which also held a can of beer.

Ecstatic, I heaved my suitcase into the backseat and climbed in after it, ready to go wherever this deus ex machina would take me. While I got in, the one-armed man, holding his beer telephone-style between his jaw and his shoulder, availed himself of the opportunity to step to the roadside and take a leak, which allowed me a moment to size up my new circumstances.

The car's only other occupant was a redheaded woman at the wheel, a real looker, an eyeful, I noted, despite (or maybe to some extent because of) rhinestone-studded cat's-eye shades and a prodigious quantity of make-up. To protect her flaming auburn coif from the wind, she wore a green scarf tied at the back of her neck, a style that for whatever reason reminded me of Susan Hayward, who to my post-teenage libido represented the very pinnacle of ambition. She had the road-weary but still dangerous look of a woman who had seen a lot . . . and had perhaps been seen a good deal as well—in short, a regular floozy, as my mom (and your mom) would've said.

Just now the Regular Floozy was impatiently tapping the accelerator and drumming her ruby-red fingernails on the horn-ring and darting menacing sidelong glances at her traveling companion, who, circumstanced as he was in the matter of available digits, was apparently having trouble buttoning up.

"F'crissakes, Chick!" she snapped, racing the motor. "Hurry up and put it away, will ya!"

Chick, still fumbling at his fly, obediently crept back into the car. "Aw now, Fondelle, baby, you know I—" he began, but the lady thus denominated slammed the accelerator to the floor and scratched off, fishtailing up the road while he was still trying to close the car door.

That accomplished, Chick turned to me with a sheepish grin. "Fondelle's in a big hurry, see. 'Cause her and me is headed to New Orleans to get married. She can't hardly wait," he chortled. "Can you, baby?"

"That's right," Fondelle said, through clenched teeth. "I can't wait. Hardly." She viciously punched in the cigarette lighter, fished a Pall Mall from the purse on the seat beside her, and fired it up. "Where you headed, boy?" she flung back at me over her shoulder, the words, accompanied by a streaming plume of cigarette smoke, riding the blessed cool air rushing in through the windows.

"WELL, ACTUALLY," I shouted into the wind, "I WAS KIND OF GOING TO NEW ORLEANS MYSELF, MA'AM. SEE, I—"

"You're a lucky boy, then," she said. And those were the last words she addressed to me for the ensuing hundred miles.

But Chick proved much more communicative. "Chick Brewster is my name," he said, extending his hand to me over the back of the seat, "and Arbuckle, Oklahoma, is my station. Now Fondelle here," he added proudly, "she's from New York City, New York!"

Trying hard to forget Chick's recent difficulties in responding to that call of nature, I reluctantly shook his hand—and as I did, realizing that he was waiting for me to complete the round of introductions, I heard myself whoop, to my own utter astonishment, at the top of my wind-blown voice:

"HOWDY! I'M . . . STERLING PRIEST!"

It was the name I had decided back in high school would be my nom de plume if I ever managed to become a writer. But why I chose to haul it out that night for Chick and Fondelle—for the first and only time in all my life, before or since—remains a perfect mystery to me even now, after almost fifty years. I was pretty sure that when I said the name I saw, in the darkening rearview mirror as we sped along, the shadow of a knowing smirk cross Fondelle's face.

"So, Squirrelly," Chick inquired, pausing to take a long pull at his beer, "are you a married man?"

Me? A married man? "NO!" I shouted. Immediately, Betsy's image rose up out of the suitcase on the seat beside me like a genie from a bottle, grim and scowling. "BUT I'M ENGAGED!" I added hastily, and Betsy vanished as swiftly as she'd come.

"Well, that's good, Squirrelly, that's good," Chick assured me, leaning intimately over the back of his seat. ("Sterling," I objected feebly, but Chick didn't seem to notice.) "Me and Fondelle has been engaged since day before yesterday ourself! This little lady is gonna set Arbuckle afire, buddy-ro!" I declared, as assertively as I could, that I didn't doubt it for a minute. "Fondelle, doll baby," Chick said, "lemme show Squirrelly that newspaper." Fondelle shrugged her indifference to the proposition, and Chick passed me a well-worn clipping of a grainy photo from a New York tabloid, datelined about a year earlier, of four people, three men and a woman, gathered over drinks around a table in what appeared, judging by the potted palm trees and the scantily clad cigarette girl in the background, to be a swanky nightclub. I recognized the gents right away: Leo Durocher, Walter Winchell, and Jack Dempsey. The woman—a real eyeful—was intriguingly familiar too, but I had to look twice before it came to me that she was, in absolute fact, Fondelle.

BUSMAN'S HOLIDAY read the caption. "Prominent restaurateur and former heavyweight champ Jack Dempsey and his date Manhattan showgirl Fondelle Fontaine share a table at the Stork Club with Dodger manager Leo Durocher and columnist Walter Winchell."

"Gosh!" I cried, upwind. "Jack Dempsey!"

Chick probably hadn't heard me, but he caught my drift. "Ain't she a pip!" he exulted. "Ain't she a goddamn pistol!" He drained the last of his beer, pitched the empty out the window, and, reaching somewhere beneath his seat, came up with a full pint of hundred-proof Wild Turkey. He clamped the bottle between his knees, popped the cork with his solitary thumb, took a slug, and turned to offer it to me—but Fondelle quickly put the quietus on my hopes by smacking his hand and observing that one shit-faced drunk in the car at a time was as many as she could stand.

Maybe even one more than she could stand. It was beginning to occur to me, dimly, that the reason Fondelle had picked me up in the first place was that, after three long days of prenuptial togetherness, she was sick and tired of being Chick's only audience; maybe she still had to hear him, but at least she didn't have to listen to him. From here on, that would be my job—which meant that I'd need to stay upright and vaguely sentient (hence no Wild Turkey) at least as long as Chick did.

Chick proved an indefatigable if not wonderfully scintillating conversationalist, so all I had to do, really, was settle back in my seat and holler an occasional "REALLY!" or "GOSH!" or "IZZAT SO?" and otherwise let him carry the load, while Fondelle drove and smoked and cracked her gum and listened to loud, scratchy pop music on the radio.

Over the next couple of hours, as night fell and we plunged on through the black Louisiana swamplands, I learned that Chick was the Standard Oil distributor in Arbuckle, county seat of Trench County and home of the World's Largest Hog-Ring Factory (I made a feeble attempt at interjecting here the equally interesting fact that Maysville, *my* hometown, boasted the World's Largest Pulley Factory, but Arbuckle had the floor and wouldn't yield), and that as a Purple Heart veteran of World War II—he lost the arm to a land mine at Anzio—yours truly Chick Brewster was much honored and highly regarded amongst your finest hoi polloi of Arbuckle, and was on a first-name basis with the absolute owner of the hog-ring factory. Wherever he went in Arbuckle, Chick asserted with a sly chuckle, folks would say, "Here comes Chickie with his Purple Heart on!" So when Chick Brewster brought his new bride home to Arbuckle—and here he laid his hand on Fondelle's shoulder in a proprietary manner, but she savagely brushed it off, as though it were some loathsome swampy thing that had flown in through the window—those fine folks were gonna treat the little lady like a goddamn queen!

"Yeah, that's me," Fondelle muttered. "The Purple Hard-On Queen of Arbuckle, Oklahoma."

But Chick was too busy talking to notice the aside. As he rattled on—and on, and on—I availed myself of the opportunity to contemplate at my leisure the happy prospect of spending a couple of exciting days in New Orleans, which according to my understanding was populated exclusively by artists and bohemians, similar to the ones I had read about in the Henry Miller novels I'd smuggled in from my week in Paris the previous summer. I was anxious to get a look at some artists and bohemians for myself, and I figured I'd better do it pretty quick because I was reasonably sure that Betsy wasn't partial to the type.

Chick had a whiney, adenoidal voice and a Fuller Brush man's way of insistently boring in on his listener, which I soon discovered (like Fondelle before me) made it almost impossible to ignore him. He had come to Dallas, he told me between snorts from the pint, for a convention of highway contractors who were about to get rich on all those new interstates the government was planning to punch through. The legislation hadn't even passed yet, but blue-ribbon commissions and congressional committees had been formed, and rumors were flying. The very first stretch would be inflicted upon the state of Oklahoma, reliable sources held, and behind the scenes the money was already flowing.

Naturally, the convention hotel had been swarming with politicians and heavy-equipment salesmen and union people and materials suppliers and small-time deal-makers like my excellent new friend Chick, who was looking for palms to grease in hopes of getting the bid to supply petroleum products to whichever outfits were to build the stretch of interstate that was sure to pass through Trench County. On the first day of the convention, he bought one congressman a two-hundred-dollar suit of clothes and another dedicated public servant a case of whiskey; the second day cost him a Harris Tweed sport coat, plus porterhouse steak dinners for a party of six contractors. It was an exshpensive way to do business, Chick acknowledged with a grand flourish of the now half-empty pint, but you gotta shpend money to make money.

That philosophy was shared by the big shpenders who'd put the convention together and were so flush with future prosperity that they'd decided to enliven the proceedings by flying in a planeload of "hostesses" from New York City—which was where Fondelle came in. Chick met her when she served him a drink while he was shooting craps—and trying hard not to win—in a hotel room with a bunch of contractors and politicians. They fell in love on the spot, Chick assured me, and the next day he proved his love by buying her the Olds 88.

"She won't even let me set behind the wheel," he giggled. "Will ya, baby? You won't even let sweet daddy dwive your widdle tar, willums, baby doll?" By this point in his narrative, Chick was getting pretty loose. Several times along the way, he'd appealed, in baby talk, to Fondelle's affectionate nature, and each time she'd replied with a monosyllabic grunt. This time, though, she had a rather more emphatic response:

"You bet your one-armed ass I won't!"

Abruptly, she wheeled the Olds into an all-night gas station and diner. It was around midnight, and we were on the outskirts of Lafayette, Louisiana. Fondelle told the attendant to fill it up and marched off to the ladies' room. Chick more or less fell out of the car, stuffed the pint into his hip pocket, and lurched away toward the gents' facility. Like Fondelle, I too was growing a little weary of Chick's loquacious company, but nature obliged me to follow him in and join him at the reverse watering trough. As before, Chick was having some difficulty dealing with the mechanics of the operation, which gave him ample opportunity to buttonhole me—figuratively speaking—for further inebrious fraternization.

"So tell me, Shquirrelly," he inquired, "you got a shoot in that shoo—s-s-suitcase of yours?"

Chick's articulation—especially in regard to the sibilants—was rapidly deteriorating (although his voice was no less annoying for that), and when he directed his question to me, the Wild Turkey fumes overwhelmed even the breath-stopping reek of the hockey-puck disinfectant discs in the urinal.

But as a matter of improbable fact, I did have a suit—a snappy little seer-sucker number, complete with a white, short-sleeved, button-down wash-and-wear shirt, and a skinny repp-stripe tie in the charcoal-and-pink combo that was all the rage that year on college campuses. I can't imagine what earthly use I'd supposed I was going to have for this getup on a road crew in Yosemite; nonetheless there it was, still stuffed away in my suitcase, exactly where it had been since I carefully packed it there last June.

Sure, I told Chick, I've got a suit. But why do you ask?

Chick wasn't tracking so good, conversation-wise, but he had a proposition in mind, and he resolutely pulled himself together and laid it on me.

Why, he said, he was thinking maybe I could stand up with him when he and Fondelle got married tomorrow. Because he didn't know nobody in New Orleans, and he didn't want some damn shtranger (which, it crossed my mind, described me to a tee) as his best man. Now Fondelle, Chick went boozily on, she had a girlfriend there, a real pretty girl named, uh, Mary, yeah, that was her name, Mary, beautiful girl, who'd be standing up with her, and after the wedding we'd go out and drink champagne and all. And who knows, maybe Mary and I—beautiful girl, Mary, just a beautiful girl, and when she got a loada me decked out in my sh-suit and all, who knows, maybe we'd hit it off and get married too, and we'd all go back to Arbuckle, and he'd set Mary and me up in a nice little house and give me a job driving one of his tank trucks because there'd be big money to be made in Arbuckle when this new intershta-interstate goes through. So tomorrow morning his people back in Oklahoma would be wiring him some cash, a thousand or two for his honeymoon, y'know, the boss's honeymoon. In the meantime, though, he was a little short because Fondelle, she was the banker in this outfit, she had charge of all the dough, heh heh, and he was a little short of pocket money. So—just till tomorrow morning, Shquirrelly, when the wire comes in—maybe I could let him have . . . twenty dollars?

By this time Chick had at last mastered the intricacies of his fly, and now he stood before me, swaying a bit unsteadily on his feet, his (only) hand extended, making that imperious little "c'mon, gimme" gesture with his thumb and fingertips, as though I owed him the twenty dollars. And simpleton that I was, temporarily under an enchantment, mesmerized by the shining image of the gorgeous, hitherto unimagined Mary and a wildly erotic future with her in Arbuckle, Oklahoma, a non-Betsy future that I hadn't even dreamed of two minutes ago, I forked it over.

We caught up with Fondelle in the diner, sitting in a booth drinking coffee and smoking impatiently. She didn't look wonderfully pleased to see us. I was famished—except for that Baby Ruth and the pack of Nabs I'd scarfed when Reverend Hoakem stopped for gas many hours ago, I hadn't eaten a bite since lunch—so I ordered two grilled cheese sandwiches and a chocolate shake. Chick asked for a cup of coffee and, as soon as the waitress delivered it and turned her back, slipped his pint out of his hip pocket, clamped it into his left armpit by means of the stump inside his shirtsleeve, deftly unscrewed the top, and added a generous dollop to his coffee.

"Jee-zus Christ," Fondelle said with palpable disgust.

"Aw, baby," Chick whined, "my stump's a-hurting me!"

"Good," she muttered through her teeth.

Chick tried a different tack. "So guess what, shweetheart, Squirrelly's gonna stand up wimme! He's got a suit an' all!"

"Whoop-de-doo," rejoiced the bride-to-be.

I longed to ask Fondelle to tell me about her sublime friend Mary, but she was clearly in no mood to discuss anything related to the forthcoming hymeneal rites. I also had a burning desire to know just what it is that a Manhattan showgirl *does* exactly, but that question didn't seem quite politic either. So I asked her instead what Jack Dempsey was really like.

"Jack's a real sweetie," she said almost wistfully, with a scornful glance at her dashing fiancé, who had collapsed, more or less insensate, in the seat beside her as if he'd sprung a leak and was slowly deflating. "Jack knows how to treat a girl."

What about Leo Durocher and Walter Winchell? I ventured to inquire.

"Horses' asses," Fondelle said without equivocation. "Two royal horses' asses."

The waitress, who serendipitously arrived just then with my order and no doubt thought Fondelle was referring to Chick and me, rolled her eyes and murmured, "I'll say" as she set my sandwiches before me.

Fondelle, clickety-clicking her alarmingly red fingernails on the tabletop, told me to eat the hell up; she wanted to get the hell on the road. Nonetheless, my questions about her illustrious connections had evidently rendered her a bit more talkative. While I was bolting my sandwiches, she volunteered that she had "worked" lots of conventions in New Orleans (I was beginning to get a better idea of what a showgirl does for a living), and that she knew her way around the city like Carter knows Little Liver Pills. She always stayed at the Monteleone, she said, which she led me to understand was the ritziest hotel in the French Quarter.

Emboldened, I asked whether she happened to know of any not-so-ritzy hotels in the neighborhood. Yeah, Fondelle said, there was a place on Canal, eight dollars a night, just around the corner from the Quarter. In fact, she added, Goldilocks here—referring to Chick, who was by now thoroughly comatose and blowing spit-bubbles with every snore—Goldilocks here would be staying there himself tonight, although he didn't know it yet.

Because she was gonna be dog-tired by the time we got to New Orleans—hell, she was dog-tired *now*—she needed her beauty sleep, and she did not have no intention whatsoever to spend another night in a wrestling match with a damned one-armed dipso.

It was just at that exact moment, as I was stuffing the last bite of my third triangular half of a grilled cheese sandwich into my mouth, that I fell utterly and irretrievably in love. Now the attentive reader may have observed that I tended, at that period of my young life, to fall in love rather readily. In addition to the omnipresent Betsy and her bevy of predecessors, there had been, in rapid succession, two or three teenage Yosemite nymphets, Jayne Mansfield (a mere dalliance), my friend Jay's lovely sister in Oakland, a couple more nymphets back in Yosemite, a dark-eyed señorita by the name of Marta in Juarez just three days ago (who, I was to discover a few days later, had presented me with a small but rapidly multiplying family of tiny migrant stowaways), and, finally, only fifteen or twenty minutes ago, Mary, the goddess who quite possibly existed only in my own fevered imagination and in the wily machinations of a one-armed, stone-drunk Standard Oil distributor from Arbuckle, Oklahoma.

Nonetheless, in love I absolutely was . . . again. Fondelle had long since put aside her shades, and she was certainly dog-tired; there was a sort of bruised look about her eyes, part weariness and part smeared mascara, that spoke to me of experience, of worldliness, of ill-usage and ruin, of commingled toughness and vulnerability. It made me think of that Rita Hayworth line "Armies have marched over me!" in *Miss Sadie Thompson*, still the sexiest line ever uttered on the screen. Fondelle was older than I'd thought, maybe thirty-five or so, but that only added a certain poignancy to her mystique. My heart welled with tenderness and desire; I would dedicate my youthful vigor to comforting her as she slipped almost imperceptibly into early middle age, coughed consumptively a few times, and expired in my arms. Afterward, I told myself as I slurped the dregs of my chocolate shake, I would carry on somehow. But first, I had to make my move.

"So, um, Fondelle," I purred, lowering my voice to its most suavay, most seductively continental tone. "Tell me, is Manhattan right *in* New York City, or is it in the suburbs?"

For the first time all evening, Fondelle cracked a smile, then she snickered, then she snorted coffee through her nose. "Hell's bells," she said, still laughing as she policed herself up with a paper napkin, "you're green as grass, kiddo!"

(I was beginning to notice, by the way, that Fondelle's inflections—"Hail's bails, yore grain as grace!"—smacked more of my own neck of the woods than of New York City. I was clearly no expert on matters Manhattan, but I could recognize an upper Ohio Valley twang when I heard one.)

Fondelle turned to Chick and punched him pretty smartly on the shoulder. "Wake up, sunbeam," she said. "Let's make like a sewer and get the shit outta here."

Together, she and I steered the mumbling, stumbling Chick out of the diner and back to the car, where Fondelle summarily confiscated the remains of the pint of Wild Turkey and ordered Chick to take my place in the backseat and sleep it off. Settling herself behind the wheel, she put the Wild Turkey on the seat between us and told me, as she wheeled the 88 back out onto the highway, that I could finish it off if I wanted. Guiltily, I glanced back at Chick, but he was already dead to the world—and anyhow, I saw when I held the jug up to the light, there was only one pretty good belt left. So as soon as Fondelle had us rolling again, I knocked it back, a double shot of Ole Liquid Plumber that went down like swallowing a hot poker. Following Chick's example, I chucked the empty out into the Louisiana night and sat back to take the evening airs.

I awoke when Fondelle pulled to a stop in front of a small Canal Street hotel—I don't recall the name, so let's call it the Metropole—and began rather abrasively admonishing Chick and me to wake the hail up and get the hail out of the car; it was two-thirty in the morning and she needed to get the hail to sleep. As we groggily disembarked, Chick whined quite piteously to the effect that he was being denied his last night of non-conjugal bliss, but Fondelle was unmoved. Nothing doing, she said; he had already drove that into the ground and broke it off. She dug a ten-dollar bill out of her purse and gave it to Chick for his hotel room and left us standing beside our suitcases in front of the seedy old Metropole, blinking in the neon glare of countless Canal Street we-never-close bars. Despite the lateness of the hour, the sidewalks were crowded with pedestrians, mostly drunken gents in fezzes—a Shriners' convention was evidently in town—many a bemused and fezz-betopped gent with his own personal Manhattan Showgirl on his arm. It was all strangely disorienting, as if I'd been suddenly dropped down into the middle of the Casbah.

"I don't hardly feel like hittin' the hay right now," Chick said when the 88's taillights had merged into the late-night Canal Street traffic. He looked off down the street where, in the middle of the next block, I could see the familiar animated sign of the eternally galloping neon Greyhound. "What say me and you run down here to the Long Dog and stow our gear in a locker, and go out and have us a little drink?"

I couldn't make it, I told him; it had been a long day, and I was bushed. Chick wasn't looking so hot himself; his Hawaiian shirt was as rumpled as a fruit salad, his face was ashen and stubbly, and his eyes, in the words of the old song, looked like two cherries in a glass of buttermilk. He promised vaguely that he'd see me tomorrow, then, and picked up his suitcase and started off down Canal Street.

"Hey, Chick!" I called after him. "What time's the wedding?"

He stopped in his tracks, hesitated for a long moment as if pondering his answer, then glanced back over his armless shoulder. "Uh, three o'clock," he said, already moving on. "Three o'clock sharp."

And there went Chickie with his Purple Heart on. Listing hard to the right, struggling to counterbalance the weight of the suitcase with the arm that wasn't there, he soldiered on down Canal, looking terribly, touchingly alone and forlorn. Sadly, that was to be the last I'd ever see of him—or, needless to say, of my twenty dollars.

But of course I didn't know that then, and thus I awoke the following morning in my tiny, stifling hotel room, filled with a powerful sense of purpose: I had to get to a dry cleaner right away, to have my seersucker suit pressed for the wedding! Ah, and for Mary!

Hastily, I washed up at the sink in my room (in the Metropole the bathrooms were, as the night clerk had told me when I checked in, "conveniently located down the hall"), got dressed, and set out with my shapeless wad of crumpled seersucker in search of an establishment that could coax it back to life. I inquired of the ancient black gentleman in the rusty-looking call-for-Phillip-Morris livery who operated the Metropole's rickety elevator (and who had been there when I checked in last night, and was still there this morning, and would be there every time I came and went for the next twenty-four hours, and for all I knew absolutely resided in the elevator, like some garrulous old raven in a relentlessly upsy-downsy cage)—and Old Bikey (as he called himself) directed me and my seersucker bolus to a Chinese laundry a few blocks down Canal.

I paused at the desk to inquire whether a one-armed party by the name of C. Brewster had checked in and was informed that no person of that description had been seen or heard of. Okay, I figured, maybe he weaseled his way into Fondelle's bed in the Monteleone after all, or had enjoyed his little drink or three and then slept it off in the Greyhound station. On the way to the laundry, I popped into the Long Dog and looked around, fruitlessly, for a snoozing Chick, and even asked a porter whether he'd seen my distinctive one-armed friend; he hadn't, the porter said, but then he was on the day shift, and the night shift had gone home a couple of hours ago. So, following Old Bikey's directions, I hoofed it on down Canal, deposited my suit at the No Tickee No Washee, and sallied forth into the French Quarter to take me a gander at some of them bohemians.

The bohos, I discovered, weren't necessarily early risers; I wandered about amongst throngs of tourists for quite a while without spotting a single one. With the impending nuptials in mind, I treated myself to a shoeshine administered by a grinning urchin whom I tipped a shiny new fifty-cent piece, doing so with a magisterial air that befit my status as best-man-to-be. Then I manfully downed a cup of chicory-laced tar-water in a sidewalk coffee shop, watched a profusely sweating one-man band's futile effort to make "When the Saints Go Marching In" fresh and scintillating, ate (against my better judgment) a fried-oyster po'boy on a park bench in Jackson Square . . . and, all the while, I kept one eye out for artistic types and the other out for Chick.

The latter sighting never happened, but I did finally come upon a guy with a beret and a goatee and an artist's smock, parked on the sidewalk on Dauphine Street with an easel before him, executing over-priced charcoal caricatures of susceptible tourists. I stood there looking over his shoulder for a few minutes, contemplating my Betsy's unalloyed delight when I returned to her with a handsome portrait of handsome Me destined to hang in some prime location in our vine-covered cottage—or, on the other hand, whether the divine Mary mightn't appreciate it even more when she and I installed the masterpiece in our little love nest out there in Arbuckle, Oklahoma. Unfortunately, the caricatures themselves were uniformly so inept, so mean, and so ugly that I couldn't quite see the efficacy of paying myself that particular homage, especially since it would've cost me twenty bucks to be thus immortalized. So I moved along.

I picked up my suit around one o'clock and, on my way back to the Metropole, peeked in at the Greyhound station one more time. No sign of Chick. At the Metropole, I inquired at the desk whether Sterling Priest had had any calls and was informed that he had not. Delivered upstairs by the ever-faithful Old Bikey, I found the bathroom down the hall available and locked myself in for a long, much-needed shower. Back in my room, I laid out my freshly pressed suit, my short-sleeved button-down shirt, my repp-stripe tie, and my newly shined cordovans, shaved my meager whiskers at the sink, slapped my callow cheeks vigorously with copious quantities of Mennen Skin Bracer, applied a whopping great glob of Wildroot Cream Oil to my unruly locks, dressed myself with infinite care, observed at length my much-improved image in the shaving mirror, and at last determined myself ready to undertake my assignment.

When I stepped onto the elevator, Bikey rolled his rheumy old eyes at me and whistled softly under his breath and said, "Whoo-ee!" These compliments cost me another fifty-cent gratuity, but they were worth every penny of it; I sauntered out of the Metropole and strolled down through the Quarter to the Monteleone (again following Old Bikey's directions) feeling every inch the quintessential Best Man.

The Monteleone's lobby, small but elegantly appointed, fairly swarmed with fezzes and showgirls. Seeing no sign of my wedding party, I peeked into the bar—it was called The Carousel—but they weren't there either. So I turned back to the lobby and located, between a potted palm and an elephant ear, an unoccupied (and, it soon developed, excruciatingly uncomfortable) Louis Quatorze chair that commanded a view of, at once, the front door, the elevator, and the entrance to The Carousel, wherein a brisk trade was transpiring even though it was only three o'clock in the afternoon.

Three-fifteen came and went and was followed, in due time, by three-thirty and three-forty-five—and still no Chick and Fondelle. Lovely ladies came and went the whole time, beauteous young things any one of whom could have been—but evidently wasn't—the Mary of my dreams, while I squirmed and sweated, much to the disadvantage of my suit, on this chair that Louis of Yore must have intended for his torture chamber. Inside The Carousel, the actual bar itself, a circular affair in the center of the room, was slowly, almost imperceptibly rotating in a clockwise direction, a strangely disagreeable phenomenon, even from afar. I couldn't help wondering if that oyster po'boy was finally checking in on me.

Along about four o'clock, a beefy, unaccommodating sort in an ill-fitting brown suit approached me and, addressing me as "Sir" in a growling, insinuating tone, inquired whether I was "expected" by a guest of the establishment. Now I had read enough cheesy detective fiction out there in my bunk in Yosemite to know that this hard-boiled party with the ugly squint was what I had learned to call a "House Dick"; so I says, Yessir, I am, heh heh, but maybe I'll just step over here to the desk and see if my party's been, um, detained. Why don't you do that, says he. Okay, says I. Okay, okay.

Under the house dick's watchful eye, I sidled up to the desk and asked the clerk to ring Miss Fontaine's room on the house phone. He consulted his guest ledger with the most perfunctory of glances, then looked down his supercilious nose and assured me that no Miss Fontaine was registered there and wondered aloud whether I might possibly have the wrong hotel.

"Surely there must be some mistake," I implored. "Fondelle Fontaine? From Manhattan? In New York City? Redhead? A real . . . a real eyeful?"

"Sonny," said the clerk, languidly closing his book, "there are probably at least a dozen ladies of that description in this hotel right this very minute."

Baffled and disheartened, I turned to slink away when suddenly the elevator doors slid open and—like the cover of one of those dog-eared Yosemite paperbacks—say, *The Case of the Purple Hard-On* by Celebrated Freelance Author Squirrelly Priest—out stepped Fondelle herself: white stiletto heels, black net hose, skin-tight black sheath dress, dangerous décolletage, the familiar cat's-eye shades, auburn hair spilling like molten copper from beneath a huge white picture hat . . .

"Hail's bails," she murmured, drawing up short when she saw me standing there amidst the potted flora of the lobby, with floozies and fezzes passing to and fro about us like butterflies and hookah-smoking caterpillars, "look what the cat drug in." Clearly, she'd forgotten that I existed.

"Fondelle!" I said. "Where's Chick?"

She glanced warily around the lobby. "He ain't *here*?"

For the longest, stupidest moment, I thought she was about to lambaste me for having failed, as best man, to deliver the groom. Then I realized that what alarmed her was exactly the opposite possibility.

No, no, I assured her, he went out drinking last night and never came back to the hotel.

Fondelle was visibly relieved. "You wait right here (*rye cheer*) a minute," she said. She turned and sashayed over to the desk where, out of earshot, she chatted briefly with the clerk, with whom she appeared to be on familiar terms. He responded, laughing and rolling his eyes; then he glanced at me, rolled his eyes again, and they both laughed. She came back and, without a word, took me by the elbow and steered me into The Carousel.

The dyspeptic house dick had posted himself like a scowling, squinting Cerberus by the door, next to a potted palm. As we walked by, Fondelle greeted him with a wave and a breezy "How ya doin', Eugene!" and he responded with a grin so huge it threatened to shatter his stony visage. "Hi'ya, Miss Fontaine!" he said warmly. At the Monteleone, Fondelle was indisputably a member of the family.

We found seats at the circular bar amongst the assembled revelers, and Fondelle asked the bartender (she called him Bob) to bring us two Sazeracs. I had no idea what a Sazerac might consist of, but the name fairly reeked of dissolution and debauchery, so I was hopeful. No telling what-all might be in it. According to my sources, you could get just about anything you wanted in New Orleans—and hadn't I seen a place called the Old Absinthe House in the French Quarter that very morning? Absinthe? It was too much to wish for.

When our drinks arrived, I made as if to pay up, but Fondelle said I should put my money away and told Bob to start a tab for her. In the backbar mirror, I saw her treat Bob to a sly but knowing wink behind her shades. He grinned and said, "Sure thing, Fondelle," and lit her Pall Mall with a dexterous flip of his Zippo.

"Don't worry about it, hon," she said when he was gone. "Bob's run many a tab for me, and I ain't paid one yet."

"So . . . where's Chick?"

"On his way home to Arbuckle," Fondelle answered with one of her expressive shrugs, "I most sincerely goddamn hope."

The Sazerac turned out to be a tea-colored potion in a tall glass. When I raised it to my lips, it gave off a faint effluvia of . . . licorice! And when, with my first cautious sip, I detected a subtle but distinct understatement of Black Jack chewing gum, my darkest suspicions were confirmed. Absinthe, sure as hell! Was Fondelle plying me with intoxicating liquors in order to lure me up to her hotel room and use me horribly? I most sincerely goddamn hoped so!

Whatever her motives, Fondelle was proving a lot more sociable than she'd been last night—and a great deal more forthcoming. Indeed, she was eagerly telling me the whole story:

When she first hooked up with Chick back in Dallas (she was saying, sounding less Manhattan and more West Virginia with every syllable), she'd thought he was actually sort of cute, y'know, for a one-armed guy. He was trying to act like a big shot, of course, she could see that; still, he was sweet and generous, spending his money like there wasn't no tomorrow and introducing her to everybody as the future Mrs. Brewster. Which at first she thought was just the usual line of bull, but then when he went and bought her that Olds 88, she told herself, *Well, hell (Wail, hail), I could do this. I could be Mrs. Chick Brewster and play canasta with the high uppity-ups* out in Arbuckle, Oklahoma. And besides, a one-armed man ought to be easier to handle than a regular one, even if he did have a Purple Heart and a Standard Oil dealership.

(The roisterous presence of all those celebratory Shriners and showgirls gathered about the bar was imposing a certain intimacy upon us; Fondelle's lovely, delicately ravaged countenance was but a heavy breath away. Trembling within, confident only that my barstool stood poised on the brink of perdition, I ventured a second sip of my Sazerac—and then a third, and eventually a fourth. The creeping rotation of the bar was faintly nauseating; I felt ever so slightly giddy, fuzzled, as though the absinthe were already going to my head. The panoramic mural of the French Quarter that lined the walls of the room crawled along, clockwise, at about the pace of a really tedious carriage ride. It was enough to make a person swear off absinthe altogether.)

But hon (Fondelle went on), the guy was so full of it! He would talk the hind leg off a dog, him and that dentist-drill voice of his. They wasn't two hours out of Dallas yesterday morning till she felt like she had met half the people in Arbuckle, and hoped to God she never had to meet the other half. Because once a person has been out on a date with Jack Dempsey, she's just not gonna be all that impressed by a hog-ring manufacturer. She didn't run off from West Virginia, Fondelle declared, just to get talked to a frazzle in the state of Oklahoma.

So when she picked me up last night, she said, I was just what the doctor ordered; with me on board for Chick to talk to, and the radio turned up loud, she could finally hear herself think. And what she mostly heard, listening to herself think, was that she did not intend to marry this one-armed dipso under no circumstances whatsoever, not in no way, shape, form, manner, or means, period, end of story. She had already been married to several dipsos and had not enjoyed it one bit. The problem was how to get shed of this one and get her ass to New Orleans without having to marry him. She would've drove off and left Chick and me in that filling station men's room, except she just hadn't been raised that way.

Any-hoo (Fondelle continued, shifting gears), by the time we got to New Orleans she had it all doped out. After she ditched us at the Metropole, she had went straight to the Monteleone—where, I might've noticed, she's well known—and parked the 88 in the hotel garage. At the front desk she asked Artie, the night clerk, for an envelope, and in the envelope she put the car keys and the title and the garage parking stub, and sealed the envelope and wrote Chick's name on it and gave it back to Artie. Tomorrow morning, she told him, a certain one-armed john is gonna come around asking for Fondelle Fontaine, and I want Wally (which that was Wally out there right now, the day clerk, the guy she was just talking to) to give this to him and tell him that Miss Fontaine was, uh, that she was called out of town on urgent business, and wouldn't be coming back.

And then, Fondelle said, she checked in under her real name, Arletta Skeens, and slipped Artie two fivers—one for him and one for Wally—and went up to her room and crawled into bed and slept till two o'clock this afternoon.

The absinthe had rendered me almost speechless, but I managed to croak, "Arletta Skeens?"

"That's right," said Fondelle Fontaine with yet another sly but knowing wink, just between us impostors. "That's right, Sterling Priest."

"Actually," I admitted sheepishly, "it's Eddie McCla—um, Ed McClanahan." Hoping to redeem some tiny smidgen of my dignity, I added, "Sterling Priest is just my, um, pen name."

If Fondelle—I wasn't quite ready for Arletta Skeens—if Fondelle had the foggiest notion what on earth a pen name might be (the name I went by when I was in the pen, maybe?), she didn't let on. She just shrugged again, as if to say, "Well, either way, it's a poor excuse for a name," and went on with her story.

"See," she confided, speaking with renewed urgency, "I *coultn't* keep the man's car. I mean, he's a damn war hero, hon! I lost my daddy in that old war." She sniffled, lifted her shades, and dabbed a tear in the corner of her eye. "I just kinda, you know, took a notion."

Exit Fondelle Fontaine, Manhattan showgirl, consort to the stars, heartless gold digger. A fond farewell to the fair Fondelle. Enter Arletta Skeens, good ole gal from West Virginia, who had took a notion. And now I saw at last why she had been so eager to tell me the story—because she had done a great thing, Arletta had, something fine and grand and noble and self-sacrificing, and I, this wet-behind-the-ears hayseed best man in the rumpled seersucker suit, was perhaps the only person in all the living world who could fully appreciate the magnitude of the deed—the only person, for that matter, who would even believe it, ladies in the gold-digging line not being in the habit, ordinarily, of refunding Olds 88s to rejected admirers.

"But I ditn't wanna be married to him for the rest of my damn life, neither," Arletta said with a little shudder. "Not under no circumstances whatsoever."

Afterward, whenever (increasingly infrequent) thoughts of the waiting arms of Betsy crossed my mind, I would remember that little involuntary shudder of Arletta's and experience my own tiny tremor of pre-connubial dread.

Just at the present moment, however, I was lost in a reverie of an entirely different description: I found myself staring straight down into the alluring depths of Arletta's cleavage, and in my absinthe-inflamed imagination, I was transported to somewhere in the mountains of West Virginia, scaling snowy peaks.

Not surprisingly, I was a little slow in realizing that Arletta had just spoken to me. "Watch out now," she'd cautioned with a generous giggle. "Don't fall in."

I raised my eyes and saw my guilty blush light up the backbar mirror. But Arletta's enterprising attention had already turned to the business at hand.

"God amighty!" she exclaimed, surveying the roomful of schooling conventioneers as though she were casting an invisible net and calculating in advance the weight of the catch. "This place is broke out in Shrinies! You better drink up on your cocktail, hon. I've got a date with . . . somebody."

She said the last almost tenderly, yet all my instincts told me that my idyll in the West Virginia hills was over. Feeling like I was about nine years old, I clambered down from my barstool and drew myself up to my full, seer-suckered nine-year-old height and thanked her politely for the lift and the Sazerac cocktail (the effects of which were rapidly evaporating). She kissed me soundly on the cheek and instructed me to be sure and have a good time in New Orleans, now, and not do nothing she woultn't do.

I stopped in the men's room, and when I came out I saw that there were two Shrinies in close conversation with her, one on either side, the tops of their fezzes peeping like bashful mushrooms from behind her picture hat. Possibly they were vying to determine which one got the privilege of paying her (and my) bar tab. Despite her shades, I caught Arletta's eye in the backbar mirror, and we exchanged diffident little farewell salutes. Out in the street, I realized that I'd forgotten to ask whether she happened to have a girlfriend named Mary—but I was pretty sure I knew what the answer would be, so I let it go at that.

Anyhow, I really didn't have time to dawdle, for Arletta's good deed had stirred something within me, and now, pricked on by conscience as I hurried through the Quarter in the late-afternoon heat, I was a man—a Best Man— on a mission. At the Metropole, when Bikey bowed me into the elevator, the lipstick imprint on my cheek, in conjunction with my disheveled suit, elicited another whistle, but I was so preoccupied that I forgot to tip him. I went straight to my room and sat down on my little bed and picked up the phone and called . . .

Not (perhaps to my eternal discredit) Betsy. But on the plus side of the ledger, in accordance with the Best Man Code of Honor, I did sit there and ring the emergency room of every hospital in the New Orleans phone book, as well as two or three police precinct stations, the highway patrol, and (a late inspiration) the coroner's office, to inquire whether a one-armed guy from Oklahoma in a '54 Olds 88 had checked in. Had the rejected suitor attempted, in his despair, to end it all, or to drink his way out of the slough of despond? Apparently not; at any rate, no one-armed Oklahoman of record had been jailed or hurt or killed lately. After an hour on the phone, I could only conclude that by now Chick must be safely rolling along in the 88 on his way home to Arbuckle to await the coming of the Intershtate, driving one-handed, of course, and probably doing a pretty respectable job of it since he didn't have the other hand to tipple with.

In any event, Best Man felt that he had done his duty and deserved a little nap. So he stretched his heroic self out and took one, suit and all.

Well, from this point forward our story—okay, *my* story—will progress at a greatly accelerated pace. Indeed, except for a few loose ends, the story is over: Chick and Arletta and Fondelle and the evanescent Mary were, as we presciently say nowadays, history—along with the Reverend and Mrs. Hoakem, and Jay's unattainable sister, and Señorita Marta (though not her insidious little colony of illegal immigrants, who had yet to make their presence known), and all those other phantoms and phantasms who had populated what I supposed would be my last summer of single blessedness, the whole motley lot of them receding irretrievably into the past, going, going, gone.

Later that evening, I ventured into the Quarter for one more shot at getting a little local color on me. I landed, eventually, at the Old Absinthe House itself, which, to my delight, was aswarm with the species boho—or, more probably, faux boho. I downed an untold number of Sazeracs, and in the process somehow fell amongst the poets, in whose company I regaled myself until, along about two in the morning, I noted with alarm a poetic hand upon my knee. I stole away and straggled back to the Metropole without incident—except that the oyster po'boy that had shadowed me all day finally mugged me in an alley off Dauphine and pretty much finished off my seersucker suit.

From that night forward, by the way, I have struggled against the impulse to make a mental association between poets (absinthe guzzlers that they are, down to the lowliest verse-monger) and oyster po'boys. And maybe I should also seize this opportunity to mention that it was to be many years before I would learn that the licorice in a Sazerac is mere flavoring; otherwise, oh my honeys, it's all rye whiskey and imagination, and not a drop of absinthe.

Nonetheless, I awoke the next morning with a Sazerac hangover the size of a Greek tragedy. I was, as we used to say of the hangovers of my youth, too sick to die. So, lacking that attractive option, I packed up, consigned my ruined suit to the trash, purchased Old Bikey's eternal loyalty with a farewell dollar bill (in penance for the deplorable condition in which I'd come in last night), and lugged my suitcase down to the Greyhound station. It had been my intention to take a bus out to the edge of town, where I planned to start hitching home to Maysville, the last leg of my great adventure. But so debilitating was my hangover, so sickly and dispirited had it rendered me, that when I crept up to the ticket window, I heard myself ask meekly for a one-way ticket to Maysville, Kentucky, please.

There ensued thirty-six sleepless hours of mobile misery, punctuated by brief interludes of bus station waiting rooms, bus station cafés, and bus station men's rooms—stationary misery, so to speak. That pernicious hang-over—the nastiest and most tenacious I've experienced in sixty years of dedicated tippling—had taken possession of me for the entire duration of the trip, loyal as a succubus. Meanwhile, my nether person was more and more disturbed by those other little fellow travelers, who had at last begun to bestir themselves, and were soon gamboling about as if they owned the place.

During a five AM layover in Nashville, after my wee beasties had no doubt infested the latest of a dismal procession of Greyhound men's rooms, I went to the café for an ill-advised cup of Greyhound coffee, where I idly picked up a discarded newspaper and came across an item headlined FIRST SECTION OF NEW INTERSTATE HIGHWAY SYSTEM SLATED FOR KANSAS. Poor Chick; he'd had a bad week. Perhaps it would've been some small consolation to him to know that his erstwhile best man was suffering, too.

Yet, sick and exhausted though I was, scruffy, smelly, and (not that any-one would've noticed) unshaven, busted (after I'd paid for my bus ticket, Betsy's ring fund stood at twenty-seven lonesome dollars), brokenhearted (Ah, Fondelle! Ah, Mary!), beset by pubic grasshoppers (Ah, treacherous Marta!), despite all that, jouncing along hour after hour in that Greyhound meat wagon came to seem, amazingly, both a fitting conclusion to my sum-mer of adventure and a quixotic fancy in its own right, a latter-day version of riding the rods, of becoming One with the Great Unwashed. And to be taking home with me, as souvenirs from exotic climes, not just a severe case of the galloping dandruff, but what I firmly believed was a real, live absinthe hangover . . . Oh my, it was a dreadful trip; I wouldn't have missed it for the world.

These entertaining diversions notwithstanding, I found time along the way to make two firm promises to myself: First, I did not intend—not under any circumstances whatsoever—to marry Betsy. Second, no power on Earth could keep me from going back to California. And may I precede myself just long enough to say that I kept both resolutions? (Which is how it came to pass that one year later almost to the day, still in a state of blessed singleness, I would be heading west again, this time in my Bel Air, bound for Stanford University, where I hoped to learn the tricks of the freelance writing trade.)

Any-hoo (Ah, Fondelle, Fondelle!), when the Greyhound paused briefly to drop off a passenger in Washington, Kentucky, a scant three miles south of Maysville, I was struck by a sudden inspiration. Leaping to my feet, I grabbed my suitcase from the overhead rack and got off, too. As soon as the bus pulled away, I stuck out my thumb and, after a very few minutes, I caught a lift with an old guy in a pickup, who was hauling a big crate of live chickens to town. Perfect! He let me out ten minutes later in downtown Maysville, where, by another delicious stroke of luck, an old high school buddy happened along just in time to witness my arrival.

"Hey, Eddie," he called, eyeballing the suitcase. "Where you been, Dad?"

"California," I answered happily. "I just hitched in from the coast."

THE DAY THE
LAMPSHADES
BREATHED

"We must all be foolish at times.
It is one of the conditions of liberty."
Walt Whitman

Like just about everybody else who lived in California during the 1960s, I Went Through a Phase. I grew me a mustache and a big wig, and got me some granny glasses and pointy-toed elf boots and bell-bottom britches (which did not, Charles Reich to the contrary notwithstanding, turn my walk into "a kind of dance"; *nothing* could turn my walk into a kind of dance). I threw the Ching. I rocked and I rolled. I ingested illicit substances. It was *épater le bourgeois* time, baby!

But this was not my first attack of *mal de Californie*. I'd been through it all before.

By way of explanation, let me go all the way back to 1952 just long enough to say that after that uninspired freshman year at Washington & Lee, I moved on for three more uninspired years at Miami of Ohio, where I majored in 3.2 beer and blanket parties on the golf course and published uninspired short stories in the campus lit mag. In 1955, I went to Stanford to try my hand at creative writage in graduate school.

Stanford was too many for me. I lasted just two quarters before I received a note from the chairman of the English Department inviting me to drop by and discuss my highly improbable future as a graduate student. I declined the invitation but took the hint, dropped out, and slunk back home to Kentucky to conclude a brief and embarrassingly undistinguished graduate career at the state university in Lexington. Thence to Oregon, and four years of honest toil at Backwater State College, in the freshman composition line.

But California had left its mark on me. For I had gone west as the blandest perambulatory tapioca pudding ever poured into a charcoal-gray suit, and I came home six months later in Levi's and cycle boots and twenty-four-hour-a-day shades, with an armpit of a goatee and a hairdo that wasn't so much a duck's-ass as it was, say, a sort of cocker spaniel's-ass. I had been to San Francisco and seen the Beatniks in North Beach, I had smoked a genuine reefer, I had sat on the floor drinking cheap Chianti and listening to "City of Glass" on the hi-fi. I'd been Californified to a fare-thee-well, and I'd loved every minute of it.

So when I weaseled my way back into Stanford—and California—in the fall of 1962 via a Wallace Stegner Fellowship in Creative Writing, it was a case of the victim returning to the scene of the outrage, eager for more. Immediately, I sought out my old Stanford roommates, Jim Wolpman and Vic Lovell, who were now, respectively, a labor lawyer and a grad student in psychology, living next door to each other in a dusty, idyllic little bohemian compound called Perry Lane, just off the Stanford campus. Among their neighbors was Ken Kesey, himself but lately down from Oregon, whose novel *One Flew Over the Cuckoo's Nest* had been published just a year ago and was in fact dedicated to Vic—"Who told me dragons did not exist, then led me to their lairs"—for having arranged Ken's enrollment as a test subject in a drug-experiment program at the local VA hospital. And the neighborhood was fairly crawling with writers and artists and students and musicians and mad scientists. It was just what I was looking for: a bad crowd to fall in with. I moved in a couple of blocks down the street and started my mustache.

In a lot of ways, it was the same old California. We still sat on the floor and drank cheap Chianti, though now we listened to Sandy Bull and called the hi-fi a stereo, and the atmosphere was often murky with the sickly-sweet blue smaze of the dread devil's weed. The manner we'd cultivated back in the fifties was sullen, brooding, withdrawn but volatile, dangerous—if not to others, then at the very least to ourselves. Its models were Elvis, James Dean, Marlon Brando in *The Wild One*. The idea was to seem at once murderous, suicidal . . . and sensitive.

(Locally, our hero in those days had been, improbably enough, the president of the Stanford student body government, George Ralph, who'd campaigned in sideburns and *Wild One* leathers behind the sneering slogan "I Hate Cops." George's campaign was a put-on, of course—between those sideburns was a dyed-in-the-wool Stevenson Democrat—but he had the style down cold, and he beat the cashmere socks off the poor Fraternity Row cream puff who opposed him.)

But six years can wreak a lot of changes, and by 1962 the future was already happening again on Perry Lane. "We pioneered"—Vic was to write* years later, with becoming modesty—"what have since become the hallmarks of hippie culture: LSD and other psychedelics too numerous to mention, body painting, light shows and mixed-media presentations, total aestheticism, be-ins, exotic costumes, strobe lights, sexual mayhem, freakouts and the deification of psychoticism, Eastern mysticism, and the rebirth of hair." Oh, they wanted to maintain their cool, these pioneers, they wanted to go on being—or seeming—aloof and cynical and hip and antisocial, but they just couldn't keep a straight face. They were like new lovers, or newly expectant mothers; they had this big, wonderful secret, and their idiot grins kept giving it away. They were the sweetest, smartest, liveliest, craziest bad crowd I'd ever had the good fortune to fall in with. And their great secret was simply this: They knew how to change the world.

"Think of it this way," my Perry Lane friend Peter, who never drew an unstoned breath, once countered when I mentioned that my TV was on the fritz. "Your TV's all right. But you've been lookin' at it wrong, man, you've been bum-trippin' your own TV set!"

For a while there, it almost seemed as if it might really be that easy. The way to change the world was just to start looking at it right, to stop bumming it out (ah, we could turn a phrase in those days!) and start grooving on it—to scarf down a little something from the psychedelicatessen and settle back and watch the world do its ineluctable thing. Gratified by the attention, the world would spring to life and cheerfully reveal its deepest mysteries. The commonplace would become marvelous; you could take the pulse of a rock, listen to the heartbeat of a tree, feel the hot breath of a butterfly against your cheek. ("So I took this pill," said another friend, reporting back after

---

* In *The Free You*, the newsletter-*cum*-magazine of the Mid-Peninsula Free University of Palo Alto.

his first visit to the Lane, "and a little later I was lying on the couch, when I noticed that the lampshade had begun to breathe . . . ") It was a time of what now seems astonishing innocence, before Watergate or Woodstock or Vietnam or Charles Manson or the Summer of Love or Groovy and Linda or the Long, Hot Summer or even, for a while, Lee Harvey Oswald, a time when wonder was the order of the day. One noticed one's friends (not to mention oneself) saying "Oh wow!" with almost reflexive frequency; and the cry that was to become the "Excelsior!" of the Day-Glo Decade, the ecstatic, ubiquitous "Far out!" rang oft upon the air.

The first time I ever felt entitled to employ that rallying cry was on Thanksgiving of 1962. That evening, after a huge communal Thanksgiving feast at the Keseys', Ken led me to his medicine cabinet, made a selection, and said matter-of-factly, "Here, take this, we're going to the movies." A scant few minutes later, he and I and three or four other lunatics were sitting way down front in a crowded Palo Alto theater, and the opening credits of *West Side Story* were disintegrating before my eyes. *This is . . . CINERAMA!* roared the voice-over inside my head as I cringed in my seat. And though I stared almost unblinking at the screen for the next two hours and thirty-five minutes, I never saw a coherent moment of the movie. What I saw was a ceaseless barrage of guns, knives, policemen, and lurid gouts of eyeball-searing color, accompanied by an earsplitting, cacophonous din, throughout which I sat transfixed with terror—perfectly immobile, the others told me afterward; stark, staring immobile, petrified, trepanned, stricken by the certainty, the absolute certainty, that in one more instant the Authorities would be arriving to seize me and drag me up the aisle and off to the nearest madhouse. It was the distillation of all the fear I'd ever known, fear without tangible reason or cause or occasion, pure, unadulterated, abject Fear Itself, and for a hundred and fifty-five awful minutes it invaded me to the very follicles of my mustache.

Then, suddenly and miraculously, like a beacon in the Dark Night of the Soul, the words "The End" shimmered before me on the screen. Relief swept over me, sweet as a zephyr. I was delivered. The curtain closed, the lights came up. I felt grand, exuberant, triumphant—as if I'd just ridden a Brahma bull instead of a little old tab of psilocybin. If they'd turned off the lights again, I'd have glowed in the dark. Beside me, Ken stood up and stretched.

"So how was it?" he inquired, grinning.

"Oh, wow!" I croaked joyfully. "It was fa-a-ar out!"

And in that instant, for me, the sixties began. Characteristically, I was about two years late getting out of the gate, but I was off at last.

Ken Kesey was a singular person, as all who knew him will attest. But these were *all* singular people, this lunatic fringe on Stanford's stiff upper lip. I should probably keep this to myself, but to tell the truth, the thing I remember best about the next few years is the parties. We had the swellest parties! Parties as good as your childhood birthday parties were supposed to be but never were; outrageously good parties, parties so good that people would sometimes actually forget to drink!

The best parties were immaculately spontaneous. Typically, they began with some Perry Lane denizen sitting at the breakfast table, staring out the kitchen window into the dappled, mellow perfection of a sunny California Saturday morning, resolving: Today, I'm gonna take a little trip. By early afternoon, two or three friends would have dropped by and signed on for the voyage, and together they'd choke down either some encapsulated chemical with an appetizing title like URP-127 or an equally savory "natural" concoction like peyote-orange-juice upchuck or morning glory seeds with cream and sugar (don't try it, reader; it ain't Grape-Nuts, and there's nothing natural about it), and then for the next half hour or so they'd lie around trying not to throw up while they waited for the lampshades to start respiring. A similar scene was liable to be transpiring in two or three other Perry Lane households at the same time, and it wouldn't be long till every lampshade in the neighborhood was panting like a pufferbelly. The incipient party would have begun to assert itself.

Under the giant oak by Vic's front door—the very oak in whose shade Thorstein Veblen was alleged to have written *The Theory of the Leisure Class*—half a dozen solid citizens with pinwheel eyeballs might be banging out an aboriginal but curiously copacetic sort of hincty bebop on upturned wastebaskets, pots and pans, maybe an old set of bongos left over from the fifties, Vic himself laying down the basic bop lines on his favorite ax, a pocket-comb-and-tissue-paper hum-a-zoo. Next door at the Keseys', they'd have drawn the blinds and hung blankets over the windows, and Roy Sebern, a wonderfully hairy artist who lived, apparently on air, in a tiny box on the back of his pickup in a succession of backyards, would be demonstrating his newest creation, a rickety contraption that projected amorphous, throbbing blobs of luminous color all over the walls and ceiling like lambent, living wallpaper, to the murmuring chorus of "oh-wows" and "far-outs" that issued from an audience of several puddles of psychedelicized sensibility on the Kesey carpet. Over at my house on Alpine Road, Peter and I would be feverishly juicing peyote buttons in my wife's brand-new Osterizer.

In the late afternoon, Gurney Norman, another apprentice writer from Kentucky, might turn up, sprung from Fort Ord on a weekend pass. Gurney had made his way to Stanford and Perry Lane a couple of years earlier (it was he, in fact, who'd spotted the original breathing lampshade), and had then gone into the army to complete an ROTC obligation, and promptly bounced back to California in the guise of a first lieutenant, running recruits through basic training down at Ord during the week and expanding his horizons at Perry Lane on the weekends. The military was doing great things for Gurney's organizational skills; within minutes of his arrival, he'd have a squad of giggling beardy-weirdies and stoned Perry Lane–style Wacs in muumuus hut-hoop-hreep-hoing up and down the street with mops and broomsticks on their shoulders, in an irreverent gloss on the whole idea of close-order drill.

Eventually, the party would assemble itself somewhere, more than likely around the corner at Chloe Scott's house, to take on victuals and cheap Chianti. Chloe is at all odds the most glamorous woman I've ever known. A professional dancer and dance teacher, redheaded and fiery, a real knockout and a woman of the world, Chloe Kiely-Peach of the British gentry by birth, daughter of a captain in the Royal Navy, she'd come to America, to New York, as a girl during the Blitz, and had stayed on to become, in the early fifties, part of Jackson Pollock's notoriously high-spirited East Hampton social circle. Along the way she married a dashing young naturalist and spent a year on the Audubon Society's houseboat in the Everglades, fell briefly under the spell of a Reichian therapist and basted herself in an orgone box, and at last, divorced, made her way west to settle in as one of the reigning free spirits on Perry Lane. At Chloe's anything could happen.

And, as they say, it usually did. For starters, Neal Cassady might fall by, the Real Neal, Kerouac's pal and the prototype for Dean Moriarty of *On the Road*, trailing adoring fallen women and authentic North Beach beatniks in his wake, looking like Paul Newman and talking as if he'd been shooting speed with a phonograph needle—which, come to think of it, he probably had: "Just passing through, folks, don't mind us, my shed-yool just happened to coincide with Mr. Kesey's here, and all that redundancy, you understand, not to mention the works of Alfred Lord Tennyson and the worst of the poems of Schiller, huntin' and peckin' away there as they did, except of course insofar as where you draw the line, that is, but in any case I believe it was at, let me see, Sebring, yes, when Fangio, with the exhaust valves wide open and the petcocks, too, that you've sometimes seen, starting with Wordsworth, you see, and working backward, in the traditional fashion, straight through Pliny the Elder and *beyond*, though it's much the same with the fusion of the existential and the transcendental, or, if you will, the universal and the transmission, as in the case of the 1940 flat-head Cadillac 8, why, you naturally get your *velocity* mixed up with your *veracity*, of course, and who knows what that's cost us? So I'll just say how-d'ye-do to my friend Mr. Kesey, and then we'll be on our way, have to get there in plenty of time, you understand . . . " Neal never stuck around for long, but he was terrific while he lasted.

Then there was Lee Anderson, a roly-poly, merry little apple dumpling of a PhD candidate in some obscure scientific discipline at Stanford, who could sometimes, at very good parties, be prevailed upon to . . . play himself! Bowing to popular demand, blushing bashfully from head to toe, Lee would strip down to his skivvies (an effective attention-getting device at any party), wait for silence, and at last begin rhythmically bobbing up and down to some inner tempo, as though he were about to improvise a solo on an invisible stand-up bass, now lightly slapping himself with his open hands on his plump little thighs and roseate tummy—*slappity-slappity-slappity-slap*—now cupping one hand in his armpit and flapping the arm to produce a small farting sound like a tiny tuba—*slappity-slappity-poot-poot, slappity-poot, slappity-poot*—now shaping his mouth into an oval and rapping on his skull with the knuckles of first one hand, then the other, then both, making of his mouth a sort of reverb chamber—*pocketa-pock, pocketa-pock, pocketa-pecketa-pucketa-pock*—picking up the tempo, working furiously, sweat flying, the whole ensemble tuning in—*slappity-pock, slappity-pock, slappity-pocketa-poot, slappity-pocketa-poot, pocketa-poot, pocketa-pecketa-poot, pecketa-pucketa-poot, slappity-pucketa-poot-poot, slappity-pucketa-poot-poot* . . . It wasn't the New York Philharmonic, maybe, but Lee's was a class act just the same—as Dr. Johnson might have put it, the wonder was not that he did it well, but simply that he could do it at all—and it always brought the house down.

I'm not exactly sure what Vic means by "sexual mayhem," so I won't try either to confirm or to deny it. I'll just say that during one party I opened the door to the darkened bedroom where the coats were piled on the bed and heard a muffled female voice say from the darkness, "Close the door, please, Ed. We're fucking in here."

Basically, though, the parties were just good, clean, demented fun. At any moment the front door might burst open and into the celebrants' midst would fly Anita Wolpman, Jim's wife, with the collar of her turtle-neck sweater pulled up over her head, hotly pursued by Jim, brandishing an ax gory with ketchup. Or Bob Stone, a splendid writer who has also done some Shakespeare on the stage, might suddenly be striding about the room delivering, with Orson Wellesian bombast and fustian, an impromptu soliloquy, a volatile, irreproducibly brilliant admixture of equal parts Bard, King James Bible, *Finnegan's Wake*, and (so I always suspected) Bob Stone. Or Lorrie Payne, a madcap Australian jack-of-all-arts, might wander in with a skinned green grape stuffed halfway into one nostril and part the horrified multitudes before him like an exhibitionist at a DAR convention. Or one might find oneself—literally find oneself—engaged in one or another of the goofy conversations that would be ensuing in every corner of the house, as did Gurney and I the night we determined that behind the peg-board on Chloe's kitchen wall lurked an enormous baby chick, ready to pounce on us, bellowing, in a voice like Bull Moose Jackson's, "PEEP! PEEP!" Or somebody might cut open an old golf ball and start unwinding the endless rubber band inside, and in moments a roomful of merrymakers would be hopelessly ensnarled in a rubbery web, writhing hilariously—a surreal tableau that, to my peyote-enchanted eyes, was astonishingly beautiful, and was entitled "We're All in This Thing Together."

At one party, Gurney maneuvered ten delirious revelers into the back-yard, looped Chloe's fifty-foot clothesline about them, and endeavored to create the World's Largest Cat's Cradle. "Awright now, men," he kept bawling at his troops, "I want all the thumbs to raise their hands!"

Well, okay, you had to be there. No denying there was plenty of unmiti-gated adolescent silliness in all those hijinks—just as there's no denying the unfortunate similarity between my experience at *West Side Story* and that of the celebrated Little Moron, the one who beats himself on the head with a hammer because it feels so good to stop. But like the man in the aftershave commercial, we needed that, some of us, to wake us from the torpor of the fifties. To be sure, there were casualties—those who couldn't put the hammer down till they'd pounded their poor heads to jelly, those who blissed out or blasted off, those for whom dope was a purgative and every trip a bad trip, an exorcism. And I'm also perfectly willing to concede, if I must, that there were just as many others who successfully expanded their consciousnesses to wonderful dimensions through the miracle of chemistry.

But for weekenders and day-trippers like me, psychedelics were mostly just for laughs; they made things more funny-ha-ha than funny-peculiar. And for me at least, the laughter was a value in itself. I hadn't laughed so unrestrainedly since childhood, and the effect was refreshing, bracing, invigorating—aftershave for the psyche. Nor had I ever in my life allowed myself to fall so utterly in love with all my friends at once. And there were several occasions, in the highest, clearest moments of those high old times, when I caught a glimpse of something at the periphery of my vision that shook the throne of the tyrannical little atheist who sat in my head and ruled my Kentucky Methodist heart.

It was all too good to last, of course. Quick as the wink of a strobe light, Kennedy had fallen to Lee Harvey Oswald, the Vietnam issue was as hot as a two-dollar pistol, the country was aboil with racial unrest . . . and Perry Lane had gone under to the developers. The times, they were a-changin', and not for the better either. The first day of the rest of our lives was over.

LITTLE ENIS: AN ODE
ON THE INTIMIDATIONS
OF MORTALITY

> LAWYER: *Yer Honor, my client Joe Hogbristle*
> *wants to change his name.*
> JUDGE: *Well, I can certainly understand that.*
> *What does he want to change it to?*
> LAWYER: *He wants to change it to Fred Hogbristle.*
> *Says he's tired of people saying, 'Hello Joe,*
> *whaddya know!'*
>
> 1001 Jokes for All Occasions

H ere, straight from the source's mouth, is how Carlos Toadvine, a poor country boy from Hogue Holler, Kentucky, got transmogrified into Little Enis, the All-American Left-Handed Upside-Down Guitar Player: *Well, it was an Eye-talian name, to start with. 'Todavinney,' they called it, and they used to speak that Spanish all the time. But I got the name of Little Enis at the Zebra Bar, back in '55 or '56, because the name of Carlos Toadvine was too big and too long of a name to put on the marquee. And I was imitatin' Elvis Presley quite a bit in those times; I was younger and thinner, and so I just said, 'Well, he is quite famous, I'll just foller along and do like he does.' Just like ever' other musician in the country, I sang his songs, y'know? So they was this joke goin' around, see, about Elvis the Pelvis? And his little brother Enis? The Penis? So they just looked at me, I was stocky and all, and they said, 'Enis . . . '*

In the early 1970s, when I first began to write about Little Enis, it seemed to me my main problem was that I had an assortment of beginnings and a great snarl of loose ends at my disposal, but no true denouement anywhere in sight. In the intervening years, you should perhaps know, the inevitable denouement of a tale such as Enis's came to pass; since 1976, he's played left-handed upside-down guitar in Rockabilly Heaven. But that, as they say, is another story—or several other stories, actually. Enough for now that we get some of the loose ends of this one untangled.

As far as my part in it is concerned, it began one night in the fall of 1956 in Lexington, Kentucky, when I walked into the Zebra Bar—a musty, murky coal-hole of a place across Short Street from the Drake Hotel (IF YOU DUCK THE DRAKE YOUR A GOOSE!! read the peeling roadside billboard out on the edge of town)—walked in under a marquee that did, sure enough, declare the presence inside of one "Little Enis," and came upon this amazing little stud stomping around atop the bar, flailing away at one of those enormous old electric guitars that looked like an Oldsmobile in drag—left-handed! He's playing it left-handed! And upside down besides!—this pugnacious-looking little banty rooster with a skintight gold-sateen cowboy shirt and an underslung lower jaw and a great sleek black-patent-leather Elvis Presley pompadour and long Elvis Presley sideburns and a genuine Elvis Presley duck's-ass *(You know, people sometimes asks me what I think of these people like you, which has got the long hair and all. And I just say, 'Well, they've got their thing to do.' Because actually, see, I've had long hair my own self since I was fifteen years old. I mean, I was the first one that created long sideburns in Lexington! I had 'em down to here!),* this five-foot four-inch watch-fob knickknack of an Elvis up there just a-stompin' and a-flailin', laying down a rendition of "Blue Suede Shoes" that would have done the master proud. In fact, he was even (oh, blasphemy!) *better* than Elvis, his guitar playing distinctly saltier, his inflections ("You c'n do *ennythang* that y'wanna *dew* / But onh-onh, honey, lay *offa* my shews!") just a shade flatter, twangier, down-homier, his bump 'n' grind at least as lewd and spirited as anything the Big E himself had thrown at us on *Ed Sullivan* a few Sundays back. We all flashed to him instantly, and hastened to settle our sodden selves into a booth so that my roommate, Willie Gordon Ryan, the evening's patron live one, could spring us to the opening round.

We. That would have included, let's see, Ryan, who was in college at last after a four-year hitch in the Air Force (as a matter of fact, that's what we were celebrating that night; it was the day Ryan's monthly GI Bill check came in), and several well-saturated running mates of ours, Tommy Cook and I. Jay Weaver and Little Billy Whealdon and Buster Kline and . . .

And me, the loosest end of all, some might say. For this was but a few months after my triumphant return from my first stint at the Harvard of the West, where, I'll remind you, I had distinguished myself by flunking out of graduate school. So I hadn't come home with that old sheepskin to nail to the wall, but I did bring back my armpit goatee and my spaniel's-ass haircut and my shades and Levi's and cycle boots, in which Califinery I currently ornamented the campus of the University of Kentucky—where I was flunking out of graduate school. Already I ranked right up there with Adolph Rupp's roundball coliseum and the Agricultural Experiment Station among the sights not to be missed on the UK campus. On football weekends, whole carloads of old grads would screech to a halt in heavy traffic to stare and point; fraternity men's upper lips automatically curled into sneers the instant I came into view; sorority housemothers hastened to gather their maidenly charges behind their skirts at the very mention of my name.

But now about this Toadvine. Well, in a way, he saved my graduate career, such as it was. Because up until the moment I walked into the Zebra Bar that night, I'd been persuaded that there was no way in the world I could stand Lexington long enough to get my MA and, as the saying went, make like a sewer and get the shit out of there. *Maybe I'd just chuck the whole deal,* I told myself darkly, *and join the army, where they knew how to appreciate us nonconformists.* But suddenly there he was, Little Enis, all the evidence I could ask for that even out here in the un-illumined heart of the provinces, careful inspection was liable to turn up some cultural phenomenon worthy of an enlightened man's condescension.

Enis took to flattery like a duck to water, poor innocent. All I had to do was buy him a seventy-five-cent Zebra Zombie at his first break between sets, and advise him that, as a noted folklorist from the university (where, in fact, I was currently pulling a low C in the only folklore course I ever enrolled in), I was satisfied that he and his understudy Elvis constituted the single most cosmic event in the history of American ethnosecular music (a genre that I invented on the spot), and that I was prepared to embark on a study of him that was a cinch to make us both as famous as Silly Putty. And that was it; I had me an Artifact to patronize. My military future would have to be postponed.

For the next two or three weeks, I paid court to Enis at the Zebra as often as I could finance a field trip down to Short Street. When he left the Zebra and hired on at Martin's, a breathtakingly unsanitary country-and-western tavern over on the north side of town, I took my trade there too—at some peril, I might add, for the clientele at Martin's tended to look at me unsociably out of the corners of their eyes. And when Enis moved on to the Palms, a cement-block *moderne* cocktail lounge between a drive-in theater and a varmint-burger stand out on the Northern Beltline, I practically took up residence in the place.

Now, the Palms had lately fallen into the hands of a certain Linville Puckett, who until that very autumn had been an almost-All-American guard on the UK basketball team, but who had come to a parting of the ways with Baron Rupp—some small dispute over training rules, as I recall—and had turned in his jock and moved around to the business side of the bar to become a night-life impresario. He'd taken over this dingy roadhouse, complete with the pair of dusty plastic potted palm trees that flanked the ladies' room door, and renamed it Linville Puckett's Palms, and installed the slickest dance floor in town and the liveliest jukebox in town and the hottest attraction in town, which was my excellent friend Little Enis and his new combo, the Fabulous Tabletoppers. *(Yeah, they was quite a few stars out there at that time. I was about the biggest thing in Lexington, so they would all say I was a big star, and Linville, he was a basketball star. So that was quite a good drawin' card, Linville Puckett, the All-American basketball player, and Little Enis, the All-American Left-Handed Upside-Down Guitar Player.)* Within a week the Palms was jumping every night, Puckett's most avid admirers showing up right after work when he was usually tending bar, early enough to drink their suppers, blue-collar sports fans and UK fratties drunkenly maneuvering for choice barstools all through vespers, hoping to hear the defrocked Wildcat tell how he'd told Der Baron he could take his basketball and shove it up his coliseum. By around eight o'clock, Enis would generally have joined them at the bar, knocking back a few whiskey-and-Cokes or a couple of cool ones to clear his head before the first set. *(When I was drinkin', I'd live each day from day to day, that's how I lived during my drinkin' years. And when I'd go to sleep I wouldn't even think about gettin' up. And then the next day, I'd get up and party again. I finally went out here to Eastern State Hospital to get me some help. That shrinker said to me, 'Are you a alcoholic?'*

And I said, 'Well, if you call drinkin' a quart of whiskey before you can read the Sunday paper a alcoholic, then I reckon I must be one.') Along about eight-thirty, the guys with dates would be falling by, here a Deke out a-slumming with his Tri Delt, there a TV repairman hustling the wife of a client who worked the night shift at the Dixie Cup factory; and by a little after nine, maybe a few unattached girls would have turned up, telephone operators and typists from the IBM typing pool and students from the Fugazzi Business College and the Vine Street Academy of Beauty, gathering themselves in jittery little coveys here and there at tables closest to the dance floor, where the light was better. They'd sit there glaring at those oblivious stiffs crowded around the bar until finally one of them, say an aspiring beautician working on her PhD in beehives at the academy, would get so pee-oh'd she'd pick up her Tom Collins and sashay over to the jukebox and plug it with her own quarter, punching out maybe "Fever," and "Raunchy," and Elvis's latest, "Paralyze"; and when Little Willie John suddenly whumped out those few heavy bass notes and growled, "Never know how mu-uch I love you!" the guys at the bar would look up, startled, to discover that the night was as young as the day was old, and immediately begin to undergo the metamorphosis from sports fans to just plain sports, their eyeballs ticking off their calculations like Rupp's new electronic scoreboards as they checked out the action in the other room.

By the time "Raunchy" was half over, there'd be four or five newly acquainted couples on the dance floor, raunching away, doing a sort of post-jitterbug, pre-twist bop, standing there at arm's length, grimacing and hunching their pelvises at each other in a kind of dirty-boogie face-off, and while Elvis was groaning his way through "Paralyze," Enis and the Fabulous Tabletoppers—a wonderful sax honker named Bucky Sallee, and a piano player named Frank, and a guy named either Johnny or Jerry on drums—would mount the bandstand beside the jukebox and start tuning up. As Elvis wrapped it up and Enis, cradling his guitar in that weird way of his and grinning an utterly wicked, lickerish grin, stepped forward into the Palms' feeble greenish-yellow spotlight, his pompadour glinting like obsidian, his tidy little torso all a-shimmer in the gold-sateen cowboy shirt, his tiny white hands poised above the first fleet notes of "All Shook Up" (*Well, my daddy was a farmer in Hogue Holler, over here by Danville, and I swear he couldn't play the reddy-o without gettin' static on it. But my mother, she* sung in church, and I would've walked a country mile to hear her sing a song, she had the most beautiful voice you ever heard. And her people, they was entertainers, years ago they was with Red Foley at Renfro Valley. My uncle, he was the state fiddlin' champion on the old breakdown fiddle at the state fair. So they would all get together of a Sunday afternoon, and everybody'd bring their music instruments, and I was just a little thing, y'know, but I'd santer around th'oo that crowd and directly I'd pick up somebody's guitar, and the first thing you know I'd be a-bangin' on it!), stepped forward into the Palms' blare and reek, and with the spotlight glaring in his eyes, the only thing he could make out would be . . .

Me again. The old loose end again, the noted folklorist again, drunk again. Sitting there right under Enis's nose at the table nearest the bandstand, wearing those ridiculous shades and that ridiculous Levi's suit and that ridiculous haircut, drunk as a lord since three o'clock in the afternoon, when I had inconspicuously departed from my Romantic Poetry Seminar at the tea-and-cookies break and had fled to the revolting pigsty of an apartment I shared with Willie Gordon Ryan upstairs over the Southern Girl Beauty Salon, and had found Ryan there busily cutting freshman English, and had straightway sallied forth once more with Ryan at my side, as faithful a Sancho Panza as e'er a Quixote could've asked for (it being the day *my* check came in, bearing my father's customarily reluctant-looking signature), to an establishment called the Paddock Club, where we drank Oertels '92 beer straight through till seven-thirty, excepting one time-out for a fried baloney sandwich, and where I had once again made a jackass of myself by authoritatively informing some indignant coed that the doodles in the back of her *Family and Marriage* textbook revealed "a definite tendency toward the Freudian concept we call penis envy." And also where I. Jay Weaver and Tommy Cook, on their way home to study for a Poultry Management exam after a leisurely dinner of beer and pickled eggs and pinball at the Scott Hotel Bar, dropped by for a spot of Oertels '92, just to clear their palates, and from which the three of us (Sancho Ryan having already committed his iron to other fires that night) repaired forthwith to the Palms, I. Jay and Cookie to juice some more and dance them dirty-boogie dances and hustle the ladies a bit, I to do my noted folklorist act—dancing is not my strong suit—for the third time that week. And to juice some more.

Thus had I arrived at my present sorry state, drumming my thumbs against the tabletop with inebrious, a-rhythmical abandon, while on the bandstand just above me Little Enis—his feet planted in that classic Presley straddle, his groin thrusting like the machine-tooled private parts of the Great Fucking Wheel, his left leg jiggling spasmodically inside his pants as if he really *was* a-eetchin' lak a bug on a fuzzy tree—tore like a man possessed into Elvis's repertoire, segueing out of "All Shook Up" straight into "Hound Dog," then laying back ever so slightly with "Teddy Bear" (the lively lovelies of the Palms squealed like bobby-soxers over that one—because, as I overheard one of them sigh when Enis purled "Run yo' fangers th'oo mah hair an' cuddle up real tight!" and hove a lusty dry-hump in her direction, "I could cuddle *that* sweet thing to *death*!"), then cranking it up again with "Blue Suede Shoes" and, for variety, Little Richard's "Long Tall Sally" and Fats Domino's "Kansas City," then tying off the set with a "That's When Your Heartaches Begin" so mellow and lachrymose that Colonel Parker would have shed a tear in his Hadacol if he'd been there to hear it.

And through it all, there sat the Palms' own noted folklorist and resident greaser, thumping away at my tabletop like a tone-deaf Sal Mineo auditioning for *The Gene Krupa Story*, applauding furiously for every number, calling out requests at the top of my voice between songs—"Hey, Enis, do 'Rip It Up'! Do 'Jailhouse Rock'! Do 'Hound Dog' again!"—generally pulling out all the stops, so that he would come and sit at my table during his break and let me buy him an Oertels '92 and patronize him some.

Oh, there were plenty of times when a tableful of admiring Palmettes would snag him first ("That little son-of-a-buck will get laid where most men couldn't get a drink of water," a Palms bartender confided to me one night. "I heard a couple of these old girls say he's *awful* heavy hung. They was talking about somebody named Old Blue, and it turned out they was referring to Enis's pecker!"); but for all their charms, they were wanting in that sophisticated appreciation of his Art that he could always depend on finding at my table. So at least once or twice an evening he'd join me—and, if the pickings on the dance floor were running slim, I. Jay and Cookie—for a quick one, and I'd tell him how he was the biggest thing in troubadouring since Allan-a-Dale, and he'd tell me about all the offers he was getting from Dot Records, and all the albums they were begging him to cut, and all the road tours he was going on . . . and one night, when my panegyrics had left him in an especially expansive mood, he confided that he was temporarily working days as a "maintenance engineer," shoveling coal into the Lafayette Hotel's furnace, and that his real name was Carlos Toadvine. He never did quite get my name, by the way; his best effort was the time he introduced me to a barmaid as "Ted Flannigan, he's gettin' his doctor degree on my life story, out at the colletch."

Throughout that fall and early winter, I was liable to drop by the Palms as often as three or four nights a week to pay my respects to Enis; it got so the waitresses would deliver an Oertels '92 to my ringside table as soon as I walked in the door. Then in January I finally met a Lexington girl who, although her tastes in music were a good deal tonier than mine (the first present I ever gave her was a 45 of Chuck Berry's "Roll Over, Beethoven"), was content to sit there while I rattled our beer glasses with my tattooing thumbs (the first present she ever gave me was a set of bongo drums) and told her about the master's thesis I planned to write, audaciously entitled "The Influence of the Celtic Bardic Tradition upon the Work of Carlos Toadvine."

Fortunately for the general state of *belles lettres*, I never got around to writing it; because in the spring of '57 there occurred the two most momentous events of my young life: I got married, and I flunked my master's oral. Flunked it cold as a wedge; I hadn't been in that room with those three professors fifteen minutes before my California cool had turned into an iceberg on my tongue. I couldn't have told them so much as the date of the Battle of Hastings—much less who fought it, or who won. "Get a grip on yourself, McClanahan," the trio of professors chorused sternly, shaking their hoary heads in unison; quit hanging around bars pretending to be some kind of Beatster or whatever they call it, and start applying yourself to the study of the history of English literature, and come back next year and try again.

Shaken to my very cycle boots, I did as I was told: I put in a whole year writing a master's thesis audaciously entitled "A Selective Bibliography of Critical Approaches to the Poetry of Robert Browning, 1935–1950," and sitting in on sophomore literature surveys, memorizing names and dates and titles, and the rhyme scheme of the sonnet. True, I didn't altogether abandon my old identity: Every now and then I'd suit up in my Beatster best (except for the goatee, which had gone down the drain of the Southern Girl Beauty Salon apartment's bathroom sink on the morning of my wedding day) and drop by the Palms and trade a little fried baloney with old Enis. But it wasn't the same, somehow; my head had got so full of titles and dates, and Enis's head so full of fans and plans, that we never seemed quite able to center the way we used to on the only thing that was really going on between us: that awkward little dance our two egos always did whenever they encountered one another.

For the most part, I stayed close to home that year, the way an earnest newlywed grad student is supposed to, and attended to hearth and desk. So that when spring rolled round again, and those ogres on my orals committee summoned me once more into their lair, I was all primed and cocked for the occasion ("Now then, Mr. McClanahan, perhaps you could name several, ah, female Victorian novelists for us?" "Why yes, certainly, there was . . . *were* . . . um, the Brontë sisters, that's three right there, and then there was George Eliot, who was actually a woman, as you probably know, and . . . uh . . . Jane Eyre?"), and sweating like a piglet on a spit, I acquitted myself with a performance that the chairman of the committee allowed they might consider passable if I'd clear out of the state by sundown and swear never to reveal to a living soul where I'd secured my sheepskin.

In June, when I struck out for Oregon to seek my fortune in the writing-and-teaching game, I was sped on my way by the stiff westward wind that the UK English Department's collective sigh of relief had given rise to.

Well, *plus ça change, plus c'est la même chose,* as they say in that Eye-talian Spanish. Get this, for instance: In the summer of 1971, when I hadn't written a printable word for months and months, when my ostensible career at the Harvard of the West had only lately perished of an anemic bibliography, and when, for all manner of other reasons there's no need, thank goodness, to go into here, my life seemed to me to be ticking away inside my breast like a time bomb planted there by some insidious cosmic assassin, at midnight on the eve of a family trip to Kentucky, intending merely to take a teensy little taste to enliven the last-minute packing of the McClanavan, I accidentally dosed myself with about two thousand micrograms of what is said to be the most stupefyingly powerful acid ever circulated around San Francisco, and spent the next twelve hours clinging like a shipwrecked sailor to the sides of my king-size California water bed, awash in my own terror, drowning all night long in the fathomless deeps of the certainty that I was going mad, dying, dead . . .

Now, an experience such as that will bring a man to give some serious thought to the matter of his own mortality. And as our mutual destinies would have it, mortality was also very much on Carlos Toadvine's mind just then. For on approximately the same morning that I, a survivor after all, came to among the flotsam and jetsam on that westernmost beachhead of my sanity, Enis had awakened in a Lexington hospital bed to the news that his liver would soon rival the size of his guitar, and that his next few parties would surely be his last.

(*Well, just bein' in the clubs day in and day out, why, people was just constantly sayin', 'Enis, have a* drank *with me, buddy!' and all, and I got to where I just constantly had a drink in my hand, funnelin' it down. An arn man couldn't of stood up under what I was a-drinkin'. I would, uh, consume at least two quarts of whiskey. A day. Not countin' beer. And they was several times when I would catch myself gettin', you know, fairly drunk.*)

I didn't know that then, of course; in fact, I'd been in Lexington for weeks before the night Enis and I crossed paths again, the night when, in a fit of nameless angst, I went out driving aimlessly about town in the vain hope that the flickering pyrotechnics in my head would shed some new light on how I might go about piecing together the myriad fragments of my life and mind.

I suppose it must have been an hour or so after I'd set out that I found myself idling my motor at the Southern Railroad crossing out on South Broadway, a workingman's neighborhood of tobacco warehouses and hardcore bars and fleabag hotels and secondhand clothing stores, while an endless freight train oozed along before me; and after I'd sat there for several minutes, my ill-used consciousness reluctantly informed me—for even a busted clock has to tell the right time twice a day—that I was just then situated directly across the street from the Scott Hotel.

The Scott Hotel is a great, ugly old four-story pile of gray-green brick with a sprinkling of quasi-Victorian afterthoughts—turrets and gables and oriels and cupolas—haphazardly affixed to its upper reaches, and a neon rooms-by-day-or-week sign in the lobby window, and, around the corner, a scummy old spittoon of a tavern where, back in the days of my callow youth, I used to go sometimes with I. Jay Weaver and Tommy Cook to drink beer and rub shoulders with the hoi polloi, the way any would-Beat worthy of his whiskers was supposed to do. The tavern, though, had evidently acquired both a new name—Boots' Bar, according to the sign—and a whole new entertainment policy, something rather livelier than the six-flipper pinball machine that used to be its main attraction; for emblazoned on the wall facing the street, in awkwardly painted letters two feet tall, were the words GO-GO GIRLS!

For the merest fraction of a moment, thinking perhaps to make some sense of the future by contemplating the ruins of my history, I considered going in for a shot or two of Old Blast from the Past; then, just as quickly, I thought better of it. Because South Broadway's notion of Southern hospitality didn't necessarily extend to loopy-looking long-hairs in bell-bottom britches. I may be crazy—I admitted, revving the motor—I may be crazy, but I ain't insane.

The train's caboose was in my headlights, and I had already slipped the car into gear, when I glanced back and noticed that, in three-inch letters above the GO-GO GIRLS!, with clumsy little musical notes leaping off the words like fleas leaving a sinking dog, and the letter *P* scrawled in by some wag with a can of spray paint, the sign said:

THE MAN WITH A GOLDEN VOICE
LITTLE*P*ENIS!

And the next thing I knew I was hooking a hard left into the Scott's parking lot, and the next after that, I was standing beside a blaring jukebox at the rear of a large, dark, low-ceilinged room with so much smoke in the atmosphere that I could already feel the nicotine condensing on my eyeballs, and dead ahead of me at the far end of the room was a flimsy little stage, and on the stage, bathed in pellucid greenish light, stood a lady about a hundred and fifty-six years old, wearing green Day-Glo pasties and a black bikini bottom and white Easter Parade spike heels, her bosoms a-dangle on her rib cage like two Bull Durham sacks half filled with buckshot, her stomach as scarred and dimpled as an old golf ball, her meager legs sheathed in torn nets of varicose veins, her sequin-spangled crotch thrusting fitfully to some obscure beat that she alone seemed able to discern in the strident rhythms of "Resurrection Shuffle," which is what the jukebox happened, appropriately enough, to be playing at the moment.

"Pour it *on*, Lucille!" someone hollered from somewhere out there in the murk, and someone else hollered, "Let's see them titties fly!" And I saw that there were maybe twenty-five or thirty customers in the place, nearly all of them men, sitting in clutches of twos and threes at the tables closest to the stage, and half a dozen next-thing-to-bare-ass-nekkid ladies plying the sea of smoke with trays of drinks. I spotted an empty table over near the wall and made for it.

I needn't have worried about my hair. For I'd no sooner sat down than there emerged out of the gloom a tray-bearing damsel—she looked young enough to be Lucille's granddaughter—appareled in tasseled pasties and a sort of sequined diaper, with breasts scarcely bigger than a pair of green persimmons and a face as amiably homely as a beagle pup's, and she walked straight up to me and put out her hand to stroke my hair and said, loudly but to no one in particular, in a voice so nasal it twanged like a broken guitar string, "Shit fire, I wisht you'd look at the heada *hair* on hee-yim!" Then, holding my locks back with her free hand, she leaned over and planted a kiss as wet as a raw oyster smack in my left ear.

"Whatcha havin', California?" she inquired, rising. Suddenly I felt like Randolph Scott, when he strides into the Barbary Coast Saloon with the dust of the trail still on his boots, and the dance-hall queen sidles up to him and murmurs appreciatively, "Sa-a-a-ay! Whatcha havin', Tex?"

"Well," I said, "I guess I'll have another one of those, to start with."

"Aw, naw," she said, grinning. "One to a customer, now."

I told her I'd settle for an Oertels '92, then, if she had one. On the stage the venerable Lucille, unresurrected but still gamely shuffling, creaked her way through the last few bars of her number, and a man's voice, hoarse with phlegm and static, issued from a two-bit loudspeaker, wheedling, "Awright, fellas, don't set on your hands, these girls'll work hard for you if you let 'em hear it." The disembodied voice paused to accommodate a listless spatter of applause, along with two or three equally halfhearted catcalls, then droned on. "That was the lovely Lucille, with skin all o-ver her bod-eh! The title of that little number was called 'It Won't Get Well If You Picket.' It's one of them good ole union songs."

"Who's that talking?" I asked the girl when she came back with my beer.

"Oh, him," she said sourly, gesturing vaguely toward the back of the room, where a seedy-looking middle-aged sport in a porkpie hat was sitting at a table by the jukebox with a glass of beer, three empty bottles, and a microphone before him. "That's Billy Bob Todd. He's supposed to be some kinda comedian."

"Well, what about Little Enis? Is he going to . . . ?"

But Billy Bob Todd was already answering the question for me. "And now," he was saying, "here he is, the Man with a Golden Voice, and a Million Friends, Little Pee—uh, Little Enis!"

"Thank you, Billy Bird Tur—uh, Billy Bob Todd," said a familiar voice, and I looked back to the stage and there he was, perched atop a tall stool, cradling an upside-down twelve-string acoustic guitar in his arms, old Enis himself in the more than ample flesh, a rotund little bodhisattva in a polo shirt and sporty white wing tips, and slacks so snugly cut that Old Blue showed himself in bas-relief inside them, dressing left; Enis and Blue, that immortal pair, indivisible as Damon and Pythias, Abbott and Costello, Ferrante and Teicher, travelin' along singin' a song, Enis and the friend that sticketh closer than a brother.

Now there's Enis, grinning impishly above his guitar to acknowledge the laugh he's won at the expense of Billy Bird Turd, Enis's tiny right hand already fingering the frets over the top of the guitar's neck after his own heretical fashion, Enis's left hand rising involuntarily to smooth back that black-enamel hair, Enis smiling as he checks himself out in the full-length mirror mounted on the wall stage right and finds himself good, the best of all possible Enises, Enis bending to his mike to say, "Welcome to Boots' Supper Club, here in the beautiful Hotel Scott-Hilton, overlookin' the Southern Railroad tracks . . . Now here's a song I used to play when I was a boy down in Hogue Holler."

Out there in the raucous darkness I sat poised on the edge of my seat, waiting for the opening licks of "Blue Suede Shoes" or "Rip It Up" or "Shake, Rattle, and Roll"—or even "Love Letters in the Sand"—to send me tripping off down memory lane, telling myself what a card old Enis was. Why, Enis playing "Rip It Up" in Hogue Holler would be like E. Power Biggs playing "I Took My Organ to the Party" at Carnegie Hall.

But chances are they do play "Wildwood Flower" in Hogue Holler, and that's what Enis was playing now, flat-picking little clusters of notes as sweet and delicate as periwinkles, tiny nosegays cascading down from the scratchy old loudspeaker overhead.

"How about it, California? You gonna pay me for that beer or not?"

"Oh, sorry," I said as I dug a dollar from my pocket. "But I don't think I ever heard Enis play bluegrass before. He used to play just rock 'n' roll, mostly."

"Well," she said, "far as I'm concerned, I've done heard enough of that old hillbilly shit down home in Crab Orchard to do me for a lifetime. But Enis's been sick in the hospital, you know, he can't jump around that way no more. Hey, I bet they don't play that old hillbilly shit out there in California, do they? Shit fire, I wish I was in California, and Crab Orchard, Kentucky, had a feather up its ass. Then me and it'd both be tickled."

"You better stay where you are," I told her. "These days, everybody in California talks about coming to Kentucky."

"Well," she said gloomily, "I shore do hope some of 'em comes to Crab Orchard then."

She started to move on to the next table, but—especially since she was escaping with my change still on her tray—I figured I was entitled to another question. "Hey, Crab Orchard," I called after her, "how's Old Blue? He hasn't been sick too, has he?"

"Blue?" she said, already moving off again. "I don't know nobody by that name."

Uh oh, I thought, *this could be serious*. (How was it that old folksong went, the one about the hound dog? "When Old Blue died, he died so hard / He shook the ground in my backyard . . .") But Enis sure didn't *look* like a sick man, up there blithely plucking those bouquets of wildflowers off the face of his guitar like Mary, Mary, Quite Contrary. In fact, he looked perfectly fine, fat and sassy and full of vinegar, his hair still black and sleek, his eye still aglint with that old devilment, his jaw still jutting with that old bulldog audacity, a ringer for J. Edgar Hoover's renegade kid brother, the wild one that ran away to join a rock 'n' roll band twenty years ago.

And when he polished off "Wildwood Flower" and eased on into "Loose Talk" and began to sing ("When I go out walkin' / There's lots of loose talkin' . . . "), his voice seemed to me clearer and stronger and surer than ever; in the refrain ("We may have to leave here / To find peace of mind, dear . . . "), it fairly rang with the doleful, plangent tones of that chronic melancholia that, in country music, almost inevitably afflicts backstairs lovers, like a kind of psychic venereal disease.

But it was a tough house—mostly, they were there to see them titties fly—and such applause as "Loose Talk" pulled down was sparse and indifferent. Enis followed up with "Six Days on the Road," Dave Dudley's truck-driver classic, but that failed him, too; this time I clapped for him almost alone, and the sound of my applause disappeared without a trace into the general hubbub of social intercourse.

"Awright now," Enis said dispiritedly, "I'm gonna play somethin' real soft this time, so I can hear you all talk."

He did an "I Kept the Wine and Threw Away the Rose" that could only have been sung by a man who'd lived it, but the trouble was that half the audience had lived it, too, and evidently they weren't quite drunk enough just yet to want to be reminded of it. Then he took a shot at "Release Me," but for all his Golden Voice, Enis was no Engeldinck Humperbert, and that one didn't move them either. He filled out the set with "Sam's Place" and "Your Cheatin' Heart," and then, looking really dejected, he mumbled something about taking a break and switched off his mike.

"*Thank* you, Little Enis!" cried Billy Bob Todd. "Give him a nice hand, fellas! Enis was brought to you tonight by the makers of Black Draught. He'll be back in a little while, brought to you by the makers of Blue Ointment. But *now* . . . "

At Billy Bob's urging, they finally rewarded Enis with a tolerably respectable little hand, and he smiled and waved and bobbed his head in the approved how-sweet-it-is fashion, like a diminutive Jackie Gleason. But when he eased himself off his stool, a sudden pain somewhere in his vitals pinched off the smile into a fleeting grimace, and I knew then that Crab Orchard's report was on the money: Little Enis, the original Glutton for Punishment, was definitely not a well man.

"But *now,* fellas," Billy Bob went on as Enis stashed his guitar and stool in the wings, "we got a very beautiful girl for you, this girl comes from a very large family—one mother and twelve fathers—here she is, the Queen of the Jungle, the lovely Edna!"

Little Richard struck up "Boney Moronie" on the jukebox and the Lovely Edna, a portly, double-chinned dumpling in a foot-tall blond bouffant wig and tasseled pasties and leopard-skin bikini bottoms, waddled onstage and began sort of marching in place to the music, phlegmatically hunching her suety loins every so often but mainly just picking up first one foot and then the other, as if she needed to go to the bathroom and had found the door locked.

"Sooo-ooo-ooeeeey!" Billy Bob hollered. Edna, sullen beneath her wig, flipped him the bird and trudged on.

The next time Crab Orchard steamed past with her tray, I flagged her down and ordered another beer. When she brought it, I asked her what it was that had put Enis in the hospital.

"I thank it was his liver," she told me, almost gaily. "They say the whiskey's just about eat it right out of him."

But she said if I wanted to talk to him during his break, I'd find him sitting in the little room beyond the bar (I looked where she was pointing in time to see Enis, his ovoid silhouette ballooning up from those pegged pants cuffs, trundle through the doorway like a toy top wobbling on its spindle), and—same old Enis—there wasn't nothing in this world, she said, that he liked better than for somebody to go back there and make over him a little.

All right, I thought when she was gone, suppose I do go back and talk to him, what then? It's bound to be another downer, I figured. First there'd be the awkward inevitabilities—"Uh, Mr. Enis, uh, you probably don't remember me, but I used to . . . "—and then we'd settle down to a leisurely, carefully considered discussion of . . . what? "The Influence of the Celtic Bardic Tradition upon the Work of Carlos Toadvine"? The fact that I'd been "doing him" ("Do Enis, Ed! Do Enis!") at cocklety factail parties for nearly fifteen years now? The fact that the world was going to hell in a handbasket and both of us were going with it?

"Looka there, fellas!" Billy Bob whooped. "Ain't that the loveliest sight you ever seen?" He was directing the beam of an oversized flashlight through the smoky dimness at the Lovely Edna, Queen of the Jungle, who now stood with her back to her audience. As the beam of light settled on her already almost naked backside, she reached behind her and hooked her thumbs in the waistband of her leopard-skin panties and lowered them to the tops of her thighs, the better that we might admire her opulent embarrassment of riches.

"Edna, honey," Billy Bob implored, "show these boys how you can make that right one wink at 'em, now! Watch that right-hand one, boys!" Edna obligingly bunched and twitched the muscles in her right buttock and set it to jiggling like a dish of vanilla pudding. "*Look* at that, fellas! I tell you, boys, a man could write a *book* about a thing like that!"

Well, by God, Billy Bob, a man could, at that, couldn't he? Not a book, of course, and not about Edna's ass, of course; but if a man was half a writer, he could situate old Enis in this place, this Boots' Bar where human frailty seems endlessly on parade, and do an interview or something that might—if a man was half a writer—reveal a whole hell of a lot about fame's dereliction and fate's treachery; about . . . mortality.

Sure, why not? I could go back into the past and fulfill that ancient promise; it would be a sort of second chance to set at least that one small alcove of my untidy history in order. Maybe I'd even learn something in the process, maybe he'd tell me what it was *really* like to go down for the third time and then come to and find oneself still struggling against the tide of circumstance. And right outside in the bus, buried beneath the debris of my travels, didn't I just happen to have my trusty little tape recorder? The times, they were a-wastin'!

In a trice I was outside in the McClanavan, rooting through moldy sleeping bags after my tape recorder, and in another trice I was standing over Enis's table in the back room of Boots'—where Enis sat alone and glumly pensive over a cup of Pennzoil-colored coffee—holding out the tape recorder so he couldn't miss it, saying, "Uh, Mr. Enis, uh, you probably don't remember me, but . . . " and Enis, instantly perking up and eyeing the tape recorder as thirstily as though it were a fifth of J. T. S. Brown, was saying, "An innerview, huh? You know, when I was with Jerry Lee Lewis, we was innerviewed just about ever' day, by ever' reddy-o station between here to Australia. Yeah, that guy over there was real comical, the way they talk and all."

And suddenly The Ed 'n' Enis Show was on the air again, Enis and I caught in our own intimate little time warp, me telling Enis how the article I intended to write about him would surely make him even richer and more famous than my master's thesis would have done; Enis telling me how he'd once been all set to get rich and famous on his own, how he'd gone on the road with Jerry Lee and played Lost Vegas with Fats Domino, how he was doing all right for himself until he came back to Lexington and the bottle brought him down (*When I was out here to the nuthouse, tryin' to get myself straightened out, they put me in this occupational therapy, you know? To occupy your mind? So they give me this big wad of clay and says, 'Now, you make whatever's on your mind, Enis.' So I made me a little canoe, see, and a little Indian' a-layin' in it. Not doin' nothing, just a-layin' there! And painted it blue! The whole thing, boat and Indian and all! And that shrinker says to me, 'Now, Enis, what do you reckon that stands for?' And I says, 'Why, it looks to me like that's just what was occupyin' my mind! Nothin'! Not one damn thing! I reckon I'm just like that old Indian!), and how . . .*

Along about here on the tape is where the Lovely Edna, carrying an empty tray in one hand and cupping the right side of her jaw in the other, comes slouching in and sinks into a chair and moans, "Aaaaah shit, I *can't* wait no more goddamn tables, I got a goddamn abscess tooth! *Plus* it's my goddamn period. Lemme hide out back here with you all for a minute."

Out front somebody is indifferently plucking at a guitar. I tilt my chair back to where I can look through the door into the other room. Billy Bob Todd has mounted the stage and is sitting on Enis's stool, with Enis's guitar across his lap. He is getting about as much music from it as Enis would from flat-picking a barbed-wire fence.

"That son-of-a-bitch Billy Bob is gonna get my guitar outta tune again," Enis grumps. "He thinks he's a picker. Sheeit. He couldn't pick his mother out of a spastic parade."

Edna, gingerly probing along her gumline with a grubby forefinger, notices the tape recorder mike at her elbow. "What're you all doin'?" she snickers around her finger. "Broadcastin' to outer space?"

(Well, *hidy*, out there in the void, friends and neighbors! This here's your Ed 'n' Enis Show, where all the action's at! We got it all right here, we got crude dudes and lewd nudes, we got Ed and Enis and Edna's Ass, we got Old Blue and Billy Bird Turd, we got Twenty Girls Twenty, we got . . .)

"This boy here," Enis is telling Edna, setting her straight, "this boy here is Ned McManahan, he's a p'fessor over at the colletch. He's fixing to write a book on my life story."

We got, like I said, the same old Enis. But Edna coolly appraises me and is plainly not impressed. "This nerve is dying," she declares as her finger disappears into her mouth again. "The gobgamn nerve is dying."

And how (Enis went on) this last time the high life had almost laid him low for keeps: *Well, we was playin' out here to Comers Bar, and I just keeled over, right there on the stage, and never woke up till eight days later. And when I come out of my coma, that doctor told me that if I was to start in drinkin' again, I wouldn't live a good two weeks. See, they had went up in me with a tube and tuck a picture of my liver, and it was just a-floatin' in there! So what I mean, I cannot consume no amount of alcoholic beverages whatsoever, hardly. 'Cause you just as well start talkin' to the Good Man Upstairs when your liver goes out on you.*

I heard the click inside the tape recorder that told me we were out of tape, which was just as well, because a moment later Crab Orchard came in to remind Enis that it was almost midnight, time for his last set.

"Hey, Enis," I said, "Crab Orchard here tells me she's never been introduced to Old Blue! How'd you let that happen?"

Despite the miseries in her tooth, the Lovely Edna managed a knowing smile at the memory of Old Blue. But Enis took my remark at face value and answered the question accordingly:

"Well," he said gravely, "your liver, see, controls all the har-mone cells in your body. And after I come out of that hospital, I just didn't have no harmones left, hardly. But they been givin' me these shots, and they say it won't be long now till . . ." Noticing Crab Orchard standing over him looking characteristically perplexed, Enis grinned and patted her naked haunch. "Aw yeah, Crab Apple, honey, you'd like Old Blue, if you just knowed him. He's got a head like a housecat and ribs like a hungry hound."

This time Crab Orchard got it. She giggled and slapped lightly at Enis's hand and said, "Why-Enis-you-awful-thang-you," but she didn't really mean it. She even blushed a little, as if something within her recognized that his very lubricity bespoke a crazy kind of boyish innocence, that after his own fashion he was being a perfect gentleman, he was being *courtly*. Old Blue was his Excalibur, and Enis had presented him to her even as the gallants of King Arthur's court must have offered up their swords in service to their ladies.

"Listen here, you dirty man," Crab Orchard said, "if you're so hot to trot, whyn't you go out there and play me some rock 'n' roll? I'm *tard* of that ol' country shit."

"Hey, yeah!" I put in. "Do some Jerry Lee songs! Do Elvis!"

"Oh, Lordy," Enis said, wincing as he struggled to his feet, "I don't know, I got awful bad water on the knee tonight, I don't know if I can . . ."

He'd do it, though, I realized as I watched him go gamely hobbling off after Crab Orchard; he'd do it because there was a show happening in his head, too, a one-man spectacular starring Carlos Toadvine as the Incomparable Enis, and *that* show must go on, water on the knee or not. He'd do it because he was a trouper, a real little trouper. And besides, if Carlos Toadvine missed a performance, who else could play the role?

"Sounds like Old Blue's been under the weather too," I said to Edna as I gathered up my gear to move back into the other room.

Edna favored me with yet another smile, a wistful one this time. "Aww, that Enis," she mused fondly, a faraway look in her eye. "He sure used to be somethin', he sure did." I started to ask her if she'd care to make a statement to that effect for publication, but just then a sudden twinge in her tooth brought that wet slug of a finger back into her mouth, so I reconsidered and went on out.

By the time I'd picked up a beer at the bar and found myself a table, Enis was onstage, perched on his stool re-tuning his guitar after Billy Bob's irreverent trifling. His melancholia had evidently passed; he was grinning, and that old roguish gleam was in his eye, that incorrigible vintage-Enis cheekiness that, inscribed upon this roly-poly latter-day Enis's chubby little features, put me in mind of a concupiscent choirboy, a randy cherub. Right then it wouldn't have surprised me in the least if Old Blue himself had come dancing out on Enis's knee, spiffy as Mr. Peanut, with a little top hat and a monocle and a tiny black bow tie and a walking stick, Stage-Door Johnny Blue doing a sprightly buck-and-wing to the tune of "Fit as a Fiddle," Old Blue in the pink again, fit as a fiddle and ready for love. Somehow I was already beginning to suspect that this set just might turn out to be an altogether different story from the last one.

"The girls'll be back in a minute, fellas," Billy Bob advised us. "They're shaving, right now. But here's the man you've all been waiting for, the Man with a Golden Voice, the one and only, the *fabulous* Little Enis!"

A pit-a-pat of applause greeted the announcement, but the audience was still restive, still a good deal more taken up with its own concerns—ordering another round, going out to take a leak, grab-assing the waitresses—than it was with whatever Enis had to offer. This time, though, Enis was up to the challenge; he was eyeing his indifferent audience as cockily as the lecherous pissant in that old joke, the one who crawls up an elephant's leg with seduction on his mind.

But the first order of business is to get the elephant's attention. "Now, here's a nice little song," Enis said, "if you like nasty dirty old songs." He picked off a tantalizingly swift run of warm-up notes, then added, "But this song ain't really dirty. It's just all dependin' where your mind is at."

> *Any ice today, ladies?*
> *Any ice today, ladies?*
> *How about a little piece today?*

That did it; as the song went on ("There's a lady lives on Ninth Street, / Her name is Missuz Brown; / She takes ice most ev'ry day, / Got the biggest box in town"), it got ranker ("There's a lady lives on Tenth Street, / Her name is Missuz Green; / She don't get no ice today, / 'Cause her damned ol' box ain't clean") and ranker ("I'm a very nice iceman, / I won't cheat you, of course; / But if you want a bigger piece, / I'll have to get my horse"), and the ranker the song became, the more clamorously the crowd acclaimed it; it woke them up and broke them up, jacked them up and cracked them up; they cheered and clapped and stomped and whistled so lustily that by the end of the last verse ("I'm a very nice iceman, / That's very plain to see; / But hurry up and put it in, / It's drippin' . . . on . . . m' knee!"), the din of their enthusiasm nearly drowned out the final chorus.

"Aw, yeah," Enis said as soon as they'd settled back a bit, "I'm a go-getter. My wife works, and I go get 'er!" With that he launched into a "Salty Dog" as spiritedly priapic as a sailor home on shore leave; and in the little theater inside my head Old Blue danced onstage again, an amorous old salt in navy bell-bottoms and a tiny white swabbie cap cocked low and rakish on his beetled brow, like Gene Kelly in *Anchors Aweigh*. As Blue took his bow and cakewalked off into the wings, Enis stopped a go-go lady who was just then passing before the stage—a hefty, hulking, heavy-breasted girl in a wig like a double-dip cone of Dairy Whip—and said, "Hey, Big 'Un, honey, would you brang me a Co-Cola? Maybe I can *drownd* this goddamn liver." While she shambled off to fetch the Coke, he killed time with a few more bars of "Salty Dog," just idling his motor, letting us know he wasn't finished with us yet, not by a long shot. When the Big 'Un came back with his glass of Coke, he tossed the whole thing off in one long swallow and wiped his mouth with the back of his hand.

"Now then, sweetheart," he said, pointing the bottom of the glass at her orange-tasseled natural endowments, "let's me and you show these boys how you can start them things by hand on a cold mornin.'"

The Big 'Un, recognizing her cue, nodded happily and set down her tray and turned to face the audience, and Enis said, "Now, here's a little number I learnt when I was on the road with Jerry Lee Lewis" and laced into "Great Balls of Fire," and the Big 'Un, bouncing in double time on her toes, grabbed herself a handful of her left breast, gave it a fierce counterclockwise flip, and set its tassel to spinning, slowly and erratically at first, like the prop on

Jimmy Stewart's plane in one of those old You-can't-send-the-kid-up-in-a-crate-like-that movies, then faster and faster as she warmed up, as *Enis* warmed up—"*Hook* it, Enis!" somebody hollered. "*Hook* it, son!"—and then she laid hold of her right breast and cranked it up the way she had the other one, clockwise this time, she was a DC-3 revving up on the runway, her prop wash swirled the smoke about her, and now Enis was really digging in, getting after it—"'Y' shake m' nerves and y' rattle m' brain, / Too much *luhhhv* / Drives a man insane!"—the All-American Left-Handed Upside-Down Guitar Player had his chops back; that big twelve-string rang out as though Jerry Lee himself had crawled inside it, Jerry Lee and a concert grand and the entire New York Philharmonic Orchestra—"'Y' broke m' will, / But what a *threeell*"—the *Enis Hour* was on the air, brought to you in living Eniscolor through the miracle of Enisvision, featuring the interpretive dance stylings of the lovely Big 'Un and the noted impressionist Old Blue, and starring the Enis the World Awaited, the Man with a Golden Voice and a Million Friends, the Man with . . .

Good-nis gray-shus, gret *balls o'fie-yer!*

But how about that curious-looking long-haired party out there in the audience, the one in the California getup, the one with his fortieth birthday hard upon him and his mind blown as full of holes as Enis's liver, the one who's leaping half out of his chair, hollering, "Do Elvis, Enis! Do 'All Shook Up'! Do 'Hound Dog'! Do 'Lawdy Miss Clawdy'! Do . . . "?

Uh, huh; me again. The old Loose End again, the noted scribbler again, stoned again. The more things change, the more they stay the same, and here comes another one, just like the other one. Because suddenly Enis was down off that stool and on his feet, and his left knee—water and all—was pumping inside his pants as though he wore a jackhammer for a peg leg with a hot-water bottle for a kneepad, and he was seesawing his guitar back and forth across the swell of his belly and cranking away at the face of it like a demented organ grinder, singing, "Well, bless-a mah soul, whuzz-a wrong wi' me? / Ah'm a-eetchin' lak a bug on a fuzzeh tree," and the Big 'Un was about to take off into the wild blue yonder, and I was belaboring my tabletop with all my old abandon—like Enis, at least for now I had my chops back—everything had slipped back into sync, I could *recognize* myself again; I mean, I'd know that guy anywhere, no matter what disguise he wore, that's just old Fred Callahan, the noted Enisologist from out at the colletch, he's been trying to find his way back to this moment for nearly fifteen years, and now at last he's here; he and Enis and Old Blue, too, they're a little the worse for the wear, maybe, but they've all made it this far more or less intact, Old Blue can still rise to the occasion when he gets his booster shots, and the Enis That Shook the World can shake it still, and their accompanist Jed Mackrelham, the old California mutant, is still the premier tabletop percussionist in all of Rockabillydom, just *listen* at 'em wail, just listen at that "Lawdy Miss Clawdy," that "Hi-yo, Silver," that "Hound Dog," that "Kansas City," that "Blue Suede Shoes"; why, these boys coulda been *stars* if they'd just kept that act together: Enis would be on the cover of *Rolling Stone, Playboy* would run a full-color spread of Lucille and Crab Orchard and Edna and the Big 'Un and all the Enisettes, *The New Yorker* would do a four-part profile of Old Blue, *Psychology Today* would editorialize on the phenomenon of Enis envy in American culture, and Professor TedNedFredJed McHammerclam would deliver a brilliant lecture entitled "The Influence of the Celtic Bardic Tradition upon the Work of Carlos Toadvine" at the Juilliard Colletch of Musical Knowletch; they coulda made it big, they coulda played Carnegie Hall, they coulda been, by God, *immortal*!

Ah, but what voice is this I hear, croaking down at me across the years from the pedagogical summit I so long ago aspired to? "Now then, Mr. McClanahan, in his 'Ode on Intimations of Mortality,' Wordsworth asks himself the rhetorical question 'Whither is fled the visionary gleam? / Where is it now, the glory and the dream?' Perhaps you could tell us—*pull yourself together, man!*—how the poet, in his maturity, consoles himself in the poem's closing quatrain for the loss of that youthful vision of immortality?"

Why, certainly, Dr. Earwigg (I might've answered if I hadn't skipped out on all those seminars), I do believe the lines in question are, if memory serves, the following:

> *Thanks to the human heart by which we live,*
> *Thanks to its tenderness, its joys, and fears,*
> *To me the meanest flower that blows can give*
> *Thoughts that do often lie too deep for tears.*

JUANITA AND
THE FROG PRINCE

WELCOME TO BURDOCK COUNTY, hails the peeling road-side billboard out at the county line, THE ASPARAGUS BED OF THE COMMONWEALTH.

Not that anyone in Burdock County actually *grows* asparagus in any noteworthy quantity; we're in tobacco country here, and asparagus makes, at best, an indifferent smoke. It's rather just that the noble vegetable is reputed to insist upon the choice spot in the garden for itself, and civic-minded Burdock Countians like to suppose they're at least as discriminating as a stalk of asparagus.

At what is purported to be at once the highest point of ground and the exact geographical center of the county, the Burdock County courthouse, an ash-gray pile of colonnaded, crenellated stucco, bulks exceeding large, with the village of Needmore, nine hundred citizens strong, abjectly huddled round it, and the wrinkled hills and dales of Burdock County tumbling off to the four horizons like a vast unmade bed. Until recently, the predominant color in this great rumpled patchwork vista would have been green—the bosky verdure of woods and thickets, the paler shades of meadows and cornfields and tobacco patches—but the harvest season's over now, and the first frost has come and gone; and on this day, a certain fine late October Sunday afternoon in 1941, the orange and dun and russet hues of autumn are in the ascendancy.

Atop the courthouse, that imposing eyesore, is situated yet another imposing eyesore: a bulbous, beehive-shaped cupola with four clockfaces the size of mill wheels, each asserting with all the authority of its hugeness four entirely different times of day. Two sides of the clock have, in fact, long since concluded that being right twice a day is better than never being right at all and have taken their stands at, respectively, 9:14 and 7:26. The remaining pair toil on, not in tandem but quite independently, one gaining several seconds every hour, the other just as resolutely losing them. There is, moreover, a bell in the clock tower that has a timetable all its own and is liable to toll midnight at three in the morning and noon at suppertime. The dedicated public servants in the courthouse learned long ago to ignore altogether the two broken clocks and the bell, and to come to work by the slow clock and knock off by the fast one. They regard their singular time-piece as a labor-saving device, and treasure it accordingly.

"... that the said defendant Luther Jukes, a.k.a. Two-Nose Jukes, in the village of Pinhook in the county of Burdock, on the twenty-third day of August, AD 1941, and before the finding of this indictment, did unlawfully, feloniously, and maliciously, with force and arms, deposit at, in, and near a doorway on a porch being that of the Bludgins Texaco Station and Garage, owned and operated by Lonzo W. Bludgins, a.k.a. Lugnut Bludgins, and the place where Lonzo W. Bludgins was then employed and did work, a package consisting of a Dutch Masters cigar box enclosing a deadly weapon, to wit: a weight bomb loaded with nitroglycerin, batteries, nuts and bolts, nails, hinges, and similar hard, egregious, and explosive substances, the said Luther Jukes, with the felonious and malicious intent then and there to kill, wound, and injure the said Lonzo W. Bludgins, a human being, by means of said deposit, and the said Lonzo W. Bludgins not then knowing that the said package contained nitroglycerin and/ or explosive substances did place his hand upon it and that, as a result thereof, the said package did explode, thereby wounding the said Lonzo W. Bludgins in, about, and upon various portions of his anatomy, body, and person, and from which shooting, explosion, and wounding, death did forthwith occur..."

The Burdock County jail occupies the entire northwest corner of the court-house grounds and complements its larger sister by presenting to the mer-cantile establishments across the street an equally grim visage, rendered in the same ashy stucco complexion. The structure weds a stolid gray bungalow of inconsolably gloomy aspect—here reside the duly elected county jailer, currently Dutch Louderback, and his family—to a miniature Bastille, replete with barred embrasures and steel shutters and little fake oriels and battle-ments. This edifice squats, ogreish and ominous, against the bungalow's posterior and is not infrequently the temporary residence of one or another—or several—of the jailer's in-laws, the Souseleys, who tend to drink a little.

In recent weeks, however, there has languished in the jail's coziest—in respect to elbow room—and most secluded cell a sojourner vastly more distinguished than the usual assortment of weekending Souseleys and other small-time miscreants, misanthropes, and misfits. Indeed, the present occupant of Jailer Louderback's dank little accommodation has distinguished himself in all three of those areas of endeavor: in miscreancy by having summarily dispatched to a better world the said Lugnut W. Bludgins by means of the said infernal device; in misanthropy by cordially despising the entire human race and everyone in it; and in misfitted-ness by looking at the world from behind a physiognomy that boasts, among sundry other remarkable features, precisely twice the regulation number of noses—which is to say, two. Noses.

By way of description—to get it over with—let's just say that the two olfactory organs are situated side by side, that they share a common nostril (for a grand total of three), and that neither is of anything remotely approaching noble stamp. Above this distinctive bifurcation, its proprietor's dark eyes glitter with malign intelligence; below it, due to some structural facial anomaly attendant upon the excess of noses, his lips are twisted into a crooked grimace, the fixed, malevolent parody of a grin. His complexion is of a strange gray-green cast, not unlike that of the jail itself, a condition that has given rise to speculation that he was sired by a Chinee, or a Hindoo, or a Portagee, or even, in the opinion of two or three local Flash Gordon fans, a Martian or a Moonman. And for good measure, he is as bowlegged as a terrapin, the result of a childhood bout with rickets, and his ears stand out from his head like a Ford coupe with both doors open.

The proper name of this understandably irritable personage is Luther Jukes, but human nature being what it is, all his days he has been called—though rarely to his ill-conditioned face—"Two-Nose," a soubriquet that, carelessly employed, cost the late Lugnut Bludgins his very life. Yet even that extreme measure hasn't had the desired effect, for now, as he awaits trial, certain conviction, and life without parole, Two-Nose Jukes owns the most celebrated name in Burdock County.

Juanita Sparks, hoosegow scullery maid and orphaned niece of the jailer's wife, stands at the jail-yard clothesline with a mouthful of clothespins and an armful of wet convict underwear. She has felt like s-h-i-t all this livelong day, ever since she woke up with morning sickness for the fifth time in a row. When she thinks about the way those old boys, Warren Harding Skidmore and Sharky Vance and Dime Logan and them, have been a-wallering her in the backseat of Warren Harding's car lately, hopping all over her like fleas on a hog-lot dog, she's about decided that this old s-e-x ain't half what it's cracked up to be.

And now it's a regular old boogeyman she's got on her hands, a downright murderer, that two-nosed thing, that Jukes. Juanita can't hardly bear to look at him herself; her eyes land on his forehead every time and then just slide off his face like two fried eggs out of a skillet. But one time she came in to mop when he was on his bunk, asleep, so for the first time she could stand there and just look and look at him, staring at him with all the eyes in her head, till all at once his own eyes popped open, and she seen that he was wide awake, grinning at her as though they shared some awful secret.

Juanita didn't say a word, she just grabbed her mop and fell to mopping like she was killing snakes. But ever since, whenever she feels him looking at her, she knows that if she looks back that terrible grin lies waiting for her, just like a boogeyman in the dark.

Here lately, though, whenever there's nobody else around, he's been trying to talk to her, saying the strangest things. Like one morning, as she was mopping along in front of his cell, he'd said, right out of the blue, "Maud Muller on a summer's day, raked the meadow sweet with hay."

Don't you know the difference between a rake and a mop? Juanita had thought. But she didn't say a word.

Another time, he said, "I ain't nowhere near as bad as people says I am. Since when was genius found respectable?"

Only a day or two ago, just as she was finishing up the corridor, he'd sung out, "No one is so accursed by fate, no one so utterly desolate, but some heart, though unknown, responds unto his own. You'd like me, sister, if you just knowed me better!"

Juanita never could make heads or tails out of it herself; she always just kept on mopping and pretended like she hadn't heard him. Still, the words stayed with her, even the big ones, and she turned them over and over in her mind, wondering about them.

But she did recognize the poem about Maud What's-her-name from

Miss Gantley's English class. It told a story about this Maud, which was a farm girl that loved a judge which come riding up on a big horse. It was the one that ended, "For of all sad words of tongue or pen"—to this day, Juanita can't hardly think about it without getting a tear in her eye—"the saddest are these: 'It might have been!'"

Wearily, Juanita picks up her empty basket and heads back to the jail basement for another load, wondering what in the Lord's name ever took a hold of her to make her quit school and go into cleaning up after a bunch of old jailbirds anyhow. Old drunkerts a-puking and dirtying theirselfs and carrying on all night long about the rats and snakes and spiders that can't nobody see but them. She don't care if most of them *is* her own mommy's kin, you just don't meet your finer high uppity-up quality of people in a jail.

If anybody in Burdock County should've known better than to address Luther Jukes as "Two-Nose," Lugnut Bludgins was the man, considering that he had made the same mistake more than twenty years before, when they were schoolmates, and had received a brickbat to the side of the head in return for the compliment. But Lugnut was nothing if not a nincompoop—indeed, it might be argued that he was nothing *but* a nincompoop—and so when he saw Luther for the first time in years, walking through Pinhook with a ragged hobo bindle on his shoulder, he greeted him, with even less wisdom than wit, as follows: "Well, look who's back! Where you been, Luther Two-Nose, Hollywood?"

Where Luther had been lately, as it happened, was in the state penitentiary in Missouri, serving eighteen months for assault with intent to kill a deputy sheriff who had unburdened himself of a similar jocularity. His cellmate there had been an accomplished safecracker with a pedagogical bent, and Luther had proved an apt apprentice. And so it came to pass that on the very night of Lugnut's little indiscretion, a certain resourceful party broke into a storage shed at the county highway department and made off with a quantity of nitroglycerin and dynamite caps. The following morning, Lugnut Bludgins received the transmogrifying parcel, and instantly was no more.

There had been several witnesses to Lugnut's ill-advised pleasantry of the day before, and within hours Luther Jukes was lodged in the county jail, where he has abided ever since. His trial is now just weeks away, yet he steadfastly refuses even to discuss his case with the attorney appointed to defend him.

"There's two sides to any story," he told the attorney, "and there's two sides to this one. My side is, some people is just too goddamn dumb to live."

Otherwise—except for those inscrutable musings he's shared with Juanita—the only person he's talked to at any length is his grandmother, a dreadful old harridan named Sallie Jukes, who made her way to town on foot just once to visit him at the window of his cell, where they conferred through the bars in hisses and whispers, like hostile serpents.

Two-Nose Jukes is a local product—or, more accurately, a local by-product. He is the fatherless issue of the wayward daughter of the irascible, gimlet-eyed old Sallie Jukes, who has lived since time immemorial on Morgadore Creek, a couple of miles down the road from Pinhook, in two or three rooms of a great, gloomy old log house that has been otherwise abandoned and in ruins for generations.

The widow Jukes lost her husband aeons ago to a serving of her own home-canned green beans, delicately seasoned, legend has it, with a pinch of rat poison and offered at supper on the very day that she discovered him in the barn fraternizing a bit too intimately with the livestock.

The daughter—"Sweaty Betty," as she was affectionately known by her admirers—eventually made herself charming to every unfettered male in the neighborhood, perhaps to ensure that Sallie's woodpile would keep growing even during the longest winter. Betty ran off with a passing tramp around the start of the First World War, urged on by the heartfelt curses of her abandoned parent, and didn't reappear until the early twenties, when a neighbor of old Sallie's recognized her one wintry day walking down the road in the direction of her mother's home, with a child, muffled to the eyeballs against the bitter cold, trudging at her side. A few hours later the neighbor saw her pass again, alone, never to return.

Now these were dark and ignorant times, long before the land had been enlightened by yet another world war, and Sallie Jukes's uncomely visage, her habit of muttering angrily under her breath about male perfidy and falseness, and especially her line of work—she sewed shrouds and laid out bodies for a Pinhook mortician—had long fostered among her neighbors the suspicion that she had access to sinister forces, and was up to no good.

The neighbors believed, or professed to believe, that she was surreptitiously fixing them with the Evil Eye, predisposing them to stub a toe or catch a thumb in the rattrap or drop the brand-new Monkey Ward catalog down the privy. "Bad-Cess Sallie Jukes," she was called. A glance from her could sour milk, it was said, or start a toothache, or induce a cake to fall. Over the years, the sheer volume of mischief attributed to Bad-Cess Sallie Jukes would have put a moderate natural catastrophe to shame.

Sallie augmented her shroud money by gathering herbs, roots, and berries for the manufacture of a line of soothing balms and purgative nostrums, which she concocted in her famous kitchen and peddled door to door. Her clientele bought her wares not out of any abiding confidence in their curative powers but rather as talismans to ward off the venerable apothecary's pernicious influence.

And when she began turning up on their doorsteps with her own personal little hobgoblin at her side, who stood there grinning as though he were enjoying some unspeakable private joke, her fame was much enhanced, and business at her roving pharmacy increased twofold in a single season.

There's too many squirrels in that family tree, people told each other knowingly—there's a dead cat on the line somewheres. In the more benighted reaches of the county, where darkness and superstition still hadn't given way to progress, there was general agreement that those curses the old woman had hurled after her departing daughter had devolved upon the child, surely to Sallie's infinite satisfaction.

In due course, an ad hoc committee of local eminences determined that in the interest of preserving the scenic beauty of Burdock County, an effort should be made to persuade old Sallie to turn her unsightly ward over to the Commonwealth, trusting that august body to find a spot for him in some dank corner of one of its more remote institutions. To advance their proposal, they dispatched a delegation of three—led, perhaps significantly, by Amos Bludgins, father of the ill-fated Lugnut, accompanied by a neighboring farmer and Pinhook's only barber, in whose shop the plan was hatched.

But Sallie, cradling her late husband's rusty double-barreled twelve-gauge in her arms, received them in her dooryard, the reputed Imp of Satan peeking out from behind her voluminous skirts, grinning hospitably, as if he'd like nothing better than to dash out and bite the company on its several ankles.

"Git," the old woman welcomed them.

"Now, Mother Jukes," Amos began, removing his hat and gamely stepping forward, "we just . . ."

Sallie brought the shotgun to her shoulder, sighted down the barrel at the balding Bludgins pate, and said, in a voice as bleak as ashes, "How'd you like me t' jump yore head off?"

"Now, Miss Sallie, now," said Amos, backpedaling a step, "we're good Christians, we wouldn't want to get mixed up in nothing like that."

Sallie drew back a firing hammer with her thumb. "Git, then," she said. "Hesh up and git."

The committee adjourned itself on the spot and retired in disarray. But at the end of the lane, Amos Bludgins did look back long enough to see old Sallie point the shotgun to the sky and fire it, first one barrel then the other, while the bandy-legged Imp of Satan danced about her with antic glee.

Within the ensuing month, lightning struck the farmer's henhouse and fricasseed his entire flock of leghorns, and the barber, in an absentminded moment, snipped off the tip of Amos Bludgin's earlobe and had to close up shop and leave town in disgrace. Clearly, it did not pay to mess with Bad-Cess Sallie Jukes.

In due time, the county prevailed upon Sallie to send the boy to school, where he proved, to universal astonishment, to be a remarkably quick study, picking up the three R's so handily, by some mysterious osmotic process, that it almost seemed to his teachers that the skills were already there inside his ugly little head, a wellspring just waiting to be tapped. His capacities, the teachers sensed uneasily, went beyond mere intelligence into the realm of the unnatural, as though he knew more than they did.

In all other respects he turned out to be as intractable and truculent as old Sallie herself. Small for his age, he was nonetheless as tough as toenails and would fight at the drop of an insult or the merest flicker of a disparaging stare, with whatever weaponry came to hand, rock or stick or claw hammer or coal scuttle, all the while grinning like a frolicsome gargoyle. On more than one occasion, he augmented his education by kicking teachers in the shins. It was even rumored that when cornered, he had the power to regurgitate upon his enemies at will, as certain poisonous toads are said to do.

So his acquirements did little to enhance his popularity, and when he failed to show up for the fourth grade, there was rejoicing at Pinhook Elementary, and no one gave the first thought to calling out the truant officer.

In the basement, standing at the washing machine running coveralls through the wringer, Juanita can hear the crazy old one-legged street preacher, the one they call Baloney Jones, stumping on his crutches up and down the steel-plated floor between the cells and the drunk tank, squawking at the drunks the way he does every Sunday afternoon, talking long distance to Jesus on the toy telephone he carries around his neck, telling him what a viper's nest of sinners Brother Baloney finds himself among today—just as if Jesus didn't know all that already, or why would they be in jail in the first place?

It was that Miss Gantley, Juanita reminds herself grimly as she feeds another pair of coveralls to the wringer, Miss Gantley the eighth-grade homeroom teacher, which was just plain j-e-double-l-o-u-s when Juanita came back for her second year in eighth grade bigger in the bustline than old puny-tits Miss Gantley her own self, and when Sharky Vance tried to feel of them in the cloakroom, and she kicked him in his textacles the way her own daddy told her to before he went and died of sclerosis of the liver, Miss Gantley sent her—Juanita!—to the office with a note that said *she* was a bad influent!

Well, Juanita seen right then and there whichaway the land laid, and from then on she just let Warren Harding and Sharky and Dime and them play with her bustesses any old time she felt like it. Which that turned out to be not near as often as *they* felt like it, them boys, and it wadn't long till they'd about drove that old s-h-i-t into the ground.

So she quit school in the ninth grade, the day she turned sixteen, and her Uncle Dutch got her on with the county, doing the laundry and swabbing up after the jailbirds, and now she's went and got herself pragnent, which that is why—watching the last pair of coveralls issue from the wringer, as flat and inky blue as the indigo shadow of the man who'd worn them—which that is just exactly why Juanita wishes with all her heart that little Miss Puny-Tits Gantley had went and got the big bustesses instead of her. It'd serve her right, the old b-i-c-t-h.

"Now listen to me, O my honeys!" Juanita hears Brother Jones implore his little flock as she lugs her wash basket up the cellar stairs. "Sinnin' is like drinkin' outta the spittoon, don't you see! For it's all in one piece, O my honeys, and oncet you start, you can't quit till you've drunk 'er dry!"

Lord, Lord, Juanita sighs. Like s-h-i-t warmed over, that's exactly how she feels.

In his early manhood, young Luther Jukes took up the most solitary trade available: He became a woodsman, a hunter, a very Nimrod stalking the countryside with his grandfather's ancient shotgun on his shoulder and a pack of vicious, half-starved curs surging all about him. Thus did he keep old Sallie's stubbled chin well greased with varmint drippings.

Later, during the second half of the 1930s, Luther left the old woman to her mutterings and set forth to make his way in, of all things, the religion game, taking to the road as the disciple—or, if you please, accomplice—of a barnstorming reprobate tent preacher who billed himself as the Right Reverend P. C. Rexroat, DD, Archbishop of the Canvas Cathedral of the Resurrection, the Light, the Divine Afflatus, and the Main Chance.

The archbishop, as it happened, had been casting about for a square-up act, an attraction rather less ephemeral than the Holy Spirit to entice flocks of potential Lambs of God into the Canvas Cathedral for a good fleecing. When, in his travels, he heard reports of the Burdock County prodigy, he made a pilgrimage to Pinhook at the earliest opportunity.

Like the Bludgins committee before him, he was obliged to stand in Sallie's dooryard and pay his compliments down the twin barrels of the shotgun—wielded this time by young Luther while the old woman stood by with a pitchfork at the ready. But unlike his predecessors, Reverend Rexroat never even flinched—for he was sustained not only by his faith in the Creator of Us All (of which the theologian actually possessed the minimum, though he did not scruple to invoke Him at every opportunity) but also by his complete confidence in a far more reliable certitude, that of irreducible human avarice.

"Madam," he began, in a voice like oil on troubled waters, "our Creator enjoins us against hiding our light beneath a bushel. This lad"—he indicated Luther with a bow—"is a national treasure. It is our sacred duty to exploit that treasure in the service of the Lord."

"Git," came the response, predictably. It was accompanied by a menacing feint with the pitchfork.

"My good woman, kindly desist until you've heard me out. It is true that the Lord has put us in this vale of tears that we might earn our way into His kingdom by our good works, yes, indeed. But in the meantime, He also wishes us to do *well,* you see, to reap the rewards *of this* world for our labors in His vineyard. This young man's face"—the reverend struggled to suppress a shudder at the thought—"could be our fortune. In short, madam, what would you say to, ah, eight dollars a week, direct to you via the U.S. mail?"

"If you would've said ten," Sallie allowed, lowering the pitchfork ever so slightly, "I mighta heered you better."

"Ten it is," the reverend conceded. "I meant to say ten."

"And keep?"

"Ten and keep," he sighed.

"Luther," said the old woman, "put that shotgun down and go fetch this preacher a drink of water. He's got some talkin' to do."

Monday mornings are the worst, as far as Juanita is concerned. They turn loose all the drunks on Sunday evening, so her first job of a Monday is to hose down the drunk tank and swab it out, which is enough right there to make a person ashamed of being a Souseley.

And if that's not bad enough, when Juanita come out of the johnny this morning after she had her morning sickness, she noticed her Aunt Jimmie looking at her real funny, and then Aunt Jimmie looked over at Uncle Dutch and kind of rolled her eyes, like, and Juanita just *knew* they smelt a rat somewheres.

So later on, when they're eating breakfast, she leaves off her wet-mopping and sneaks down the hall to the kitchen door, where she can listen in on them.

"Do you reckon," Aunt Jimmie is saying, "that a man could have got to that child?"

"Well," says Uncle Dutch, sucking his teeth, "a good big boy coulda done it."

Then Aunt Jimmie sets down her coffee cup so hard Juanita can hear it smack the table, and says she's got half a mind to march the girl right straight down the street to Dr. Winnaberry's office. "We run a nice Christian jail here," Aunt Jimmie declares. "If Doc Winnaberry was to say the little snip's in trouble, I'd send her back to the homeplace so fast it'd make her nose bleed. That'd learn her not to go around with her titties stuck out!"

"Some of them says she's runnin' after that Skidmore," Dutch offers. "Maybe he'll marry her."

"Pshaw!" Jimmie snorts. "That worthless thing ain't gonna marry nobody, and there ain't one single Souseley that's man enough to make him!"

Almost reeling, Juanita turns and tiptoes away, holding her breath to choke off a sob. And it is just at this most dismal moment that she remembers something her girlfriend Harletta Porch, who lives in Pinhook, once told her about Bad-Cess Sallie Jukes.

In the gloomiest chamber of the dark inside Juanita's head, a little light comes on. Suddenly she knows what she must do: She has to talk to Luther Jukes.

Philander Cosmo Rexroat was a sky-grifter of the old school. In the fair-weather seasons, he plied the back roads in an ancient LaSalle sedan the size of a locomotive, towing a ramshackle house trailer with a stubby crucifix mounted atop it like an overgrown sarcophagus. The cross bore on either side the modest legend:

$$
\begin{array}{c}
\text{R} \\
\text{E} \\
\text{X} \\
\text{R E X R O A T} \\
\text{R} \\
\text{O} \\
\text{A} \\
\text{T}
\end{array}
$$

His plan, as Rexroat disclosed it to old Sallie, was to effect the instant metamorphosis of young Luther Jukes into a former heathen whom His Eminence, through the sheer vigor of his enunciation of the Word, had brought to his knees at the feet of the Lord during the latest Canvas Cathedral missionary expedition to the godless Orient.

To that purpose, Rexroat, after studying his subject's dingy, leaden complexion for as long as he could bear it, uttered an "Aha!" and plunged into the trailer. A good deal of noisy, expletive-punctuated rummaging ensued, until he finally emerged with an old gray flannel bathrobe, a pair of worn Mexican huaraches with tire-tread soles, a white chiffon window curtain with a fringe of little yarn snowballs, and an extra-wide, hand-painted, gravy-embellished necktie depicting a bucolic autumn scene, complete with falling leaves, pumpkins, Thanksgiving turkeys, and tiny square dancers.

After Luther had stripped to his drawers and donned the flannel caftan and the sandals, the reverend, averting his eyes from his new protégé's cloven mug as best he could, fashioned the curtain into a sort of rudimentary burnoose and secured it by tying the autumnal cravat as a headband around Luther's brow, square dancers do-si-doing up and down his spine, little snowballs a-dangle on his forehead. Rexroat took up the chiffon train and flung it, with a Lawrence of Arabia flourish and an audible sigh of relief, about the lower portion of Luther's visage, then stepped back and declared his creation a worthy rival to the Sheik of Araby.

"Behold, madam!" he exulted. "Out of Egypt have I called my son! Behold Abdul the Assyrian, the Infidel with the Mark of Satan upon His Countenance and the Love of Jay-zis in His Heart!"

"Yas, Jay-zis!" echoed the Infidel. "I'm gone, Grannie! Amen goddamn, I am gone!"

"Hesh, mister!" snapped the doting matriarch. "I'll have that first ten cash on the barrelhead," she announced, turning to Rexroat. "I need to git me some good baloney, for I have et all the groundhog I can stand."

Within the hour they were on their way. Rexroat and Luther rode together in the LaSalle's front seat, His Eminence waxing theosophical at the wheel, Luther riding shotgun, grinning behind his veil as if he found the archbishop's every utterance immeasurably enlightening. The backseat was the exclusive domain of Rexroat's other disciple, a decrepit elderly wino roustabout by the name of Prince John, who served as a sort of curate of the Canvas Cathedral.

"And now, my sons," the reverend declaimed after their first few miles on the road, waving his unlit stogie at the windshield as though he were conducting a symphony of himself, "let us take sweet counsel together. Why do the heathen rage, you ask? I'll tell you why, my lads. Because the way of the transgressor is hard! Because the serpent abideth in the garden! Because the king of terrors stalks the Earth, while Hell enlarges itself daily! Yea, verily, I have seen all Israel scattered upon the hills, as sheep that have not a shepherd, and doubtless there are those among them that wouldn't pay a nickel to see a pissant eat a bale of hay! But *we* shall shepherd them, Luther my boy! Together, you and I shall drive the wolf from the fold and teach the children of Israel that above all things, the Lord loveth a cheerful giver!"

"Amen, by God!" cried Abdul the Infidel.

"On the dot!" Prince John chimed in from the backseat. "On the dot, Reverent, on the dot!"

"Wherefore," quoth His Reverence, "take unto you the whole armor of God, that you may withstand the evil day! For the worm shall feed sweetly, my sons, on those that rebel against the light! And as for thee, Luther, dear boy, thou shalt become an astonishment, a proverb, and a byword among all nations."

Rexroat proved as good as his word in the matter of faithfully mailing Sallie her weekly stipend—perhaps because, as a man of the cloth, he was also something of a metaphysician and could claim a healthy respect for the Weird Sisterhood, and he understood all too well that anything—absolutely anything—is possible.

Anyhow, he could afford it, for the Assyrian Infidel proved to be a great success among the heathen Pentecostals, and the Canvas Cathedral World-wide Missionary and Universal Temperance Fund was bringing in the sheaves. When Luther, unveiled, stood at the pulpit and sang, in a cracked but surprisingly sweet and plaintive tenor—a voice, people said, not unlike the peeping, piping tones of the tree frogs on a summer's evening—"Just as I am, I come, I come / O Lamb of God, I come, I come," no Christian heart could have remained unmoved, no Christian purse untapped.

Thus did a certain grinning little green incubus insinuate himself into the bad dreams of more than a few virtuous farmwives.

In due time, the reverend gentleman introduced his acolyte to the pleasures of Four Roses Blended Whiskey, and in the Canvas Cathedral many a midnight toast was lifted to the great Crusade for Universal Temperance.

As a sideline, meanwhile, Rexroat industriously worked the widow-woman dodge at every stop, finding his way several nights a week to the dinner table—and not infrequently to the bed and the bank account—of one or another lonely local matron. Often he returned to the tent with a plate of leftover cold fried chicken and biscuits, a generous donation to the Missionary Fund—and a glow of immense personal satisfaction.

"Hiho, lads!" he'd hail his disciples, hoisting a fresh pint of Four Roses. "Arise from your beds, shake the dew off your lilies, turn up the lamp, break out your tin cups, and let us have ourselves a taste of ignorant oil! For I have caused the widow's heart to sing for joy, and payday comes upon the morrow!"

While Luther and Prince John ate, Rexroat would regale them with tales of his conquest of the evening, never failing to express his gratitude to the Almighty for having placed in his humble servant's way such a cornucopia of blessings.

"Y'know," said Luther one evening, ruminatively gnawing the last drumstick, "I shoulda been a preacher. I like fried chicken and dicky-doodle better'n anybody."

"On the dot!" Prince John whooped, his wit by now well lubricated by more than his rightful share of ignorant oil. "And gets lesser of it, too, I reckon . . . with all them noses!"

"Never you mind, Luther, my chuck," soothed the archbishop as Prince John helped himself to another generous allotment from the pint. "The Lord tempers the wind to the shorn lamb, and sweeter than sweet are the uses of adversity! He who is despised and rejected of men, yea, verily, he who is ugly and venomous like the toad—nothing personal, dear boy—he is a man of sorrows, acquainted of grief . . . yet he wears a precious jewel in his head! Let us find tongues in brooks, and sermons in stones and what have you, and good in . . . Well, let us find good wherever we are so fortunate as to discern it."

"Say again the part about that precious jewel," Luther wheedled.

"In days of yore, my lad, the lowly toad was held to be a sacred beast, possessed of the wisdom of the ages and the sages. And upon its death, its brain was thought to ossify and become, over time, a certain small gemstone—the precious jewel, don't you know, because in the right hands it has, ah, remarkable properties. It's . . . Egad! See here!"

Suddenly Rexroat fell to his knees on the floor of the tent and began pawing through the straw, as though he'd spotted something of great value, perhaps—zounds!—the very object under discussion!

"See here! What cosmogonic confluence of the cosmos is this?"

Rexroat held to the light a small, plum-colored stone—which Luther instantly snatched from the reverend's hand and popped into his mouth, then just as promptly spat it out again, depositing it livid and shimmering in his palm.

"What the billy goddamn hell?" he demanded.

"Gadzooks, lad, it's . . . a toadstone!"

Luther eyed it suspiciously. "Be damn," he said, "I thought it was a chicken liver."

"This, my chub, is the tenth migration of the ossified malignum! Formed by the miracle of petrifaction upon the perfect corpus of the sacred toad! Keep this sanctified artifact upon your person at all times"—he took Luther's other hand and closed it over the one that held the stone—"and look to it in times of trouble, for there might be no end of luck in it, no end of luck and power and magic!"

"Well then," Luther demanded, "if it's such a booger, how come you don't keep it yourself?"

"Because, my boy, I don't believe in toadstones, and so it would be of no use to me. *I* believe, as you have perhaps observed, in the Main Chance, and although there are those who can tailor their beliefs to suit the demands of the moment, I am not, alas, amongst that happy number. But if I were you, dear boy, circumstanced as you are in the matter of, ah, affinities and what-have-you, I should declare my faith in toadstones, indeed I should."

"Be damn." Luther peeked between his fingers cautiously, as though he half expected the captive stone to slither free and go bounding off for the nearest toadstool.

"Watch out now!" Prince John hooted. "Them rocks is hard to catch!"

"Be not deterred by Philistines and skeptics, dear boy! There are millions of rocks, millions and billions, but precious few are toadstones! Who can say what powers reside within it? You and I are but poor students of the great mystery of life, and the first lesson we must learn is to take nothing for granted! Nothing!"

"On the dot!" howled the Prince, in a perfect royal transport of Dutch courage. "Specially not when some lyin' ol' shit-pitcher like Rexroat tells it to you!"

Luther and Rexroat exchanged a look that would have sobered Prince John on the spot if he hadn't been too drunk to appreciate it. Then Luther pocketed the stone, hooked back his last drop of Four Roses, and took himself off to bed, to dream, we must assume, of widow women and fried chicken.

When Prince John awoke the next morning, he found himself under a blazing sun in the middle of a vacant lot, with no Canvas Cathedral sheltering him and no LaSalle, no trailer, no Rexroat, no Luther, no payday, and most lamentable of all—considering his condition—not a dram of ignorant oil. Yet Prince John was withal more fortunate than he knew—for Luther had stoutly urged the reverend to run over him a time or two on their way out.

Back at her wet-mop, Juanita labors grimly, struggling to prepare herself for what she knows she has to do.

Warren Harding Skidmore is the daddy of this baby that's inside her, and sometimes Juanita halfway wishes she could just go ahead and have it, just for spite—because, being his, it will have red hair, and everybody will know he was the one that did it.

But there's another thing: In her heart, Juanita fears that if she has this baby, she will love it more than she can stand—and that if she doesn't have it, she will hate herself forever—and all because Warren Harding is its daddy.

Warren Harding Skidmore is the only child of a briefly successful Burdock County insurance salesman who died young and left behind a tidy little property, a hopelessly chuckleheaded widow, and an infant heir who proved constitutionally disposed to take full advantage of both circumstances. The widow Skidmore, in her grief, lugubriously pampered and petted and indulged the boy to a high gloss, thereby assuring herself of a son who would grow up devious, dissolute, thieving, and mean. At ten he was a tormentor of cats and turpentiner of dogs, at twelve a lifter of little girls' skirts; by fifteen he was stealing his despairing mother blind; by seventeen he'd wrecked three cars, two of them while trying to run down small animals.

Recently, to reward the likely lad for having finally cheated and bullied his way through high school, his feckless parent had bought him the Pinhook Texaco Station from the estate of the lately dispatched Lugnut Bludgins— and then promptly dithered and fretted herself into a fit of apoplexy and an early grave when she found out he used the station mostly as a place to pitch pennies and play gin rummy and lay up drunk with the local sporting set.

One afternoon back in the early autumn, Juanita's Uncle Dutch had taken Luther Jukes out and handcuffed him to a lawn mower and put him to mowing the courthouse yard, and while he was mowing (Juanita saw the whole thing from the courthouse porch, where she was washing the windows of the sheriff's office), Warren Harding drove around and around the block hollering smart remarks—"Hey! You cut grass like a man with two noses!"—and one time, he leaned out the car window and threw an apple core and hit the prisoner on the leg.

Juanita is scared spitless of the two-nosed man, but she ain't the kind that likes to see anybody get tormented.

But the meanest trick of all—Juanita reflects, often and bitterly—was the one Warren Harding did on Juanita her own self. Because if you must know, she really, truly loved him, see—that red, red hair, y'know, and . . . oh! them freckles!—and that's why he was the first one she had ever, you know, *went* with, if you can call it going with somebody which never took her anywheres except the graveyard, to park and get in the backseat. Many a time he'd have her back at the jail inside of thirty minutes. But a person needs something nice in their life even if it don't last but thirty minutes, so she put up with it.

Then, one night a couple of months ago—the very night that Juanita was planning to tell Warren Harding that she had missed her curse again this month, and what did he aim to do about it?—Warren Harding got out of the car after he was done and went around and opened up the trunk, and . . . and out come that sneakin' Sharky Vance! So then Warren Harding went over and set down on a tombstone and commenced to clean his fingernails like he thought he was the King of Sheba, while Sharky just politely hopped in the backseat with Juanita!

At first, Juanita thought she would just kick Sharky in his textacles again, like she did in eighth grade, and then get out and walk home. But she seen in her heart that Warren Harding didn't give a poot what happened to her one way or the other, and if Sharky Vance hopped around on her till next Tuesday she couldn't get no more pragnent than she already was, and anyhow she felt so low-down and lonesome that she was halfway glad for the company.

So one thing led to another thing, and directly here she is two months later, still p.g. and not but one person in the world which can tell her where to turn, and that's a person with . . . two noses.

·   ·   ·

Disencumbered of Prince John, Abdul the Infidel had become, under Rexroat's tutelage, ever more indispensable to the archbishop's salvational exertions. The reverend gentleman coached him in how to talk in tongues—no problem for an Assyrian—and how to fling himself to the ground twitching and frothing in a paroxysm of Christian zeal, and how to rifle the ladies' purses while their owners were similarly enthralled. After every service, the two pious entrepreneurs moved among the congregation hawking—at a dollar-fifty per, marked down from five ninety-eight—autographed copies of a pamphlet entitled *Prayers for My Good Health* by the Reverend P. Cosmo Rexroat, Doctor of Natural Theosophy, Chiropractic Science, and Colonic Irrigation—who had already assiduously instructed Luther in the numerous arcane arts of shortchanging the clientele. The money changers had, at long last, turned the tables on the Christians.

His Eminence even revealed, in an attack of candor brought on one evening by a sacramental beaker of Four Roses, that the oversized volume that was always open before him on the pulpit was not exactly the Holy Bible so much as it was, in point of fact, *Bartlett's Familiar Quotations.*

Eventually, after many seasons on the road, they happened to cross trails with a carnival that employed a lady of the reverend's acquaintance, the former star attraction of a skin joint called Uncle Billy Peeper's Wild West Revue, where she'd performed as Nyoka, Queen of the Apaches. A few years back, when Rexroat was running a three-card monte flat just down the midway, they'd managed a little tumble in the hay while Uncle Billy's peepers were turned elsewhere. These days—Uncle Billy having lately overtaxed his central nervous system and been gathered unto his fathers—she was plain Wanda Pearl Ratliff once again, selling tickets for the Tilt-A-Whirl, waiting, like Mr. Micawber, for something to turn up.

"And not no goddamn hide show neither, hon," she told her confidential friend Gertrude, who worked the cotton candy stand. "It ain't polite, showin' your spizzerinctum to a bunch of strangers at my age."

When something did turn up, in the persons of Rexroat and his remarkable disciple, the two former lovers elected to throw in together and resume their raptures. Rexroat, with Luther at his side, turned immediately to his *Bartlett's,* this time falling amongst the poets. After a few hours of deep study, they took the cross off the top of the trailer and joined the carnival, setting up shop as Colonel Rexroat and His Two-Nosed Child Prodigy, Little Luther the Appalachian Frog Boy. Never mind that the Child Prodigy was old enough to vote or that his genius was represented exclusively by his ability to recite, at a snap of the newly commissioned colonel's fingers, a few lines from "Invictus," or "Thanatopsis," or "The Boy Stood on the Burning Deck."

"This, m'dear," the colonel predicted to Wanda Pearl in an aside on opening night, "will be a strong joint. The general public, you see, loves a freak with book sense best of all. It confirms their darkest suspicions about intelligence, and reassures them that when all is said and done, ignorance is still a virtue."

As usual, when it came to human nature, Colonel Rexroat had it dead on the money: It *was* a strong joint. Whether they came to admire Luther's noses or his intellect—or maybe just because it only cost fifteen cents to enjoy what the colonel, in his grind, liked to call "the whole shit-a-ree, dear hearts!"—the Two-Nosed Child Prodigy drew good crowds.

". . . She drove her daughter, great with child, from her door into the storm!" went the Rexroatian rendition of Luther's history, while Luther stood by, masked to the eyes by a red bandanna. "Yea, and with the storm raging all around her, friends, this unnatural mother cried, 'And may your firstborn be a brother to the toad!'"

However (Rexroat would explain), because the unborn child was inadvertently her own grandson, the ethics of the Sisterhood had required the crone to accompany her curse with a special endowment of some kind, a gift, a blessing. After thinking it through, she cunningly decided to grant him overarching intelligence, that he might always know he was . . . a frog.

"A cruel hoax, my friends! Better she had made the lad an imbecile! But his loss is Western civilization's gain, dear hearts, and now you can see the entire phenomenon for a mere fifteen cents, the whole in-ta-lectual shit-a-ree for three greasy little nickels . . . "

(In due time, while he languished in that Missouri prison under the tutelage of the learned safecracker, Luther, fingering his toadstone, would ruminate long and deeply upon Rexroat's fanciful account of how a likely lad such as himself came to be that which he indisputably was—a frog boy, no getting 'round it—and would eventually conclude that his own doting old grannie was indeed the bane of his infelicitous existence. Accordingly, those of us who know our Luther's character may safely assume that until he was unavoidably detained in Pinhook by the fateful encounter with Lugnut Bludgins, he was on his way to pay a social call at the old log house on Morgadore, and that Bad-Cess Sallie would not have been made comfortable by the prodigal's return.)

After the colonel had inveigled an audience into the tent, he'd break out his old three-card monte setup and, while they waited for the Prodigy to display his extraordinary properties, would endeavor—successfully, as a rule—to disengage a few among them from their pocket money.

"Lord, hon, he's slick as snot on a goddamn doorknob!" said Wanda Pearl admiringly to Gertrude. "Last night he jiggered a mark outta seventeen dollars quick as a pickpocket, and two minutes later he's got the two-nose sayin' a poem about Down by the Shores of Glitchy-Gloomy, and the mark is cryin' like a goddamn orphan!"

Alas, their success was short-lived. For at the Arbuckle County Fair in Eggermont, Missouri, that injudicious deputy sheriff saw fit to inquire how many flies Luther had et so far that day . . . and a few hours later, Luther waylaid him down by the stables and beat him senseless with a singletree. Southeast Missouri being intolerant of ill-natured Frog Boys from out of state, they charged him with the attempted murder of a lawman and set about to throw away the key.

While Luther awaited trial, Rexroat paid him a farewell visit at the Arbuckle County slam. He and Wanda Pearl, the colonel said, had bought themselves a two-headed chicken and were looking around for a few pickled punks and maybe a half-and-half. So they'd be moving on.

"We'll miss you, my lad," he said, taking his leave, "indeed we will. You could have been the strongest blow-off going. It's an incalculable loss to Western civilization. But"—Colonel Rexroat sighed, shrugged extravagantly, and turned to go—"but, as the philosopher says, that's show business."

Juanita has mopped her way almost to his cell door, and nobody in the whole jail but him and her, and she knows that if she's ever going to say something to him, now's the time. But she can't hardly just waltsch right up to him and say, "Welp, Mr. Two-Nose, how much would that old woman charge me to get rid of this here baby?" What she needs is something nice and friendly to kind of break the ice a little, something along the line of "Welp, Mr. Two-Nose, it's a nice day out, ain't it?" But then she thinks, *What's it to him, he ain't out.*

So when she stops in front of his cell to wring out her mop, she still don't have the least ideal what she's going to say. Nonetheless, steeling herself to look at him without flinching, she straightens up over the mop bucket and takes a deep breath and opens her mouth and—

"Thirty-five dollars."

"Hunh?"

"Thirty-five dollars cash on the barrelhead. Them's Grannie's rates."

The voice issues from the gloomy recesses of the cell—wherein, to her relief, Juanita sees that our Luther is wearing his bandanna, and so looks less like a monster, if more like a burglar. But the price he's named is so stupendous (the county pays Juanita nine dollars a week, Aunt Jimmie charges her six for room and board, and right now she's got two dollars and forty cents to her name) that she forgets to wonder how he's answered a question she hadn't even asked yet.

"It ain't me!" she blurts. "I was just askin' for, uh . . . Harletta Porch. This friend of mine. Is who it was."

"Listen," he says, in a voice muffled and made ominous by the bandanna, "people pays good money to look at me, but it don't cross their mind that I'm a-looking back at them. I can see through you like a drink of water."

Juanita lowers her eyes as though she stands before a stern, all-knowing judge, pleading guilty. She knows, deep inside herself, that her life has reached a turning point.

"It was that redheaded jack, I reckon. Oh, I seen you sneakin' out at night, oh, yes! I seen him pick you up out yonder in the jail yard! I knowed what you all was up to, you bet, oh, yes!"

Luther's eloquence suggests that that little matter of the apple core has not quite been forgotten.

"Anyhow," he continues, less vehemently, "you don't want to let Grannie get her hooks in you, she's a bad egg. She ain't the one you need."

"Who, then?" Juanita pleads.

"Why, me, that's who. Me, myself, and I. Now I can't knock that baby for you, that's Grannie's line of work. But lookahere"—he steps to the bars and lowers his voice to a conspiratorial whisper—"there's more than one way to skin a cat. What if I could show you how to make that Skidmore do right by you?"

Juanita, in her desperation, has even prayed to God to help her out, but it looks to her like the Devil is the one that answered.

"You can make him—?"

"I can make him marry you!"

"How?"

"All right," he whispers, "you know them shoe boxes in the office?"

Juanita does; he means the ones on the shelf behind Uncle Dutch's desk where the jailer keeps the odds and ends he takes out of prisoners' pockets when they go to jail.

"Well, one of them boxes," Luther goes on, "has got my name on it, and in that box is a little purple rock, about so big. You sneak in there this afternoon while he's out 'lectioneering, and you get me that little rock and bring it to me around about midnight, when they're all asleep, and I'll show you a secret trick that works like . . . a charm."

"Uh-huh," says Juanita. "And what's this trick gonna cost me?"

"Not a penny. But when you come"—he points out of the gloom to the key ring at her waist—"you bring them keys."

"Oh, Lord," Juanita gasps. "You ain't aiming to run off? Uncle Dutch'll wring my neck!"

"Run off? Hell, no," he tells her, with a dry little laugh. "I ain't coming out, you're coming in."

Now here's Juanita sitting in the dark in her little room, waiting for midnight. She sits near the window, hands in her lap; her right hand, palm up, cradles the toadstone. A harvest moon hangs over Needmore, and a vagrant moonbeam has singled out the Sanctified Artifact, so that it seems almost to glow with an inner light as Juanita gazes abstractedly down upon it, trying to figure out what in the h-e-double-l she ought to do.

Yes, she had stole the rock, like he told her to, but she could put that back any old time, Uncle Dutch'd never know the difference. And she never has been one to take much stock in spells and curses and rabbit feet and all. She ain't a bit religious.

On the other hand, she remembers the time her little brother Herschel got the mumps, and Grandma Souseley tied a blue silk ribbon around his waist to keep them from dropping on him, and they never did drop. So who knows, you can't tell, maybe there's something to it after all.

Although Juanita's heart is as capacious as the bosom in which it is lodged, she realizes she's not no Miss Gantley in the brains department. Still, she can see just exactly what will happen if she lets Uncle Dutch and Aunt Jimmie send her back to the homeplace to have the baby. There wouldn't be no peace for her in this life, that's for sure. Old spiteful Aunt Augusta wouldn't let her out of her sight; the only social life she'd have for the rest of her days would be cleaning up after all them Souseleys. Which, when you think about it, ain't that different from her social life right now, except the Souseleys wouldn't be locked up in the drunk tank, they'd be running around loose. And her sweet little redheaded baby, even though it'd be a Sparks by name and half Skidmore by blood, would be bound to get some Souseley on it while it was growing up.

All this Juanita sees as plain as day, almost as if it has already happened. Yet if she did but know it, at this very moment she holds, literally in the palm of her hand, an altogether different future. For the toadstone encompasses all knowledge, and if it could speak—or rather, if she knew how to listen to it—it would tell her things she's never dreamed of.

But Luther Jukes hears the toadstone's voice, clear as a nightingale's; it sings to him of luck and power and magic, exactly as told by the prophet Rexroat. If Juanita brings the plenipotentiary relic to him in his cell, she'll discover that other life which, we devoutly hope, awaits her . . .

Tomorrow morning, just as the sun is coming up, she will awaken from a sleep so deep and so untroubled it could almost have been a kind of trance. She'll be in Warren Harding Skidmore's car; he is at the wheel, and she's been sleeping with her head pillowed on his thigh. She knows whose car it is and whose thigh it is, because the first thing she sees when she opens her eyes is this raw-knuckled, freckled hand on the suicide knob, with the 1941 Burdock County High School class ring on the ring finger, a hand she knows almost as well as the hand knows her.

There's a voice somewhere inside her head, saying—no, not a voice, exactly, just the words theirselves, kind of scratchy and screechy, like a memory of something Miss Gantley could've wrote, one time long ago, on the blackboard:

The iron tongue of midnight hath told twelve;
Lovers, to bed; 'tis almost fairy time.

Juanita has no idea where she is or where they're going, yet a warm, delicious feeling of contentment and perfect trust steals over her. Gratefully, she closes her eyes again and drifts back into sleep, and as she does she will hear, oh my, the most amazing thing: Warren Harding Skidmore, somewhere far above her, murmuring, ever so softly, "Maud Muller on a summer's day, raked the meadow sweet with hay . . . "

Back in the jailer's house in Needmore, Aunt Jimmie, as she sleepily goes about assembling breakfast, will chance upon a note on her kitchen table. "Me and Waren Harding S.," it reads, "has run off 2 get maried." The note is signed, "You're neace, Juanita Sparks."

And even as Aunt Jimmie stands there shaking her head in disbelief—"The child don't know poop from apple butter!"—the morning quiet will be rent by a bloodcurdling shriek of anguish from the jail, of which, as we know, Luther Jukes is currently the sole inhabitant.

The prisoner has awakened under a strange delusion: He believes—or at any rate he hysterically professes to believe—that as recently as last night he had been a free man and that the free man he had been was, of all people, Warren Harding Skidmore. Last night, around about midnight, after dropping off his running mates Sharky and Dime, he—Warren Harding Skidmore—under the influence of a few (quite a few) beers, had pulled into the jail yard—hoping, perhaps, that Juanita's dreams would inspire her to go out walking in her sleep, looking for him—and had gone to sleep himself instead . . .

He awakes in jail. Bringing his hand to his aching head—whoever made off with the corporeal Warren Harding S. having neglected to take along his hangover—he discovers that overnight he has somehow acquired—Aieeeel—a second nose!

This likely story will be greeted, predictably, by a chorus of derision and ridicule. The vast preponderance of opinion will hold that of course the murderer, in his infernal cunning, hopes to cheat the hangman by pleading insanity; a much smaller contingent will choose to believe that he has in fact lost his mind, because only a genuine lunatic could concoct such a story in the first place.

Tomorrow evening, the return of the newlyweds—for such they are, absolutely—will affirm that Warren Harding Skidmore's outer man is thoroughly intact and appears to be none the worse for the purported transmigration of his soul.

When the prisoner, confronted with this new evidence, persists in banging his head against the bars and tearing his hair and, variously, shrieking and screaming and howling and moaning words to the effect that he is Warren Harding Skidmore—even though the fact that he's Luther Jukes is (in the amused opinion of Warren Harding, who almost overnight seems to have metamorphosed from rather a dullard into what passes locally for something of a wag) "as plain as the noses on his face"—a few neighborhood ancients will begin reminding each other that the rottenest apple falls nearest the tree, and Lord knows what all a grandchild of Bad-Cess Sallie Jukes might do.

But when the howling and shrieking and head banging—"Sounds like he's in there playin' dodgeball with a brick!" quipped Warren Harding, on the occasion of his first supper with his new in-laws, the Louderbacks—and moaning and screaming and so on and so forth continue unabated throughout the next few weeks before the trial, the weight of public sentiment will have shifted, gradually but inexorably, toward the conclusion that the unhappy prisoner is indeed quite mad.

Then too, as the trial date approaches, those who had known Lugnut Bludgins in life will perhaps acknowledge to themselves that they can't honestly say they miss him much; their eulogies of him rarely extend beyond Luther Jukes's own encomium to the effect that Lugnut was, in fact, too goddamn dumb to live. In any event, by court day there will have developed in the public mind a certain sympathy for the afflicted wretch who's been setting up such a hee-cack in the county jail.

At his trial, Luther Jukes—he who is called Luther Jukes—has to be dragged into the courtroom in a straitjacket; and as the sheriff's deputies seat him in the dock, an evil-looking old crone amongst the spectators—Bad-Cess Sallie, of course, showing remarkable agility for her years—will leap to her feet and point a long, yellow-nailed finger at the defendant, screeching again and again, "It ain't him! It ain't him! You bloomin' idjits, it ain't him!"

She will have to be escorted from the courtroom, while the prisoner in the dock, quiescent for once, looks on uncomprehendingly.

After that brief outburst, justice will move swiftly, and before the day is done Luther Jukes—he who is called Luther Jukes—will be declared innocent by reason of insanity and committed to spend the rest of his days in a padded cell in the Commonwealth's most dismal madhouse—quite possibly the same institution to which, many years before, the Bludgins committee had sought to consign an earlier manifestation of our amiable friend—where perhaps he may find time to mourn all the small animals he's run over.

As the deputies lead the wretched prisoner away, there will rise above the general hubbub in the spectators' gallery a male voice cheerily calling out, "And forever, O my brother, hail and farewell!" Several nearby spectators later agree that the voice was that of Warren Harding Skidmore—of he, that is, who calls himself Warren Harding Skidmore. Certainly, however, not one among them suspects that the former dullard's words were borrowed from Catullus.

That very night, the peaceful dreams of downtown Pinhook will be broken by the clang of the village fire bell—too late, alas, for the old log house on Morgadore will have burned to the ground, with Bad-Cess Sallie in it, by the time the fire engine turns down her lane. Officially, the fire can only be attributed to a defective coal oil heater, but there will always be those in Burdock County who believe—who profess to believe—that the flash point was old Sallie herself in her featherbed, and that the cause was spontaneous combustion.

The ruins smoldered for days, they say, and the stench of sulfur fouled the air for miles around.

The new Mr. and Mrs. Skidmore, meanwhile, will have gone to housekeeping like any other young couple, and Warren Harding—the new Warren Harding—will have utterly thrown over his old wicked ways and bad companions, as every young breadwinner must, and buckled himself into the traces and gone to work. By the time the excitement of the Jukes trial has begun fading into history, Skidmore Texaco, fresh as paint and elbow grease can make it, is the tidiest, most forward-looking business establishment in downtown Pinhook, and Harletta Porch is up to her plucked eyebrows in plans for her friend Juanita's baby shower.

Before the year is out, America will find herself yet again in the toils of a great war; the following spring, Warren Harding's number in the military draft will come up on the same day that Juanita presents him with a ruddy, squalling, redheaded draft deferment. And every eleven months for the duration of the war, dependable as the seasons, she will repeat the ceremony, so that by the war's end there will be four spanking new Skidmores, with a fifth on the way, and Warren Harding won't have been required to dodge a single bullet.

Skidmore Texaco will by then have become Skidmore Used Cars, soon to be Skidmore Used Cars and Ford-Ferguson Tractors, then Skidmore Ford ("Out of the High-Rent District!"), then Skidmore Ford-Mercury-Lincoln (by now W. H.—as he calls himself—is much in demand at the annual Lions Club Fourth of July Picnic for his famously stirring recitation of Longfellow's immortal "Paul Revere's Ride" and is widely regarded as Burdock County's leading patriot and intellect), and so on down through the years until the dealership acquires so many titles, both domestic and foreign ("Skidmore Ford-Mercury-Lincoln-Porsche-Volvo-Toyota-Hyundai-Peugeot-Subaru") and occupies so much territory that at last it positively swallows whole the village of Pinhook and becomes a sort of city state in its own right, populated largely by automobiles . . .

. . . by which time those five little Skidmores will have taken over the several ethnic neighborhoods of the dealership, each to his or her own little principality, and Warren Harding and Juanita are safely ensconced in a condo—"condominimum," W. H. calls it, with a flash of his old wit—in West Fungo Beach Golfing Community in West Fungo Beach, Florida, where Juanita whiles away her golden years playing canasta with some nice Jewish ladies while W. H. goes a-golfing, his lucky toadstone keeping company with the loose change in his pocket.

But none of this has happened yet, and for all we know it will never happen—for Juanita, remember, is at this moment still sitting at the window in her lonely little room, glumly pensive, pondering the decision that will seal her fate. In her palm, the toadstone seems almost to pulse with light like a tiny, luminous heart, beating hard, as though it were trying desperately to tell her something.

And now the courthouse clock tolls thrice. It must be midnight.

A MISDEMEANOR
AGAINST NATURE

*"A man should be jailed for
telling lies to the young."*
Lillian Hellman

August 1968, the very week of the Democratic Party's unhappy soiree in Chicago, and all across the length and breadth of this great land (as the politicians on TV had been bleating all week long) there hung a sulphurous cloud of suspicion and malevolence as foully palpable as smog, and there I was in what had to be among the worst places in the continental U.S. for a man of my political and social inclinations at the time, just pulling into the parking lot of the Penington Club Tavern on Highway 52 in Aberdeen, Ohio.

This stretch of Highway 52 winds along the north bank of the Ohio River for about twenty miles, from Ripley through Aberdeen to Manchester, and there was a time in my life when I knew it as well as I know the way to my own bathroom. At Aberdeen, there's a toll-free bridge across the Ohio to Maysville, Kentucky, the hometown of my high school and college years . . . and since Ohio permitted the sale of 3.2 beer to eighteen-year-olds, whereas in Maysville you couldn't darken a tavern door until you were twenty-one— and then only until ten o'clock at night—that bridge loomed as large as the Golden Gate in the landscape of my adolescence.

For the Buckeye he is a crafty breed, and in the days of my youth, Highway 52 was fairly lined with taverns—the Top Hat and the Terrace Club and the Bay Horse and the Penington Club and a dozen others—rank, musty, low-ceilinged places with puke in the urinals and Cowboy Copas on the jukebox and lighting feeble enough to allow a fifteen-year-old to pass for eighteen if the bartender wasn't in a mood to split hairs, which he hardly ever was. Some of those havens have long since yielded to mom-and-pop motels and Col. Seersucker's Kentucky Possum Tartare stands, but in 1968 a remarkable number of them were still unscathed by progress. And the unscathiest of all was the scrofulous old Penington Club, where even then I had already been wasting my substance in riotous living off and on for almost twenty years.

To which purpose I found myself that August night, as I did every summer when I came home to Kentucky for a visit, about to sally into the Penington Club once more. Ordinarily a happy moment for me, this, a moment filled almost to bursting with anticipation; nostalgic nitwit that I am, I can be moved to the point of tears by the raunchy familiarity of such places, the sweet memories of revels best forgotten.

By 1968, you may as well know, I had become a to-the-manner-born New Age Californian, with all the rights, privileges, and irresponsibilities that are the natural birthright of that favored race. I had also become, improbably enough, a bona fide member of the faculty of Stanford University, my Wallace E. Stegner Fellowship having miraculously transmogrified itself into an Edward H. Jones Visiting Lectureship way back in 1963.

Clearly, though, I was no visitor. I was more like the Man Who Came to Dinner; they couldn't have run me out of California with a stick. Since 1966 I'd lived, with my first wife, Kit, and our burgeoning family, in a big old house in downtown Palo Alto that had become a sort of southern way station for Bay Area freakdom. Kesey and his troupe, the Pranksters, were in and out all the time, as was a steady parade of peace activists, revolutionaries, *Whole Earth Catalog* visionaries, associate professors of touchy-feely from the Free University, Black Panthers, White Panthers, Gray Panthers, Red Guards (they lacked the sense of humor to call themselves Pink Panthers, so I'll do it for them), dealers and dopers and Diggers, gurus and swamis and Sufis, psychodrama honchos, Hairless Krishnas, the occasional Hell's Angel . . . and, once, the FBI. It was like living in the national center of gravity, or in one of those ubiquitous California tourist traps called Mystery Spots, places where gravitational and magnetic forces are supposedly concentrated in such a way as to inspire water to flow upstream, marbles to roll up inclines, birds to fall from the sky like rocks. I pretended I was working on my novel—but you can't write a novel in a place like that; the words just won't stay on the page.

Naturally, my enthusiasms had continued to manifest themselves in the form of certain subtle changes in my outward aspect: As I pulled into the Penington Club parking lot that night, I was wearing high-heeled, pointy-toed, zip-up frootboots and tie-dyed bells and an over-the-collar mod-bob and a Genghis Khan mustache and round, mellow-yellow granny glasses—a set of accessories not likely to take the best-dressed barfly award in Penington's, where the clientele's taste ran at its very dandiest to bowling shirts and engineer boots, and not the first sign of a facial hair below the eyebrows. Already my little affectations, modest as they'd seemed at home in Palo Alto, had won me wide-eyed stares on the streets of Maysville. It was the specs, I think, that did it, those piss-muckledy-dun Ben Franklins, which, representing as they did a fairly substantial commitment of cold cash, seemed to confirm what my other trappings strongly hinted at: *It's a hippie, it's a yippie, it's a Commie, it's a California crazy, it's a fruit-cup, it's a freak!* Not exactly the sort of reception a sensible and prudent thirty-six-year-old pedagogue and father of three would ordinarily choose to be accorded by the usual Friday-night crowd in Penington's—farmhands and construction workers and beer-truck drivers on a busman's holiday, any number of whom would no doubt just as soon knock me on my California ass as look at me. Indeed, would very much rather.

And as a matter of convenient fact, it just so happened that I had my regular old black horn-rims right in the glove compartment; put them there myself, if you must know, against just such a contingency as this. But were there not matters of principle involved here? Had I not the inalienable right—the duty, even!—to go about looking like a perfect simpleton if I chose? And hadn't I always prided myself on my success at turning my conservative Stanford colleagues' hostility into curiosity into what passed, at faculty cocktail parties, for communication? And although I'm probably the most inept bar fighter since Ethelred the Unready, was I not big enough to *look* fairly formidable to a not-too-discerning eye?

Unto the breach, then. In a matter of moments I was sitting at the Penington Club bar with a beer in front of me, sitting there in the neon smaze and the blare of shouted conversation and beery laughter and Red Sovine mourning "Little Rosa" at the top of the Wurlitzer's electronic lungs, and so far not a soul had uttered an unkind word, or even looked too very askance at me. So it was just paranoia after all, I scolded myself, just hippie-dippy paranoia compounded by my own unseemly willingness to think the worst of my countrymen. Clearly I owed them an apology, perhaps a musical salute to demonstrate that, despite my alien getup and my California appetites and my *à la mode* politics, I stood foursquare with them against the barbarian hordes.

Taking my beer along, I left my barstool and ambled over to the jukebox, plugged it with a couple of quarters, and picked myself a nice bouquet of country songs. Then I made my way between the tables to a booth over against the wall, where I settled down to drink my beer and listen to Patsy Cline sing "I'll Sail My Ship Alone" and watch a two-hundred-pound lady and her one-hundred-pound gentleman friend play shuffleboard.

But no sooner had I set my leaky rowboat of a mind adrift with Patsy's ship in these familiar and relatively tranquil waters than I became aware of some sort of minor turbulence at my shoulder, a gentle but insistent jostling, and I looked up to find a large, lubberly young Penington Clubber towering over me, shaking my shoulder with a heavy hand and grinning down at me in a way that did little to enhance my peace of mind. Instinctively, I glanced toward the door. ("Whenever they get his chickenshit up," a college drinking buddy used to sing of me, to the tune of "Clancy Lowered the Boom," "McClanahan leaves the room-room-room.") But this crew-cut young stalwart had had the foresight to position himself between me and the exit, so strategic withdrawal was not among my options. Essaying a friendly—not to say craven—little grin of my own, I looked up at him inquiringly and squeaked some idiotic greeting.

"Hey there, Hairy," he said, almost—but not quite—affably, "you're kinda hairy, ain't you?"

The question seemed pretty strictly rhetorical, so I ventured a hangdog "Who, me?" gesture and, in the wisdom of my years, kept my big California mouth shut.

"You see that guy over there?" He pointed to a nearby table, where, in fact, two guys sat watching us. But there wasn't the least doubt which of the two he had in mind.

The big scrapper. The big, thick-necked, dark-haired lout of a youth who was even at that very moment favoring me with an indolent, almost pitying smile. His smaller companion, who was crumbling oyster crackers into a bowl of bean soup, eyed me as though I were a foreign body that had turned up in his soup spoon.

"I mean that black-headed one," the crew-cut explained unnecessarily. "You know what he called you, Hairy? He called you a fucken punk."

Well, here it is, hotshot, I told myself. *Your big moment, your chance to become the youngest old crock in history to cross the Generation Gap on a tightrope . . . backward.*

"No, wait now," my interlocutor ponderously corrected himself, "I got that wrong. He never said you was a fucken punk, he just said you was a punk. *I* was the one that said you was a fucken punk."

He turned to the other table. "Hey, Estill!" he called above the din. Estill rose and shambled toward us, growing taller and broader by the step. He was carrying his empty beer bottle by the neck. A bad sign.

"Hey, Estill," the crew-cut said, "I was just tellin' old Hairy here that we called him a fucken punk."

Estill flipped me a diffident little two-fingered salute with the hand that wasn't holding the beer bottle. "Naw, Parky," he said, "now you know we never said he was a fucken punk. All we said was, he *looks* like a fucken punk."

"Well," I offered hopefully, "I guess you all are entitled to your own opinion."

Estill heartily concurred in my championing of the fine old principles of democratic egalitarianism. "You better believe it," he said. "And my opinion is, if you ain't a fucken punk, you woulda done got up and kicked the livin' shit out of us."

"Whaddya say, Hairy?" Parky chortled. "Has Estill got your number?"

"I'll tell you what," I said, begging the question. "How about if you all sit down and let me buy you a beer instead. Maybe we'll get along better than we think."

Speak swiftly, Kesey used to say, and carry a big soft.

Suddenly a lot was riding on what happened next. Because wasn't this exactly what the Richie Rich revolutionaries at Stanford were forever exhorting us to do, to take our ideals out among the People, and Make the Revolution? And there was also the sobering fact that if somebody did get the livin' shit kicked out of him, I could be reasonably sure it wouldn't be Estill or Parky.

Those stout defenders of the status quo, meanwhile, were exchanging smirks, as if to say, "Well, if the fucken punk wants to buy us a beer before we kick the livin' shit out of him . . . " Then Estill slid into the other side of the booth, and Parky, following his lead, dropped into the seat beside me. Breathing a little easier, I signaled anxiously to the barmaid, who'd been keeping a watchful eye on the proceedings, for three more beers.

"Listen," I began, fumbling for the beer money, "in the first place, I'm too damned old to fight with you guys, if I can get out of it. I'll bet I'm half again as old as either one of you all."

It was not, let me hasten to explain, that I imagined I looked notably younger than my years; just that I suspected Estill and Parky hadn't yet seen through my flower-child getup to the doddering old trentagenarian behind it. And they were still young enough themselves that they might be impressed by my seniority.

"Shit you are," Estill said. On the TV screen behind the bar, a space-helmeted Chicago policeman was beating some poor long-hair senseless with his nightstick.

"Well, I'm thirty-six. I graduated from Maysville High School in 1951. That's over seventeen years ago."

"Shit you did," said Parky. "You mean to tell me you're from Maysville?"

"I sure am. I grew up in Brooksville, over in Bracken County. But I went to Maysville High for three years."

"Wait a damn minute," Estill said. "I've lived around here a long time, bud, and I never seen nothing looks like *you* in Maysville." He said "you" as if it tasted bad.

"I don't live here anymore," I told him. "I live in California now."

"California!" Parky marveled. "Sure enough?"

Far out, as we Californians say; Parky was already coming around. But Estill would be another matter.

"California?" he pressed me. "What do you do in California?"

"I'm a schoolteacher. I teach English."

"Shit you do. You ain't no damn schoolteacher, lookin' like that."

"Well," I said, "they don't pay as much attention to that kind of thing in California, I guess."

"Must not," Estill sneered. "What grade do you teach?"

"I teach in college, actually."

"He could be tellin' the truth there, Estill," Parky said. "When I went down to Briarhopper State that semester, they had some English teachers down there that was queer as three-dollar bills."

"They might have some of those where I teach, too," I had to allow, "but I'm not one of them. I'm a married man, myself. In fact, I've got three kids."

"They tell me some of your biggest queers is married men," Estill grumbled. "Hey, Rick," he called across the room to their companion, who was polishing off his bean soup at the other table, "this guy says he went to Maysville High."

"He shit, too," Rick demurred. He got up and stalked over to our booth, bug-looking me all the way, and sat down next to Estill. "When were you ever at Maysville High?" he demanded, glaring across the table at me as if the very suggestion amounted to a desecration of the Temple of Learning.

I went there three years, I told him; I graduated in '51.

"You shit, too. Because listen here, I went to Maysville High School all my life, by God, and my whole damn *family* went to Maysville High School, and my brother Jerry, by God, *he* graduated in '51! So don't you tell *me,* by God, that you . . ."

"You're Jerry O'Dell's little brother! You're Rickie-O! Hey, I went to *school* with Jerry!"

Saved! Singled out by Fate's fickle digit, that I might live to revolute again! Little Rickie-O, whose brother Jerry-O had been one of my favorite copilots when we'd cruised the midnight streets of Maysville in my fabled Chevy Bel Air! Old Digger O'Dell! Why, we'd logged more flight time together than Van Johnson and Dana Andrews! And here was little Rickie-O!

But in my delight at this unexpected turn of events, I'd momentarily forgotten that Rickie-O still didn't know who *I* was. In fact, he was at that very moment leaning across the table peering intently at me without the slightest flicker of recognition. Seventeen years is a long time; what if he didn't remember me?

"My name's Ed McClanahan," I prompted, searching his face for some reaction. For the first few seconds, nothing. Then, spurred by sudden inspiration, I took off my glasses; and as I lowered them, Rickie-O straightened slowly, raised his eyes to the cobweb-festooned ceiling, and dramatically clapped a palm to his forehead.

"Eddie McClanahan!" he cried. "Why, you stupid sons of bitches, this guy went to school with Jerry! Why, this here was one of the smartest guys in Maysville High School! Why, this guy teaches college somewheres, ain't that right, Eddie? Why, this goddamned hippie is twice as old and twice as smart as both of you two half-asses put together, and you all wantin' to punch him out!"

Then Rickie-O was pumping my hand energetically, and we were both grinning and giggling, and Estill was hiding his face behind his hands in mock humiliation. "Hey, Park," he said, "you know what you are, don't you?"

"Yeah, Estill," Parky snickered. "I'm a fucken punk."

Well, it was the beginning of a brief but otherwise perfect friendship. I spent the next couple of hours in the Penington Club drinking beer with Estill and Parky and Rickie-O, and the next couple of hours after that drinking coffee with them at the truck stop down the road. And while we were together I told them all I knew—and a good deal more besides—about the vital social issues of the day, about peace and love and civil rights and cops and dope and hippies and yippies and swingers and nude beaches and topless shoeshine parlors, and by the time we parted company they'd learned more about some of those matters, perhaps, than was good for them. As I drove home, giddy in the dawn, I congratulated myself happily for having finally pitched in and propagated the counterculture on my home turf, and lived to tell the tale. Mess with an English teacher, would they! Up the revolution!

I wish I could also testify now that, in my hour of triumph, I'd remembered to toss a few crumbs of credit to Estill and Parky and Rickie-O, who'd had the good grace to spare a Perfect Simpleton his comeuppance, and the good manners to listen politely to his heresies—and possibly even to have taken a few of them to heart. But I'm afraid that when it came to credit, I gathered most of it unto myself.

And not until years and years later, when I too had become a Kentuckian again, did it come to me that in the Penington Club that night, in my own small and, I trust, ineffectual way, I had aided and abetted a ravishing of innocence: the Californication of Kentucky.

THE ESSENTIALS
OF WESTERN
CIVILIZATION

Way out there at the far edge of the country, just off the campus of Arbuckle State College of Education in Arbuckle, Oregon, that most anonymous of towns, Assistant Professor of History Harrison B. Eastep, MA, had once, in a previous existence, lived a largely anonymous life in an anonymous apartment at an anonymous address, toiling by day deep in the bowels of Lower Division Humanities at Arbuckle State (there was no Upper Division), holing up at night in his apartment to grade papers and drink blended whiskey and smoke dope and listen to his increasingly unfashionable "progressive" jazz albums, while contemplating The Meaning of It All. His second marriage had by now—let's say midwinter of 1967—been dead almost three years, or about twice as long as it had lived. ("You know what I think, Harry?" his wife, Joellen, had said tearfully on her way out. "I think you're just *hiding* behind all that cheap cynicism! You're just scared, Harry!" (*Cheap?* he'd asked himself when she and the boy were gone. *If it's so fucking cheap, how come it's costing me so much?*) For the last couple of years, he'd been carrying on a half-hearted affair with a woman named Marcella, a divorced librarian at the state university in Eugene, forty miles away, but neither of them was enjoying it much (in large part because Marcella's three teenage daughters persisted in treating Harry like The Degenerate Who Came to Dinner), so Harry only saw her every couple of weeks or so, when the sexual imperative asserted its insistent self. Between times, blended whiskey (along with immense nightly cloudbanks of marijuana smoke) provided all the solace he could handle.

Joellen had been right, actually: Cynicism did come cheap in Arbuckle, whose residents took great civic pride in the fact that they lived in the seat of the only county west of the Continental Divide to support Alf Landon for president in 1936.

Fort Leonard Wood, Missouri—where, as a clerk-typist in the U.S. Army, Harry had spent two dismal years mindlessly typing requisitions for laundry soap and toilet paper—remains the only public facility in his experience that could rival Arbuckle State for pure ugliness. The institution had begun life as a teacher's college, but over the years its mission had gradually expanded to include agriculture, engineering, home economics, nursing, accounting, and a host of similarly romantic disciplines, with the result that the campus itself was a preposterous confusion of uniformly unimaginative yet utterly contradictory architecture. The stateliest buildings were the ones that made up the original campus, a cluster of eight or nine low, homely but serviceable crenellated red-brick farewell salutes to the Industrial Revolution. They were closely surrounded by several nice stands of elms and maples; in the spring the trees became leafy ambuscades for great raucous flocks of grackles and grosbeaks that unloaded their sodden ballast only when Humanities faculty happened along the sidewalks below. One learned not to mind it much; in Oregon it was always raining something or other anyhow.

But looming over this bucolic little patch of relative serenity was a farrago of towering slabs of steel and glass and concrete, thrusting themselves skyward as if to blot out the very sun itself (on those rare occasions when it endeavored to shine on this gloomy Joe Btfsplk of a campus), each of them—like the new Food Technology Building, which the student newspaper proudly dubbed "the largest erection on the Arbuckle campus"—as impersonal and heartless as . . . well, as the largest erection on the Arbuckle campus.

About the feet of these noble piles crept, kudzu-like, an impenetrable maze of interconnected one-story frame barracks, olive-drab relics of the Navy's wartime V-12 officer-training program. Here, in shabby oblivion, resided (or was bivouacked) Lower Division Humanities, including the Departments of Art, Languages and Literature, Social Studies, Band (not Music), and History, an Augean stable where Harry and his friend Gil Burgin shared a stall and plied their inglorious trade.

Humanities was a two-year "Service Division," ranking just above Maintenance & Janitorial. Its minions were regarded by the larger Arbuckle faculty much like the famous redheaded stepchild at the family reunion: Assistant Professors of Poultry Management looked down their beaks upon Western Civ instructors as if at indigestible insects; football coaches treated the poor devils who labored in the freshman composition line like something they'd stepped in by mistake. A distinguished Professor of Sanitary Engineering once openly referred in the faculty senate to required humanities courses as "a damned nuisance," and further denounced these la-di-da garnishments to a liberal education—in a soaring flight of rhetoric such as was rarely heard in that august chamber—as "frills, fluff, and frippery!" Students who evinced an unwholesome interest in the humanities were sent packing after their sophomore year, before the condition became contagious.

When Harry first came to Arbuckle, he'd supposed that he was under some personal or moral or even intellectual obligation to do his best to teach a little something, so he included an essay question in his first exam: He asked his students to discuss briefly some of the influences of the Great Plague of London on the religious climate of the time. The first paper he read began, "In this modren world of ours today, our modren medical science . . . " The second paper began, "Daniel Webster, in his dictionary, defines 'influence' as . . . " The third, "In his dictionary, Daniel Webster defines 'climate' as . . . " Harry round-filed the whole batch of papers then and there and began immediately to make out another test, multiple-choice questions only ("The Great Plague was spread by: a. dirty doorknobs; b. old paper money; c. rats; d. illicit sexual intercourse"). Later, he discovered that true-false questions ("Sir Walter Raleigh caught the Great Plague from an Indian maiden in America and brought it home to London with him. T or F?") were even less bothersome to mark, and henceforward he relied on them to the exclusion of all other forms.

So it came to pass that over the years Harry's dedication to pedagogy eventually eroded to such an extent that when his mother first hinted, in a letter, that he might want to consider taking early retirement and coming home to Kentucky to go into the antiques business with her, he found himself, he confided to his office mate Gil Burgin, seriously entertaining the possibility.

"What?" cried Gil, as he scurried off to knock down yet another Western Civ section. "And give up the Life of the Mind?"

·   ·   ·

"HELL NO, WE WON'T GO!" shouts Assistant Professor Harrison B. Eastep, MA, in unison with some two or three hundred youthful—and a few, like Harry, superannuated—resisters of the military draft, gathered on this sweet spring morn with their arms linked at the elbows to block the entrance to the Portland, Oregon, Induction Center, a four-story beige building of no architectural distinction whatsoever, ugliness excluded. It being Saturday, the Induction Center is closed, and no potential inductees are scheduled to arrive until Monday morning—a mere technicality, so far as both the demonstrators and their antagonists, a large, heavily armed contingent of the Portland police department, are concerned.

"HELL NO, WE WON'T GO! HELL NO, WE WON'T GO!"

Now let it be clearly understood that there is not the slightest possibility that Harry Eastep will ever be obliged to "go." After all, he's thirty-six years old, he's a father (albeit an absentee one), and he's already a veteran. (What would the troops at Fort Leonard Wood have done for toilet paper, were it not for the heroic efforts of Pfc. Eastep, bravely typing requisitions in the quartermaster's office?) No, Harry is putting his aging but still serviceable person on the line in solidarity with one of his favorite students at Arbuckle State, who has claimed conscientious-objector status and on whose behalf Harry has written several wonderfully artful letters of support to the student's local draft board, testifying to the deeply religious nature of the earnest young man's pacifist convictions, despite the fact that the young man in question is at best an agnostic, quite possibly a pagan, and most assuredly Professor Eastep's dope dealer.

Not to suggest, even for a moment, that Harry Eastep is any less staunch an opponent of the odious Vietnam War than the next right-thinking person. But up till now, his opposition has taken the form of appending his signature to supplicatory petitions and letters to the editor, participating in polite little on-campus peace marches, and bravely adorning his automobile with a bumper sticker bearing the ubiquitous, iniquitous footprint of the American chicken. In other respects, however, he has made himself a bit more of a spectacle, having zealously taken up (being between marriages) certain other accouterments of the Now Generation—such as long hair, a droopy mustache, bell-bottoms, and granny glasses, not to mention all the sex, drugs, and rock 'n' roll he can stand. He opposes the war, of course, but he has been, let us say, distracted.

But there is something about the looming presence of a couple of hundred cops in the parking lot directly across the street—some astride great horses like centurions, some bearing tear gas grenade-launchers, some with slavering, ravenous-looking dogs on leashes, the rest sporting huge cold-cocks and flak vests and space helmets with spooky plastic masks—which, to borrow Dr. Johnson's well-used expression, concentrates the mind wonderfully. The air in the no-man's-land between the adversaries is poisonous with bullhorn commands, vile imprecations, tear gas. At this particular juncture, despite the defiant slogans and locked arms and revolutionary good intentions, Assistant Professor Eastep has only one thought in his highly refined, pedagogical mind: how to get the fuck out of here unbusted, with his long-haired noggin unbludgeoned and his bell-bottomed lower person intact.

On Harry's immediate left is his friend and favorite student Freeman Jackson "Freejack" Harmon, recently defrocked Arbuckle State backup halfback (he and the coach didn't quite see eye to eye in regard to training rules), proprietor of an Afro so immense he could wear a peck basket for a fez, dealer in Acapulco Gold and other exotic enhancements to everyday human cognition. And right now, Freejack has Harry's intellectual-feeb left arm locked in the iron grip of Freejack's ex-halfback right arm to such an unrelenting extreme that there is not the slightest chance that Harry can escape without tearing his own arm off at the shoulder, like some small animal springing itself from a steel trap in tiny agony. Harry, in turn, has a nearly equivalent death grip on the left elbow of Gil Burgin, who is participating in this demonstration solely because Harry, as his friend and colleague and office mate, had appealed to his conscience (misery loving company, Harry had actually allowed himself to use that portentous word, though he did so with his own conscience as guilty as sin) and prevailed upon Gil (who also bought a little weed now and then from Freejack) to do his duty and join hands in expressing their unanimous, unswerving opposition to the draft and the war.

"HELL NO, WE WON'T GO! HELL NO, WE . . . "

Hell's rejoinder to this imprudent challenge arrives straight out of the luscious blue springtime Oregon heavens with a hollow *thwok!* on the pavement almost at Harry's feet, a hissing, spitting, fuming tear gas canister the size of a Colt 45 Malt Liquor can, hot as a two-dollar pistol, bouncing along in the gutter, spewing hateful, noxious vapors. Freejack—who all morning has been wearing, mysteriously, a leather glove on his right hand—instantly turns loose of Harry's arm and reaches with his gloved hand for the canister as if noxious vapors were exactly what he'd been thirsting for, scoops up that scorching, virulent, vehement missive, and in the same motion, hurls it with all his considerable pacifist might straight back into the advancing ranks of the minions of the Dark Angel, looks back just long enough to holler "Scratch gravel, White Wind!" over his shoulder to his troops—both of them—and takes off up the street through gathering clouds of tear gas. Harry and Gil exchange horrified glances, then break ranks and haul ass in hot pursuit.

After a few blocks Freejack swings down an alley and they catch up with him—which is to say, Freejack slows down, then stops and waits for them. When they arrive, breathless and staggering, ashen with terror, Freejack is exultant.

"You dudes!" he cries, laughing helplessly and slapping his knee. "Man, you the palest ofays in Portland!"

Gil Burgin is hugging a lamp post, gasping for breath. "Y'know," he wheezes, "Snakeshit had it right."

How so? Harry manages to inquire.

"Conscience," Gil says. "It really does make cowards of us all."

For all of Harry's carping and cavilling about his soul-destroying labors in the salt mines of Western Civilization, he eventually came to realize, over the years, that he'd somehow become rather good at the work. His classes were regularly over-subscribed, and in 1969, to his own astonishment and his department head's vast annoyance, his students voted him what the sponsoring student newspaper annually and invariably called "the Coveted Teacher of the Year Award." Harry's department chairman at that time, a reactionary middle-aged young man who liked to be addressed, in correspondence and intramural communications, as Dr. Nelson R. Peckler, Head, denounced the award as a glorified popularity contest—true, but Coveted nonetheless, especially by Dr. Nelson R. Peckler, Head—and strongly hinted that Harry owed the accolade solely to his penchant for getting palsy-walsy with student lefties and acidheads and dope smokers—also true, perhaps, but quite irrelevant, considering that Nelson Peckler wouldn't willingly have allocated Harry a ten-dollar raise if he'd won the Nobel Prize for his tireless labors on behalf of the propagation of the Essentials of Western Civilization.

Harry and his pal-to-be Gil Burgin and Nelson R. Peckler, EdD, had joined the History Department of Lower Division Humanities of Arbuckle State College more or less simultaneously in the autumn of 1958. Gil bore an MA from Berkeley and a wife and two kids; Harry logged in with his measly MA from Ohio State, but was otherwise unencumbered; Nelson Peckler came loaded for bear, armed with that EdD from some quasi-ephemeral institution in remotest Manitoba along with an overweening Sasquatch of a wife and four (and counting) toothy little Pecklers who would just as soon bite you as look at you. Harry and Gil entered as instructors, "Dr." Peckler (he would not have appreciated the quotation marks) as an associate professor on the fast track for advancement. In 1962, in lockstep accordance with incomprehensible department policy at the time—four years up or out—Gil and Harry, having committed no sins quite egregious enough to get themselves fired, both made assistant prof, and were granted perpetual tenure and simultaneously assured that, as regarded rank, they had reached the apex of their careers at Arbuckle State and might want to consider some other line of work. Peckler, in the meantime, had already made full professor and was scrabbling up the ladder to Headship, a distinction that he was destined to achieve within a few more years.

Harry had liked Gil, his new officemate, right away. A lanky, handsome, young hipster with a chiselled Dick Tracy profile, astonishingly black eyebrows, and a fast lip, Gil was double smart, he read books, he played piano with an ad hoc campus jazz combo, he voted left, he had even smoked a little weed in grad school (as had Harry, a time or two, in Columbus's murky mid-1950s dens of Bohemian iniquity). Because they both liked to come into the office at night, when the place was abandoned and quiet, to grade papers and work up the next day's classroom blather, they logged a lot of hours in each other's company. Gil and his wife, Marge, took pity on Harry during his periodic (and ultimately chronic) bachelorhood and regularly invited him to dinner, so that he became an intimate of their household, and a sort of de facto uncle to their kids, for whose innocent delight he recited the poems and riddles and tongue twisters ("Sherman Schott and Noah Knott shot it out. Knott was shot and Schott was not, so it was better to be Schott than Knott . . . ") that his granddaddy had taught him on the front porch swing at the homeplace down in Kentucky all those years ago.

And Gil and Harry had another bond: a mutual, overarching loathing for their colleague and boss-in-waiting Nelson Peckler, coupled with that eminence's reciprocal contempt for the two of them. Peckler—"Nelson R. Pecklerhead," as the two young wags had taken to calling him, between themselves, years before he'd actually scaled those Olympian heights—was a large, soft-bodied, wide-rumped, one-time third-string football player for a third-rate state college somewhere in Missouri, an individual scant of hair and intellect and principle but hungry, withal, for power of the more petty varieties: the power to schedule Saturday morning eight o'clock classes for insubordinate subordinates, the power to impose his mossback politics on curriculum and textbook selection, the power to pat and pinch department secretaries (observed) and the occasional student cutie (rumored) whenever he could get away with it. ("Peckler the Inspector," the secretaries called him or, alternatively, "the Handy Man.") Despite his vaunted EdD, he knew but little history, and his classroom lectures were reputed to be crashingly dull—much as he lusted after it, he would never win the Coveted Teacher of the Year Award—nor was he popular among his colleagues, who were regularly galled by his ambition. But these deficiencies did not at all impede his rise, for, as a former third-string jock, he was an ardent fan of Arbuckle State's athletic teams, the Beavers, and those Beavers who signed up for his classes (they were legion) found Professor Peckler to be, in their case at any rate, exceedingly generous in the matter of grades, a fact that did not escape the notice of the grateful, sports-happy Arbuckle State administration—especially that of the president, an unreconstructed old warthog named August L. Shitemeister—and that went far to make the professor's ascendancy through the ranks both swift and sure. In 1968, a scant ten years after he arrived on campus, he was enthroned, and so became, in very truth, Dr. Nelson R. Peckler, Head.

It was never in the cards that Gil and Harry would become fast friends with Nelson Peckler. In the first place, their own educations had taught them, if nothing else, that even a puny master of the arts could trounce a doctorate in education any old time—that, indeed, the "EdD" appended to Peckler's name branded him not as a learned man but rather as something of an ignoramus. Unfortunately, they weren't as successful as they might've been at keeping their estimation of him to themselves: Their first fall term at ASC was barely under way when Gil, during a departmental committee meeting, openly corrected Peckler's grammar ("That was actually a kindness," Gil told Harry afterward. "If he'd said 'the reason is because' one more time, I would've had to shoot him.") And later, at the annual Homecoming Day Alumni Barbecue, at which new faculty were expected to dish up lunch for the alums, Peckler made bold to take charge of the operation and imperiously order Harry to don a paper apron and cap and hand out Dixie Cups of ice cream at the dessert table, whereupon our hero did—in very truth—suggest that Dr. Peckler go take a shit in the ocean. Thus was their enmity sealed early on, and forevermore.

Over the ensuing decade, as Nelson Peckler marched inexorably toward dominion, Harry and Gil engaged in many small skirmishes against him, and actually won their share of tiny victories; for despite the rising Peckler influence within the department, change was coming just as inexorably to the college as a whole:

Way back in 1961, the pacifist son of the Beaver wrestling coach, of all people, had strode onto the football field during an ROTC halftime Homecoming Day parade bearing a sign declaring, before countless thousands of non-plussed Beaver football fans, MILITARY EDUCATION IS NOT EDUCATION FOR DEMOCRACY! President Shitemeister endeavored to expel the renegade transgressor, but failed, thanks to a petition signed by a heavy majority of his faculty and vigorously circulated within the history department by Gil and Harry, over the violent objections of the president's new protégé, Professor-in-Waiting Peckler, who branded them (plagiarizing his own hero, the late junior senator from Wisconsin) "handmaidens of the Communist conspiracy."

It developed that the young pacifist had fired the first shot of a revolution that would mightily shake the Arbuckle State campus, as similar incidents would soon be shaking campuses everywhere. In 1963, the faculty dress code—coats and ties at all times in the classroom—came tumbling down. (That didn't do much for Gil, who continued to look ultra-cool in those skinny suits and ties of the era; but Harry immediately took up jeans and sweatshirts and, eventually, bell-bottoms and frootboots and paisley-printed, big-sleeve pirate shirts. Gil had the history department's first beard, Harry its first ponytail. Needless to say, Nelson R. Peckler was mortally offended.) In 1964, a Young Turk professor in the English Department ventured to teach Vladimir Nabokov's dangerous novel *Lolita*, and the maiden lady who served as Dean of Students sent a student spy with a tape recorder into his class; the tape recorder was discovered, and the incident became a scandal that brought down Arbuckle State's entire system of *in loco parentis* rules, and allowed boys and girls to cohabit in the dorms, and girls to stay out until two or three or four o'clock in the morning if they chose to do so. Then came the resistance to the Vietnam War and teach-ins and sit-ins and be-ins, and even—in Harry's case, between marriages—the occasional love-in. Again needless to say, Nelson R. Peckler . . . did not participate.

There was even talk that Arbuckle State College might someday soon— once it had disencumbered itself of the current administration of August L. Shitemeister—finally declare itself a genuine university, and offer degrees— even *advanced* degrees!—in those formerly despised fields known contemptuously as Lower Division Humanities.

In the final days of 1967, Arbuckle State College's venerable president August L. Shitemeister was gathered at last unto his fathers, but not before, as one of his final official acts, he had assured the elevation of his pet professor to the exalted position of head—or, rather, Head—of the History Department. Later that same academic year, Arbuckle State University did absolutely become a reality and began to expand its offerings accordingly. Among the new programs was a Department of American Studies, which outraged the highly refined sensibilities of the History Department's distinguished Dr. Pecklerhead by incorporating in its curriculum, along with all manner of other licentious—possibly subversive—childish infatuations, the study of such low-life musical diversions as Nee-gro blues and jazz, as well as folk and soul and hillbilly trash and even that incomprehensible, unsavory new phenomenon, rock 'n' roll.

Now it happened that Harry Eastep, notoriously tuneless and tone-deaf though he certainly was, knew a little something—more than a little—about those very subjects, as well as about other arcane areas of the American Studies curriculum, including motion pictures and popular culture and literature, and especially about the work of his personal literary hero, Erskine Caldwell, in Harry's opinion the most overlooked, underrated writer in America.

(Except for rock 'n' roll, a late arrival that synthesized its predecessors, all these enthusiasms had come to Harry in the bloom of his youth way back home in Needmore, Kentucky. He had, for instance, fallen hard for "race" music when he was fifteen, the very first time he heard, on late-night radio out of Nashville, a stirring tune called "Work With Me Annie"; had learned to love Hank Williams on the Craycraft's Billiards' jukebox while shooting nine-ball with his pal Monk McHorning; had become enamored of the movies while popping popcorn at the New Artistic Theatre; and had come to admire the sublime work of Erskine Caldwell while standing by the revolving paperback rack in Conklin's Drugstore, surreptitiously reading *God's Little Acre*.)

Over the aeons that Harry had been affiliated with what had become, for him, the Department of the Essentials of Western Civilization, he had been contributing essays and articles about all those subjects to obscure academic journals of American folklore and popular culture. But the pre-Peckler department chairman, a doddering old gent named Dr. Summerset, himself a Shitemeister-annointed wart-piglet, would have regarded such publications as Communist-inspired incursions on Western Civilization, so Harry hadn't even bothered to report his little successes to his nominal superiors, figuring they would probably count against him anyhow.

Nonetheless, his efforts hadn't gone for naught in the grander scheme of things, for it happened that the up-and-coming chair of the new American Studies department, young Dr. Toddler, had been reading Harry's work for years—had in fact cited it and quoted from it liberally in his doctoral dissertation at Brown—and was amazed to discover, when he arrived at Arbuckle State, that this Fount of All Knowledge was ignominiously slaving away in the bowels of what had until recently been Lower Division Humanities, teaching four sections of Western Civ. He summoned Harry to his office and offered him a proposition: Dr. Toddler aspired to publish, under the aegis of his spanking new department, a quarterly—*The Northwest Journal of Popular Culture*—and he hoped that the eminent Assistant Professor Eastep could be persuaded to become its editor. In the course of their conversation, it quickly came to light that they were both admirers of the Grateful Dead (which hinted at other certain affinities), and that they would both certainly have been at Altamont if only they hadn't had to be somewhere else that day.

In short, they hit it off splendidly, and Dr. Toddler proposed a shared teaching position with Harry's department: halftime in the trenches of Western Civ, halftime at play in the editorial fields of the Lord.

The fly in this delightful ointment was in the person (so to speak) of a very large insect of the genus Peckler, who would have to sign off on the whole scheme, and was hardly likely to be cooperative. Last spring, when Harry and Gil and Freejack had been under siege in that Portland daisy chain, they'd been featured the next morning in a large photograph on the front page of the Sunday paper, *The Oregonian*—the three of them arm-in-arm, Gil in his usual sharp black suit and narrow tie, Harry long-haired and bell-bottomed and tie-dyed to a fare-thee-well, and Freejack with his prodigious Afro like a giant, black dandelion—above the caption ASU PROFS, EX-JOCK DEFY DRAFT! On Monday morning, bright and early, Peckler callled Gil and Harry on the carpet and charged them with bringing disapprobation and contumely upon all of Western Civilization, or at any rate upon the Essentials thereof, and sternly reminded them that, henceforward, their every move was under the intense scrutiny of . . . The Head!

At the time, the threat didn't mean all that much to Harry—his tenure protected him from getting fired, and he was already condemned to eternal Saturday morning eight o'clocks anyhow—but it presented a major problem for Gil, who, during the years while Harry had been writing paeans to his rustic idols in the quarterlies, had striven mightily to earn a PhD at the *real* state university, forty miles down the road. Gil had finally taken his degree, with distinction, just weeks after that infamous episode at the Induction Center; and with the expanding curriculum, he hoped that he might fall heir to the occasional advanced class, maybe even a promotion. But der Pecklerhead had proved unforgiving, and now, with a new academic year well under way, Gil was still an assistant prof, still doing, perforce, his usual four sections of involuntary servitude while he grimly plotted his appeal to the faculty grievance committee.

So of course when the American Studies proposal came along, Harry knew immediately that he, too, had a problem. He explained the difficulty to his new best friend Dr. Toddler, who was sympathetic, and readily granted Harry a few weeks to come up with a strategy. Later, Gil and Harry had talked their situations over at great length, and gloomily concluded that the grievance committee—which was, unpropitiously, Peckler-appointed, and therefore under his pernicious thumb—might have to be their only recourse.

· · ·

On a Sunday afternoon a couple of weeks later, Freejack dropped by Harry's apartment to see if he was interested—and he was, he was—in a lid of newly arrived Maui Wowie. The transaction completed, they tasted and, like the song says, got wasted; and eventually, during the rather aimless conversation that ensued after they regained the power of speech, Freejack mentioned, apropos of nothing in particular, that Harry's boss—here Freejack was unable to suppress a marijuana giggle at what he was about to say—Harry's boss must be one hip dude.

"Peckler?" Harry scoffed. "A hip dude? C'mon, man!"

No lie, Freejack assured him, explaining, with many more giggles of the same description, that a certain chick of his acquaintance who sometimes babysat the wee Pecklers, and who called herself Rainbow (Harry knew Rainbow from his affinity group at a teach-in a year or so ago, when she was still Mary Lou Suggins) was telling her closest campus friends (among them Freejack and a select few of his associates whom Rainbow sometimes condescended to ball) that Dr. Peckler, while driving her home night before last after a babysitting gig, having somehow discovered that she occasionally modeled for life-drawing classes, confessed his own long-suppressed artistic yearnings, and offered her forty dollars to let him take her picture, topless, with his new Polaroid.

And when Harry declared that he didn't believe a word of it, Freejack showed him what he claimed were the very same two twenty-dollar bills that Dr. Pecklerhead had paid Rainbow for the Polaroids he had taken of her in his office yesterday afternoon—an away-game Saturday afternoon when the campus was basically shut down—the very same two twenty-dollar bills that Rainbow had, in turn, paid Freejack not two hours ago for a lid of the very same most excellent weed that Harry himself had just purchased and, indeed, the very same weed that he and Harry had, with such exceedingly satisfactory results, just smoked.

"Twenty bucks a titty, dad!" Freejack added happily, slapping his knee. "Rainbow's cool, she could care less. And"—he stuffed Peckler's pair of twenties back into his pocket—"the bread was right."

As soon as Freejack left to continue his rounds, Harry twisted up, for meditative purposes, a fresh doob, torched it, and sat back to think the whole thing over. There had to be a way—he told himself, as his fading high magically bloomed once again inside his head, and with it his resurgent hopes for becoming the exalted editor of *The Northwest Journal of Popular Culture*—there had to be a way to turn this information to advantage.

Peckler wouldn't dream of taking such pictures home, Harry reasoned, not with that great beetle-browed brute of a wife looming over him; so if said pix existed at all, they would reside somewhere in Peckler's office. This circumstance was actually quite heartening, in light of the fact that he and Gil, during their midnight explorations of the premises, had been surreptitiously invading that forbidden sanctuary off and on for years, having discovered long ago where Mrs. Sowersby, the department secretary, stashed the key, in a little niche in the top drawer of her desk in the front office.

The first time they went in, during the reign of old Dr. Summerset, Peckler's predecessor in the chairmanship, they were looking for the personnel files, for the purpose of ferreting out any unfavorable disclosures about themselves. (Gil's were clean, but Harry found a letter of "recommendation" from one of his former history professors at Ohio State deriding as "Freudian trash" a term paper in which Harry had propounded the theory that the impetus of the Westward Movement was rooted in the infamous twinned myths of *penis captivus* and *vagina dentata*. Harry instantly pulled the letter from his file and tore it to bits and boldly dumped the pieces in Dr. Summerset's own wastebasket.) Later, they'd gone in several times to get a look at forthcoming departmental exams, with an eye to preparing their students accordingly. More recently, after Peckler's ascension, they'd gone so far as to poke around inside his very desk on a fishing expedition, but had found nothing more damning than a stack of three-by-five cards bearing astonishingly stupid limericks ("There was a young man from Corvallis / Who had a very large phallus . . . ") in Peckler's own hand, suggesting—though not proving—authorship. The discovery was nonetheless an eye-opener, in light of Inspector Peckler's massive venting about moral decline on the campus during the *Lolita* scandal. But hypocrisy isn't an actionable offense, not even in academe—especially not in academe—so in the end they were obliged to let it pass.

The trick, then, would be not so much in getting their hands on the evidence, as in figuring out how to take advantage of it when they did. For a brief, delicious moment, Harry envisioned another headline in the Sunday *Oregonian,* something like PECKLERHEAD EXPOSED BY UNDERLINGS! TITTIES TELL TALE! But that wouldn't advance either Gil's promotion or

Harry's own editorial aspirations, and anyhow he knew that neither of them had the stomach for that sort of direct assault on their persecutor. Nor was out-and-out blackmail an option; sweet as it would be to have the upper hand at last, Harry really couldn't imagine either himself or his almost equally mild-mannered colleague making that hoarse, hankie-muffled, midnight phone call: *"Okay, Peckler, play ball—or else!"* Despite their readiness to sneak like, yes, burglars into Inspector Peckler's private office and pry into his very own personal effects and private art collection, there wasn't a criminal bone—well, hardly a criminal bone—in their liberal pinko bodies. Still, a few titty pix might go a long way, a very long way indeed, toward righting certain wrongs against the underclass . . .

Next morning in the office, Harry regaled Gil with Freejack's toothsome tale, to their mutual delight. But they both understood that nothing at all could happen till they had successfully verified that the pictures did, in fact, exist—and they agreed (almost without even saying so) that they'd best not let the grass grow under their feet: That very night, it was written, they would once again invade the realm of the Prince of Darkness, and see what they could see.

Having blown—thus far—two short-lived marriages with nothing to show for them except his lost baby boy and an enthusiasm for good eats (fostered by the fact that both wives had been excellent cooks), Harry had, of necessity, taught himself the rudiments of culinary art. Accordingly, in preparation for the evening's hugger-muggery, he fortified himself with a bacon-wrapped filet mignon, a baked potato, and three generous glasses—call it a bottle—of an exceptionally nice little red, a favorite of Gil's from his own Napa Valley hometown. Then, anticipating a small late-night celebration in the event of a successful conclusion to their larcenous work, Harry stashed a second bottle of the Napa Valley red and a substantial fat-boy of Freejack's finest in his briefcase, along with a draft of the essay he was currently working on—"Criminality, Judgement, and Redemption in the Delta: Howlin' Blind Muddy Slim and the Epistemology of Despair," for *Backbeat Quarterly: A Journal of Undiscovered American Genius*—and, around nine, betook himself back to the office for their date with destiny.

Gil was already there, diligently poring over the weekly essay exams that he alone, of all his Western Civ colleagues (certainly including his friend

Harry), still resolutely inflicted upon his students—and, of necessity, upon himself as well. Both he and Harry knew what was coming and felt no need to talk about it; Harry planted himself before his Olivetti and began pecking away at his own essay, glad that, at any rate, he wouldn't have to submit it to Gil for a grade.

They fretted away at their separate chores, more or less in silence, till almost midnight, when Mr. Dingus, the night watchman, came through the building on his final round. As was his habit, Mr. Dingus stopped in their doorway to make his usual remarks about still burning the old midnight oil, eh?, and about the weather—damp, of course—and to remind them to be sure and lock up after themselves, now, and then trekked off into the night.

"Welp," said Gil resolutely when the back door had slammed shut behind Mr. Dingus, "it's gumshoe time, old son."

Together, Gil and Harry made their way down the dimly lighted hallway—each manfully resisting the impulse to tiptoe even though they both knew perfectly well that there wasn't another soul anywhere in the building—and let themselves into the front office. Gil went to the mimeograph machine and began copying tomorrow's pop quiz—a ruse, in the highly improbable event that they would have to explain what they were doing there in the first place—while Harry invaded Mrs. Sowersby's desk and extracted the key to Fort Peckler, as per the ground rules they'd adopted during many a clandestine midnight foray into the enemy's redoubt. Then, with the mimeograph machine clattering away, Harry opened Peckler's door just wide enough to let Gil slip inside the darkened office and close the venetian blinds.

That accomplished, Harry hit the light switch, the flourescent overheads flickered, and suddenly the room was flooded with light, featuring Peckler's desk as though a spotlight blazed down upon it. Grinning conspiratorially, Gil and Harry briefly pantomimed the old Alphonse-Gaston routine, and then Harry, after the approved fashion of spies, cat burglars, and similar snakes in the grass since time immemorial, did the honors, sliding the shallow drawer all the way out to reveal, in the furthermost left-hand corner, the stack of three-by-five cards bearing, on the top card, Peckler's latest contribution to the collective poesy of Western Civilization ("There was an old man from Eugene / Whose penis could scarcely be seen . . . "), and, underneath that, another little stack of . . .

Polaroids! Yes! Titty pix galore, eight of 'em in all, the entire product of what was, for the primordial Polaroid cameras of the day, a whole roll of film, eight fetching little black-and-white shots of the amply endowed Rainbow with her peasant blouse gathered down around her waist and wearing, from there up, only an insuppressible smirk—not unlike the well-known Mona Lisa smile, although perhaps rather more condescending toward the artist—that graced each and every photo.

"Ho-lee shit!" Gil and Harry murmured, almost in unison, when the photos were all spread before them on the desktop.

Despite her youth, Rainbow proved to be, in the titty department, somewhat droopy. But that had hardly discouraged her avid portraitist, who featured the celebrated appendages in every picture, usually at the expense of the top of poor Rainbow's head, which, like a mad scientist in a two-bit horror movie, he had lopped off quite indiscriminately. And best of all, every single one of the photos showed, in full view on the wall just over Rainbow's naked left shoulder, the tiny but perfectly legible image, as good as a signature on each and every masterpiece, of the framed diploma of Nelson R. Peckler, EdD!

"So," Harry wondered aloud, after a long moment of silence while he and Gil stroked their chins in deepest cogitation, "what next?"

"Okay," Gil said, finally, "here it is: You take one, and I'll take one, and we'll put the rest back just like they were."

Harry was aghast. First thing tomorrow morning, he protested, Peckler, being Peckler, would no doubt sneak a peek at his new treasures, and would know right away who . . .

"Exactly," said Gil. "Just so."

Now Harry got his drift: Of *course* Peckler would know that his two bitterest enemies, who were on the premises almost nightly, were the prime—indeed, the only—suspects, but what could he do about it? He was not without a blustering, bullying sort of courage, but, like Dickens's Mr. Bounderby, he could see as far into a grindstone as the next man, and he'd soon realize that, given his situation (PECKLERHEAD EXPOSED!), discretion was his only refuge. His goose was cooked, his ass was grass, they had him by the shorthairs; they could forget the heavy-breathing midnight phone calls.

Harry and Gil exchanged quick grins and muffled chortles (which spoke volumes as to their estimation of the Peckler intellect), then Gil grabbed two photos while Harry scooped up the remaining six and tucked them neatly back into their nook in Peckler's desk. They turned off the lights, re-opened the blinds, locked the door, replaced the key in Mrs. Sowersby's desk, gathered up Gil's quizzes from the mimeograph machine, and beat it back to their own office, where they collapsed into their respective desk chairs in paroxysms of mirth and self-congratulation.

After they had more or less regained their composure, they turned the two photos titty-side down and shuffled them on Gil's desk, blindly selected one apiece, and filed them in manila folders in their respective file cabinets under *T*. That done, Harry went to his briefcase and brought out the celebratory bottle while Gil produced the corkscrew from his desk drawer (they had a long-established celebration ritual, usually reserved for the end of a grading period), and they each dumped out the paperclips from the innocent-looking café glasses on their desks and poured themselves two brimming slugs of the nice little red.

(The two Polaroids, by the way, are destined to repose on file until the following spring, when Peckler, to the surprise and delight of all of Western Civilization—or at any rate of the Department thereof—will announce that he is resigning to accept a position as Superintendent of Public Schools of Fungo County, Alabama—and Gil and Harry, hearing the news, will gleefully tear the little photos to shreds and festoon each other with titty-photo confetti.)

So there they were, just raising their glasses to toast the success of their midnight mission, when there came a soft tap-tap-tapping at their office window. His heart in his throat, Harry spun in his chair, expecting to see, at best, Mr. Dingus and, at worst, Peckler, the Dean, the entire campus police force, and the House Un-American Activities Committee all assembled on the lawn outside the window like an out-of-season band of malevolent Christmas carolers . . . and beheld instead just one dark face, grinning maniacally.

Freejack.

As Harry, giddy with relief, rose to go to the back door to let him in, Gil put his finger to his lips in the traditional mum's-the-word gesture, to which Harry acceded with a nod. By the time Harry returned with Freejack in tow a couple of minutes later, Gil had found a clean coffee cup and was pouring their guest a welcoming dram of the nice little red.

Freejack shook the raindrops out of his Afro and sat down, meanwhile explaining that he'd been walking across the campus after a party somewhere, and had seen their light on, and thought he'd come in out of the rain for a minute. Harry, remembering his manners, dipped into the briefcase again and came up with the fattie, fired it up, and passed it over to him.

"Thanks, Teach," Freejack said, taking his hit and passing the smoldering doob on to Gil. "So what's happenin'? Looks like you dogs havin' a little party your ownselves."

"Ah, yes," said Gil, ready as usual with the exit line: "'Tis a naughty night to swim in."

Then, noting that Freejack looked more than a little puzzled, Gil took his toke, winked at Harry, and added an attribution: "Snakeshit."

But any proper academic treatise (which this chronicle certainly aspires to be) ought to have a few footnotes. So . . .

The following morning Dr. Nelson R. Peckler, Head, showed up bright and early, entered the front office whistling merrily, picked up his mail, gave the long-suffering Mrs. Sowersby an affectionate—albeit unwelcome—squeeze, and softly closed the door of his sanctuary after him, securing it with a click of the inner lock. After ten or fifteen minutes (according to later reports from the other secretaries), the door burst open and he stepped out, glowered about him as though, like his own flesh-eating children, he were looking for someone to bite, then turned on his heel and went back in and slammed the door. He stayed closeted, out of sight, until he knew that Gil's and Harry's eight o'clocks were over, then came storming out again and stomped down the hall toward their office, steam fairly issuing from his ears. He arrived at their door glaring ferociously and found both miscreants seated at their desks, dutifully taking care of business.

Harry and Gil, having individually run through, overnight, numerous mental rehearsals in preparation for this moment, put on the most disarming smiles they could muster, and blithely bade him good morning. Peckler, venomous toad that he was, puffed himself up and opened his mouth to spew forth what would surely have been an unprecedented volume of invective, opprobrium, and calumny—and then, almost visibly, thought better of it, brought himself up short, snapped his great mouth shut again, swallowed hard, and slowly deflated to his normal cumbrous proportions. The jig, he had seen as plainly as though the terrible fact were lit by lightning, was indisputably up.

"Morning, fellas," he said at last, in honeyed tones accompanied by a smarmy leer that put their own disingenuous smiles to shame. "You fellas have yourselves a lovely day, now."

And with that, he slunk off down the hall and, for all practical purposes, out of the picture for good and all.

The following week's edition of the inter-departmental newsletter announced that Assistant Professor Gilbert Burgin, PhD, had been promoted to Associate, with all the perquisites attendant thereto (next term, though of course he doesn't know this yet, Freejack will be enrolling in Associate Professor Burgin's new upper-division Literature as History seminar, where he will inadvertently get some Snakeshit on him and decide to become a writer), and also that Assistant Professor Harrison B. Eastep, MA, had been appointed editor-in-chief of the new *Northwest Journal of Popular Culture*.

Neither of them was ever assigned another eight o'clock.

GREAT
MOMENTS
IN SPORTS

O the clear moment, when from the mouth
A word flies, current immediately
Among friends; or when a loving gift astounds
As the identical wish nearest the heart;
Or when a stone, volleyed in sudden danger,
Strikes the rabid beast full on the snout!
              Robert Graves, "Fragment of a Lost Poem"

Like everybody else, I've told my favorite sports stories
so many times I almost believe them myself. For instance:

When I was twelve years old (stop me if you've heard this), Happy
Chandler gave me an autographed baseball. I once rode on an elevator
with Jim Thorpe. I know a guy who knows a guy whose father once stood
next to Lou Gehrig at a urinal in Yankee Stadium. I saw Ewell "The Whip"
Blackwell pitch a no-hitter for the Cincinnati Reds in 1947, and Tom Seaver
duplicate the feat in the next Reds game I attended—thirty-one years later.
Gay Brewer, Jr., the golfer, once bird-dogged my girlfriend. My friend Gurney Norman claims to have tossed a ping-pong ball into a Dixie Cup from
twenty feet away. (I believe him, of course—but hey, what are friends for?)
Waite Hoyt once let my uncle buy him a drink. In college, I was employed
as a "tutor" by my university's athletic department, in which capacity I took,
by correspondence, an entire sophomore English literature survey course
for a first-string All-American tackle.

("Now don't get me no A," my protégé cautioned, the night before I was to take the final for him. "Get me about a C+, that'd be about right." It was a line I would put to use twenty-five years later in my one and only novel, *The Natural Man*, still available at fine booksellers everywhere.)

Well, I could go on, but modesty forefends; my record in Vicarious Athletics speaks for itself.

Yet there were a few times when I actually got into the fray in person, in the quest after that elusive Perfect Moment. Like the time I ran fourteen balls in a game of straight pool (and had a straight-in shot at the fifteen—and scratched). Or the time I won a dollar and thirty-five cents in half an hour pitching pennies on the courthouse steps (and lost it all back in the next twenty minutes).

Or the time twelve guys on our high school basketball team came down with the flu, and I was abruptly—not to say precipitously—elevated from second-string JV to the furthermost end of the varsity bench, and suddenly found myself, deep in the third quarter, not only in the game but endeavoring to guard the great Cliff Hagan, then of Owensboro High, later of the University of Kentucky Wildcats and the St. Louis Hawks. On the first play he broke for the basket and went twinkle-toeing up my chest like he was Fred Astaire and I was the Stairway to the Stars.

Hagan—Mr. Hagan—accumulated eleven points during my two-minute tenure, mostly on shots launched from some vantage point afforded him by my reclining anatomy. If there were a statistic called "percentage of defensive assists," I'd have set some kind of record.

Still, every mutt has his Moment, and mine was coming up.

By the spring of 1950, when I was a junior at Maysville High and my glory days on the hardwood were but a distant memory ("Mac," our estimable Coach Jones had said, drawing me aside one day after practice, "Mac, you're a good, hard-working boy, but son, your hands are small, and I just don't believe you've got the equipment to make this team"), I had long since limited my athletic exertions to the rigorous pursuit of female companionship.

In other words, I was spending a disproportionate amount of time mooning about the house and grounds of a certain Mr. and Mrs. T.C. Stonebreaker, who had four beautiful daughters still at home. Alas, I was but one of many, a restive, milling herd of rampant teenaged billy goats strutting our dubious stuff before the less-than-awestruck Misses Stonebreakers. On Saturday afternoons (when Mr. Stonebreaker usually beat a strategic withdrawal to his euchre game at the Moose Lodge while Mrs. Stonebreaker did her grocery shopping), the testosterone level in Stonebreaker Hall could have peeled the wallpaper.

For these occasions, we trotted out all our highly developed social skills—which is to say we maligned and demeaned and bullied and belittled one another mercilessly, in the hope of raising our own stature in the eyes of the four (largely indifferent) fascinators; we cut up and showed off like drunken sailors, and talked as indelicately as we dared, for the edification of that beguiling audience.

Such was the scenario on that memorable Saturday afternoon in the spring of 1950, the day of my Personal Best Great Moment:

Mr. S. is at his euchre, Mrs. S. is out shopping, and the house fairly teems with post-pubescent boys of every size and description, from eighth graders vying for the attentions of Gracie, the youngest Stonebreaker, to a couple of pipe-puffing college freshmen home for the weekend expressly to pay court to Mary Margaret, the eldest, who graduated from high school last year and now has an office job at the cotton mill. Once again, the objects of our affection have reduced us all—even the college guys—to the developmental level of the eighth graders, who themselves are behaving like fifth graders. Naturally, there have already transpired numerous episodes of pantsing, not to mention various hotfoots, noogies, and wedgies; and the atmosphere is redolent of bathroom humor so sophisticated that it has left the sisters Stonebreaker fairly gasping with (let us hope) admiration.

I'm there too, of course, but for once I've held myself aloof from these adolescent proceedings, having somehow cornered Bernice, who is to my mind the fairest Stonebreaker of them all, over by the piano, where I and my Lucky Strike are demonstrating my prowess at French-inhaling, blowing smoke rings, and—like Tony Curtis on the cover of the paperback of *The Amboy Dukes* ("A Novel of Wayward Youth in Brooklyn! Now a Thrilling Motion Picture!")—making suave conversation while the Lucky is parked roguishly in the corner of my mouth. I have also lately cultivated, in the wake of my departure from the uniformly crew-cut Bulldog squad, a pro-digious Wildroot-lubricated pompadour, complete with a lank Tony Curtis forelock that dangles ornamentally over my right eye; and I'm sporting my brand-new oh-so-cool two-tone jacket with the collar turned up—just like Tony's!

("How come you've got your collar turned up that way, Eddie?" Bernice has just interrupted my suave conversation to inquire. "It's not a bit cold in here!")

And now into this tranquil domestic circle swagger the last two guys in all of Christendom whom the rest of us—the males, I mean—want to see, namely the dreaded Speedy Little Guards (so-called in the local press), a brace of Bobbys—let's call them Bobby One and Bobby Two—indispensable Bulldog mainstays, One a razzle-dazzle ball-handler, Two a nonpareil set-shot artist, both of them brash, bandy-legged, and, in the unanimous opinion of the Stonebreaker girls, devastatingly cute.

Bernice quickly escapes the narrow confines of our tête-à-tête and joins her sisters, who are gathered 'round the Bobbys to admire their new Bulldog letter-sweaters, acquired just last night at the annual awards banquet. (*How come they're wearing sweaters?* I hear myself grumbling inwardly. *It's not a bit cold in here!*) Then we all troop dutifully outside to see Bobby Two's new short—actually his mother's new short—a dumpy, frumpy 1950 Nash Rambler, whose contours, come to think of it, are not unlike those of Mrs. Two herself.

Still, the Nash is profoundly snazzier than the scuffed penny loafers that at present constitute my own principle means of locomotion, and I am positively viridescent with envy. And this condition is further aggravated by my growing certainty that if Bobby Two has his way, he and Bernice will be snuggling up in that goddamn Rambler at the RiverView Drive-In Theater tonight.

Once we're all back inside the house, the two Bobbys, along with Marcella, the second-eldest sister, and (sigh) Bernice, promptly disappear into the kitchen, from whence soon begin to issue various muffled giggles, sniggers, chortles, titters, and similar sounds of suppressed merriment. Meanwhile, the eighth graders are entertaining Gracie with a tiny-tuba ensemble of rude armpit noises as the pipe-puffers regale Mary Margaret with BMOC tales (featuring, of course, themselves), leaving the rest of us Lotharios to loll about the living room shooting pocket-pool while we feign indifference to the jolly goings-on behind the kitchen door.

After ten or fifteen minutes the merrymakers emerge, the girls still all a-giggle behind their hands, the Bobbys all a-smirk. Each Bobby is carrying, inexplicably, an egg.

"Okay," Bobby One announces, stepping to the center of the room, "now let's see which one can bust his egg on the othern's head!" With that, he and Bobby Two begin comically bouncing around the room on their toes like sparring sperm-weights until, after a brief and thoroughly unpersuasive flurry of pseudo-fisticuffs, Bobby One, egg in hand, smacks Bobby Two on the noggin and—how could I have been so surprised by this?—*mirabile dictu*, the egg's not loaded, there's nothing in it. The empty shell shatters harmlessly on Bobby Two's crew-cut pate.

Of course the Bobbys—being Bobbys—act like this is the greatest joke since the chicken crossed the road. There wasn't nothing to it, they aver, clapping each other on the back in the throes of their hilarity; we just punched little pinholes in them eggs and blowed the insides out.

And right there is where I make the dumbest move of my young life.

"Let's see that one," I hear myself saying, unaccountably, to Bobby Two, whose egg—whose eggshell—is still intact. "Lemme take a look at it." To this day, I don't know what in the world I was thinking of.

"You wanna see the egg?" says Bobby One. "Hey Bob-o, Clammerham wants to see the egg!"

Bobby Two is grinning, and there is a gleam in his eye that should have given me pause. Could that be a corresponding gleam in the eye of Bernice, who is standing just behind him? Why do I feel like I'm in a play, and everybody knows the script but me?

"Sure, Hammerclam," says Bobby Two, putting his hands behind his back. "Which hand?"

Christ, I'm thinking, *it's only an eggshell*. But hey, I got my forelock, got my Lucky hangin' on my lip, I'm cool. So I play along.

"Uh, the left?"

"Nope," he says, showing me his left hand, in which there is, of course, nothing at all. Meanwhile his right hand—in which there is, of course, not an eggshell but an *egg*, in all its fullness—is describing a high, sweeping arc from behind his back to the top of my head, where it arrives with a disgusting splat, much to the disadvantage of my pompadour.

"Sorry," says Bobby Two, wiping his palm on my Tony Curtis lapel, "wrong hand."

So there I stand in the Stonebreaker living room with a coiffeur nicely dressed out in egg yolk, a viscous thread of egg-white trailing, like a sneeze gone terribly wrong, from my forelock to my Lucky Strike, and all about me a tumult of eighth graders rolling on the floor, college boys roaring, Stonebreaker girls hugging themselves in their mirth, Bobbys pounding each other on the back to the point of bodily injury. My dignity, I fear, has been seriously compromised. Time to regroup.

To which purpose I slink off to the kitchen, where I stick my sodden head under the faucet in the sink and shampoo my hair as best I can with dishwashing liquid, dry it with Mrs. Stonebreaker's dishtowel, and sponge off my jacket with her dishrag. Then I comb my hair; the egg-yolk residue is beginning to set up, which actually helps a little in the reconstruction of my pompadour. Finally, I go to the refrigerator and help myself to two more of Mrs. Stonebreaker's eggs. Thus armed, I return to the scene of Clamhammer's Humiliation.

In the living room, things have sorted themselves out predictably, in accordance with the New Social Order: The armpit ensemble has resumed serenading Gracie, and the college stuffed shirts, solemn as owls, are once again puffing industriously away on their calabashes, throwing up a smoke screen around Mary Margaret as dense—and certainly as aromatic—as an enchantment. But now Bobby One is cozying up to Marcella on the sofa, and Bernice, that Jezebel, has joined Bobby Two over by the piano—in *our* corner!

Such is the sordid scene that Clamhammer the Redeemer bursts upon, with blood in his eye and vengeance on his mind.

"Awright, you sorry bastids," I thunder—yes! I actually thundered!— brandishing an egg at first one Bobby, then the other. "Now I would hate to have to throw this right here in Mrs. Stonebreaker's living room, but I've got one of these apiece for you two sonsabitches, and if you're not outta here by the time I count to three, you're definitely gonna get egged! One!"

The Bobbys exchange stricken glances, and I know that I am terrible in my wrath.

"Two!"

Now Bobby One half-rises from the sofa, while the craven Bobby Two endeavors to shield himself behind Bernice.

"Three!" I cry, and with that the Bobbys break simultaneously for the doorway into the front hall, and I am in hot pursuit, my throwing arm cocked at the ready. But not for nothing do their admirers call them the

Speedy Little Guards, for by the time I make the hall, they are scrambling out the front door. And the truth is that, despite my threat, I am not quite willing to throw an egg within these sacred premises, owing to the certainty that Mrs. Stonebreaker would forthwith banish me from the temple forever and ever, world without end.

So I hold my fire, and in another instant I'm on the front stoop and the Bobbys are already legging it across the street toward where the Rambler awaits them. I reach the curb just as Bobby Two arrives at the Rambler's driver's-side door, and I have a clear shot at him, a perfect target inasmuch as, even if I miss, I'll still hit his mommy's car. Then, just as I'm going into my windup, what suddenly looms up between us but a city bus, lumbering along as huge and pokey as a steamship. And when the bus is out of the way at last, I see that Bobby Two is at the Rambler's wheel, revving up, and his door is closed. Bobby One is just opening the passenger-side door; I can see his head above the roof of the car, so I uncork a desperation throw at it, not a bad throw, actually, except that he sees it coming and ducks into the car as the egg sails over his head and splatters abortively against a telephone pole. Then Bobby Two pops the clutch, and the Rambler scratches off more spiritedly than I would've dreamed it could, while I stand there on the curb shaking my fist after them, a masterful study in futility.

But wait, what's this I see! Down at the far end of the block, the Rambler is hanging a U-ey! Can it be that they're actually going to come back past me? Yes they are; the Rambler has wallowed through its turn and is headed back in my direction. Maybe they've forgotten that I still have an egg in my arsenal—and this time, I am vowing grimly as I palm my egg, I won't miss.

As the Rambler rolls slowly past, Bobby One has his thumbs in his ears and is making donkey faces at me behind the passenger-side window. I draw a bead on his ugly mug and cut loose a vicious Ewell "The Whip" Blackwell sidearm bullet that I know even as it leaves my hand is a wild pitch, and that it will miss the strike zone by half a yard.

Now there are those who will maintain that an egg is, after all, only an egg, a stupid, insensate, ovoid article of no cognitive power whatsoever unless and until it somehow gets a chicken in it—itself a species not conspicuous for its intellect. But that does not describe *this* egg. For this is *my* egg, friends, as surely as if I'd laid it myself, and this egg is smarter, even, than its proud parent; it has a mind of its own and knows *exactly* where it wants to go. And this egg of mine has *eyes*, dear hearts, and as it spins off my fingertips it sees what I have not seen, which is that although Bobby One has his window snugly closed, his wind-wing—that little triangular vent that all cars used to have, back in the days when car-makers were smarter than, say, chickens—his wind-wing is . . . wide open!

And this little egg of mine *finds* that tiny opening with all its eyes, and it flies as true as Cupid's arrow straight through the vent and explodes in a bright golden sunburst all *over* the interior of Bobby Two's mommy's brand-new short, all *over* those accursed Bobbys and their goddamn letter-sweaters! Thus have I struck the rabid beast full on the snout!

Luck? You dare call it luck? Was it luck that directed Gurney's ping-pong ball into that Dixie Cup? No indeed. Luck, I think, is synonymous with money; it's strictly a business proposition, wherein good luck produces a payoff, bad luck a payout. Nor, of course, was it skill; neither I nor Gurney could duplicate our feats in a thousand thousand years. No, this was destiny, pure and simple; we had, each of us, a blind date with Immortality. Did Cliff Hagan ever toss a ping-pong ball into a Dixie Cup at twenty feet? Did Ewell the Whip ever fling an egg through the wind-wing of a moving car?

And while I'm asking questions, I'll ask these: Were the Stonebreaker girls all watching from the stoop when my egg burst like a de Kooning master-piece inside the Rambler? Did they scream and squeal like bobby-soxers when this miracle of art and magic and athletic prowess transpired right before their very eyes? Did Bernice and I go to the movies that night—the sit-down movies, not the drive-in—and did I, when I took her home after-wards, kiss her on the lips on that very stoop?

No, sports fans, I'm afraid not, I'm afraid not. But . . . O the clear moment!

KEN KESEY,
JEAN GENET,
THE REVOLUTION, ET MOI

"He is not a tame *lion."*

C. S. Lewis

I hold here before me a tattered and barely legible duplicate draft registration card, issued to me in August 1955, after I'd lost my original card, along with the rest of the contents of my billfold and the billfold itself, one night earlier that summer in a place called something like El Rancho Gringo in Nuevo Laredo, Mexico, under circumstances that, if I could remember them, I'd just as soon forget.

I've never been back to Nuevo Laredo, and never lost another billfold, so I've carried the duplicate ever since, although the fine print on the card advises me that I should have destroyed it as of my thirty-sixth birthday, more years ago than I care to count. I've hung on to it for sentimental reasons, rather the way one clings to the ticket stubs from some memorable concert or evening at the theater—for once upon a time, as a matter of fact on almost the very eve of that long-gone thirty-sixth birthday, I was sure that my old draft card was about to become my ticket to the glory of revolutionary martyrdom.

Indeed, I already had a lifelong history of flirtations with subversion. Was I not the only closet agnostic in Daily Vacation Bible School (having suffered a couple of boils myself at a tender age, I was privately of the opinion that Job had got the rawest kind of deal), and the only Marxist-Leninist-Stalinist-Fascist Eisenhower Republican (this was purely for the sake of argument, you understand) in my freshman class at Washington & Lee, and the only proto-crypto-pseudo-semi-quasi-California Beatnik in the University of Kentucky English Department's graduate program in 1956? And wasn't I, in 1958, among the very first English instructors at Backwater State Teachers' College to sign the petition defending Gus Hall's right to speak on campus, despite the college president's assurance that this seditious act would pursue the signatories to their academic graves—which, he trusted, would prove both deep and early? Damn straight I was; don't mess with Robespierre, daddy-o.

So when I landed back in California in the 1960s, working the Visiting Lecturer in Creative Writing circuit, it was no surprise that in due time I could be observed on or about the premises of the institution we'll call the Harvard of the West, bedecked in peace symbols, love beads, Martin Luther King Jr. memorial armbands, "Free Huey!" buttons, marching here, sitting-in there, protesting this, supporting that, locking horns with the Establishment wherever it reared its ugly reactionary head, Bakunin of the Suburbs, a bomb in my pocket and a slogan ever at the ready on my lips . . .

Truth to tell, I'm afraid I wasn't really cut out for the revolution business. Whenever I tried to chant "Ho-Ho-Ho Chi Minh!" or "Hey, hey, LBJ!" my tongue went limp, in an adamant little protest of its own. At demonstrations, I tended to wander dazedly from faction to faction, listening to the incessant arguments about goals, strategies, tactics, and whose-turn-is-it-to-go-for-Cokes until I was half drunk on other people's rhetoric, a lost soul seeking his Affinity Group. Once, during a rousing Stop-the-Draft riot outside the Oakland Induction Center, I gleefully set a curbside trash basket afire—and then, in a paroxysm of remorse, dashed through a traffic jam of police cars to the Doggy Diner across the street, slapped down a couple of quarters for a large Pepsi to go, dashed back across the street, and poured it on the blaze. There was, it seemed, a sort of spoilsport moral plumb bob somewhere inside me, an Automatic Equivocator that brought me back to perpendicular whenever it caught me listing too far to the left. I may have had the heart of a firebrand, but mah feets was moderate to the bone.

My career as a revolutionary reached its nadir that night in October 1968, just three days short of my thirty-sixth birthday, when I went all the way to Berkeley for the express purpose of torching my tattered old duplicate draft card at a huge hell-no-we-won't-go! rally on the hallowed steps of Sproul Hall, that most sacrosanct of Movement temples. I arrived with a head full of newsreel footage of how it was going to be: When they asked for volunteers, I'd be the first to come forward, an aging sacrificial lamb throwing his poor old body on the line just three days before it reached the safety of eternal deferment. Not that it wasn't perfectly safe already; in fact, I'd been classified 4-F for years, thanks to a cooperative allergist who'd described my occasional hay fever as "chronic debilitating asthma" in a letter to my draft board. But my invulnerability merely added luster to the noble sacrifice I'd be making. For of course the government would have to prosecute such outright defiance; doubtless J. Edgar Hoover would dispatch his thugs to snatch me off to jail while the ashes of my draft card were still smoldering. "Free Ed!" the cry would ring across the land, ten thousand voices strong. "Free Ed! Free Ed!"

What actually happened, comrades, is that I stood around for hours, draft card in hand, listening to interminable speeches by a parade of posturing malingerers who were probably even more invulnerable to the draft than I was—and that at last, sometime around midnight, when the FBI had long since gone home to bed and the crowd had thinned out to the point that there weren't even enough warm bodies on hand to mount a respectable "Free Ed!" rally, someone passed among the stragglers with a metal wastebasket, collecting draft cards for the ritual immolation. I returned my card to my billfold, for a souvenir, and when the wastebasket came my way I tossed in an out-of-date fishing license instead. "Right on, man! Right on!" piped a couple of youthful voices here and there, with feeble enthusiasm. Following, for the first time since I outgrew "Crime Does Not Pay" comics, the good example of the FBI, I too went on home to bed.

From then on, my revolutionary ardor cooled considerably. I still dutifully showed up for marches and what-have-you, but I was just along for the walk; my heart wasn't in it anymore.

During the last days of 1969, as the Now Generation took its final tokes, there came into brief vogue the social phenomenon upon which Tom Wolfe was soon to pin the tag "Radical Chic," and in so doing to deal the fad a mortal wound, skewering it on the spot like some exotic but exceptionally short-lived butterfly.

Radical chic was, of course, that practice among prestigious, socially prominent people of throwing fund-and-consciousness-raising parties in their homes for the benefit of certain fashionable political causes—the antiwar movement, the civil rights movement, the grape workers, the environmentalists . . . and, notably, the Black Panthers. The Panthers took New York penthouse society like Grant took Richmond; in fact, it was Leonard Bernstein's party for the Panthers that Wolfe would perforate with such fatal accuracy, in the famous essay first published in *New York* magazine in June 1970.

But for a while there, the Panthers were the hottest thing going, and a lot of loose change was being turned in the course of these curious fraternizings. So in early 1970, the Oakland chapter of the Panthers, who like Dickens's Mr. Bounderby could see as far into a grindstone as the next man, put together a traveling Panther-in-the-parlor act of their own, complete with a special imported extra-added attraction, the celebrated French pederast cutpurse incendiarist Marxist-Leninist writer and all-around fruitcake Jean Genet, fresh out of prison for who-knows-what heinous offenses against whatever passes for human decency in France. They shipped Genet in by way of Toronto, where he laid over long enough to hold several press conferences in which he rather shrilly expressed his conviction that the FBI planned to snuff him the instant he set foot on American soil. The FBI didn't oblige him; when he landed in Oakland they evinced no more interest in him than they had in stopping the "Free Ed!" movement. Undaunted, the Panthers tricked him out in a tiny Panther Junior Auxiliary black leather jacket (Genet would wear about a boys' size 12), like some preposterous little mascot, and began exhibiting him around the neighborhood. Within a few days I got a phone call inviting me to a hastily arranged wine-and-cheese social that very afternoon at the home of an eminent Harvard of the West professor, to enjoy a warm excoriation of myself and selected other white liberal Enemies of the People, administered by those experts at the work, Jean Genet and the Black Panthers.

Which is where Ken Kesey comes into the picture.

Ken had long since left California to its own infernal devices and moved back to Oregon, but it so happened that when the party invitation came, he and I—Ken being between planes on his way home from Los Angeles—were sitting at my kitchen table in Palo Alto, talking Black Panthers. A friend had recently taken him to a Panther rally, Ken's been telling me, and all the whites in attendance were subjected to a weapons shakedown at the door, a procedure that Ken's experience has taught him is demeaning to both parties, frisker and friskee alike.

"It's a cop trip," he insists, "and it's a big mistake. They shouldn't be trying to out-asshole the assholes, they should try to be the good guys."

He goes on to tell me how, up in Oregon, his brother Chuck's creamery business sponsors a basketball team in the local municipal league, and how there are a couple of spades (still a term of endearment among us diehard old hipsters) on Chuck's team, and how, one recent night, the team found itself involved in a game the referee of which was evidently persuaded that only black players committed fouls.

"So we all started callin' *him* on it," Ken says. "Whenever he called a foul on our guys, we'd jump up off the bench and call one on *him*. And pretty soon the crowd could see it too, and they got into it, everybody was on his case, and we shamed the guy till he *had* to call a straight game . . ."

Along about here the phone rings, with the invitation to the professor's at-home, to meet the winsome enfant horrible, as well as David Hilliard, the acting Exalted Grand Sachem of the Oakland Panthers (Bobby Seale, Huey P. Newton, and Eldridge Cleaver being either incarcerated, exiled, or otherwise indisposed at the moment). After I've hung up, I explain the deal to Ken and ask him if he'd like to come along.

"Far out," he answers. "I'll wear your shirt."

Now, I realize that introducing a commonplace shirt into my narrative at this critical juncture risks trivializing the momentous issues with which we are concerned here. But this is *not* a commonplace shirt, this is my Errol-Flynn-Goes-to-Frisco Buccaneer Blouse, my Polk Street Sike-O-Deelic Swashbuckler, the silky, silvery one with the shiny blue paisleys as big as quahogs and the mother-of-pearl buttons and the huge, billowy sleeves and the tight three-button cuffs and the cantilever collar and the gullet-to-sternum décolletage, my Saturday-Night-at-the-Fillmore shirt, which is even now hanging right there on the kitchen doorknob, where I hung it this morning when it came back from the dry cleaner. Ken has had his eye on it ever since he walked in. But does he really intend to wear that to a Panther party? He'll go over like a transvestite at a Green Beret reunion.

Well, he certainly does; he intends to wear—and he does wear—not just the shirt, but also his neon red-and-white-striped hip-hugger bells and his bug-eye blue reflector shades and his American-flag front tooth and his new twelve-tone hand-painted Day-Glo sneakers, a little something he's just picked up in L.A. He goes off and suits up in this insane ensemble, and when he comes back into the room, he looks so smashing that I applaud him, and declare on the spot that the shirt is his forevermore.

On our way out the front door we meet our mutual pal Gordon Fraser, the only dealer still in the business who actually sells an Original Lid—a Prince Albert can, stuffed good and snug. Naturally, we go right back in and buy one, and refresh ourselves accordingly. Soon we're off again, this time taking Gordon with us, over his protests: "Panthers? I dunno, wait a moment, wait a moment . . . " Gordon has pulled a couple of years in the Joint himself, and the prospect of fellowshipping with Black Panthers is not his idea of a good time. But he's game, and off we go—as a matter of fact in Gordon's car, just for the ambiance.

The Eminent Professor lives in the Harvard of the West faculty ghetto, a lavish suburb-within-the-suburbs just off the campus, where the university has installed some of the finest minds of Western civilization, on the theory that if you put a fine mind in a nice Eichler split-level, it will sit right down and get busy thinking important thoughts. We know we're at the right house when we spot what have to be Panthermobiles—a matched pair of sleek black Citroëns with photo-gray no-see-um windows—parked at the curb outside.

We are met at the garden gate by the resident fine mind's minion, his graduate teaching assistant, who is checking a guest list, to keep out the riffraff that commonly prowl the faculty ghetto streets. I happen to know this particular grad student; he's notorious on campus for calling everybody over thirty "Doctor"—textbook salesmen, typewriter repairmen, grounds keepers—just in case. Now he stands there all agog, with his chin on his chest and his pencil frozen above his checklist, as Ken, blazingly resplendent in the brilliant California afternoon, strides past him as though he were part of the shrubbery. Gordon follows Ken, but the grad student never even notices him.

"I know you're on the list, Dr. McClanahan," he gulps when he finds his voice, "but who—?"

"That's Dr. Kesey," I tell him. "He's with me."

"Ken Kesey!" he cries happily. "Oh wow! Wait'll I go tell Dr. Cheesewitz!

Ken Kesey!" He scurries off into the garden, rubbing his hands together as if (as Tom Wolfe likes to put it) he's making invisible snowballs.

Inside the gate, a fairly good-sized party, maybe forty or fifty people, has assembled itself on the lawn and is tucking into the wine and cheese with an excellent appetite and chatting convivially with itself. Mostly, I note as I hurry after Ken and Gordon, they're folks I know, at least by sight if not by name, junior faculty and wives and grad students and, here and there, the odd progressive young lawyer, doctor, dentist, or Unitarian minister; the crowd that always turns out for the milder, more restrained rallies, nice, earnest liberals whose greatest happiness is in marching along arm in arm under the CONCERNED CITIZENS banner, singing "We Shall Overcome" with revolutionary fervor. Senior faculty—except for our host, the estimable Dr. Cheesewitz, who is at this very moment approaching me through the crowd with his hand already extended in greeting—is largely unrepresented here today.

"How do you do, Mr. Mackrelham!" exclaims Dr. Cheesewitz, pumping my hand warmly as he peers over my shoulder, looking for Ken. "So good of you to come! Mumford here"—out of nowhere the graduate student materializes beside him, manufacturing snowballs at a phenomenal rate—"Mumford here tells me you've brought us . . . ah, Mr. Kesey!"

Ken has turned, and now he looms prodigiously before us, as gaudy and gorgeous as a Christmas tree. For just the merest moment, you could knock Dr. Cheesewitz's eyeballs off with a broomstick. But he recovers quickly and grabs Ken's hand, prattling, "Awfully good of you to come, Mr. Kesey! I've admired *One Fell Out of the Cuckoo's Nest* for years! So pleased to meet you, so nice to have you, such an unexpected pleasure!"

Ken is suffering these effusions politely, but he is not moved to say how delighted he is to be here, or what a wonderful time he's having. A bit desperately, the professor turns to Mumford. "Aren't we fortunate, Mumford, in having *two* famous authors with us?"

"Fame," Ken says. "Let me tell you about fame." Dr. Cheesewitz leans attentively toward him, waiting. "Fame," says Ken solemnly, "is a wart."

"A . . . wart," the professor repeats. He waits, but Ken is inscrutable behind his Plastic Man shades, and no elaboration is forthcoming. "Hmm, yes, a wart. Just so. Ha ha. That's very good. 'Fame is . . . a wart.' Isn't that good,

Mumford? Say there, Mumford, be a good fellow, won't you, and take Mr. Kesey and his friends over to meet our"—he hesitates, as if something in him balks at the encomium—"our guest of honor. Thank you so much, Mumford . . . " Dr. Cheesewitz turns away and drifts off into the crowd, shaking his head distractedly.

Mumford, bowing and scraping like a Chinese headwaiter, leads us toward a little clutch of people gathered in the far corner of the yard, Gordon and I bringing up the rear, Gordon murmuring, "Wait a moment, wait a moment!" all the way. At the fringes of the little assembly, the crowd falls away from Ken as if, bedazzled, they fear they'll be struck blind by so much splendor, and I see that the center of attention is—or was, until Ken got there—one very small, very pale, very unprepossessing Frenchman, bald as your thumb, flanked by two very large, very dark, very imposing Black Panthers, all three decked out in matching Panther leathers and the two big bodyguards in black berets as well, like . . . like an act, see, like Gladys Knight and the Pips, or The Two Hits and a Miss. There's even a backup group behind them, half a dozen more uniformed Panthers, among whom I recognize David Hilliard, and a thin young white woman with rimless glasses, a pinched look about the mouth, and her hair pulled back so severely into a bun that the circulation to her nose is apparently compromised— for its tip is already turning a frosty white. This fetching dose of salts— Madamoiselle Deadbolt, let's call her—is with us today courtesy of a Berkeley cell of feminist Maoists, to translate for Monsieur Genet, who has no English.

The two bodyguards glare balefully at Ken as he approaches, but Genet is goggle-eyed; in France they haven't seen this much finery since the Folies Bergère moved to Vegas. Ignoring the Panthers, Ken plants himself before the diminutive prodigy, grins a big, warm, friendly American grin— complete with a tiny American flag smack in the center of it!—thrusts out his hand, and announces, in the extra-large voice that most of us employ when addressing foreigners, "I'm Kesey!"

Genet manages a wan smile and a limp handshake, but it is plain he has no idea under heaven what a kee-zee is, or why they get themselves up this way.

"And this"—Mumford is doing the honors—"is Dr. McClanahan and, uh . . . "

"Dr. Fraser," I put in, as Gordon reluctantly comes forward. "He's in the Pharmacology Department."

The larger and more menacing of the two bodyguards taps Mumford smartly on the shoulder and commissions him to "run an' git M'shoo Jenay a little glass of that Boojalaize." Mumford doesn't need to be told twice; he excuses himself and scuttles off.

Genet, having shaken hands all around, rocks back on his heels to find Ken still rooted there before him, grinning resolutely. Who is this *grand bouffon*, Genet is surely wondering, and why does he not move along? Ken, meanwhile, is just as surely thinking, Now if I could just take this weird little booger aside and explain to him, straight from the shoulder, famous author to famous author, jailbird to jailbird, baldhead to baldhead, about how the Panther trip is a cop trip, about how they shouldn't try to out-asshole the assholes, about how up in Oregon his brother Chuck's creamery basketball team . . .

So there they stand, Ken with his arms folded over his great paisley chest, Genet fidgeting somewhere beneath him, shuffling his feet, glancing furtively about in search of someone else to shake hands with, rolling his eyes heavenward, only to find a whole paisley skyscape grinning down upon him, hastily lowering his gaze to the ground, where it lights upon—*Zut alors! Quels sabots!*— the twelve-tone hand-painted Day-Glo L.A. sneakers!

"L.A.!" Ken says expansively, still in his heartiest all-foreigners-are-deaf voice. "Los An-je-lus! L.A.!"

"Eh? Los . . . ?" Suddenly Genet brightens. "Los Angeles! Eh? Eh? Los Angeles!" Ken nods, urging him on, whereupon Genet points to his own feet—he wears the cunningest little tan Hush Puppies, brand-spanking-new ones—and squeaks, *"Toe-ron-toe!"*

Unfortunately, we have only just arrived at this breakthrough in international understanding when Mumford returns with a paper cup of wine for Genet, and word that it's discussion-and-castigation time, and that Dr. Cheesewitz proposes we gather in the living room, where we are to hear a prepared statement by Genet and get what's coming to us.

Genet is quickly led away by his handlers, and the rest of the crowd drifts after them. Ken and Gordon go on inside, but I peel off at the front door and veer across the deck for the wine bar and a little last-minute taste of Boojalaize. On the way I meet my friend and cohort Fred Nelson, who is covering the occasion for *The Free You,* of which he is managing editor and guiding genius. Fred is carrying a tape recorder.

"Why don't you encourage Kesey to get into the discussion?" he suggests, with a cagey eye to spicing up his story.

I decline the honor in a hurry, pretty well satisfied that the Panthers wouldn't find the Springfield Creamery basketball team parable all that edifying. But I don't imagine Ken will require much encouragement, if it comes to that.

By the time I've wined myself up and found my way into the house, Dr. Cheesewitz's living room is knee-deep in white liberals sitting on the carpet, with Genet perched in an immense La-Z-Boy in the far corner of the room, imperious as the frog prince on his throne. To either side of him is a couch, upon which is seated a rank of unsmiling Panthers. At Genet's feet hunkers Mlle. Deadbolt, looking snappish, and to his immediate left sits David Hilliard, a large, dark, dour man with a handsome black leather attaché case across his knees. The entertainment is in progress, with a vengeance; young Dr. Chutney, an assistant professor of sociology with an immense Tolstoyan beard, is on his legs before the fireplace, reading aloud from the translation of Genet's prepared malediction. I spot Ken and Gordon standing in a little alcove off the rear of the room and ease myself over to join them.

The statement is a lengthy one, all cant, rant, and invective, undefiled by any taint of grace or wit or sense. We are, Genet is here to tell us, a nation of white racists, wherein the "dominating caste," the police, is in cahoots with the Mafia to distribute drugs to black people, the better to oppress them; we terrorize our intellectuals, as evidenced by the fact that the Harvard of the West has yet to offer Eldridge Cleaver a professorship; we are white slave drivers, colonialists; we are either pawns or perpetrators of the international banking conspiracy; we'd better stop the trial of Bobby Seale, or else; if we don't arm ourselves and take to the streets *tout de suite,* we're in a fair way to get our white academic asses handed to us on a silver salver, come the Revolution.

Throughout Dr. Chutney's spirited rendition of these (and many similar) compliments, their amiable author sits bolt upright, darting quick, avid little glances about the room as though he were hungry and looking for flies. When Dr. Chutney finishes his number and throws the floor open for discussion, Genet is first to speak, his voice shrill, hectoring, and incantatory:

"*Vous intellectuels, vous professeurs, donnez-moi une leçon! Si vous n'êtes pas d'accord avec . . .* "

"You intellectuals, you professors," echoes Mlle. Deadbolt, with equal rancor, "give me a lesson! I begin by accusing the people in this room! Your power isn't great, but it's comfortable power! You are the accomplices of the great American banks and corporations that dominate the world! If you do not agree, correct me *right now*, so I can rectify it!"

("Wait a moment," Gordon murmurs, "wait a moment, wait a moment!" Beside him, Ken stands the way he always stands, stock-still, as intransigently stationary as a statue of himself. Inside his head, the creamery basketball team has already begun to rally.)

"A good professor cannot give a lesson, but can learn a lesson," Dr. Chutney is venturing to observe, reverently but unfathomably, from the abject prostration into which he seems to have collapsed upon the carpet. "So I, for one, am here to get a lesson."

Genet promptly takes up the lash again—"*Faites attention! Vous intellectuels, vous êtes complices de . . .* "—and proceeds to administer Dr. Chutney and his fellows a lesson in humility they will not soon forget.

And for a time, this exchange—vituperative tongue-lashing answered by craven whimper—sets the tone and pattern of the discussion period. The more enthusiastically Genet reviles the assembled champions of democracy, the more meekly they—all right, *we*—receive the indictment; we know we must be guilty, because we *feel* guilty all the time. Even when Genet acknowledges, proudly, that his credentials as a revolutionary derive from his having been sent to prison for theft, it is we who are somehow made to take the blame, as though we were the thieves ourselves. Our scourge, meanwhile, is having the time of his life; the words fly from his mouth like tiny bats, shrill and malevolent. He never knew Americans were so much fun.

But every worm has his turning point, and after Genet and Mlle. Deadbolt have favored us with fifteen or twenty minutes of friendly exhortation, someone—Mumford? Could that be Mumford?—dares to inquire who is financing Dr. Genet's current adventure in international diplomacy. Genet replies, with a Gallic sniff, that his books and plays have brought him "a little fortune," which, he seems to suggest, he has placed entirely at the disposal of Bobby Seale, Ho Chi Minn, and Chairman Mao. *Toutefois*, he goes on, we should not allow ourselves to be sidetracked by such trivial concerns;

we should instead be concentrating on saving the Black Panther Party from the savage clutches of the bloodthirsty American judiciary.

But how *do* you stop a trial? Mumford—hanging in there—wants to know. Why, Dr. Chutney volunteers, you simply put thousands of people in the streets, like at the Moratorium, and you . . . Okay, someone else breaks in, but then what happens when . . . Now, as Mlle. Deadbolt struggles frantically to catch up, little arguments break out like chicken pox in several corners of the room at once: "Well, I don't think that by arming and by violence you can . . . " "This country's going completely Fascist, and . . . " "But they'd get wiped out, if . . . " "Now at the Moratorium, they . . . "

"ORDER!"

The resounding imperative has issued from David Hilliard, who accompanies it by hammering on his attaché case with a fist like a three-pound lump of anthracite. Hilliard's been around these scenes enough to know that intellectuals tend to be more tractable when they can be prevented from squabbling among themselves. And when he wants order, he gets order; the room is suddenly as still as a moment of silent prayer.

"We are not here today," he says at length, in a voice that would freeze vodka, "to waste words tryin' to tell you people what to do, 'cause we know you're not gonna do it." Eldridge, he reminds us, busted his hump running around talking to professors and intellectuals, and what did it get him? He got run out of the country, that's what. Anyhow, it is the judgment of history and the considered opinion of the Black Panther Party that this country ought to take a good bloodbath every so often, whether it needs it or not. Fortunately for those of us here today, there's a nice class struggle coming up any minute now, but we'd better step lively if we want to get into it on the winning side.

"You have to pick up guns," he admonishes this roomful of desperados, most of whom would sooner shoot themselves than point a gun at someone else, "and you have to move against the criminals, against the disturbers of the peace, against the lawbreakers! And *that*"—he deals the attaché case a heavy blow, the first of four—"is your *judges,* your po-lice *officers,* and your other *symbols* of the *state!*"

Well, that does it. "Wait a moment!" Gordon exclaims, out loud this time, and I turn to see Ken step forth from his alcove and, heedless even of besmirching his Day-Glo sneakers with white liberal guilt, intrepidly wade in among the supine pedagogues, saying, "Let me tell you about the Springfield Creamery basketball team . . . "

Vainly, Hilliard tries to cut him off. "I think we should stick to serious . . . "

"Now my brother has a creamery up there in Springfield, and there's a basketball team, and the team is made up of my friends and my brother and people I know well, and . . . "

"Order! Order!" Hilliard beats a furious tattoo on the hapless attaché case. "I think we should stick to . . . "

"So these two spades from up there, these two Negroes up there that I know well, they were . . . "

"Get out of here!" shrieks Hilliard. "We didn't come here to talk crazy, we came here to talk about . . . "

"No, let me go through with it now, let me . . . "

Hilliard is on his feet, shaking the attaché case menacingly at Ken. "We will leave if this man continues to . . . " Beyond Hilliard, Genet's eyes are as big as teacups, rendering him even froggier than before.

"So the referee started calling fouls, and he was calling them heavy on the color—on the black people, right? And so everybody there could see it, they could *see* it! As soon as a foul was called, it was right there where they could . . . "

Pandemonium! If some faculty ghetto anarchist had chucked a bomb through Dr. Cheesewitz's picture window, it could hardly have cleared the room any more efficiently. By the time Ken is ten words into his narrative, everybody in the place is making for the door—first Hilliard, screaming "Let's go! Let's go!" as he storms out; then Genet's two bodyguards, hoisting their small, staring charge between them with such rigor that his little Hush Puppies barely touch the floor; then Mlle. Deadbolt, who glowers at Ken as if she'd like to bite him; then the rest of the Panthers, several of whom angrily declare, in passing, their aversion to all forms and manifestations whatsoever of jiveass red-neck honky intellectual bullshit; and, finally—as the air is rent by the racket of Citroën doors slamming, Citroën engines revving, Citroën tires squealing—come milling masses of bewildered academics all a-twitter, entreating one another to explain what on Earth just happened. Among the last to leave is Ken himself, pursuing his analogy right out the door and into the front yard, trailed by Mumford and a small but rapt band of listeners.

"We blew the whistle on *him,* see, and when the fans got on his case it took his power away. More of his Fascism had showed, see, than he had known was there! And from then on we had the game won, because . . . "

Most of the guests are heading for their cars, but a few little knots of people have gathered here and there on the front walk, Talking It Over, as academics will. Dr. Chutney is still skulking around behind his whiskers, looking unfulfilled, but when he mutters something to the effect that the famous Ken Kesey now stands revealed as a reactionary racist swine, one of his brother savants immediately scoffs, Oh, come off it, Chutney, and that's the last we hear from the Sociology Department.

"So the real power of the movement thing, the civil rights thing, is way up there in the back row. But the Panthers, now, they can't generate that sort of response, that affection that gets the back row to rooting *for* them instead of . . . "

While Ken, by sheer doggedness and main strength, brings the analogy to the ground and finishes it off, Gordon comes over to say that if I can line myself up another ride, he'll drive Ken directly to the airport to catch his plane. Sure, I tell him, Mumford there will run me home.

" . . . And our job," Ken says, wrapping it up, "is to watch the ref and keep him honest. But overthrowing the law, the *idea* of the law in its pure form, that's a mistake. Because without the ref, see, you can't play the game."

"Mr. Kesey," asks Mumford eagerly, "do you think the Panthers really wanted to . . . to have a dialogue with us? Because otherwise, why didn't they stay and talk?"

"I think," says Ken, "that they were looking for a bunch of zombies. And some of us"—he bestows his fabled, flag-bedizened all-American grin on Mumford, a regular Medal of Honor of a grin—"some of us just didn't qualify."

Moments later, Mumford and I stand together on the sidewalk watching Ken and Gordon pull away in Gordon's little yellow VW Beetle, with the smoke already rolling from its windows.

"Wow, Dr. McClanahan," Mumford giggles, as they buzz off into the sunset, "who *was* that masked man?"

"Mumford," I tell him happily, "that was no ordinary man, that was the leader of the Free Ed movement."

THE CONGRESS
OF WONDERS

This way, this way, this way, this way, it's sensational, it's terrific, it's educational, it's scientific! Marvels and monstrosities, freaks of nature and facts of life, miracles of modern medical science, throwbacks to the Dark Ages of his-toh-ree! See the immortal Lord's Prayer engraved by the finest Hebrew scribes of ancient Abyssinia upon the head of a priceless sterling silver pin! See Little Big, the World's Smallest Midget Donkey! See the lovely and talented Bearded Contessa, toast of seven continents! See the Chicken Boy, Miracle Baby of Bunchburg, in the great state of Tenn-oh-see! See it all, my friends, right here at the Burdock County Fair, amaze yourself and amuse yourself at the incredible Congress of Wonders, brought to you at exorbitant expense by yours truly, Professor Philander Cosmo Rexroat, BS, MS, and *Pee*"—Professor Rexroat lowers his megaphone, ceremoniously doffs his pith helmet to the milling midway, mops his damp, florid brow with his shirtsleeve, and covers his thinning silver senatorial locks again—"Aitch Dee, direct from the Instituto del Experimento Scientifico of Nuevo Laredo, Mexico, internationally acclaimed explorer, globe-trotter, author, archaeologist, zoologist, ichthyologist, herpetologist, lepidopterist, philatelist, cosmologist, natural theosophist, minister of the Gospel, and licensed practitioner of colonic irrigation! This way, this way, this way! See the lovely and talented Patagonian Mermaid, whose charms have sent many a dee-lirious seaman to the briny deep! See the Two-Headed Pig, the Hairless Jackanape, the Five-Legged Calf, the Three-Eyed Tasmanian Boa Constrictor, the Fur-Bearing Web-Footed Hornswoggle, see curiosities previously exhibited only before the crowned heads of Europe!"

The professor's spiel rumbles on, an oily fount of hogwash. Professor Rexroat, general all-around Man of Science, Man of Letters, and Man of

God, is withal a smallish gent, and his improbably large, dirgelike baritone, issuing from beneath his Frank Buck pith helmet like the sepulchral croak of a bullfrog under a toadstool, strikes a lugubrious note against the tinkling gaiety of the midway. Yet it casts no pall—for this is 1944, the summer of Normandy, the summer of the taking of Guam and Tinian and Saipan, the very week of the liberation of Paris, and in America we are at last beginning to allow ourselves to hope again, and to celebrate such happiness as the war has left to us. So, even as the bright lights of the midway dispel the gathering dusk and the evening chases the sullen heat of the dog-day afternoon, so too does the spirit of rejoicing dissipate the professor's gloomy monotone.

From the painted canvas backdrop behind him, the misbegotten prodigies whose little idiosyncrasies the professor is heralding gaze down in lurid color, all apparently very much alive and enjoying vigorous health, notwithstanding the unhappy fact that inside the Congress of Wonders tent, the vast majority of its star attractions are basking in glass vessels of formaldehyde. Nor, indeed, does the professor feel it necessary to notify the public that more than a few among his little troupe of pickled artistes owe their interesting anatomies to the resourcefulness of a certain alcoholic taxidermist in Idabelle, Alabama—who fashioned, for instance, both the Chicken Boy and the Patagonian Mermaid in a single afternoon by dismantling a deceased rhesus monkey, a Rhode Island Red rooster, and a large Perdido River mud cat and then reassembling their several parts according to his recollection of some rather unsettling dreams he'd been having lately. ("Yass, Doc Woosley had a way with leftovers," the professor has often remarked to Jojo, his hermaphrodite, of his old drinking buddy. "The, ah, remains of the rooster furnished the two of us an excellent coq au vin that evening, so only the fish head went to waste.") But in his spiel, Professor Rexroat keeps these little particulars close to his gravy-spangled vest and rumbles on.

"See the death-defying Signorina Electra Spumoni, my dear friends, see this lovely and talented little lady, born to the court of the kings and queens of the Holy Roman Empire, see her cruelly strapped into a genuine authentic certified simulated regulation electric chair, an exact similar replica of the infernal engine in which the lowest elements of modern society meet their untimely end, see her receive into her fair, unblemished, highly refined young person *fifty thousand deadly volts* of pure electric power! Enough electricity, friends, to run a trolley car nonstop from New York to Los Angeleeze, in the state of Cal-oh-fornia! And back again!"

. . .

Near the professor's podium, at a wobbly card table parked before the entry-way to the tent, sits a hulking, scowling woman in a long, none-too-clean dressing gown and dusty carpet slippers, smoking furiously, her large head studded like a hand grenade with fierce henna-tinted pin curls. This rara avis is Professor Rexroat's business manager, consort, soul mate, and ingénue, the lovely and talented Signorina Electra Spumoni herself, née Wanda Pearl Ratliff of Ardmore, Oklahoma. On the table before the Signorina are a cash box and a roll of tickets, and directly above her spiky noggin hangs what purports to be her own portrait—a stunning depiction of a bathing beauty wearing a coronet and brandishing, Zeus-like, two fistfuls of lightning bolts, a figure that might have been the result had old Doc Woosley conjoined Betty Grable's gams, Dorothy Lamour's torso, and Shirley Temple's coun-tenance. That the professor will shortly be requiring his clientele to accept this vision as a likeness of the actual Signorina Ratliff in the ample flesh is a testimony to his boundless faith in the credulity of his fellowman.

Almost at Wanda Pearl's shoulder, just outside the rope that separates her table from the midway throngs, stands a boy, a towhead of some twelve or thirteen years, eating a candy apple and gazing raptly up at the masterpiece above him. On the back of his head is perched a white sailor's hat, deeply soiled by much affectionate fondling with grubby fingers.

"Hey, lady," says the boy to the all-too-real Electra at his elbow, never lowering his eyes from the bogus one on the canvas banner, "where's that there 'lectric girl *at*?"

"Inside," says Wanda Pearl, without a flicker of hesitation. "You got a quarter, admiral, you can come in and look at her till yer ship comes in."

"Ain't she pretty, now," he murmurs.

"Pretty as pie," Wanda Pearl assures him. "Girl about your age, too, mm-hmm."

"This way, this way, this way!" drones the professor, deep-mouthed as the grave. "See it all right here at Professor Rexroat's Congress of Wonders! See Joseph/Josephine, the Human Enigma! One half a pu-u-u-ulchritoodinous, vo-o-o-looptuous female in the full bloom of her womanhood, one half a vee-rile male with all his manly faculties intact!" (The extraordinary per-sonage so described is, according to the representation of it on the ban-ner, divided vertically, its right side a mustachioed circus strongman in a leopard-skin undershirt, its left a curvaceous cutie in a tutu.) "The entire

Mystery of Life wrapped up in one lovely and talented young body! So shocking that each and every ticket includes, absolutely free of charge, a one-thousand-dollar life insurance policy! Ladies cordially invited!"

"I haven't got no money," the boy owns ruefully. He looks off into the midway crowd, searching, and adds, "My brother and them's got some, though. They got aplenty."

"Is that him?" Wanda Pearl inquires, peering off in the same direction. "The sailor boy?" The sailor she's got her eye on is across the midway at the baseball pitch, throwing at the flip-overs of Hitler and Tojo and Mussolini. Another young man, in civvies, and two girls stand by, cheering him on. "I tell you what," she proposes. "You get them four to come in here, I'll let you in free. Won't cost you a penny."

The boy is doubtful. "I dunno," he says. "Him and Skinner just took up with them girls a minute ago. They was aiming to take 'em on the Tunnel o' Love, I think. I dunno if they'll . . . "

"Aaaah, sure they will. Tell 'em about the morphadyke. Tell 'em it's a thing they ort to see."

"Well . . . " Then he decides, and suddenly he's off like a shot, already calling, "Hey, Sonny, hey!" A second later Wanda Pearl sees him through the crowd, tugging at the sailor's sleeve and pointing in her direction. Ain't that cute now, she chuckles. She always did have a soft spot for little old boys like that, ever since she was a girl back home in Ardmore.

The professor's pitch is beginning to reel 'em in. Approaching Wanda Pearl's table now is a tall, shambling rube with a look of irremediable puzzle-ment about the eyes. He is accompanied by two women, one work-worn and old-looking, the other—his daughter, to judge by her own long chin and idiot eyes—no more than fourteen or fifteen, both enormously pregnant, the latter doubtless bearing a likely candidate for one of the professor's jugs of formaldehyde. Christ on a crutch, Wanda Pearl reflects, sighing, while the rube digs three quarters from his old leather snap purse. What a world, what a goddamn world. It's more freaks outside the show as inside, nowadays.

The two young men over at the baseball pitch are Gunner's Mate Third Class Wilbur D. "Sonny" Capto, Jr., USN, and his old pal Skinner Worthington, 4-F. Sonny Capto, a perfect picture of a lad, with crinkly, golden curls and eyes as blue as cornflowers and a head as empty as all outdoors, is presently enjoying the sixteenth day of his last twenty-one-day shore leave; some eighteen hours from now, he will board a train in Cincinnati, and four days later—though of course this is a military secret, so Sonny doesn't know it yet—he'll pass beneath the Golden Gate Bridge aboard the MS *Avenger*, a minesweeper bound for the South Pacific. His companion, Skinner Worthington, a gangly youth with an incipient potbelly and a million-dollar heart murmur, can claim no such exciting prospects; tomorrow morning— and every workday morning for the ensuing forty years—he will be at his post in Worthington & Son's Ladies' Footwear Emporium in Needmore, across the street from the Burdock County courthouse.

Sonny and Skinner have been running mates since Burdock County High School, a partnership to which Skinner has traditionally contributed the wheels and finances while Sonny has put up the good looks. Tonight, having already secured them the attentions of a tolerably pretty girl for Sonny and a tolerably homely one for Skinner, their collaboration seems to be functioning about as successfully as it used to. And the girls—a brace of consummately trashy gum-popping blondes named, by odd coincidence, Rosemary and Rosemary—appear ready, willing, and indefatigably able to send Sonny off to war and Skinner back to his daddy's shoe store in a state of blissful enervation. But there's a hitch in this evening's delightful project, in the innocent person of Wado Capo, Sonny's little brother, whom Sonny has brought along over Skinner's grumblings and who is even at this very moment plucking at the sleeve of Sonny's middy blouse, breathlessly imploring him to consider including the Congress of Wonders in the evening's entertainment.

"They got a two-headed pig, and a five-legged calf, and . . . "

"Hot damn, Sunset," Skinner chortles, nudging Sonny with an elbow, "sounds like your old man's farm!" Skinner's own idea of the evening's entertainment, consistent with his standard wooing procedure, is to get one of these Rosemarys into a dark place somewhere and run his hand up her leg and see what happens. He ain't studying no two-headed pig.

" . . . and a chicken boy," Wade goes on, undaunted, "and a three-eyed boar conscriptor, and . . . "

"Is this yore baby bruvver, Sonny?" whoops Big Rosie, a strapping Aphrodite with the voice of a bugling coonhound. "Ain't he a doll!"

"Lookit his li'l sailor cap!" shrieks the dumpy Little Rosie, with less volume but equal stridor. "He is such a doll!"

"Kid thinks I hung the moon," Sonny modestly confides, tossing a baseball from hand to hand. "He hasn't hardly took off that swabbie hat since I give it to him. Have you now, shipmate?"

Wade ignores them all as best he can and presses on. "And they got the Lord's Prayer on a pinhead, and a . . . a marthadyke, and . . . "

"Nah," Sonny is declining, "see, shipmate, me and Skin, we . . . "

"Hold it, kiddo," Skinner breaks in. "They got a morphadyke, you say?" Wade has hooked himself a live one.

"Oooo, icksy!" the two Rosemarys scream, as in a single voice. "A old morphadyke! Let's go see it, you all!"

"It's a thing you *ort* to see!" Wade urges, remembering the ticket lady's exhortation. "And they got one of these fish-girls that don't wear no clothes on her . . . "—he gulps, and blushes as red as his candy apple, and lowers his voice almost to a whisper, but he gets it said—"on her . . . boozems, and . . . "

Amid peals of girlish laughter, Skinner turns to Sonny and says, with a wink and a smirk, "Whaddya say, Cap'n Capto? I reckon we could take these gals to see the morphadyke, don't you?"

Sonny grins his accord, takes off his swabbie hat and claps it, starched and bleached white as a new tooth, atop Big Rosemary's towering, mustard-colored upsweep. Then he wheels and lets fly with the baseball, and pops old Tojo right between the eyes, flipping him over to show his naked, bristly yellow hiney. The attendant hands Sonny a pea-green monkey on a stick, which Sonny straightway passes on to the clangorously ecstatic Big Rosie. If she hadn't been there, it would've been Wade's monkey, sure. From beneath his own soiled cap, Wade glares at Big Rosemary as though he can't believe they're in the same navy.

"See it all, see it here, see it now!" they hear the professor calling from across the midway. "See it all at the amazing Congress of Wonders! It's scientific, it's sensational, it's . . . "

"C'mon, shipmates," Sonny says, throwing an arm around Big Rosemary's shoulders. "Anchors aweigh. Let's go reconnoiter that there morphadyke."

"See the amazing Bodiless Head! A human head actually *severed from its body,* yet kept alive by the very latest scientific methods! Nothing like it in captivity! It talks, it sings, it eats, it drinks, it laughs, it cries like a lit-tle ba-a-a-by! The Bodiless Head sees all, knows all, tells all—and it never, never lies! See it right here at the incredible Congress of Wonders! See Little Big, the World's Smallest . . . "

As soon as Wanda Pearl has admitted Skinner—who, as usual, is funding the entire expedition—and his party to the tent, she jams a fresh butt in the corner of her mouth, fires it up, slaps her cash box shut, and rises from her table, wreathed in smoke. "Can it, Phil," she calls to the professor. "We've done got ten or twelve inside. Let's do a show."

"Right-o, pet," Professor Rexroat says obediently, breaking off in mid-spiel. "Any, ah, philanthropists among them, do you think?"

"Nah. That funny-lookin' duck with the sailor might be good for a few bucks. The rest is deadheads."

"Right-o," he says again. Wanda Pearl generally assumes, with his blessing, rather broad managerial responsibilities in Professor Rexroat's enterprises. Nonetheless, as he steps down from his podium, the professor adds, with a certain firmness in his tone belying the apology, "Ah, beg pardon, my lamb, but the fetch-it will be along shortly, and you know tonight is Friday, and on Friday nights after the show Jojo and I always enjoy a little taste of . . . "

"Oh, yeah," Wanda Pearl sighs, resigned. "And every other damn night of the week besides. Y'know, Rexroat"—she opens the cash box and extends it to him—"if you don't make that morpho cut down on the 'shine and eat a little bite now and then, it ain't going to last you. It's as yeller as a Chinaman."

"Now, now," he purrs, helping himself to several bills (and an extra quarter for the fetch-it), "you know Jojo has her own little habits, lambie, even as you and I."

(Long ago and somewhat arbitrarily, Professor Rexroat had assigned his current Joseph/Josephine—latest in a long line of Jojos—the female gender, perhaps largely because, his old palship with Doc Woosley notwithstanding, he generally prefers the company of ladies. Wanda Pearl, however, noting the tiny, childlike, but undebatably male anatomical features among the peculiar assortment of charms the hermaphrodite exhibits at every show, is not quite prepared to certify Jojo as a member in good standing of the fair sex; she favors the nondenominational pronoun.)

"Well," she persists, "it's pretty near your whole show, the poor thing—it's your bearded lady and your talking head and your fortune-teller and your half-and-half—it's the only real square-up act you got, and you don't pay it nothing, hardly, and you make it sleep with the donkey, and . . . "

"Business, pet, strictly a business arrangement. And Jojo's needs are really very small, you know. She dines, I believe, quite satisfactorily on the midway."

"Yeah, outta the trash cans, poor little possum. Phil Rexroat, you ort to have your . . . "

But the professor has enjoyed a sufficiency of this examination of his business practices; he is already at the entryway to the tent. "Show time, dearest," he says, stepping inside. "You run along back to the trailer now, and slip into your little costume. You needn't worry your pretty little head about these trifles." He draws the curtain across the opening and is gone.

"You ort to have your butt kicked," Wanda Pearl admonishes the curtain, "is what you ort to have." Then she flings her cigarette to the ground, tucks the cash box under her burly arm, and lumbers off around the corner of the tent, muttering vehemently under her breath.

"Call that thing a meermaid?" Skinner Worthington snorts disdainfully. "I seen bigger tits on a sowbug. That damn kid . . . "

Skinner is peering into the murky urine-yellow depths of Miss Patagonia's formaldehyde beauty bath, in which Doc Woosley's shriveled dreamgirl floats serenely beneath her tiny horsehair wig. Sonny Capto is at Skinner's side; Wade is over at the far side of the tent, waiting in line to look through a microscope at the Lord's Prayer on a Pinhead, and the two Rosemarys are admiring, with many a shrill "Oooo, icksy," the ineffable allurements of the Chicken Boy.

"Yeah, she ain't sunk no ships lately, has she?" acknowledges the gunner's mate third class, scrutinizing the Patagonian Mermaid with an old salt's coolly appraising eye. "But hey, Skin, don't blame the kid. He was just goin' according to the picture outside. She looked fine, setting there on that rock. Maybe they had to shrink her to get her in the bottle."

But Skinner's one-track mind has already moved on to the next stop down the line. "Listen, Cap'n," he wheedles behind his hand, "howzabout we shake the kid and take these hides to the parkin' lot?"

"Aw, I don't know, Skin, beings as it's my last night and all, and I been promising Daddy all week long I'd . . . "

"Hey, c'mon! I got a pack of cundrums and a half-pint of sloe gin in the glove compartment—man, we'll tall-dog 'em, we'll thrill 'em and drill 'em! Here"—he fishes a small roll of bills from his pocket and peels off two singles—"slip him a couple of bucks for the rides, and tell him to catch a lift home with Burdette there. He'll be fine." Burdette Pence, the long-chinned fornicator with the vacant look who entered the tent earlier, is the hired hand on the farm next door to Wilbur Capto's. "Let's stay till the morpha-dyke comes on, though," Skinner adds, as Sonny, no slave to constancy, tucks the bills into his pocket. "I heard some of them at the poolroom say they seen one screw itself, one time. Them babes see a thing like that, they'll be all *over* us!"

Wade Capto, just stepping up to the Lord's Prayer on a Pinhead microscope, can't hear a word his brother and Skinner are saying, but he has caught them glancing at him out of the corners of their eyes, and as soon as he sees the two dollars disappear into Sonny's pocket, he understands perfectly the drift of their deliberations. ("The Lord give my good looks to Junior," runs Wilbur Capto's favorite family joke, "but he saved his mama's brains for Wade.") *They're gonna pay me out,* Wade tells himself bitterly, *they're gonna pay me out and slip off with them two hoors.* He wishes now that he hadn't seen the money change hands; then at least he could've pretended to himself that it was a real present—and from Sonny, not from Skinner Worthington. It'd suit Wade just fine if Skinner Worthington caught a social disease this very night, preferably a fatal one.

Not Sonny, though, please not Sonny. Every day Wade prays to God that Sonny won't catch a social disease, and that he won't get killed in a car wreck, and that he will come home from the war OK. There is much, very much, that Sonny Capto doesn't know and never will, but one thing he's got right as rain: His little brother thinks he hung the moon. Wade and Sonny's mama—"the brainy one of all them Hurtle girls," everybody says—died of the childbed fever when Wade was born, and ever since Wade can remember, it seems as though he's had this worry in him, like an heirloom she'd entrusted to him, this little lump of fear that something bad would happen to Sonny, that Sonny's beauty wouldn't see him through. Wade loves his brother with a mother's love—and he fears for him as a mother fears.

The Lord's Prayer on a Pinhead turns out to be a gyp; you can tell right away that the words are printed inside the microscope somehow, and not on the pin at all. He won't count on the electric girl either, Wade resolves; if they'd mess with the Lord's Prayer, they'll mess with anything.

Behind the tent, in the half-light from the midway, Wanda Pearl stumbles over the stake to which, during the off-hours when a show is not in progress, the professor tethers Little Big, the midget donkey who is in fact the only living nonhuman member of his menagerie. Cursing and grumbling, she moves on through the darkness toward the trailer until she comes upon what appears, in the shadowy lee of the back wall of the tent, to be a shapeless heap of rags among the trampled weeds. Wanda Pearl pauses and nudges it gently with her foot.

"Wake up, Jojo," she says. "Wake up, now. It's show time, hon; he'll be wanting you inside."

The heap stirs itself, whimpers, struggles to rise, an orderless form, vaguely human, draped head to foot in a chaos of greasy rags, the lower part of its face heavily veiled, its eyes as red-rimmed and bloodshot as open sores. As it rises, it is preceded by a powerful stench.

"Phew!" Wanda Pearl whistles softly. "Christ on a crutch, hon, you gotta quit sleepin' with that damn donkey!"

Even at its full height, Wanda Pearl towers over this malodorous apparition, and she can feel those upturned mendicant eyes upon her face, beseeching her for what she cannot bring herself to give it, the merest touch of a human hand. Instead she says, "You scoot now, and check your talking head setup. After the show, maybe I'll fix you something good to eat."

"Hokay," it answers, in a cracked, androgynous little whisper. "Hokay, missus." And it scuttles off into the shadows.

My sweet Jesus Christ on a crutch, Wanda Pearl says to herself as she mounts the steps to the trailer. *If I had some ham, I'd fix it ham and eggs, if I had any eggs.*

". . . And now, my friends, allow me to direct your very kind attention to one of the most remarkable creatures that ever slithered out of the mudflats of the mighty Amazon onto the sunbaked sands of the Sudan, the Mammoth Three-Eyed Tasmanian Boa Constrictor"—the bottled and marinated reptile the professor indicates *is* a large one, and it does have three indisputably genuine eyes, all in a row and all its own; but it is rather less a Tasmanian boa from the mudflats of the Amazon than it is a cowsucker from a West Virginia corncrib—"captured on my last safari into the jungles of Borneo in the heart of darkest Madagasca-a-a-ar . . . "

Professor Rexroat moves among his trophies and treasures, enlarging upon their histories and personal anomalies, his audience trailing raggedly in his wake. And when, at the glass redoubt of the Argus-eyed cowsucker, he pauses to describe how he and Momo, his trusty and devoted native bearer, bagged the monster just as it was preparing to sink its venomous sandwich-clamps into a particularly tasty portion of the beauteous number-one wife of a great Ethiopian Pygmy chieftain—thereby earning the professor the eternal gratitude and protection of all Ethiopian Pygmies everywhere—Skinner Worthington perceives a golden opportunity to advance the cause of romance, and seizes the moment.

Taking the two girls by the elbow and motioning to Sonny with a jerk of his head to come along, he steers them across the tent to the corner where Little Big, the World's Smallest Midget Donkey, is on display. Wade, noting the maneuver and suspecting at first that Skinner and Sonny are trying to sneak off without even paying him his two dollars, follows at a discreet distance.

The diminutive Little Big, a sleepy-eyed beast about the size of an Aire-dale, stands in his corner reflectively chewing his quid—dreaming, perhaps, of some colossal and gorgeous Shetland filly, for he sports an immense erection, gun-metal gray and dangling almost in the sawdust at his tiny hooves. Skinner, determinedly belaboring the obvious, urges the two nattering, tittering femmes fatales closer for a better look.

"Wouldja glim the boner on that little bastard!" he exclaims to Sonny out of the side of his mouth. "Them babes get a load of that, they'll . . . "

Disgusted, Wade tosses the remains of his candy apple to a grateful Little Big and turns away, and as he does he notices some small movement behind the old pink chenille bedspread that curtains off the opposite corner of the tent. Professor Rexroat, meanwhile, has moved on from the Three-Eyed Boa Constrictor to the Hairless Jackanape—in fact a stuffed armadillo with "Souvenir of El Paso, Texas" emblazoned on its underbelly—which, he sol-emnly avers, he and Momo subdued after a monumental struggle wherein the valiant Momo shed the last drop of his life's blood upon the jungle floor in the noble cause of the international advancement of science and human knowledge. Wade, hoping to catch an unauthorized glimpse of some rather less insensate Congress of Wonders phenomenon—even of Signorina Electra Spumoni herself, that fabled beauty!—eases around in back of the spellbound audience and lifts the curtain for a furtive peek.

Behind the bedspread, against the back wall of the tent, stands a low wooden shelf or table, which is bathed in wan, faintly viridescent light and seems somehow to float, legless, above the grassy floor. The table is laid with a scarlet sateen cloth with a gold fringe, and a large, silver-plated meat platter. And on the platter, all hairy and hideous in a pool of blood, is a human head, looking back at Wade with terrible, red-rimmed, all-seeing eyes. Their eyebeams meet, the head utters a tiny squeak of terror or surprise, Wade starts, drops the curtain, and as it falls he sees the head, as though it has opened its own throat and swallowed itself, disappear into a bottomless hole in the middle of the platter.

In the trailer, Wanda Pearl sits before her mirror, putting on her Signorina Spumoni face. Through the open window behind her, she hears the hubbub of the midway, the distant piping of the carousel, the agonized greaseless creak of the Ferris wheel, and faintly, from within the tent, the professor's eulogy of his late associate Momo.

That old rip, Wanda Pearl muses fondly; he'll get more use out of a make-believe slave than most people would out of a real one.

She applies a final touch of crimson to her Kewpie-doll lips, smacks them noisily for the mirror, takes up her eyebrow pencil and haphazardly describes a pair of lopsided arches on her lowering brow. That the two new eyebrows look as if they belong on two different foreheads doesn't bother Wanda Pearl in the slightest, any more than it bothers her to go around on the street, sometimes, wearing one black shoe and one white shoe. If she was all that hipped on having things just so, she never would've hooked up with a pickled-punk show in the first place.

Poor little Jojo. The professor is always claiming there's no need to feel sorry for freaks—"Because," according to him, "the worst has already happened to them, you see. And so they need not fear the Unknown, as other mortals must." Which you can't depend on nothing Rexroat says, Wanda Pearl reflects, dabbing rouge on a corduroy cheek; he's got the Gift of Gab and can't help it. But they've had half a dozen different Jojos down through the years—they billed them all as Joseph/Josephine, so they wouldn't have to repaint the banner—and some of them was real morphos and some was gaffs, and as far as Wanda Pearl is concerned they was all real pathetic. They just didn't know what they was, poor things.

Wanda Pearl halfway wishes she hadn't seen that sailor boy out there;

he reminds her too much of Rodney, the boy she ran off from Oklahoma with, that got killed working on this very Ferris wheel ever so many long years ago. Rodney was the pretty-boy type himself, just like the sailor. He'd had a mean streak a yard across, the little sneak, but she had loved him anyhow, loved him and loved him. If that Ferris wheel hadn't broke down, and Rodney had lived, and her and him had stayed together till she'd had to kill him herself, the sneak, and if they'd've had a little baby and it had been a boy, it would be a whole lot like that other kid by now, the sailor's little brother. Rodney Junior, she would've called it, and it would be the sweetest thing that ever drawed a breath.

The thought of Rodney Junior brings two fat tears to her eyes. As they course down her cheeks, tracing twin rivulets like snail tracks in the rouge and powder, she comforts herself with the certain knowledge that at least there ain't any little Rexroat Juniors running around loose, telling lies and keeping people all mixed up.

According to Professor Rexroat's reliably exhaustive introductory remarks, when Signorina Electra Spumoni's sainted mother, great with child, was struck down by a bolt of lightning at the midwife's very door, the central nervous system of the infant daughter pulled from the late mother's womb was discovered to have undergone a major rearrangement, leaving the child with AC red corpuscles and DC white corpuscles, thereby rendering her forever immune to the deleterious effects of electrical power. ("For God tempers the wind to the shorn lamb," the professor reminds his little flock, perhaps harking back to some long-forgotten sermon delivered in this same tent when he was in a different line of work.) And so the Signorina, having fled the old country before the jackboots of the tyrant Mussolini, has condescended to exhibit her remarkable capacities to the American public, strictly in the interest of the international advancement of science and human knowledge, with the clear understanding that all proceeds from these demonstrations be set aside for the establishment, back in her beloved homeland after the war, of a place of refuge for children orphaned by the conflict, with whom, naturally, she feels a special kinship.

Having said that much (and a good deal more), the professor stands aside and presents to his patrons' view, all the while reminding them that it is absolutely the Genuine Authentic Certified Simulated Regulation article, a large, bulky object shrouded beneath a profoundly soiled bed sheet. With a flourish, he whips aside the sheet to display a rough wooden armchair affixed with various straps, clamps, and metal plates—an exact working replica, he solemnly attests, of the principal article of furniture in the death house at Sing Sing. He then commends to their attention, mounted on a panel behind the chair, an elaborate electrical apparatus with an oversized, ominous-looking switch. This device, the professor avouches, will deliver "one *hun-dred* thousand deadly volts" of electric power into the mortal person of the chair's occupant—in this instance, happily, "the only living human being ever to survive an electrical charge of this stupendous magnitude, the scientific wonder of this and every other age, the very, very lovely and talented Signorina Electra Spumoni!"

All these compliments notwithstanding, however, the phenomenon so described is still—as the vigilant Skinner Worthington is quick to observe, indignantly—"that big bucket-headed old bag we seen outside!" This despite the fact that she has somehow insinuated herself into a strapless, liver-colored sarong with a sequin-spangled lightning bolt spanning her bosom (and a pack of Raleighs peeking from her cleavage), her hams bound in torn black net stockings, her big number nines jammed into tiny white down-at-the-heels majorette boots with ratty gold tassels, and enough paint on her face to lay down a primer coat on a two-car garage, the whole ensemble topped off with a mangy oakum wig, like the pelt of one of Doc Woosley's famous leftovers, cocked pugnaciously on her beetled brow.

"Watch that mouth, rube," Signorina Ratliff snarls, glowering inhospitably at Skinner as she settles herself in the electric throne. "I'll smack the pee-waddin' outta you!"

"Kindly refrain," Professor Rexroat puts in hurriedly, "during this highly experimental procedure, from all remarks which might upset the delicate balance of the Signorina's central nervous system . . . " As he delivers the admonition, the Man of Science is energetically lashing and clamping his subject into the hot seat—to restrain her, he hints, from rocketing through the roof of the tent when he lights her up.

"She ain't no damn Senior Rita!" Skinner protests. "She's just that big—"

"Better stow it, mate," Sonny cautions. "We wanna see the secret act of pokeration, don't we?"

"I'll pokerate *him,*" Wanda Pearl vows, "the little—" But her malediction is cut short when the professor, cognizant of the tradition that holds that the show must go on and anxious, accordingly, to keep it proceeding apace, stops her mouth by inserting into that capacious orifice the business end of "a Common Ordinary Everyday Basic Conventional Household Light Bulb," and turning on the juice.

Now Wanda Pearl, at this moment, is seriously out of sorts. She's sick and goddamn tired of turning herself into a goddamn floor lamp four or five times a night for a bunch of goddamn hayseeds that wouldn't know good entertainment from a poke in the eye with a sharp stick. Also, these little pointy-toed boots is killing her corns, and she's sure her wig has got cooties in it, the way it's itching her old head, and Rexroat has pulled the straps on the chair too tight again and pinched her arms black and blue. Plus, what with thinking about Rodney and little Rodney Junior that never was and then that smart-aleck snot calling her an old bag, her nerves is giving her fits. Sorry as she feels, sometimes, for the poor little Jojo, she's fed right up to here with freaks and geeks and rubes and carnies, and sincerely wishes she had went into some other line of work, where she could've dealt with a better class of people.

"... One *hun-dred* thousand deadly volts, my friends! Enough to light up the entire midway of the World's Fair in Chicawga, in the great state of Ill-oh-noise!"

The electricity—which is the static kind and don't hurt a bit—would make Wanda Pearl's hair stand on end except that, under the wig, her hair's still put up in pin curls; as it is, it feels as if the pin curls are about to come ripping up through the wig like innersprings in an old horsehair sofa. And when she touches the tip of her tongue to the butt end of the light bulb, it tingles like a memory, and the bulb glows as softly as a maiden's blush, as though she were having a romantic thought.

By the time Professor Rexroat accomplishes the illumination of Signorina Electra, Wade is barely watching. He's tuned in to Skinner Worthington, who in turn is talking in a low voice to Burdette Pence. As before, Wade can't hear what Skinner's saying, but as soon as he sees Burdette look over at him and grin his big slack-jawed, half-wit grin, he knows what's going on, all right: instead of riding home in style in the rumble seat of Skinner's roadster, with the moon flying high and the night air cool on his face and maybe even a sip or two of Skinner's sloe gin, just for practice, and Sonny right there in the front seat where Wade can keep an eye on him, Wade will be going home tonight in the back of Burdette's pickup truck, which he saw Burdette hauling hogs in this very morning. While the professor is freeing the Signorina from the chair's comfortless embrace, he decrees a standing offer of a one-hundred-dollar U.S. War Bond to the estate of anyone willing to duplicate her ordeal. Skinner Worthington instantly receives a small chorus of nominations from the floor and again declines the honor, emphatically if not very graciously. Wade seriously considers volunteering, figuring he could will his war bond to Sonny to help him get his start in life after the war. But Sonny would just cash it in and spend it on some old hoor, Wade reminds himself gloomily, and probably catch a social disease in the bargain.

Professor Rexroat, having reassembled the audience before the chenille bedspread, is delivering himself of a few brief remarks by way of introducing the next act, the lovely and talented Bodiless Head—which, behind the curtain, is once again resting on the silver platter, with the remainder of its remarkable person crouching beneath the table, hidden by an artfully positioned mirror. Wade, having caught this act before, hangs back to have a reproachful word with Signorina Ratliff-Spumoni, who is standing now, rubbing her wrists to get the circulation going.

"I thought you said they was a girl."

"She couldn't make it," says Wanda Pearl, with a shrug. "I had to set in for her." He's Rodney Junior made over, she thinks—look at them eyes. She has half forgotten, for the moment, that Rodney Junior . . . never was.

"Yes," the boy presses her, "but you said—"

"Listen, bucko, y' got in free, didn't ya?" Suddenly and inexplicably, she is almost angry at him, at his innocence, his goddamn country dumbness. "Never mind what I said! It didn't cost you one damn penny, did it? So why don't you wise the hell up, fer crissakes!"

Even as the kid dejectedly slouches off to rejoin the others, Wanda Pearl is already wishing she hadn't blistered him that way. But my sweet Jesus P. Christ on a crutch (she marvels as she slips behind the curtain to help the Head get ready for its act), if he was looking for somebody to tell him the goddamn truth about things, why the hell would he come to a goddamn pickled-punk show?

.   .   .

"Pew! Gag!" squeals Little Rosemary when the professor draws aside the curtain. "Gag a *maggot!*" Big Rosemary echoes, leaning over the rope to poke her monkey-on-a-stick perilously close to the baleful, baneful eyes of the Bodiless Head. "It's that old morphadyke agin!"

The Head, yellow as a boiled cabbage, resplendent now in a turban fashioned of a dirty dish towel with a ruby-red bicycle reflector affixed to it like a third eye, regards its admirers with a stare of abject, defenseless horror. If it had hands, it would hide its face in them.

"The Bodiless Head! A living miracle of modern medical science and good old Yankee know-how! Tell these fine folks, O Head, is it true that you can see into the future?"

"My . . . dee-vine . . . sign," rasps the Head, "eendo-cate . . . de few-tchoor . . . to me." Its speech is halting, mechanical, almost without inflection, as though it hasn't the foggiest notion what it is saying.

The professor turns to Skinner and the business at hand. "So how about it, my friend? Two bits, a measly twenty-five centavos, the first dime of which goes in toto to the Gold Star Mothers' Relief Fund, and this lovely and no doubt talented little lady here"—Little Rosie, hanging like a sash weight to Skinner's arm, encourages the extravagance with a walleyed gaze of deathless adoration—"this little lady here can ask the Head any question she desires! The innermost secrets of the human heart! Five trifling little nickels! Thank you, my friend"—Skinner is grumpy, but he coughs up the quarter—"the bereaved mothers of our fighting men will remember you in their prayers tonight!" Professor Rexroat approaches the Head, bows deeply, and describes a sweeping arc of obeisance with his pith helmet. "Speak to us, O Head!" he implores. "Reveal to us the ancient wisdom of the spirit world! We beseech you!"

"I know . . . naw-theeng," the Head confesses miserably, in a voice like a clock running down, "egg-zept . . . de fact of . . . my igg-no-rantz-z-z."

"The Head knows all!" the professor promptly contradicts his oracle. "Ask it what you will, little lady."

Skinner, in the interest of getting his quarter's worth one way or another, propels Little Rosemary forward with a shove and an affectionate pat on her low-slung rump. "*Quit,* stoopit!" Little Rosie snaps. Then she leans over the rope till she is almost nose-to-nose with the Head and, as if she supposes its misfortunes have rendered it hard of hearing, shrieks full into its face, "AM! I! GONNA! GIT! RICH!?!"

For a moment the Head appears to ponder the matter, chewing its answer. "Haf-fing de . . . fewest wants-s-s," it declares at last, "I am . . . near-est . . . to de gods."

"What the hell does *that* mean?" demands Skinner, still mindful of the quarter this intelligence has cost him.

"Why, who has the fewest wants, my boy? The rich man, that's who! This little lady is going to be . . . rich! Fabulously wealthy! Rich as Croesus!"

"Oh, poot," scoffs Big Rosie. "She ain't got a winder to throw it out of."

"My . . . dee-vine . . . sign . . . " the Head begins again, as Professor Rexroat closes the curtain on its act, "eendocate . . . de few-tchoor . . . "

Professor Rexroat stands before the curtain extolling the divers charms and virtues of the Congress of Wonders' final presentation of the evening's entertainment, the international star of stage, screen, and radio, the lovely, talented, and delightfully versatile Joseph/Josephine, the Human Enigma. Wanda Pearl has put on her tattletale-gray dressing gown over her costume and returned to the electric chair, where she is resting her dogs and having a smoke. Wade Capto, meanwhile, has worked his way to the front of the crowd and is attending, rather skeptically at this point, to the professor's account of how Joseph was once employed by day as a palace guard in the court of the czar, while Josephine served as the Crown Prince Rasputin's favorite concubine at night.

"Is it gonna pokerate itself?" Skinner Worthington calls out, with a cackle.

"I'll pokerate *you*," Wanda Pearl promises again, half rising from her chair.

But the professor hastily assures Skinner that the Human Enigma is "fully capable of *all* the bodily functions," indeed that it positively *specializes* in the sacred act of self-pokeration—and that, in consideration of the enormous expense of maintaining this magnificent national treasure in the style to which it inevitably became accustomed during its years with the czar, the management has deemed it necessary to require the insignificant sum of fifty cents, additional, per patron of the arts, Hollywood talent scouts of course excepted, for each and every exhibition of the enigma's remarkable gifts.

Wanda Pearl moves into the crowd—or what's left of it, after several impecunious types have departed, grumbling—to collect this final tribute to Professor Rexroat's powers of persuasion. A couple of elderly pension-ers elect to stay ("I've lived in Burdock County eighty-two years," one of them quakes, "and I'll pay fifty cents to see any dern thing that don't come from around here"), and there's also a half-drunk plumber named Pipes Marquardt, who claims to be sticking around out of professional curiosity. Burdette Pence has sent his wife and daughter out, on the grounds that "hit might mark them babies," but he manages to locate fifty cents in the bottom of his snap purse to finance his own education.

"This goes to the Home for Old Morphadykes, I reckon," Skinner gripes, handing over two more dollars to Wanda Pearl. "I don't have to pay for this here shit-heel, too, do I?" He means Wade, who turns and glares at Skinner as if he'd like to kick him in the shins.

"Nope," says Wanda Pearl resolutely, with the professor, himself for once incredulous, looking on over her shoulder. "This boy don't need a ticket. He's too little, and he ain't a-watching it."

Outside, Wanda Pearl resumes her seat at the card table, while Wade stands nearby, staring moodily at the happy throngs of revelers streaming past him. Wade's posture is mopish and sullen; he is still brooding over the insult he has suffered. Far off in the night sky, lightning flickers fitfully, like a bom-bardment in a distant war. Despite the warmth of the evening, Wanda Pearl shivers and draws her duster more closely about her.

"It's fixing to rain dishrags around here after while," she remarks, eyeing the sky warily. Signorina Electra's unique history notwithstanding, Wanda Pearl never did like lightning.

Great, Wade is thinking; *rain would sure slow down the action in that rumble seat.* Aloud, he says, in tones of deep aggrievement, "I don't see why you couldn't've let me stay and watch it. After I had brung in all those customers, I don't see—"

"Let that learn you a lesson, then," Wanda Pearl breaks in. "A shill is just the bait on somebody else's line. Ain't nothing lower than a goddam shill." She still sounds a little rougher than she means to—but she would've said the exact same thing to Rodney Junior, if he'd been there.

"It ain't even a real morphadyke anyhow, I bet," Wade sulks, consoling himself with a few sour grapes.

"Behold, the Human Enigma!" That's the professor, from the far side of the canvas wall just behind them. "Moments to witness, a lifetime to forget! Examine closely the—" Here the stentorian voice is drowned out by the screams and screeches of the two Rosies, carrying on as if their delicate sensibilities were being assaulted horribly.

"It's real enough, poor little booger," says Wanda Pearl, with a sigh.

"Well, it's a sorry-looking thing." That sounds ungenerous even to Wade, and right away he wishes he hadn't said it.

"Don't you be throwing off on that morphadyke," Wanda Pearl rebukes him, stomping out one Raleigh while fishing in her bodice for another. "It ain't had our advantages."

The Human Enigma has taken its final bow. Pipes Marquardt is first out of the tent, listing slightly and looking a little green around the gills. Then the two ancients totter into view, shaking their hoary heads in wonderment or dismay. "I went plumb to Orlando, Florida, and back in 1926," says the better-traveled of the pair, "but I never seen the beat of that." Next out is Burdette Pence, grinning hugely. As he passes Wade, he motions in the direction of the parking lot and says, "Air m'sheen's over h'yanner," which Wade, after a moment's consideration, understands to mean that the Pences' truck is over yonder.

Now Skinner and Sonny and the girls emerge, blinking in the sudden glare of the midway. Sonny's summer whites, as he approaches Wade, are dazzling, but his hat still graces the prow of the SS *Big Rosemary*. "Listen, shipmate," he says, looking Wade not quite squarely in the eye, "me and Skin, we—"

"You all go on," Wade interrupts. "I'm ridin' home with Burdette." On Sonny's sleeve, just at the level of Wade's eyes, is his gunner's mate third class patch—two tiny silver cannons, crossed, on a field of white, with a single stripe below. Wade studies it intently; the cannons swim in and out of focus like two little minnows in a jar.

"Well, here"—Sonny glances back to make sure Skinner isn't watching—"here's you something for the Tilt-A-Whirl and all." He fumbles with two fingers in the pocket of his blouse and extracts a dollar bill. Wade can see the outline of Skinner's other dollar—Sonny's now—still folded up in Sonny's pocket. Sonny holds the first bill out to him, but Wade doesn't reach for it.

"C'mon, Cap'n Capto!" Skinner calls. "These gals is ready for Freddy!"

Sonny stuffs the dollar into Wade's shirt pocket. "Wake me up early in the morning, shipmate, and we'll shoot us a few buckets before train time." Wade nods mutely, biting his lip. Sonny reaches out and squares the swabbie hat on Wade's brow, then steps back, snaps to attention, and throws him a stylish salute. "OK, sailor!" he barks. "Show us some *navy!*" Wade manages a listless salute in return and a mumbled "Aye, aye, sir." Sonny grins, dismisses him with an "At ease, shipmate!" and turns away.

"Let's *go,* you all!" Big Rosie pleads, grabbing Sonny's arm. "I hafta take a whiz!" Little Rosie pauses at the midway's edge to wipe her shoe in the grass. "Oh, shit," she laments, "I stepped in some doggy-do!" Skinner promises her a brand-new pair of saddles—wholesale price and no rationing stamps— and drags her off down the midway after the others.

"Them two young ladies," Wanda Pearl observes when they are gone, "is as common as pig tracks."

"Listen, ma'am," says Wade, with sudden urgency, "can I go back in and ast that Head thing a question?" He shows her Skinner's dollar. "I can pay, see? Just one question."

Wanda Pearl is touched; nobody's called her ma'am in the longest time. "Hon, that poor thing don't know nothing worth paying for," she tries to tell him. "Phil learnt it that stuff hisself, out of a book. Them sayings is by Socraits somebody, I don't know his last name."

"Well," the boy says stubbornly, "I gotta ast it something. It don't have to get back in its hole or nothing. I just . . . I just need to ast it something."

The little old rube's fixing to bubble up and cry, Wanda Pearl sees; his brother and that other squirt ort to have their butts kicked. "Well, hell," she says, "all right then, come on." At the entrance to the tent, she stops to say, a little less gruffly, "Put your money away, it might draw flies."

The fetch-it has come and gone; Wade and Wanda Pearl find the professor standing before the closed chenille curtain, refreshing himself with a long pull at a pint bottle containing an elixir the approximate color of the Patagonian Mermaid's formaldehyde. The Human Enigma seems to have repaired backstage, perhaps to set to rights whatever state of deshabille has resulted from its recent exertions.

"M'dear?" says Professor Rexroat, plugging his pint with a stub of corncob. "To what do I owe—?"

Wanda Pearl brushes past him, saying, "You better lay offa that jake-leg,

Rexroat. Hard telling what all's in it. You stay here," she orders Wade, and she disappears behind the curtain.

"She's gonna let me ast that Head a question," Wade explains to the professor. "It's on something I need to find out about."

"Of course, certainly, by all means. But as you will perhaps recall, there is a small, ah, gratuity connected with the Head's, ah, oracular services, and—"

"Can that, Phil," Wanda Pearl instructs from out of sight. "This one's on the house. You can open the curtain now."

The professor raises his eyebrows, pockets his pint, and does as he is told. The curtain drawn aside, the Bodiless Head is as before, a ghastly, turbaned cabbage on a bloody platter. Wanda Pearl stands off to one side, hands on her hips, waiting.

"Speak to us, O Head!" the professor importunes, with a perfunctory tip of his pith helmet and a considerably foreshortened rendition of his traditional deep salaam. "Tell us what you see, tell us all!"

"I know . . . naw-theeng," the Head avers, inconsolably, "egg-zept . . . "

"Never mind about that, O Bodiless One. Our young friend here"—Wade steps to the rope and, for reasons that are to remain forever mysterious to him, takes off his hat and bows his head—"our young friend desires to know . . . "

He defers to Wade, who hears himself say, in a voice scarcely above a whisper, "Is Sonny gonna make it through the war?"

"O-o-o-o-o . . . " groans the Head. "O-o-o . . . " Out on the midway the Tilt-A-Whirl roars, the Ferris wheel creaks, the carousel tinkles, the barkers cry, the girls scream, and there is the rumble of distant thunder. But within the tent a terrible silence prevails while the Bodiless Head struggles to speak.

"O-o-o-o-kiiii-naaaa-waaaaaaaa!" the Head intones at last. "O-o-o-kiii-naaa-waaa!"

Wade looks to the professor for an interpretation and meets with a *no comprende* shrug; the Man of Letters purports to be as mystified as Wade is. And when Wade looks back, the Head is gone, withdrawn into its hole again. On the platter is the empty turban, a wadded dish towel in a pool of painted blood.

"That's all?" Wade asks in disbelief.

"That's it, son," says the professor, not unkindly. "That's the whole shit-a-ree, as it were."

"Well, it's all a big gyp, then."

"That's as may be," admits the professor, holding back the exit flap for him. "But you must never presume upon the cosmos, my lad. That wouldn't be . . . good policy."

"Aw, *bull!*" the boy flings back angrily as he rushes out. Through the opening they see him pause momentarily at the teeming midway's edge, like a reluctant swimmer on the bank of an arctic stream. Then he plunges in and is swept away.

"Awright, Phil Rexroat," Wanda Pearl demands to know, "how come the Jojo called that poor child a Okie? You ain't been learning it to throw off on the Okies, I hope."

"The word, my lamb," says the professor, in his most sonorous, funereal tones, "is Okinawa. It's . . . a place in the war."

And he too exits through the flap.

The Human Enigma parts the ragged draperies that conceal the base of the Bodiless Head's hidey-hole and creeps fearfully into the light. As it labors to its feet, the professor, out front, cranks up his spiel for the next show.

"This way, this way, this way, this way! See the Pomeranian Humbug! See the Himalayan Quahog, World's Only Man-Eating Bivalve, Terror of the Andes! It's sensational, it's scientific, it's . . . "

For a long moment, Wanda Pearl and Jojo stare wordlessly at each other across the narrow space between them. Then Wanda Pearl opens her arms and they embrace, each patting the other tenderly on the back, as grieving women will.

DROWNING IN
THE LAND OF
SKY-BLUE WATERS

*One used-car salesman to another in the Elbow Room
Bar in Missoula, Montana: "Who made the most
money last year? I did, by God! So don't tell me
you're the goddamn epitome of virtue!"*

This all begins about where it will end, way up in the
upper-left-hand corner of the country, where I am lumbering along a Montana freeway in a cumbersome, rump-sprung old white whale of a '65 Chevy
van named Moldy Dick, headed east, into the very first sunrise of July 1976.
At my back is a U-Haul trailer and, receding into both the distance and the
past, the town of Missoula, Montana, which until this morning I've called
home for all of three years now. Ahead of Moldy Dick and me is my new
bride Cia, piloting the ageless, long-suffering McClanavan, and ahead of
her are a couple of thousand miles of eastbound highway, at the far end of
which is a tumbledown, four-room tenant house on a high bank of the Kentucky River, near the hamlet of Port Royal, in Henry County, Kentucky. In
Moldy and the U-Haul are two-thirds of all our worldly possessions; in the
VW, with Cia, is the other third. We have no money to speak of, no jobs, no
prospects. Yet, as must ever be the case with nearly-newlyweds, our hopes
are high. We are nesters, homesteaders, a weird little wagon train in the
Eastward Movement, pioneers seeking our earthly paradise.

This is not the first time Cia and I have hit this trail in hot pursuit of the
wild goose. Exactly ten months ago to the very day—on September 1, 1975—
we set out from Missoula on this same highway, in the same direction, with

the same destination—but that time it took seven weeks and seven thousand miles to get there, and another seven weeks and seven thousand miles to get back, and along the way we drank enough beer to drown the entire feline population of Ardmore, Oklahoma. There'll be no such dawdling on this trip; we're humping to make it to Kentucky in time to get a very late garden in the ground, so we'll at least have a few turnips to gnaw on this coming winter. But that other trip, that was a hoot, buddies. It liked to kilt us.

I still don't know for sure whose idea it was, but it seemed like a winner at the time. There we were in Missoula in the spring of '75, Cia working in the public library and I rounding out my second, and last, year as a utility factotum in the University of Montana's creative writing program, my career as a professional Visiting Lecturer finally about to come a cropper, apparently for good. I was still pecking desultorily away at my poor old dead letter of a novel, and Cia was writing songs and short stories during her coffee breaks at the library, but neither of us had much heart for the business. Like everyone else in Missoula—where the outdoors closes up shop in November and doesn't reopen till around the summer solstice—we spent most of our free time in the bars, soaking our anxieties in Dutch courage and cowboy blues.

And then one fateful night, probably at the Am Vets Club, where there was a fine country house band and a nice little dance floor, upon which Cia had long endeavored, with indifferent success, to improve my elephantine impression of the Texas two-step, one or the other of us—I'll take the blame—was struck by a stray bolt of lightning from a passing brainstorm.

"Hey, do you realize we could make a *living* doing this?"

"What, dancing? Are you out of your mind?"

"No, no, I mean we could hang out in places like this and *write* about them!"

"About honky-tonks!"

"Honky-tonks, dives, juke joints—!"

"About country music!"

"We could write a *book*!"

"Yeah! We could travel around, goin' to honky-tonks, and write a *book* about it!"

"Hey, yeah! We could get a *contract*, we could . . . !"

Something like that. By the time Cia got her feet out from under mine, we'd two-stepped our way into a whole new cottage industry. Within the next few weeks, with the help of several rather credulous Friends in High Places, we snagged a small option from a New York publisher, along with, more important, a letter of introduction certifying that we were accredited knights of the plume and ought to be extended every courtesy. Our plan was to stay in Missoula through the coming summer, outfitting the McClanavan for camping and getting into drinking shape for the long haul, and then to hit the road in September for a couple of months, in the general direction of Kentucky, *my* home turf, where we'd sit out the winter. Then we'd honky-tonk it back to Missoula in the spring, arriving triumphant with our manuscript in hand and our Pulitzer Prize virtually a foregone conclusion. *Saturday Night,* we'd call the book; *Saturday Night: Honky-Tonkin' in Hard Times.* Perfect!

Well, maybe not quite perfect. For one thing, we dreamed up this terrific title in 1975, about fifteen minutes before *Saturday Night Live* hit the TV and *Saturday Night Fever* hit the screen and the Bay City Rollers' "Saturday Night" hit the pop charts and Tom Waits's "The Heart of Saturday Night" hit the album charts. So our timing wasn't all that hot. And just how *do* two people write a book together? Don't ask us, because we never got ours written. Not that it matters, since it was clearly a book the world could get along without, as the world has subsequently demonstrated, to a nicety. But we did make the trip; we actually put in all that time and all those miles jukin' and jivin' and juicin' our way through hundreds— hundreds!—of bars, dance halls, roadhouses, juke joints, and "low drinking resorts" (which is what my dictionary calls honky-tonks), earnestly interviewing every musician, barkeep, and barfly we could corner, researching the definitive study in downward mobility, looking, as Tom Waits has it, for the heart of Saturday night.

And we found it. I am pleased to announce, here and now, that the Quintessential Peerless Paramount Honky-Tonk of the Known World is the Town Tavern in Osgood, Indiana—or anyhow it *was,* one Saturday night in December 1975.

Honky-tonking, see, is like stalking the Loch Ness Monster; what counts are the sightings, not bringing home the varmint's gory fleece. The quarry is at once as ubiquitous as Santa Claus and as elusive as a snipe; scarcely a citizen of the realm is more than twenty-five miles or so from a honky-tonk experience of the highest order on any given Saturday night (or almost any other night of the week, for that matter), yet even the most dogged and enterprising roisterers are assured of no reward save a repentant Sunday morning for their efforts, if luck and intuition aren't with them.

The night before we went to Osgood, for instance, at a popular country night spot in Louisville, a pall of boredom as palpable as cigarette smoke hung all evening long over a crowd of some three hundred dispirited revelers (ourselves among them), despite the best efforts of a tight, hardworking house band and the usually enlivening presence of several apparently unattached charmers in high heels and hot pants. Whereas, the very next night up in Osgood, it required only some fifteen celebrants (our vagrant selves again among them) and two road-weary old guitar-pickers named Singin' Sam and Ramblin' Joe to raise the Town Tavern's roof nigh unto outtasight.

In fact, we eventually concluded, all that's really required for the primary honky-tonk alchemy to work is a good country jukebox and a solitary beer drinker. Imagine, for example, some poor old homesick hillbilly sitting all alone in a Detroit briar-hopper beer joint at closing time, plugging the jukebox with his last quarter for one—no, *two!*—more plays of Bobby Bare's great citybilly blues song "Detroit City"—which is *about* him!—and you're as close to the fundamental implosion as it's safe to stand, probably. The honky-tonk is the crucible in which this phenomenon occurs, when artist and audience are fused in the commonality of their experience.

You can't make a sow's ear out of a silk purse, of course; Charlie Rich doth not of Caesar's Palace a honky-tonk make. But when Johnny Allen and the Memories lay into "Jolie Blonde" in BooBoo's Niteclub in Breaux Bridge, Louisiana, and four hundred exultant Cajuns storm the dance floor ... when the All-American Left-Handed Upside-Down Guitar Player keens "I Kept the Wine and Threw Away the Rose" to his audience of redneck deadbeats in some Lexington, Kentucky, dive, exhorting them—too late, alas, too late!—to beware the perils of ambition, the blandishments of bright lights and city ways ... when Bobby Bare's morose beer drinker communes with himself and his sources ("I wanna go home ... Ohh, how I wanna go home!") through the medium of the jukebox ... that's a *honky-tonk,* dearly beloved, that's a holy place!

Not to make too much of this holiness business, though; there's really nothing all that sanctified about establishments that treat so openly with the Devil.* You can get hurt in a thousand ways in a honky-tonk: you can break your heart, ruin your health, lose your religion, and get your ass handed to you; virtuous women are metamorphosed overnight into tramps, strong men are reduced to—in the parlance—knee-walkin', commode-huggin' drunks; lovers murder one another in honky-tonks; if you're the passive type, you can simply, quietly drown in beer, bad music, and other people's bullshit in a honky-tonk.

And the undertow, I'm here to tell you, is something fierce.

The fact is, we didn't know ourselves what we were getting into when we undertook this endeavor. Oh, we'd honked and tonked around some in our time, and country music had long been among our mutual abiding passions—but we certainly never reckoned with the honky-tonk blues.

The honky-tonk blues is a malady brought on by overexposure to the wild side of life. People who frequent low drinking resorts eight nights a week are liable to get—vulgarity says it best—they get *fucked up.* They are assaulted by too much truth and, at the same time, too many lies; they lose their sense of proportion, of balance; their vision of reality is chronically blurred by alcohol and elation and hangover and depression, they get manic, they are by turns garrulous and quarrelsome, their dispositions sour, they fight among themselves over imagined slights and shadowy suspicions; in the dark of their minds they brood upon mortality and, worse, upon the death of love. A dreadful affliction, all in all—and one to which writers have no more natural immunity than the veriest illiterate.

Yet from Alberton, Montana, to Breaux Bridge, Louisiana, to Osgood, Indiana . . . and back again . . . we pursued our evanescent quarry, through trials and travails, despite pitfalls and pratfalls, following our noses and our muses and, sometimes, our muses' noses, sticking whenever possible to the back roads and small towns, a hundred, two hundred miles a day,

---

* Honky-tonk music itself testifies endlessly and eloquently to the general unwholesomeness of its own environs: to genial, joyless alcoholism ("Pop-A-Top," "What Made Milwaukee Famous [Has Made a Loser Out of Me]," "Wine Me Up," "Little Ole Winedrinker—Me," etc., etc., etc.), to aimless sexuality ("From Barrooms to Bedrooms"), to marital restlessness ("The Wild Side of Life"), to the failure of religious faith ("The Lord Knows I'm Drinkin'"), to violent political resentments ("The Fightin' Side of Me"), even to the insalubrity of the very atmosphere ("Smoky the Bar").

camping or putting up in out-of-the-way cheap motels, barhopping like Hav-A-Hank salesmen, nine or ten noisy, noisome clubs a night sometimes, starting conversations, relentlessly ingratiating ourselves, asking questions, swilling toxic fluids and breathing noxious fumes, taking endless notes that regularly progressed, in the course of an evening, from lucid to addled to delirious to indecipherable, but that always included a smattering of hot tips for the next town down the road (*Rhonda waitress at Paree Lounge in Baton Rouge sez don't miss Mary Jane's in Bay Town, Tex., that's where they do the Goat-roper . . .*), clarion calls to duty that kept us pressing ever onward.

It was just such a hot tip that led us to Singin' Sam and Ramblin' Joe at the Town Tavern, up in Osgood. We'd driven nearly sixty miles to find it, on the recommendation of a bartender in a place called, I swear, the B&M Disco & Bait Shop in Carrollton, Kentucky. At first blush the Town Tavern didn't look much more promising than the B&M had proved. Although it was the very shank of a Saturday evening, there were scarcely a dozen folks on hand, and most of them looked glum and sullen, as if the two grizzled old minstrels cranking out "Waltz Across Texas" on the bandstand were keeping them awake. A couple of fat ladies were essaying a sort of ponderous mazurka on a dance floor the size of a double bed, but otherwise the Town Tavern's vital signs were pretty feeble.

Then, wonder of wonders, while we were still settling in at our table, the bartender came over to tell us that we'd just won the door prize—a case of Schlitz! How about *that,* we exulted, let's set up the house! An inspired move, for it instantly won us a dozen new friends at no cost whatsoever to ourselves, inasmuch as the new friends were simultaneously obliged to set *us* up before the night was over. Within minutes people were drinking our health and smiling upon us from every corner of the room; Sam 'n' Joe saluted us from the bandstand and picked up the tempo, a couple of skinny old boys got up to join the fat ladies on the dance floor, and in short order the joint was jumpin' like a hatful of grasshoppers. We were the life the party had been waiting for. I danced with all the ladies, Cia danced with all the gents, and after we'd discreetly put out the word that we were writers, they all wanted to buy us even more beer and tell us their life stories. Sam and Joe took their breaks at our table and told us *their* life stories ("So I had me a job all lined up with Bill Monroe and the Blue Grass Boys, and that's when I mashed my hand in my cousin Randy's trailer hitch . . . "), and then

Sam's wife, Irene, showed up and told us *her* life story ("Yeah, him and me met at the Old Dominion Theater, in Alexandria, Virginia . . . "). Sometime late in the proceedings, Joe mentioned that his real name was Howard Miceburger. Well then, I inquired, how come he called himself Ramblin' Joe? "We-e-e-el," he allowed thoughtfully, "I couldn't hardly call myself Ramblin' Howard Miceburger, I reckon." At closing time, the bartender gave us two free six-packs for the road—and told us his life story.

Neon lights, midnight madness:

In Butte, Montana, after we'd tripped the light fantastic for hours at the Helsinki Baths Bar & Grill to the lilting cacophonies of Frankie Yankovic's brother Johnny's polka band, we fell into a place called Dirty-Mouth Jean's for a nightcap, and the well-dressed matron behind the bar took Cia's order, then turned to me and said, "And what'll this prick have?"

In Clovis, New Mexico, at the Cellar Bar in the basement of the Hotel Clovis, I danced with a lady whose earrings featured her late husband's gallstones.

In Luke's Cool Spot in Carrollton, Kentucky, the bartender, a former professional wrestler named Oscar the Mountain Ox, whiled away his idle moments squashing cockroaches on the bar with the bottom of a beer bottle.

In the Wonder Bar in Walsenburg, Colorado, of all places, we ran into a melancholy young drunk named Steve, who told us he was the son of a great American athlete, an Olympic distance runner so famous that I instantly recognized the name. "I love to drink, get drunk," Steve acknowledged gloomily. "I'm angry, bitter, vitriolic. And all because of . . . track."

In the Starlite Eats & Beer, on a back road somewhere in eastern Arkansas, the woebegone old soak sitting next to me at the bar, who was drinking beer and simultaneously gumming an immense chew of tobacco, decided that introductions were in order. "M' name," he announced, in a voice as thick and damp as pond slime, "is Rrrrrraymon' Mmmmmmurphy. Rrrrrraymon' is m' firs' name. An' Mmmmmmurphy is m' las' name."

"Don't pay no attention to Raymond," interjected the bartender, swatting a fly on the back bar. "He's like these damn flies. He eats shit and bothers people."

In the parking lot behind Tex's Barrelhouse, in Bakersfield, California, we saw a cowboy sitting on the running board of an old pickup truck, fastidiously throwing up into his boot.

In the back streets of Houston late one sweltering Sunday night, we landed in a mosquito-infested open-air beer joint called Kountry Korners, where a hulking truck driver named Leon was striving mightily, though to little avail, to pass his fleshy, thirty-eight-year-old person off as a reincarnation of Elvis Presley, circa 1957. Leon had the requisite guitar, pompadour, sideburns, and repertoire, but he was sadly lacking in the talent department. He worked hard at it, though—grinding out what seemed an endless medley of old Elvis rockers and sweating like a one-man Texas chain gang—and his enthusiasm was worth a lot all by itself. At his break I bought him a beer and asked if he'd care to sum up his life story in a few well-chosen words. "Aw," Leon said, mopping his greasy brow, "I've played 'em all, from the biggest to the littlest. My biggest was a soul gig in a thirty-six-lane bowlin' alley, had a twelve-piece band and three colored girls behind me. Ever' poor boy's got the same dream, see, the same damn dream: set his mother up in a nice place."

In the only bar in Kooskia, Idaho, the barmaid pointed to her feet and said, "See these sandals? Day before yesterday, they was boots. That's what happens when you dance all weekend."

In a Holiday Inn cocktail lounge on the interstate archipelago somewhere in the vicinity of Atlanta, I asked the solitary drinker at the bar whether he happened to know of any live music in the area. "Naw," he said, "all I know is how to get back on the interstate. I never been in Tennessee before."

At the Chicken Ranch in Austin, at the break, the bandleader stepped to the mike and said, "Now, you all get you a beer, and be thankful that you drink. If you didn't drink, when you wake up in the morning, that's as good as you'd feel all day." And in the B&M Disco & Bait Shop, a hairy, leathery little backwoods hippie, who called himself Pisswilliger and looked like a three-day-old roadkill, told us he'd just finished pulling two years in the state pen. Too polite to ask what he'd been in for, we inquired instead what he intended to do, now that he was out. *"Do?"* he cried indignantly. "I ain't gonna do nothing, by God! They wouldn't let me do what I wanna do, so I just ain't gonna do nothing, by God!" Well, we asked, what was it you wanted to do, Pisswilliger? "Why," he fumed, "I *wanted* to sell pot and pills to the high school kids, by God!"

And so, on. And so, forth.

Now don't get me wrong, we went to uptown places, too, and we heard some wonderful music and met some lovely folks. We swang and swayed to the sweetest house band in the land—that'd be the nameless "bunch of Merle Haggard rejects" (their description) at J.D.'s Cocktail Lounge in Ridgecrest, California—we heard Pretty Jan Dell at the Cabin in Milltown, Montana, and the Salt Creek Boys at Ziggy's in New Orleans and the Juice Commanders at the Club Imperial in Vicco, Kentucky, and Curly Cook at the Caravan East in Albuquerque, and Lonny Mitchell's Zydeco Band at Mitchell's Lounge in Houston, and Oscar Whittington at the Democrat Hot Springs Inn in Democrat Hot Springs, California, and the White Trash Liberation Front at Mac's Bar in Thermopolis, Wyoming, and Doug Sahm at the Soap Creek Saloon in Austin, and Asleep at the Wheel at the Palomino in L.A.; we followed the great Clifton Chenier and His Red-Hot Louisiana Band from Antone's in Austin to the Bamboo Lounge in Rayne, Louisiana, to BooBoo's in Breaux Bridge; we ate steak at the Lowake Inn in Lowake, Texas, and crawfish at Elmer Naquin's Crawfish Kitchen in Breaux Bridge, and tacos and beans at La Fiesta in Clovis, New Mexico, and hot boudin sausages at Mitchell's Lounge, and cheeseburgers at the Broken Drum ("You Can't Beat It!") in Hayden, Colorado, and catfish (nobody's gonna believe this, but it's true all the same) at the LBJ Ranch; we drank more beer than the Pittsburgh Steelers and danced more miles than Arthur Murray and listened to more life stories than Sigmund Freud.

During our midwinter layover in Kentucky, we holed up in this abandoned tenant house beside the Kentucky River, just down the road from our old friends Wendell and Tanya Berry. The little house was in a bad way, but then so were we by that time; after all those days and nights in that VW, the house seemed extravagantly well appointed and as roomy as all outdoors. And the location was just grand—a pretty river at our doorstep, a garden on the riverbank, a CinemaScope view of the valley without another house in sight. It was the perfect setup for a pair of old nearly-newlyweds. As soon as we got our land legs back, we began to see that this place was definitely going to figure in our future, if we could only manage to outlive the present.

At Christmastime we went to Lexington to pay a sick call on my irrepressible old pal Little Enis. The All-American Left-Handed Upside-Down Guitar Player was in a bad way too. He had what he called "sclerosis of the liver," his kidneys were failing, his heart was beating as erratically as a one-legged drummer in a marching band, varicose veins as thick as grapevines looped his poor skinny little legs, clots the size of goose eggs coursed his bloodstream. Seeing him, I was reminded that a linguist friend of mine once suggested that "Toda-vinney" probably used to mean "all the wine." But Enis had just one regret. "I shoulda been a preacher," he declared intrepidly. "I like fried chicken and pussy as much as anybody."

Enis died February 27, 1976. We were in Austin, working west, when the word came; I sent flowers and a card that said, "So long, little buddy." Then I sat in the McClanavan and cried like a baby, in the terrible knowledge that the more things stay the same, the more they change, and not even immortality lasts forever.

This whole ramble was beginning to get to us. We'd bottomed out resoundingly in Baton Rouge one night the week before, bombing along from the Kozy Keg to the Club Riviera to Silvio's Grille to the Paree Lounge to the Sugar Patch to the Silver Dollar I to the Twilight Lounge to an oblivion so profound that neither of us has ever been able to recall where we went next. Call it the Dew Drop Inn; in a town the size of Baton Rouge, there's bound to be a Dew Drop Inn. We don't remember either exactly what occasioned our little disagreement in the parking lot as we were leaving; but we must have administered each other a pretty thorough going-over, because our bruised feelings didn't recover for days and days. This was no way to run a honeymoon, I'll tell you that.

And it kept on happening; we high-centered again, more or less similarly, in Nederland, Texas, in Tiny Richardson's Club 88, and again in El Paso at the Maverick Club, and again in Albuquerque at the Thunderbird, and again in Yuma at Johnny's Other Place, and again in Bakersfield at the Silver Spur, and again in Redding at the Oak Grove Club . . .

A chronic case of the honky-tonk blues, compounded by a touch of motion sickness; the wild side of life had just about undone us. Too much beer and bad music and bullshit—our own as well as other people's—too many renditions of "Proud Mary" by too many groups with names like the Soporifics or Randy Snopes and the New Country Moods, too many hangovers, too many fights in the parking lots of too many Dew Drop Inns. As the old Jim Reeves song says, we'd enjoyed as much of this as we could stand.

By the time we limped back into Missoula in early April of '76, we understood all too well that if our collaboration had a future, it had better be in babies, not in books. But our travels weren't over yet, for we already had our sights set on that sweet little house back there on the bank of the Kentucky, where a couple of newly minted homebodies like us could settle in and get down to some serious collaborating.

So here we are just three months later, heading east—only it isn't July the first anymore, it's July the seventh, and we've spent the past four days in Sheridan, Wyoming, high-centered once again. It wasn't our fault this time, though; we've been waiting for Sheridan's inevitable hippie VW mechanic to repair the McClanavan, after the depredations lately visited upon it by Missoula's hippie VW mechanic, the most recent of a legion of that irksome ilk.

Sheridan turned out to be a nice town, with a lovely cheap motel and two or three of the bulliest cowboy bars we found anywhere; and it was fine to make the rounds without questions to ask, notes to take, books to write. Anxious as we've been to get on the move, we've had a good time there, one last little blast before we hit that turnip patch.

Now we're back on the road, Cia still leading in the McClanavan, Moldy and I and the U-Haul bringing up the rear. For the first fifty miles or so out of Sheridan, I've tailed her pretty close, expecting her poor old spavined steed to start spewing oil all over the roadway at any moment, like it did four days ago.

But everything seems to be in good order this morning, so finally I relax my vigil and fall back a ways. These old bangers of ours cruise at about forty-five, flat out, which makes for a long, lazy day at the wheel. Any other time, lollygagging along all by myself like this, I'd sit back, pop the top of a cold Grain Belt, and tune in the nearest call-in show on the radio. There's a problem, though: Moldy Dick, which we bought for four hundred bucks just for this trip, came with a gaping hole, like a missing tooth, in the dash where the radio should have been. So, left to my own devices, too uncoordinated to twiddle my thumbs and steer at the same time, I'm casting about for something to occupy the vasty fastnesses of my mind for the next few hundred miles. And that's when I remember the Elbow Room, and the Born in the Land of Sky-Blue Waters sign.

The Elbow Room is a nondescript bar in a nondescript building that squats nondescriptly amid the used-car-lot ghetto on the south side of Missoula. It has a pool table, a good country jukebox, and a peremptorily ami-able bartender, but by and large the atmosphere is pretty businesslike, and the business at hand is alcohol (THE DOCTOR IS IN AT SICKS A.M., discreetly advises a small sign taped to the backbar mirror.) The clientele is mostly trailer-court working class—day laborers and millhands and motel maids and Granny Goose salesmen and tire re-cappers and Korean War widows and Exxon pump jockeys—and it includes a sizable contingent of full-time, dedicated alcoholics.

Now, for all my inabstinent ways, I have never counted myself among that happy number; but when we lived in Missoula I did like to fall by the Elbow Room every now and then for a nightcap or three, just to clear my head after a hard day at the thesaurus or some trifling domestic impasse or a particularly egregious outrage on the late news. The glum, podiatrist's-waiting-room anonymity of the place seemed to cool me out somehow, and many a midnight hour I've whiled away sitting there nursing a shot of Brand X bourbon and meditating upon the electric Hamm's Beer sign behind the bar, the one that bears the legend "Born in the Land of Sky-Blue Waters" beside an animated picture, which follows a rushing mountain stream down past a campsite with a red canoe, on down a riffle and over a waterfall and around an island and past a campsite with a red canoe and down a riffle and over a waterfall and around an island and past a campsite with a red canoe and down a riffle and . . . The Hamm's sign, with that mad little river rushing eternally up its own fundament, has always seemed to me an inef-fably profound representation of spiritual isolation, a sort of horizontal electric mandala for contemplative drunks, and I have long-aspired to write a country song about it.

Why not now? Sure! I'll call it "Drowning in the Land of Sky-Blue Waters"; it'll be my personal anthem, an old honky-tonker's swan song. Within the next ten miles of freeway I've got the opening lines—"I've lost my way again / Out in this neon wilderness . . . "—and something that passes, at least to my tin ear, for a rudimentary tune. By lunchtime I have the first verse all wrapped up, and by our afternoon beer break, just across the Wyoming-Nebraska border, I've made it through the chorus. And before the sun goes down that evening, I am singing—if you can call it that—at the top of my inharmonious voice, the very first song I've ever written. No doubt there will be those who say that it should be the last as well, but that's *their* problem. So, as Roy Rogers used to put it, "Now don't you worry, folks, we're a-gonna git them rustlers. But first, lemme sing ya a little song. It goes . . . kinda like this . . . "

I've lost my way again
Out in this neon wilderness,
Where the rivers run in circles
And the fish smoke cigarettes;

Where the only things that give me
Any peace of mind
Are a jukebox and a barstool
And a strange electric sign.

Chorus:
'Cause I'm drowning in the land of sky-blue waters
Since I lost the way home to you.
Yes, I'm drowning in the land of sky-blue waters;
I need you to see me through.

I've seen that peaceful campsite
A hundred times tonight,
Where the campfire's always burning
And everything looks right.

But across that crazy river,
In this godforsaken place,
A man is going under;
He could sink without a trace.

Chorus:
'Cause he's drowning . . . etc.

The Elbow Room is closing now,
And I must face the street,

Where the only rushing rivers
Are rivers of concrete.

There's no way I can cry for help;
My pride has got its rules.
But at last call for alcohol
My heart calls out to you:

Chorus:
Oh, I'm drowning . . . etc.

As we roll on into the gathering Nebraska dark, I can feel the faint mag-netic pull of all those honky-tonks out there, all the Dew Drop Inns in the Land of Doo-Wah-Diddie, neon lodestars in the night. But they're not for us, for our honky-tonkin' days are o'er—because although we won't even suspect it for weeks and weeks yet, when we pulled away from that nice motel this morning there was a stowaway among us, a tiny mite no big-ger than the dot over the "i" in Sheridan. We must wait the requisite nine months before we get to look upon her darling face and name her Annie June McClanahan. Our true collaboration has begun.

EXEGESIS:
A FICTION

CERTAIN SOCIO-PHILOSOPHICAL THEMES IN
ROBERT HUNTER'S LYRICS TO "NEW SPEEDWAY BOOGIE"
BY AUSTIN M. TODDLER, PHD

The Grateful Dead were deeply involved in planning the Rolling Stone's disastrous Altamont concert—it was they, according to most sources, who suggested that the Hell's Angels be employed to police the area around the stage—and Robert Hunter's lyrics to "New Speedway Boogie" may properly be regarded as their "official" public statement about the meaning of the grisly events of that unhappy day.

First, then, the lyrics, as sung by Jerry Garcia on the album *Working-man's Dead*:

> *Please don't dominate the rap, Jack,*
> *If you got nothin' new to say.*
> *If you please, don't back up the track;*
> *This train's got to run today.*
> *I spent a little time on the mountain,*
> *Spent a little time on the hill.*
> *Like some say, better run away;*
> *Others say better stand still.*
>
> *Now I don't know, but I been told,*
> *It's hard to run with the weight of gold.*
> *Other hand, I've heard it said,*
> *It's just as hard with the weight of lead.*
> *Who can deny, who can deny*

It's not just a change in style.
One step's done and another begun,
And I wonder how many miles.
I spent a little time on the mountain,
Spent a little time on the hill.
Things went down we don't understand,
But I think in time we will.

Now I don't know, but I was told,
In the heat of the sun, a man died of cold.
Keep on comin' or stand and wait,
With the sun so dark and the hour so late . . .

You can't overlook the lack, Jack,
Of any other highway to ride.
It's got no signs or dividin' lines,
And very few rules to guide.
I spent a little time on the mountain,
Spent a little time on the hill.
I saw things getting out of hand;
I guess they always will.

Now I don't know, but I been told,
If the horse don't pull, you got to carry the load.
I don't know whose back's that strong;
Maybe find out before too long.

One way or another;
One way or another;
One way or another;
This darkness got to give.

The song is, on the one hand, an expression of apprehensiveness and confusion and, on the other, an exhortation to a new order of wisdom, a higher
and truer vision. However, unlike the authors of most of the journalistic
postmortems on the Altamont debacle (especially those who, like "Jack"—
a.k.a. Jumpin' Jack Flash, a.k.a. Mick Jagger—insist on "[dominating]

the rap" even though they "got nothin' new to say"), Hunter is not of the Altamont-as-Armageddon persuasion, and he does not agree that the quest after salvation—the voyage that began in the Haight-Ashbury and carried us all the way to Woodstock—has dead-ended at last in the molten yellow hills of California just twenty miles east of where it started, impaled on the point of a Hell's Angel's rusty blade, skewered there like one of those suicidal Siamese frogs that travel great distances only to fling themselves upon the spikes of some rare thorn bush. Rather, the poet suggests, the journey has only just begun, and the way is long and arduous and fraught with peril; Altamont is but one dark moment in the community's *total* experience, the first installment of the dues that we must pay for our deliverance. On the Big Trip, the poet warns, the pilgrims will encounter suffering as well as joy, and those who have no heart for the undertaking would do well to stand aside, because "this train's got to run today." The song's thrice-repeated refrain, "I spent a little time on the mountain, / Spent a little time on the hill," bespeaks the poet's (or, if you will, the singer's) modest claim to have made a private, careful consideration, hors de combat, of the enlightened person's obligation* in a time of public turmoil; in fact, we must seek guidance within ourselves, since public advice—"Like some say, better run away: / Others say better stand still"—is likely to be hysterical and paralyzingly contradictory. And in the next quatrain that contradiction blooms into a full-blown paradox:

> *Now I don't know, but I been told,*
> *It's hard to run with the weight of gold.*
> *Other hand, I've heard it said,*
> *It's just as hard with the weight of lead.*

Metaphorically these lines describe and define the two equally seductive—and equally treacherous—temptations that beguile the truth-seeker, the Scylla and Charybdis between which he must thread his perilous course: on the one hand, Fortune, represented at Altamont in the opulent persons

---

* A very literal interpretation of the refrain might also make reference to the fact that the Dead, scheduled to go on after the Stones, never actually played that day; thus they had ample opportunity to climb "the hill" overlooking the scene and see that things were indeed "gettin' out of hand."

of the Stones, seen here as listing dangerously beneath "the weight of gold";
and on the other Violence, the way of the Angels, burdened as they are with
chains and helmets and Iron Crosses and all their weaponry, the hardware
of their sullen calling. Then too, of course, there is the more literal reading
of the passage, in which the relative subtlety of the metaphor is overridden
by the ominous, code-of-the-old-West caveat to the effect that he who is so
foolish as to make off with his brothers' gold is subject to end up carrying
their hot lead as well, cut down by the heavy-handed irony of a Fate against
which any admirer of *The Treasure of the Sierra Madre* could have warned
him right from the start.

Nor may we shrug off the events at Altamont as harbingers of a mere
"change in style"; rather, the minstrel contends, the change is *substantive,*
and the death of Meredith Hunter signals that when the pilgrimage arrived
at Altamont it entered into new and hostile territory, the twilight of its own
dark night of the soul. Yet "one step's done and another begun," and so the
song, even as it grieves one emblematic death and dreads the miles and
trials ahead, directs us to turn our eyes to the changes yet to come. For, as
the next verse reminds us, "Things went down we don't understand, / But I
think in time we will"—that is, however weary we are of mistakes and wrong
turns and, most of all, of the terrible burden of our desperate longing for the
destination, we can only comprehend the meaning of present events—and
of the judgments they pass—from the perspective of the next change.

And now, with the following quatrain—

> *Now I don't know, but I was told,*
> *In the heat of the sun, a man died of cold.*
> *Keep on comin' or stand and wait,*
> *With the sun so dark and the hour so late . . .*

—an almost *literal* shadow sweeps across the trackless yellow landscape of
the song, the specter of some nameless thing so unspeakably awful that its
very shadow casts a deadly chill, a pall from which no escape is possible,
no matter whether we "keep on comin' or stand and wait." It is, of course,
the specter of our own inhumanity, our selfishness, our passionless indifference, and now at last the lesson of the song—and of Altamont—is clear: The
Angels are the dark aspect of ourselves, reflections of the beast that skulks
behind our eyes; we created them as surely as we created the Rolling Stones,

fashioned them all of the mute clay of our need for Heroes and Villains as surely as we created Altamont itself that fateful day. Thus we can no more excise the bloody-handed Angels from our midst than we can cut away some vital part of our own psyche, lobotomize ourselves.

Nonetheless, that hard lesson learned the hard way, our course remains set, fixed by the iron resolve of destiny, and there can be no turning back; we can only face up to "the lack . . . / Of any other highway to ride" and, as R. Crumb puts it, "keep on truckin'." True, we travel this treacherous road at our own risk; but could we ever have supposed it might prove otherwise? And if the absence of "signs" and "dividin' lines" and "rules to guide" guarantees a hazardous journey, it also promises times when this heaven-bound ride is indescribably wild and sweet and free; things *will* get "out of hand"— "*always*"—but even that inevitability has its compensations, so long as we are among friends.

Still and all, "if the horse don't pull, you got to carry the load"—that is, if the communal vehicle and the full power of the community's combined energies will not bear one safely through, then the whole burden of care and growth must rest upon oneself. And, the minstrel cautions, it may well be that none of us is capable of that effort, that the whole enormous enterprise will come to nothing. But this is a time of testing, of pitting our strength against all the forces that oppress us—our guilt and our despair; our selfishness, our failures and our fear of failure—for "one way or another" relief *must* come, these gloomy times *must* pass, the darkness *will* give.

Thus "New Speedway Boogie" is at once a sober—if highly subjective— study of a violently traumatic moment in the course of human events, a desperate prayer for deliverance, and a hymn of hope. And when those final fervent lines—

> *One way or another;*
> *One way or another;*
> *One way or another;*
> *This darkness got to give.*

—come echoing and reechoing down like "Excelsior!" from the heights, it also becomes an anthem quite as stirring, in its own somber, introspective way, as "Onward, Christian Soldiers."

for CW

FURTHURMORE

One afternoon in the early summer of 1964—the infamous Long, Hot Summer, during which I was planning to spend the entire month of August in Mississippi, where I intended to perform ever so many as-yet-undefined acts of heroism on behalf of the civil rights movement—I stood in Ken Kesey's front yard under the California redwoods, way out there on the westernmost lip of the land, and wistfully waved goodbye as Ken's psychedelically retrofitted 1939 International Harvester school bus lumbered off eastbound up Highway 84, the Good Ship Further—"Furthur," if you're a purist—adorned stem to stern with luridly amorphous abstract expressionist psychedoodles and psychedribbles, Ray Charles's "Hit the Road, Jack" blaring from the loudspeakers mounted on the poop deck, and all my most audacious pals—the Merry Pranksters, they'd lately taken to calling themselves, Ken and Faye and Jane and Babbs and Hassler and Zonk and George and Hagen and them, and the Real Neal (Cassady, that is) at the Wheel—gaily waving back from every porthole, setting sail across the trackless wastes of America for the World's Fair in exotic, unspoiled New York City.

You dip! chided a still, small voice within me. *You missed the boat again!*

No, no, I reassured myself, you're a family man, you got responsibilities. Besides, bless their hearts, those nitwits will get busted before they're halfway to Burlingame. Go home and work on your novel, family man, think of your wife and babies, think of your adoring public. Think, you self-absorbed hedonist, of the civil rights movement!

Well, as you may have surmised by now, the civil rights movement muddled through without me (I did go to Mississippi, but I couldn't even *find* the damned civil rights movement), and while my adoring public waited another nineteen years for that novel, I became a family man . . . twice over.

So the still, small voice had it right: I'd missed the boat. The nitwits didn't get busted (actually they *did,* but that came later), and, as everybody who read Tom Wolfe's *The Electric Kool-Aid Acid Test* knows to the point of distraction, the bus trip turned out to be one of the signal adventures of a gloriously adventurous decade. Ken's loose assortment of protohippie sybarites had, almost inadvertently, administered to America its first national contact high, and they came home to California fired with missionary fervor.

They purposed, these new-minted zealots, nothing less than to turn on the world—Heads up, world!—and thereby to show it to itself in a whole new light. The issue of their resolve was an ever-burgeoning series of Bay Area parties called the Acid Tests, hosted by the Pranksters, featuring Day-Glo décor and strobe lights and throbbing-blob light shows—all Prankster innovations—and the cacophonous rock of an unheralded group by the improbable name of the Grateful Dead and—ah, yes! The refreshments!—God's own plenty of sacramental Electric Kool-Aid, liberally spiked with LSD.

Heads up, world!

Do I hear someone out there muttering that all this seems a bit . . . well, old hat? Permit me to remind you, friends, that in the mid-1960s the chapeau was brand-spanking fresh-off-the-rack new, and that the Acid Tests spawned the great Trips Festival at San Francisco's Longshoremen's Hall in early 1966, and that the Trips Festival begat the Fillmore Auditorium, which begat Woodstock, which begat Life As We Know It.

Meanwhile, after a few more adventures (so thoroughly chronicled by Tom Wolfe that there's no need to recount them here), Ken did eventually have to do a little jail time. Then he and Faye went back to their native Oregon and set up housekeeping on an old dairy farm in the shadow of Mt. Pisgah, near Springfield and Eugene.

So tempus fugited relentlessly onward, and suddenly we've eased into the 1990s somehow, and Ken has this new book out entitled *The Further Inquiry,* a sort of recapitulation of the original bus trip in the form of a screenplay about a purgatorial mock trial of the late, much-lamented Neal Cassady (who died under rather mysterious circumstances in Mexico in 1968), to determine whether his spirit is suitable for admission into Heaven.

To promote the book, rumor has it, Ken has resurrected the bus and reassembled as many of the old crew as are still (as Lord Buckley used to say) sensible to the pinch, and is preparing to embark on one last trip across the country, destination the Smithsonian, where he plans to donate Furthur to posterity, that generations yet unborn might see in it a model for liberating themselves from the constraints of some still undreamed-of Twenty-First-Century Eisenhower Era.

Now by the time reports of these goings-on reached me in Port Royal, in the waning days of the summer of 1990, I was in a bad way. Earlier that summer, my second marriage, which I'd naively supposed was indestructible, had blown up in my face as abruptly as a letter bomb. I survived, but I had suffered major collateral damage, and, so far, the progress of my convalescence was not encouraging.

So anyhow, there I am—or there, at any rate, is what was left of me—shell-shocked and bewildered amidst the rubble of domestic cataclysm, forlornly wondering wot-the-hell-next, when—*mirabile dictu!*—here comes the bus again!

Shall I do it this time? Shall I submit my aging but still serviceable person to the rigors of this unprecedented second chance, mayhap to drown my sorrows in Electric Kool-Aid? Hey, you betcher sike-o-deelic ass I shall! Make room for one more geezer, pals! Hit the road, Jack!

"The bus," Ken is fond of saying these days, "is like Zapata's horse"—which, he will remind you, ran off into the hills when its master (Brando in the movie) was cut down in ambush. According to Hollywood-enhanced legend, the noble steed roams there to this day, awaiting the first shots of the next revolution, and the coming of the new Zapata— or the return of the old one.

Could be. One thing certain, some variety of magic or miracle of regeneration has been at work here, if the bus that now stands gorgeous and gleaming in Ken's barnyard is the same one I saw mouldering into the ground on this exact spot back in 1985. The original Furthur—the Ur-Furthur, if you will—though it was painted and repainted so often that the paint itself became a sort of carapace, an inch thick in spots, always had a rather murky, haphazard look, as if it had been assaulted by a band of renegade abstract expressionist finger-painters.

(Indeed, my own daughter Kris, who in 1964 was four years old, still remembers slapping on one of the first daubs, in the company of her favorite childhood playmate, the Keseys' daughter Shannon.)

But this 1990 incarnation is a Furthur of an altogether different hue, an hallucinogenic little cream puff featuring everything from a man-sized Sistine Adam to a spotted owl to a radiant Sun God to Pogo to a school of surreal fish to the obligatory Grateful Dead death's head to Oz-inspired lions and tigers and bears to Buddhas to totem poles to seagulls to the Silver Surfer, an eye-popping panorama of intertwined images and icons, all rendered in meticulous detail ("Holy shit!" marvels a tiny Tin Woodsman, standing agog on the Yellow Brick Road), all varnished to a shimmering high gloss, all interrelated to an extent that declares, in no uncertain terms, that what you see is the product, Gulley Jimson–like, of a single, unifying vision—Ken's, of course—yet in such a wild array of styles and techniques as to make it abundantly apparent that every artistic talent within hailing distance had a hand in this paint job. Earl Scheib need not apply.

So is this *the* bus, or a ringer? More to the point, does it matter?

"Mr. Kesey," sniffed a Smithsonian spokesparty on the phone, "is running around Oregon in something he *calls* the original bus, invoking the Smithsonian's name without our permission. We are *not* interested in reproductions, facsimiles, simulations, or counterfeits of any description whatsoever."

One is tempted to inquire whether the Smithsonian's interest might be piqued if Mr. Kesey offered to have himself stuffed and mounted on the bus as a hood ornament. And one might also wonder, idly, whether the Smithsonian is familiar with that ancient Prankster caveat "Never Trust a Prankster." But one bites one's tongue and bides one's time, awaiting Mr. Kesey's rejoinder, which isn't long in coming.

"Are we dealing with the body," he snorts, "or are we dealing with the spirit? Because that's what the bus is, see, a spirit, not a bucket of nuts and bolts. Giving this bus to the Smithsonian would be like putting your balls in a golden chest and sending them to the Queen. It'd be a nice thing to do, but it would be a mistake."

This whole stunt is just a hustle, then? Just another book tour, tricked out in love beads and bell-bottoms?

"That's like saying I put on the Acid Tests to promote Tom Wolfe's book.

On these book tours, the publishers want to kiss the bookstore owners' asses, and they want the writers to be their lips. I'll never sell enough books on this trip to make any money. But the bus isn't a *thing*, it's an *event*; it doesn't work until it's full of people and music, and it begins to warble and reverberate. It wouldn't be *right* to turn it into a relic, an artifact! The Smithsonian has talked itself out of this bus!"

Intending to take full advantage of the therapeutic, restorative, recreational, and literary possibilities in this adventure, I had contrived to present myself at the Kesey farm almost two weeks before the scheduled date of departure, Major Magazine press card in my hatband, ready to ride scribe.

(Actually, I wasn't ready for much of anything, with the possible exception of a winding sheet. Stricken I was, and down in the mouth to a disfiguring degree, alone and palely loitering. Fate had deposited me on the Keseys' doorstep like so much soggy wet wash, still warm from the Maytag of life.)

Ken and Faye have made their home for many years in a capacious hay barn on a sixty-five-acre farm in the Willamette Valley, a few miles south of Springfield. It's been a haven to me since the days when I roamed the West on the Visiting Lecturer in Creative Writing circuit, searching for some modest little sinecure to call my own. More than a few of the grandest times of my life were had right here, over the years—some of the craziest poker games (Ken's favorite call is "Dukers, Jukers, and One-Eyed Pukers Wild") and craziest conversations (Mad Genius Paul Foster: "Since the number of people now alive is greater than the total of all now dead, it follows that death has been reduced to a 50 percent probability. And since the world's population is still increasing, the odds are inevitably going to improve . . . ") and craziest psychotropic cocktail parties (one memorable Kentucky Derby Day a thousand years ago, we started out on silicone shoe polish fumes, worked up to psylicibin, and ended up knocking back a few schnapps juleps) . . . In short, a hard place to be unhappy in.

Still, being of a resolute and determined nature, I managed to suffer pretty good during those two weeks, although there were a couple of moments when I was in grave peril of enjoying myself just a little.

In the mornings, say, drinking bottomless cups of coffee at the big round cluttered dining room table that is to the Kesey Corporation what the War Room is to the Pentagon, sitting there with the soft autumnal Oregon sunshine streaming through the windows, sharpening our wits with a taste of Colonel Kesey's Morning Pipe while we plotted strategy for the Great Smithsonian Shuck-Off. It was at one such session that I was elevated from (self-appointed) Dean of the School of Subjective Journalism to the exalted post of Minister of Misinformation, from which vantage point I was to fire salvos of obfuscation at the Smithsonian, via the public press—which, it being a slow season for stories about fun and frivolity, was eating this one up.

(*Hello, AP? This here's the Reverend Mackrelham, Minister of Misinformation, with the latest sound-bite from the Kommandant! Headline:* KESEY SCORNS SMITHSONIAN OFFER! *Lead:* "The Smithsonian says it wants to 'restore the original bus,' scoffed the redoubtable Sage of Oregon today, striking a defiant stance. 'I told 'em, Okay, fine, let's paint it yellow!'")

(*Hello, CNN? This here's the Imam Hammerclam, Mullah of Misinformation, with the latest . . .*)

Actually, I wasn't all that great at this line of work. In print, see, I can lie with the best of 'em—what's a writer who can't lie?—but I've never been any good at the old one-on-one shuck 'n' jive. My heart pounds so loud you can hear it over the telephone, my voice cracks as though I'd been called to the principal's office, my face flushes as if . . . well, never mind. Also, you have to be fast on your mental feet in the p.r. biz, nimble enough to stay a step or two ahead of the curve—whereas I am notoriously retroactive in the snappy riposte department, generally coming up with the right thing to say about two weeks after the appropriate moment.

I was no Marlin Fitzwater, that's the point.

Nonetheless, we were being besieged by the very targets we besieged: All the local papers—the Portland *Oregonian,* the Eugene *Register-Guard,* the Roseburg *Gazette*—ran big feature stories as a matter of course; *People* was in touch, and *Newsweek* and *Time;* the San Jose *Mercury-News* sent its ace reporter Lee Quarnstrom—himself an old inner-circle Prankster—to ride with us and do a series of pieces for national syndication; *The New York Times* and NPR were scrambling aboard. The media, I was discovering, is like a music box; *anyone* can play it.

We spent one entire day (don't ask why) fashioning, out of mylar and bent sticks and helium balloons and Day-Glo tape and good old Yankee know-how, our very own flying saucer, which, that evening, we managed to get airborne to an altitude of about forty feet, and then somehow inveigled the local TV station (call letters KEZI, believe it or not) into putting it on the eleven o'clock news. They ran it as a "Martians-Invade-Kesey-Farm-to-See-Bus-Bound-for-Smithsonian" sort of thing, an antidote to all those ominous stories about the preparations for the looming war in the Persian Gulf. Nobody seemed to notice that the diameter of the flying saucer was exactly that of the Keseys' dining room table.

So an unconscionable amount of fun was being had, and this was truly a hard place to be unhappy in.

Hard—but not impossible.

Mt. Pisgah, altitude around 4,000 feet, rises as bold and tawny as a dromedary's hump amongst the lesser hillocks in the broad Willamette Valley. At its summit, about an hour's determined hike from the farm, is a modest memorial to Ken and Faye's son Jed, their youngest, who was killed at twenty when the University of Oregon wrestling team's van fell off a Central Washington mountainside in a snowstorm in 1984. (Properly speaking, it really isn't a memorial at all, since it doesn't even bear Jed's name; rather, the Keseys and their friends caused it to be placed there as, in Faye's words, "a gift from Jed.") The marker replicates, in bronze, a basalt outcropping about the size of a stout tree stump, maybe four feet high, topped by a bronze bas-relief of the valley that spreads itself tremendously before it. From the farm, you can see the marker, a flea-bite on the dromedary's hump; from the marker, you can see the farm, distance rendering the big red barn a microscopic Monopoly hotel. The top of Pisgah is a serene, beautiful, melancholy spot, and during those sunny autumn days before the trip, I oft betook my wounded and solitary self up there to sit with my back resting against Jed's reassuringly sturdy gift, and commune with dat ole debbil Mr. Mortality.

Three months earlier, just one day after my smug little pipe dream of a world had suddenly come crashing down about my ears, I'd made another, far more desperate journey west, that time to my dear California friend KC's place, in the hills above Palo Alto. Just minutes after I arrived, very much the worse for the wear, someone phoned KC with the news that his own close friend Drew, whom I had also known and liked, had gone home from a party the night before and, despondent over the recent collapse of his marriage of nineteen years, put a bullet through his head.

Now a coincidence such as that will tend to stick with a person for a good long while—which is why I was still thinking about it three months later, on Jed's mountaintop in Oregon.

I don't mean that I was contemplating following Drew's example, but rather just that his death had brought me to a whole new, intimate knowledge of how, assaulted by a confusion of grief and disappointment and pain and despair and (oh, yes) guilt, a person could do such a thing. I couldn't have done it myself—but I wouldn't have minded too much if someone else had done it for me. In a story of mine called "Finch's Song" there's a beleaguered character whose gloomy ruminations perfectly reflected my own frame of mind:

"By little and little," I had written, "Finch's dread of his departure from this mortal coil had at last almost entirely given way to a deep, inchoate longing to begin the journey, a longing not so much to die as merely to be . . . elsewhere, to be *taken,* to join those shadowy legions known as The Departed."

Jed Kesey and his sister Shannon and older brother Zane, along with their half-sister Sunshine, had grown up with my first set of kids, Kris and Cait and Jess. As adolescents, they'd spent whole summers together at the farm; I seem to recall that Cait was sort of sweet on Jed one summer. He was a fine, high-spirited, handsome boy—"a lightfoot lad," as Housman has it—and his loss was perhaps the first my children had suffered out of their own generation. From Pisgah's heights I could see his gravesite, just beyond the barn far below me. I wished with all my heart that he and I could trade places, that Jed were up here on the mountain with his whole unlived life opening out before him, and I were burrowed deep beneath the Oregon sod, two thousand miles from the home I could no longer love.

Lee Quarnstrom, yet another indispensable old friend, arrived two or three days before the bus was scheduled to embark. One morning, Lee and I were sitting at the dining room table drinking coffee when Lee suddenly stood up and looked out across the barnyard toward Jed's grave and said, "My son was shot dead on the street on Fisherman's Wharf eight years ago. He was eighteen years old. I think about it every day."

Death, needless to say, is a fact of life: Enis and Neal, *sic transit Gloria.* Gordon Fraser, that sweet man. My old Maysville drinking buddy Loujack Collings, felled by a stroke at forty-one. Dear Fred Nelson, a suicide in his mid-forties. Lanky and Bobby Sky and good old Page Browning, three Prankster pals of mine who'd checked out early. Jed. Drew. Lee's boy. The marriage that was supposed to outlive, by an eternity, the two mortals who were party to it. After Drew's death, I wrote a little poem, another first for me. If I can be said to have a strong suit, poetry is certainly not it; so mine is doubtless a poor effort, and I offer it here in all humility. It's called "The Hosts," and, of course, it's for Drew:

> With our mind's eye
> We watch over our departed guest,
> Anxious to see him safely home.
> How brief the visit,
> How long the vigil!

The bus, the man said, is not a thing, it's an event. Hoo boy, I'll say it is. On a shakedown run to Portland the day before the big trip is to begin, while Ken is signing books in a big downtown bookstore, the bus is fairly mobbed by a traffic-blocking throng of Furthurphiles of every stripe and vintage, hippie graybeards and thistle-headed punks, literary duffers and yuppie culture-mongers crowding round to glom the magic, all thirsting powerfully for the merest taste of Old On-The-Bus, that ineffable elixir from an age when everything and anything seemed not merely possible, but likely.

I spot a couple of old friends among them, and get off and mingle a bit. After a few minutes, though, I find myself inexorably drawn back on board.

"When you first get on the bus," Ken had told me just that morning, "it seems dangerous, and everything outside seems safe. But after you've been on it for a while, that turns around, and the bus is where you want to be. The danger is outside."

Danger or no, inside the bus is definitely where one wants to be. Wonderfully wired for sound, with walls all Day-Glo whorls and swirls, and carpets and cushions enough for a pasha's tent, it is deliciously cozy, like being inside a colossal translucent Easter egg. This is the absolute domain of artist and dedicated Prankster Roy Sebern, who decorated it, and who is its guardian and protector, and will climb your frame if you come in without wiping your feet. The Secretary of the Interior, we have dubbed him. And before long,

I become almost as protective of that sweet space as Roy is. To be On The Bus, I am already discovering, is to be inside a work of art; the real pleasure is in looking out and observing the gratification and delight of the viewers. Thinking about that, I begin to understand what makes the Mona Lisa smile.

Aside from several energetic second-generation Pranksters (who cheerfully undertake, thank heavens, to do most of the real work on the trip), our basic crew is largely of the geezer persuasion. "In 1964," Ken reminds us as we make our way south to San Francisco, "we were young people, trying to turn on the old. Now we're old people, trying to turn on the young." What he doesn't say is that this time we are also damaged people, most of us; death and divorce have touched our lives, and pain and loss and failure.

"And when we show up in this bus," he goes on, "the kids see that we've made good on a promise, and they're *lifted* by that, it makes sparks go off in their hearts, and strengthens them." And the little pep-talk makes sparks go off in geezer hearts, and lifts and strengthens us as well.

In Berkeley, where we spend a day campaigning for our old friend Wavy Gravy, who's a candidate (though not, it turns out, a successful one) for a seat on the city council, Ken waxes political:

"There's a battle for constitutional rights going on," he declares, "and it's called the War on Drugs. But it's not over yet, so don't stop fighting. Give the government enough rope, my daddy used to say, and it'll step on its dick every time. They have no more right to tell us what we can put inside our heads than they have to tell women what they can do inside their bodies. *This*"—he points to his own great bald noggin—"is our last stronghold! Don't let them take it from us!"

And a day or two later, at a reading in San Francisco, he regales a large, enthusiastic audience with a riff that is fast becoming a Kesey classic, his advice-to-writers exhortation: "You writers, one of these days you'll be walking along, and suddenly you'll look up and there, across the street, will be . . . God! And he'll say, *'Co-o-o-ome to Me!* Come to Me and I will make the words fly into your ears like little bluebirds, and out of your mouth like honeybees! Come to Me and I will get you a grant from the NEA, and a good review in *The New York Times*! Co-o-ome to Me!' And it's the job of you writers to say"—now his fist comes up, with a defiant middle finger standing at attention—"it's your job to say, 'Fuck you, God! Fuck you!'" As always, it brings the house down.*

These thunderous admonitions, though, are the exception, not the rule, on this trip. "There's nothing complicated about what we're doing," he explains gently the next day to a group of sweet-faced sorority girls we've happened upon on the Stanford campus. "The bus is like a kite, or a sunset, or fireworks, or a tree in the fall. You go by and people smile, and you smile, and that's it. But it's enough."

Enough? Well, maybe—for most folks. But there are afflictions that no amount of kites and sunsets can assuage, wounds too deep for any soothing balm. Amongst countless loving friends both old and new, I was incurably, inconsolably lonesome and heartsore: awash in a floodtide of diversions, I clung to my unhappiness like a drowning man clutching a concrete lifesaver.

But first, about those diversions: I never saw any Electric Kool-Aid on this trip, but there was some very interesting orange juice circulating from time to time. (Lee Quarnstrom complained one night on the road about all those transparent purple bunnies hopping across the interstate. "Hallucinations are shy," Ken reminded him. "But if you entertain them, they'll bring all their friends, and then they're hard to get shut of.") Then, too, there was the Wavy Gravy campaign. ("A rubber chicken in every pothole! Put a *real* clown on city council!") And a Halloween party at which Huey Lewis showed up as an Elvis impersonator. (Hey, you don't believe me? I got pictures!) Paul Krassner, the *Realist* editor and sometime stand-up comedian, came on board, firing zingers from the hip. ("Used to be, you'd go to a rock concert, and some total stranger would walk up and hand you a pill, and you'd take it without a second thought. These days, we've got the Tylenol killer. That's why I never take any legal drugs.")

On the aforementioned night of the transparent purple bunnies, I even

---

* I first heard Ken deliver himself of his advice-to-writers dictum in 1988, in a speech at the University of Louisville. The friend I was with objected to his remarks, on the grounds that they were blasphemous. I disagreed but for years was unable to articulate my reasons. This troubled me until, during a reading of "Furthurmore" when it was still a work in progress, it suddenly dawned on me: That's not God, that's the Devil! And not only are the righteous *permitted* to say "Fuck you!" to the Devil, they're practically *enjoined* to do it!

roused myself out of my torpor long enough to get off a pretty good one-liner of my own. But modesty forfends—so I'll let Lee tell it for me:

"The lowest point so far," he wrote in one of his syndicated pieces, "was at Dunnigan, north of Vacaville, where we finally stopped, at 3:30 AM, after a night of Prankster music and hallucinations, to get some sleep in a crummy flat place just off the freeway. Here were a dozen or so of us jammed sideways in the bus, bodies bent and twisted between coolers and cameras and other trappings and paraphernalia, the whole joint reeking of the vaporous effects of the elk-and-bean chili we had eaten at a stopover dinner with friends up in the Oregon Vortex, none of us really comfortable enough to sleep. As we lay there, mind-goblins dancing out at the edges of our vision, each of us feeling just damned miserable, McClanahan, in a send-up of the Old Milwaukee beer commercial, said loudly:

"'Y'know, fellas, it just doesn't get any better than this!'"

Meanwhile, I too plugged doggedly away at my scribblings, laboriously (or so it seemed) taking notes for my Major Magazine assignment, but my heart wasn't in it; I still had some loitering to do, the paler the better. Old friends abounded, popping up like transparent purple bunnies (Peter Najarian! Mountain Girl! Vic! Jane! Stark Naked! Bob Hunter! Chloe! Jim! Page Stegner! Candace!), new friends (I think particularly of Wally and Roseanna and Roseanna's beautiful mother Regina, who opened their splendid Marin County home to this roving band of superannuated hipsters, flipsters, and finger-poppin' granddaddies*) raised my spirits amazingly. But some essential portion of me was still . . . elsewhere and couldn't be reached.

The day we campaigned for Wavy Gravy was one of those picture-perfect California fall days, all golden sunshine and cerulean skies with little white clouds like puffs of smoke from God's own hookah. A three-man Dixieland ensemble was tootling merrily away on the little caboose platform at the rear of the bus, and a small army of Gravyites in big flappy shoes and outsized polka-dot pants and goofy hats and Bozo wigs and rubber noses surrounded us as we rolled slowly through the winding, flower-bedizened streets of the Berkeley hills, cheering on groovy ole Gravy as he stood atop the bus in all his clownery, making madcap—or just plain mad—campaign speeches over

---

* With another tip of the McClanahat to Lord Buckley.

the loudspeaker ("Yup, I always wanted to assassinate Nixon with a ballpoint pen, so I could say, 'Eat Bic, Dick!'"). Yet even at the daffiest, dizziest apex of the hijinks, hard truths obtruded.

"See that church over there," Lee said to me, gravely, amidst the merriment. "My son's funeral was in that church."

Later that day, during what might be described as a preemptive nonvictory party at Wavy's Hog Farm commune in downtown Berkeley, I happened to be in the kitchen with Lee and Ken, while the party roared in the other room. The two of them stood there by the kitchen sink in a broad beam of late-afternoon sunlight, the featured players in what was—and is—for me, a deeply moving tableau.

"Up in the hills today," Lee told Ken, "we went past the church where my son's funeral was held."

"You never get over it," Ken said softly.

"Yeah," Lee said. "And you never want to."

"Right," said Ken. "It's how you keep them with you."

Compared to grief, I was beginning to discern, dying is a breeze.

Mutiny! On only our eighth day out, at the University of the Pacific in Stockton, while Ken is in the auditorium doing a reading and signing books, a lawless minority of the crew commandeers the bus and mysteriously disappears it somehow into the California night, leaving only its chalked outline and the cryptically disarming old Prankster motto NOTHING LASTS inscribed on the pavement.

There are rumors they've absconded to Reno to blow the booty they discovered in the hold, but the more likely story is that they took the backstreets out of Stockton, paused somewhere north of town just long enough to hide Furthur's exuberant exterior under a quick coat of water-soluble powder-blue church-bus anonymity (with MT. PISGAH SCHOOL FOR THE DUMB emblazoned on the sides), and high-tailed it back to Oregon— perhaps the only mutiny in maritime history planned down to the last detail by the captain of the ship.

What, then, was the point of it all? If he never intended to complete the journey, if he had no intention whatsoever of presenting *any* bus to the Smithsonian, or even of driving this cherry new edition to D.C. just to give the stuffy old Institution's leg a well-deserved pulling, if, fer crissakes, he wasn't even interested in promoting and selling his own book, why did Kesey go to the huge bother and expense of setting out on this foredoomed misadventure in the first place? Why assemble a crew and call in the media and assert his considerable presence upon the public consciousness once again, when he knew from the word go that the end of the line would come, God save us all, in Stockton?

As those who love Ken and know the history of his endeavors have long since come to understand, his purposes were, as ever, many and varied, great and small, selfless and self-serving, artistic and political, cosmic and comic, complex and simple-minded.

But my own short-form answer goes something like this: He wanted expressly to effect a reappearance of Furthur (remember Zapata's horse?) in this time of terrible national ennui, a time when the revolutionary spirit of the '60s seemed moribund, extinguished, buried beneath the rubble of the recent past.

And it worked. Wherever we took the bus, from the shopping mall in Roseburg, Oregon, to the streets of Berkeley, it was greeted by smiles of recognition, honking horns, upraised fists, and more V signs (okay, peace signs, if you insist) than I'd seen in twenty years. On a cold, windy weekday midnight, in the parking lot of a convenience store on the outskirts of Weed, California, it instantly drew a crowd of admirers; in Portland and Berkeley and San Francisco and Palo Alto, it drew sweet, mild-mannered little mobs. Even to those unfamiliar with its fossilology, Furthur seemed—seems— almost immediately to suggest personal liberation, artistic freedom, gaiety, joy; everywhere one sensed an almost palpable wonder in the air, and felt oneself present at the rebirth of a frail, nascent kind of hope.

"We have to reestablish the whole idea of *trust* in this nation," Kesey declared in that rousing speech in Berkeley. "The war is not on drugs, it's on consciousness. If Jesse Helms wants to lock horns with God, I can take him up there and introduce him in twenty minutes. But it won't be the Southern Baptist God with the big voice and the white beard, it'll be the God of the stars and the lights and the planets and the colors. The government says we should Just Say No. But I think we should just say . . . Thanks!"

My most treasured memento of the trip is a snapshot (taken by David Stanford, Ken's editor at Viking) of myself sitting atop the bus as we cruised down the coast highway toward Santa Cruz. The blue Pacific's on my right, the wind is in my face, and I look happier than I'd been in months.

Which reminds me: Thanks, Ken. Thanks a million.

And so it ended. I came back to Kentucky and faced up to the grim realization that even in Port Royal, the more things change, the more they change. I spent a miserable, restless winter trying to come to terms with living alone in the big, empty farmhouse that echoed mercilessly with ten years' worth of memories. The weeds had taken the garden, the dogs had taken the sheep, the possums had taken the chickens—except for four wretched roosters who'd so far survived the watches of the night by huddling together in the top of a hickory tree. Otherwise, the livestock consisted solely of my old yellow, jake-legged tomcat, Sunset, who'd lived there as long as I had, and who somehow seemed, that winter, to be exactly as sad and lonesome as I was. I contemplated writing one more country song—"Four Roosters, a Tomcat, Old Grand-Dad, and Me"—but the title pretty much said it all, so I never got beyond it.

During the winter, the possums picked off the surviving roosters, one by one, and the Major Magazine cut my allotted three thousand words to three hundred, and ran it as a photo caption under an immense depiction of Ken atop the bus in some sort of goofy pirate get-up, clowning around. It's time I stopped writing about this guy, I told myself; after all, it would be nice to be the protagonist of my own life story.

There was one more shining bus-trip moment, though: I was talking to KC on the phone one evening in the dead of that dismal winter, burdening him yet again with my usual litany of woe and affliction, when he asked me if I recalled crossing the Golden Gate Bridge in the bus, back in the fall.

I did remember it, vividly, because there had been a little group of people, gaily dressed as if they were celebrating something, gathered on the pedestrian walkway in the middle of the bridge, and when Furthur came toddling along they all got wildly excited, waving and jumping up and down and applauding and so forth; some of them, as I recalled, even threw flowers. But why did he ask?

Well, KC explained, that was a group of Drew's friends and family. They were gathered there that morning, more than three months after his death, to cast his ashes into the Bay, and say one last goodbye. And when the bus happened along at just that moment, they unanimously (and, no doubt, quite correctly) took it as a blessing, a benediction.

Just say, "Oh, wow."

By the time spring came creeping in at last, and the crocuses had pushed their little elfin heads up through the snow, I knew I'd never make it through another winter in that house. So I put it on the market and, to my surprise, sold it almost immediately. Then I went to Lexington, sixty miles away, where I had family and friends beyond number, and found a cottage that seemed ideally suited to be a disconsolate old bachelor's pad. I closed both transactions on the same day, around the middle of April 1991, and began to plan the move.

Two weeks later, on the first Saturday in May—which every Kentuckian knows from birth is Derby Day—I went to a Derby party near Lexington, and there I met a tall, beautiful Belgian piano teacher named Hilda, who had the bluest eyes and the brightest smile and the prettiest ways I've ever been struck dumb by.

She also had, as I discovered on our first date, a monumental Great Dane—Lisa—not to mention a grand piano the size of a two-car garage. Nonetheless, after we had seen each other a few times, I'd regained my eloquence sufficiently to persuade her that we could all fit very nicely into this no-longer-disconsolate bachelor's humble pad.

"Sunset," I confided to my feline associate one mellow cocktail hour around the first of June, "everything's about to change again. We're gonna move to town, and live with two tall, beautiful foreign ladies. And Sunset, old top, you're gonna love it!"

Sunset said he'd drink to that.

Hilda and I were married on the last day of July 1991, on the very spot where we'd met, three months earlier.

Lisa and Sunset hit it off famously as well, and were a loving couple until three summers ago when Sunset became, alas, a widower.

Lexington, Kentucky, June 1997

DOG LOVES
ELLIE

On Labor Day weekend of 1948, my parents and I moved from Brooksville, Kentucky, population 700, twenty miles east to the Ohio River town of Maysville, population 7,000. I had arrived at last in the Celestial City.

I was just a month shy of sixteen, an about-to-be sophomore at my new school, Maysville High. I stood six feet two inches tall—a considerable height in them days, kids—and weighed 147 pounds; a year and a half ago, I'd been five-feet-five—and weighed 147 pounds. It was rumored, quite incorrectly, that I was gonna be a helluva basketball player. Secretly, I was afraid of my new height; it gave me vertigo.

During the first week of school, when I was also at the dizzying height of New Kid popularity, I made friends with a junior named Gene Manley, a jittery, bespectacled, round-chinned little guy who I thought was just unutterably cool. Well, damn, he *was* unutterably cool; he played drums in the school band, he dated cheerleaders, and best of all, he drove this nifty little '32 Ford roadster, a mustard-yellow ragtop with painted-on crimson flames blazing back from the radiator, a rumble seat, foxtails, ah-oo-gah horn . . . a flivver straight out of "Archie and Jughead." Talk about cool! On the Friday night of my very first week in Maysville, when I somehow insinuated myself into Gene's rumble seat—up front, riding shotgun, was an equally cool trumpet player named Johnny Gantley (think Ray Anthony! think *Young Man with a Horn*!)—I was, oh, my, elevated beyond imagination.

Now I was already familiar with Maysville's many ornamental features, and the one that had always most impressed me was the bridge, that lacey, graceful, mile-long silver arc with twin silver spires spanning the broad

Ohio to the little community of Aberdeen, which, according to my infor-mation, consisted solely of roadhouses, beer joints, and similar wholesome attractions. Over the next few years, I would become as intimate with that bridge and the interesting diversions at its other end as I am, nowadays, with the route to my refrigerator. That first night, though, I knew only that every time Gene and Johnny and I putt-putted along East Third Street in Gene's flivver, past the sign pointing to Ohio, I experienced an unsettling little premonition that if I ever crossed that bridge for real, there might be no coming back.

Along about ten o'clock, on our umpty-umpth tour of East Third Street, we discovered that the entry to the bridge was blocked by a fire engine and two police cars—the entire fleet, basically, of Maysville's emergency-response rolling stock—all with their spotlights trained on the near spire of the bridge.

What was going on, it turned out, had begun one night exactly a month ago, when a notorious Maysville bon vivant named Wild Bill Dugan had clambered drunkenly but intrepidly up—and up, and up—the swooping catwalk to the very peak of the spire, a hundred and fifty vertiginous feet or so above the murky waters, before the cops and firemen hauled him down. They gave him thirty days for public drunkenness and disorderly conduct—and tonight, the minute they let him out, he had scurried straight back up, to finish off the remains of the fifth of gin he'd stashed up there . . . exactly one month ago.

But that was actually my second introduction to the high life that awaited me in cosmopolitan, metropolitan Maysville, home of the famous Browning Manufacturing Company—which was merely the World's Largest Pulley Factory, you understand—and the soon-to-be-famous Rosemary Clooney and the already famous Maysville High basketball team, the Bulldogs.

Having started life in Brooksville, where hatred for Bulldogs was like mother's milk, I grew up a loyal Brooksville Polar Bear. (Hey, I made the junior high team! I averaged eight points . . . a season!) In small-town Ken-tucky in those years, high school basketball was assumed to be one of the pillars of Western civilization—or perhaps it was the other way around. The Polar Bears came by their name honestly, the original Brooksville teams having played their first few seasons in an unheated tobacco warehouse. Later, in the early 1920s, the heyday of girls' basketball, my own mother and several of her sisters were star Polar Bears in Brooksville High's brand-new basketball palace, a modest little brick outbuilding with a playing court hardly bigger than a ping-pong table, the same gym I, too, would play in, utterly without distinction, twenty years hence. Girls' basketball, stifled by the imposition of a plethora of dispiriting rules intended to "effeminize" (or, if you prefer, "demasculinize") the sport, had by the 1940s been dropped by most Kentucky schools, including Brooksville High. Meanwhile, the boys' version of the game had become more popular than God, and the Polar Bears, despite their meager home-court circumstances, had an honorable—indeed a glorious—history: In 1939, led by Mooney and Marvin Cooper, top guns of the sixteen(!) fabled Cooper brothers, they won the state championship, a Cinderella accomplishment of *Hoosiers* proportions; and subsequent Coopers and Cooper cousins beyond number—Earl, Clyde, Dale, John Foster, the Yelton boys, et al.—had kept the Polar Bears in contention in the Tenth Region ever since.

But Maysville strode the Tenth like a very Yao Ming throughout the 1940s, and the Bulldogs were in the state tournament almost every year; in '47 they won it all, and in '48, just six months before we moved to town, they were runners-up. I, meanwhile, had largely been a plump, bespectacled little meatball plugging along in Brooksville, twenty miles down the road, striving with all my pudgy, ineffectual might to hang on to my seat at the far end of the junior high team bench—until, in the summer before my freshman year, the growth spurt struck me like Captain Marvel's transmogrifying bolt of lightning, and suddenly, unaccountably, I was looking down on people I'd long been in the habit of looking up to.

This flabbergasting development assured me of a spot in the junior high Polar Bears' starting line-up—I was, after all, the tallest kid on the team—but did little to enhance my skills: I started every game that season . . . and barely eked out my annual eight points.

The truth is, Brooksville was deeply conflicted about Maysville, which boasted, just a short Long Dog ride away, all too many of the amenities we rustics hardly dared to dream of, such as a public swimming pool worthy of Esther Williams and a dime store and the White Light nickel-burger stand and Schine's Russell Theatre (a gorgeous arabesque fantasy with a statuette of a semi-nude houri in the lobby) and Kilgus's Drugstore (where, if you were quick about it, you could sneak a peek at an astonishing little *Readers'*

Digest-sized periodical called *Sexology*, in whose pages were displayed such pornopological images as a close-up photo of a certain primitive work of female body-sculpting called the Hottentot Apron—an image so arresting that it vividly endures in my memory even now, six decades later). There was even, rumor had it, a real live two-dollar lady of the evening, if you knew how to find her. It was enough to turn many a Brooksville boy's head . . . and mine was already swiveling like a klieg light.

From the Brooksville point of view, Maysville would've been the fabled City on the Hill, were it not that, topographically speaking, it was the other way around. Brooksville stands at the highest point of ground in Bracken County—its courthouse clock and water tower (both of which I have scaled, by the way) are visible for miles around—whereas Maysville crawls along the banks of the Ohio, three miles long and only six streets deep. River Rats, we called 'em, masking our envy with disdain. In Brooksville, we knew for a fact that the wily Maysville coach Earle Jones, Evil Genius of the Hardwood, had snatched the great Kenny Reeves, one of the best players in the state during the mid-1940s, away from humble circumstances over in Ohio somewhere, and was paying him untold sums of money to play for Maysville, just so those mangy Bulldogs could routinely have their way with our Polar Bears three times a year.

For the '47–48 season, my freshman year, Brooksville retaliated by importing a hulking, menacing center named Tony Maloney, a quasi-legal transplant from an upstate orphanage whose play was brutish enough to have left at least one opposing center in tears. (Tony's fate was to become the model for Monk McHorning, the title character of my novel, *The Natural Man*.) But not even Tony could roll back the annual tide of humiliation; Maysville had dispatched us handily, as usual, in the regional, and then almost won the state championship for the second straight time.

Now my mom and dad were just as whacked out about basketball as everyone else was (and is) in our enlightened state, so every year they took me with them to Louisville for the Sweet Sixteen (as the state tournament was inevitably called), which meant that every year I was allowed, on the grounds of cultural enrichment, to cut three days of school and have my own room in the Brown Hotel and run around loose in downtown Louisville and watch a lot of great high school basketball. And every year the Bulldogs, having once again eliminated the hapless Polar Bears in the regional tournament, showed up in Louisville with the classiest teams and the most fetching cheerleaders in the Commonwealth—so that, over time, my favorite quadrupeds and secret heroes (don't breathe a word of this in Brooksville) had become not Polar Bears but Bulldogs—Kenny Reeves and Buddy Gilvin and Buddy Shoemaker and Gus Stergeos and Elza Whalen and Emery Lacey and the Tolle brothers, Fats and Shotsie, and most of all, in the '47 Sweet Sixteen, a pair of eighth graders the sportswriters had nicknamed Dog and Como, who were just my age and were already, in my personal pantheon of demigods, international celebrities.

So Labor Day of 1948, the day my folks and I moved to Maysville, was a watershed in my life. That very day I changed my name, forever and ever, from "Sonny," the diminutive cognomen by which I'd been known (if at all) in Brooksville, to the relatively Brobdignagian "Eddie," as befit my new height; and that very evening a nice old lady of our acquaintance fixed Tall Eddie up with Carla Browning, of the Browning Pulley Works Brownings, and Carla and I went to a movie at the Russell Theatre and then to Kilgus's Drugstore for Cokes, and right there on Kilgus's corner, Carla introduced me to . . . omigawd, it's . . . Dog and Como!

My apostasy was complete. Go Bulldogs!

A few months earlier I couldn't have dreamed that these two paladins of the hardwood (I myself was an aspiring sportswriter, and that sort of language was my soul's own music) would soon become not just my classmates but also my running mates and even, for one brief, inglorious season, my teammates, fellow Bulldogs.

Como was a handsome guy—some imaginative scribe had fancied, not unreasonably, that his profile resembled that of the redoubtable Perry—a fiery, red-faced demon on the basketball court but, off it, as sweet—and about as thick—as a Kilgus chocolate malt.

Dog, on the other hand, was significantly less handsome but appealing nonetheless, a stocky, eager little ball-handler and ball-hawk—the sports pages had dubbed him "Bulldog" not because they identified him with the team but just for his relentless tenacity on the floor—with deep, fawning brown eyes resembling a beagle's more than a bulldog's and an earnest, almost imploring manner that made him hard to resist when he asked you for "butts" on your current cigarette (meaning he got to smoke the last half of it) or wanted to copy your math homework or mooch a dime for the pinball machine at the White Light or even, on the basketball court, any time you had the ball and he didn't, a circumstance likely to reverse itself in your next heartbeat. When he turned those great, pleading brown eyes on you, he could steal the ball or your smoke or your homework or your dime—or, as I would find out all too soon, your heart's delight—with no more conscience than a stockbroker.

I believe I mentioned, a few pages back, something about my familiarity with the ornamental features of Maysville, and how the bridge to Aberdeen was my favorite—but that was before I'd seen Ellie Chadwick.

Ellie was—and she remains—the loveliest fifteen-year-old who's ever bedazzled my unworthy eyes. (I exclude from this equation, of course, my own three lovely daughters, each of whom was once fifteen.) Inside my head I've been humming wordless paeans to Elinora Chadwick's beauty for almost sixty years, but now that I'm obliged, at last, to attempt an actual description of her, words fail me, and I find myself grasping at the stalest of clichés: flaxen hair shimmering like a sun-struck field of . . . well, damn, of flax, I guess, eyes as blue as cornflowers, peaches-and-cream complexion, a smile to rival the lights of Broadway, a lilting voice, a figure wonderfully, sumptuously voluptuous yet at the same time as lissome as a willow switch, a girl fairly born to drive schoolboys to distraction, to inhabit their dreams both waking and sleeping, as though she'd been atomized and then dispersed all at once like a swarm of tiny Tinkerbells into the fevered imaginations of a multitude of Maysville's Lost Boys. So it was comforting—sort of—to know that at least I had company, plenty of it, legions of hopeless juvenile devotees just like me, all worshipping at the same shrine.

There was, however, one brief moment when I was *not* amongst that wretched number, one mortal instant in the measureless history of love when I alone of all the others stood before Ellie beneath a harvest moon and placed my trembling hands upon her perfect cashmere-sweatered shoulders and gently drew her to me and . . .

But I precede myself (a special talent of mine, as you may have noticed). Like every other schoolboy in Maysville, I fell for Ellie on sight, in my case in Miss Wallingford's English class on the first morning of school in the fall of '48, only twelve hours or so after Carla Browning had introduced me to Dog and Como. Carla, a very pretty girl who, unfortunately for whatever dreams I might have harbored overnight of becoming the premier tycoon of the pulley empire, went off to some fancy girls' school somewhere the very next morning after our bogus date and basically disappeared from my life forever. But Carla was no sooner beyond the city limits on that memorable morning when, downtown at MHS, just as the late bell began to jangle, the door to Miss Wallingford's ten o'clock English class opened and into my life stepped—be still, my heart!—Ellie Chadwick!

All that semester in English class, she sat in the row to the left of mine, one seat ahead, so that for fifty minutes every morning her immaculate profile was before me, a lovely, enigmatic ivory cameo. In homage to its alabaster perfection, I taught myself to write "Ellie" in the margins of my grammar workbook (the ever-popular *Keys to Good Language*) in fat, overlapping letters resembling nothing so much as a handful of amorous caterpillars at the height of the mating season.

Still, smitten and stricken beyond salvation though I inconsolably was, during those first few weeks at Maysville High, I became, as a Bulldog of far greater repute in prospect than I would ever be in retrospect, the Wild Bill Dugan of MHS society, scaling hitherto-unimagined heights of popular regard. Which brings us—almost—to that tremendous moment beneath that tremendous harvest moon. But first, a little scene-setting:

From the time I was old enough to pay attention to the funny papers, my favorite had been the strip called "Li'l Abner," by Al Capp. Abner, as everyone of my dwindling generation will recall, was a strapping, handsome young hillbilly, sweet but none too bright (not unlike my new friend Como), as evidenced by the fact that he preferred, unaccountably, the company of his pet pig Salome to that of his girlfriend Daisy Mae, a scantily clad, impossibly curvaceous cartoon rendition of . . . Ellie Chadwick! It was true! Daisy Mae really did look just like Ellie!

Okay, right, I need to take a deep breath here. But Daisy Mae *was* a dish, just as Abner was a dope, and therefore every year she pursued him, relentlessly but fruitlessly, in the annual autumnal Sadie Hawkins Day chase, wherein if a gal caught a fella, he had to marry her. And so popular was the strip that every autumn, on a certain Friday evening in practically every high school gymnasium throughout the land, there would be a Sadie Hawkins Day girl-take-boy dance, the only event of the year when the ladies were afforded the opportunity to select their escorts. And one morning in the autumn of 1948, only a couple of weeks before fall basketball practice would be exposing me (I didn't exactly know this yet, but I deeply feared it) for the fraud that I certainly was, who do you think Ellie Chadwick invited to the Sadie Hawkins Day Dance? Not Li'l Abner, not Dog or even Como, but Tall Eddie Clammerham, the Future of the Bulldogs!

It was, I think, the closest call I've ever had with immortality. I was just arriving at the door of Miss Wallingford's English class when Ellie approached me, her books clutched to her bosom in the protective manner favored by schoolgirls in those pre-backpack days, and looked up at me with those dazzling blue eyes and smiled her dazzling smile and asked, so sweetly that I could almost feel my blood sugar level soar, if she could take me to the dance next week.

Take me? cried my inner juvenile delinquent. *O God, yes, take me anywhere, and use me horribly!* Meanwhile, my candy-assed outer post-adolescent, his knees knocking like castanets as he shuffled his great cumbrous feet somewhere way down there at the bottom of his interminable legs, stammered, "Um, um, um . . ."

Somehow, we arranged it: I would be Ellie Chadwick's date for the Sadie Hawkins dance. Within the closely guarded ranks of post-adolescent boys in those days—and doubtless in these days as well—it was the practice to trumpet one's conquests to the heavens ("I got bare braw!" an erstwhile Polar Bear teammate of mine had once proclaimed ecstatically after an away-game ride home on the team bus, with the cheerleaders aboard), yet as best I could determine by discreetly inquiring amongst my peers, Ellie had never yielded so much as the first kiss. Indeed, it was said that, due to her conservative parents' restrictions, she'd never even had a date! To borrow Li'l Abner's favorite exultation, O happy day!

There was, however, one small problem: I couldn't dance. In Brooksville, girls would sometimes dance with each other, but—perhaps for that very reason—Brooksville boys generally ranked the terpsichorean arts somewhere down around needlepoint. Whereas in Maysville, many of my new friends, boys and girls alike, had matriculated at Mrs. Brown's School of the Dance when they were in the sixth or seventh grade, and by the time they got to high school they had all the moves down cold, and could dip and twirl like Fred and Ginger and jitterbug like Archie and Veronica. Making matters worse, those who hadn't gone to Mrs. Brown's had learned from those who had, so that every kid in Maysville would be dancing circles around the Bracken County bumpkin, laughing and pointing and belittling—the last being, I feared, the aspersion of choice. My new manhood, my vaunted Eddie-ness, would be puckered to the merest trifle before I'd danced a single step.

During those first few weeks of school, I'd made friends with a junior named Darrell Henson, who owned a huge, boxy, Capone-era Hudson sedan that some dead uncle had bequeathed him, and who was dating another of my pretty classmates, Lucia Traxel, who happened to live in my neighborhood. So I proposed to Darrell that we double-date for the Sadie Hawkins Day ordeal, and to Lucia that she undertake, in the scant seven days remaining to us, to teach me how to tango.

Or at any rate how to do the box-step, which, despite dear Lucia's best efforts, proved to be the very maximum that she could accomplish in those seven desperate evenings of stumbling about with me in the Traxel family's basement rec room to the dreamy airs of Guy Lumbago and His Royal Pains issuing from an ancient wind-up Victrola. As its name suggests, the box-step—one step forward, one step right, one step back, one step left, one step forward—is a stiff, plodding, robotic sort of business, the ballroom equivalent to marching in place, performed largely in disregard or defiance of whatever music actually happens to be playing at the moment. If that lonely old blind man who taught Dr. Frankenstein's creation how to smoke had also undertaken to teach the monster how to dance, rest assured they would've done the box-step.

It probably didn't help that, on the eve of Sadie Hawkins Day, I had used my sixteenth-birthday money to buy myself what I'd imagined would be the coolest footwear on the dance floor, a pair of blue suede Thom McAns with two-inch-thick crepe soles, cosmic clod-hoppers that weighed about eight pounds apiece and rendered me even taller and gawkier than I'd been in my old penny-loafers, and my lumbering box-step even clumsier and more Frankenstinian than it had been in Lucia Traxel's basement. The music, once again, was recorded; I seem to recall that the first number was "A Slow Boat to China," and being torn between the dreamy escapism of the song ("I'd love to get you . . . on a slow boat to China . . . all to myself, a-lo-o-o-one . . . ") and the more immediate exigency of somehow escaping the agonies of the moment at hand. Ellie was as supple and lissome and light on her feet as a forest nymph, but I was steering her on a herky-jerky forced march to nowhere, and as we lurched about inside our invisible little box, I could detect, through the agency of the hand that now rested ever-so-tentatively at the (sigh) small of her back, a tiny, involuntary wince—call it a shudder—at every misstep (and there were many) of those monstrous blue suede concrete blocks I was wearing. The slow boat to China hadn't even left the harbor, yet already it was sinking like a stone, and its cabin boy—that kid with the concrete feet—was well on his way to becoming a hat-rack for the fishes.

They must've played a couple more slow numbers in the early going, but hey, I was *dancing*, folks, I didn't have *time* to listen to music! I had been given to understand, I guess from movie musicals, that I was expected to initiate bright, scintillating conversation as we danced, but I was dumbstruck. Incapable of thinking and talking and dancing all at the same time—multitasking, we'd call it nowadays—I mindlessly, mutely propelled poor Ellie from invisible pillar to invisible post as, suffering like a penitente and sweating like a stevedore, I trod on her no doubt lovely little toes as though I were stomping slugs in the garden—or the graveyard—of my hopes and dreams.

That unhappy phase of my extremity ended—and another began—when someone put Glen Miller's "Chattanooga Choo-Choo" on the turntable, which of course required one—or, rather, two—to jitterbug, and in turn required me to confess to Ellie, shamefacedly, that jitterbugging was utterly beyond my powers. I got through that mortification somehow, but as I steered Ellie toward the bleachers to sit this one out, who should pop up before us but that devilishly cool rascal Gene Manley, eager to boogie. Ellie graced me with a quick, apologetic smile, and then the choo-choo jitterbugged on down the line and left me standing in the station with the other wallflowers, in a sort of penumbra of commingled regret and relief.

Gene, who was such a tightly wound little bundle of nervous energy that he had no patience for slow dancing, delivered Ellie back to me when "Chattanooga Choo-Choo" gave way to some less vigorous tune, but we had barely made it back onto the dance floor when Johnny Gantley tapped me on the shoulder, cutting in. Johnny clung to the advantage for a couple of numbers until I.Jay Weaver, a smooth-talking senior, cut in on him, and then the ever-dangerous Como cut in on I.Jay, and then I myself, Eddie the Unready, swung boldly into action and cut in on Como, but before Ellie and I had managed even one full turn around the narrow confines of the little rectangular plot of hardwood I'd staked out, Dog—him and his big, beseeching brown eyes and his ingratiating goddamn ways—cut in on me, that dirty Dog, and away they waltzed!

Well, it was that kind of evening. The enemy was legion, and He was everywhere, in the persons of Gene and Johnny and I.Jay and Como and most of all the omnipresent, indefatigable Dog. There were, of course, a host of other interlopers as well, but none with so much staying power, such irritating perseverance, such . . . dare I say it? . . . such sheer doggone *doggedness.* By eleven o'clock, when whoever was "spinning the platters" (an infelicitous locution that I sincerely hope turned into library paste in the mouth of the very first deejay who ever uttered it) signaled that the dance was over by putting Ray Noble's oleaginous "Good Night, Sweetheart" on the turntable, Dog had danced with Ellie about twice as many times as I had. Indeed, in order to dance the last dance with my own date, I had to cut in on *him*—and as he reluctantly released her to my custody (temporarily, as it turned out), he turned those great beseeching eyes on *me* . . . and hit me for a cigarette!

I'm pretty sure that after the dance, Darrell and Lucia and Ellie and I would've piled into Darrell's giant Hudson shoebox (a few months later, Darrell would put that old Hudson right through the front wall of some poor citizen's living room) and mo-gated up East Second Street to Mrs. Hedges's East End Café for carbonated aperitifs, and logistics would've dictated that we take Ellie home first. Most of that has drifted away, though, into the mists of teenage history. But I do recall, luminously, that when Ellie and I arrived at her front door, that luminous harvest moon was looking down, and Ellie's luminously lovely face was looking up, and . . .

I'm tempted to describe our kiss as having been as tender and delicate and fleeting as a butterfly taking sweetness from a flower, except that I was certainly no butterfly. Nonetheless, with uncharacteristic courage, I wordlessly claimed the kiss and, to my astonishment, was granted it. Afterward, butterfly-like for once in my life despite that dead-weight ballast of blue suede brogans, I floated off Ellie's front porch and back to Darrell's car in a perfect transport of delight. I could've plucked that harvest moon from the sky and put it in my pocket for a keepsake.

The next day, a Saturday, I was still all a-flutter until I was brought crashing back to earth when I called Ellie and asked if I could take her to the Sunday night movies at the Russell, and she apologized (not very sincerely, I must say, although she tried to be kind) for the fact that she already had a date: Dog, of course. I didn't even need to ask; I knew when I was whupped.

From that Sunday evening forward for the next three years, Ellie and Dog were as one, and to my knowledge Ellie never strayed. True love was true love, after all, and the Maysville High ladies generally kept things strictly on the up-and-up, and did but rarely go a-roaming. They were, by and large, Nice Girls, and in those days Nice Girls just didn't do that sort of thing. Despite that one delicious, indelible kiss, Ellie Chadwick, a very nice girl if ever there was one, would be, alas, forever out of reach, at least for me.

Dog, on the other hand, ran with the pack (of which I was a panting, slavering member), and on many an evening, after we had taken whatever minimal liberties were allowed us by the Nice Girls and had (metaphorically) put those vestal virgins to bed, we—the pack—were ourselves at liberty to go on the prowl, perpetrating all manner of after-hours outrages and indignities upon the public weal. Lured by those beckoning beer-joint signs, neon lodestars in the night, we crossed that stupendous bridge to Aberdeen and found our way to the Pennington Club and the Terrace Club and Danny Boone's Tavern and the Hi-Hat, and discovered that, as far as Buckeye bartenders were concerned, we were all absolutely eighteen years old, and legally entitled to drink all the 3.2 beer we required. After last call for alcohol at those accommodating venues, we were as likely as not to arrive, eventually, back in Maysville at the address of that even more accommodating— and even less discriminating—two-dollar lady down on Front Street. More often than not, Dog was an enthusiastic party to these revels, while Ellie, all unknowing, slept the untroubled sleep of the innocent.

Thus it came to pass that, heartbroke and forsook, I comforted my wounded teenage person during my high school years with tobacco, beer, pool, and all the complimentary debauchery I could get away with—not much— during double dates at the drive-in theater, and all the commercial debauchery I could afford—which, after I'd budgeted for beer and smokes and pool, didn't amount to much either. My height, meanwhile, secured me one last eight-point season, this time as an apprentice Bulldog at the far end of the JV bench, after which Coach Jones reminded me that height wasn't everything, and suggested that I look into some other extracurricular activity, glee club or debate or something along those lines.

Ellie Chadwick was a varsity cheerleader by then, but—alas, alas—she would never cheer for me. All hope must be abandoned; it was probably just as well that I'd already gone ahead and consigned my soul to the devil anyhow.

To finance my expensive new appetites, I spent most of the summer of '49 in a tobacco patch up on the hill above town, a long, narrow, mercilessly sun-baked strip of worn-out, yellow hardpan along the backbone of a ridge, chopping out weeds with a garden hoe at fifty cents per interminable row of stunted tobacco plants, which broke down to four dollars a day. I knew the story of Sisyphus and the great stone, and was frequently reminded of it during my own grim labors, by the way the weeds seemed to spring back up out of the ground almost as soon as I smote them down. But not even Sisyphus had to confront sweat bees and deer flies, armed only with a garden hoe, for four dollars a day. It was time to reconsider my career options.

That fall I accepted an after-school position presiding over the soda fountain at Kilgus's, pulling down a cool forty-five cents an hour. (The post, it seemed to me, wanted a dash of flash, so I taught myself to scoop one of those bulbous little five-cent fountain Coke glasses down into the shaved-ice bin, flip it end-over-end into the air without losing a single shaving, and catch it one-handed under the syrup spigot with the other hand already on the handle, ready to dispense a dash of the black, unpromising sludge that was the foundation of a fountain Coke.) And there were other compensations for working at Kilgus's: milkshakes to be guzzled and cigarettes to be pilfered and copies of *Sexology* to be spirited away and perused in the privacy of one's own . . . privacy. Girls came and went in Kilgus's in bewitching profusion from the minute school was out till closing time at nine (a few of them, I'm happy to report, specifically to marvel at my artistry with those Coke glasses), and the street corner right outside the drugstore was where I and all my friends hung out after hours, loafing and smoking and trading dirty jokes and trying to cadge rides to the bright lights of Aberdeen. Kilgus's corner was, in fact, the very crossroads of Western civilization . . . and don't think we didn't know it.

Ellie, like most of the high school girls, wasn't allowed to date on school nights, so Dog was usually prominent among us. Como, on the other hand, rarely showed up on Kilgus's Corner; rumor had it that he had taken up with the amorous, buxom, forty-something wife of a local grocer, and had but little time for boyish pursuits.

(Como's exertions in the backseat of the unwary grocer's car hadn't rendered him any sharper, though. Once, when he was a guest on Coach Jones's sports-talk show on WFTM, the local radio station, Coach asked him how many points he'd racked up so far that season. "Gee, I don't know, Coach," Como answered modestly. "About, oh, two hundred and thirty-four.")

After I hired on at Kilgus's, I worked evenings during the summer in the drugstore and supplemented my income with daytime jobs in construction as a hod-carrier and pick-and-shovel guy. On Sunday afternoons in the wintertime I even served a stint as a cub reporter for the Maysville *Daily Independent*—or, as one of my wiseguy fellow knights of the plume liked to call it, the *Daily Disappointment*—writing obituaries for the Monday edition, an apprenticeship from which I received numerous early and unsettling intimations of mortality.

The Bulldogs continued to prosper as a Tenth Region powerhouse, although during my tenure at Maysville High they never quite made it back to the Sweet Sixteen. Como, nonetheless, played inspired basketball, and made the all-state list every year; when we graduated in '51, he was offered a full-ride scholarship by the fabled University of Kentucky Wildcats. Dog also played brilliantly but always in Como's shadow, and by college basketball standards he was, as the unkind old joke has it, "short . . . but slow." No scholarship materialized, and as soon as Ellie left for the exclusive southern college she'd long since planned to attend, he would be enlisting in the Air Force. Her family left town soon thereafter, so she rarely—if ever—came back to Maysville during her college years. To my knowledge, she and Dog never had another date.

As for me, I too matriculated at a snooty southern college, which I loathed, and then transferred, as a sophomore, to Miami of Ohio, where I changed my name again, this time from "Eddie" to "Ed," having discovered that it was my fate to become, or rather to try to become, a writer, and calculated, no doubt mistakenly, that I'd be taken more seriously if I dropped the diminutive form. In pursuit of my muse, I eventually went west and spent most of the next twenty years writing and teaching at universities in

Oregon, California, and Montana, then landed, broke and jobless, back in Kentucky in the late '70s, this time to stay. In effect, I had re-crossed the bridge at last, very much the worse for the twenty years of wear and tear, and very glad I was to be back home again.

Como starred on the Wildcats' freshman team, but his GPA was about as robust as my old eight-points-per-season scoring average, and, as all who knew him could have predicted, he flunked out after one season. A pretty good high school baseball player, he then tried out with the Pittsburgh Pirates, who gave him a five-hundred-dollar bonus and signed him to a minor league contract. They sent him to play outfield for a Class-D team somewhere in the Midwest, but he "threw his arm away"—his term—making an ill-advised long throw to the plate in his very first game, and was home within a week. I never saw him again after that summer, and I don't know what he did with the balance of his life, but I do know that when he was in his late fifties or early sixties he got gut-shot by a woman—another predictable development—and died after months in the hospital. A friend told me that she went to see him during his final days, and that he was as handsome and sweet and sunny as ever.

The Air Force sent Dog to Japan during the Occupation, and I lost track of him for quite a while. After his tour in Japan was over, he made his way down south, went into business (snack foods distribution), married, had kids (including a daughter named, I heard, Elinora), divorced, remarried, and perhaps divorced and remarried again. In later years, whenever I came home to Kentucky to visit family and friends, I heard reports that Dog—who came home periodically for the same reasons—had never gotten over it, that the old torch was still burning bright, that he still carried Ellie's senior photo in his wallet. (I knew that photo well, having carried its duplicate in my own wallet throughout my undergraduate years.) According to one of the more romantic versions of the story, he'd even engaged a Tokyo street artist to do her portrait, taken from the same photo, and had cherished and venerated it ever since. I envisioned Ellie's portrait, flanked by the matched pair of gleaming, gold-plated All-Tournament trophies Dog had won in the Sweet Sixteen in '47 and '48, displayed in some sacred niche or grotto somewhere deep in the interior of every life he'd ever lived.

But for most of her admirers, the Ellie pipe dream went up in smoke when, after college, she married a no-doubt handsome young fellow from up east—I'm guessing he was a lawyer—went with him to New England, and became the mother of a couple of (I'm guessing again) lawyers. She eventually divorced, and never remarried.

So tempus fugited apace, and the next time I looked up, forty years had passed, and suddenly it was the spring of 1991, which would mark the fortieth anniversary of my high school graduation. As it happened, Maysville High was being gobbled up by a gargantuan new consolidated county school, and would be closing its doors forever that same spring. Plans were afoot for a grand all-day reunion of MHS alums on the first Saturday of June: There were to be speeches and recognitions and many, many soapy reminiscences, as well as a concert by the school band in which any old-timer who still had chops was urged to sit in. There would also be a sort of round-robin basketball game, in which all credentialed former Bulldogs—hey, remember that last eight-point season?—were invited to participate, cheered on by—uh, oh!—cheerleaders of yesteryear. That evening, the individual classes would split off for their own private dinners and parties.

For whatever reason, the class of '51 had never had a reunion of its own, and many of us hadn't seen each other for a long, long time. I knew that for most of my old classmates, it surely promised to be a very big day indeed. But in the early summer of 1990, my second marriage had, as I described it afterward, "blown up in my face as abruptly as a letter bomb," and ever since that dreadful cataclysm I had been wreathed in the miasma of a difficult and painful divorce. In the midst of so stygian a darkness, not even the beguiling fantasy of one last shot at roundball glory could dispel the gloom—not even with Ellie Chadwick cheering on the sidelines! The upcoming reunion was the last thing on my mind.

Then, on the first Saturday of May 1991, I dragged myself to a Kentucky Derby party in Lexington, where I met a beautiful Belgian classical pianist named Hilda and fell in love on the spot, and within two weeks we had decided that we'd marry the instant my divorce was final. As you might suppose, this prospect brightened my horizons amazingly. Suddenly, I was feelin' frisky! Go Bulldogs!

Hilda, who was still wrapping up a couple of courses in grad school at UK, couldn't make it, so I drove up to Maysville alone on the morning of the reunion, in the nifty new Dodge Dakota pickup I had just given myself as a tender little prenuptial wedding present. The town was busy, the sidewalks swarming with people, the way they used to be in the days before the coming of Wal-Mart and K-Mart and their attendant strip malls, when downtown Maysville was the Saturday shopping destination for the whole surrounding area of rural northeastern Kentucky and southern Ohio. I found a parking space just up the street from Kilgus's—remarkably, they were still in business—and set forth on foot for the MHS auditorium, where the festivities were already under way.

On Kilgus's Corner I spotted the first familiar face, that of a stocky, jowly little gent in a shiny green polyester suit and a necktie (although the day was already shaping up as a scorcher), who stood rooted there on the sidewalk like a fireplug as the pedestrian traffic surged about him. He was anxiously but furtively searching the faces of the passersby, as though he were looking for someone but didn't want to be noticed doing it. I knew immediately— those doleful brown eyes gave him away—that here was my long-ago hero and friend and rival, Dog. But just now he put me in mind of yet another canine personality, namely the bumbling old-time movie detective Bulldog Drummond. All that was wanted to complete the characterization was a derby hat.

When Dog saw me approaching, he quickly looked away, but then, tacitly acknowledging that he'd been recognized, he turned back to me and stuck out his hand in greeting.

"Hullo, Clammer," he said, forcing a smile. "How they hangin'?"

I allowed, as we shook hands, that they were hangin' pretty well, all things considered. Although it wasn't yet eleven AM, Dog's immediate aura was pungent with the redolence of what my long experience and highly refined olfactory sensibilities told me was blended whiskey, and not very good blended whiskey at that. His brow was beaded with sweat, and he was still glancing avidly at the faces in the passing parade—and I was pretty sure I knew who he was looking for. I asked him if he planned to play in the veteran Bulldogs' shoot-out that afternoon, and he answered, almost irritably, Nah, hell, no, and then—same old Dog—asked if I had a cigarette on me. I apologized for the fact that I'd stopped using them years ago, and he said Yeah, he had quit awhile back too, but for some reason he was really wanting one this morning. I laughed and said Hey man, a guy's *gotta* smoke on

Kilgus's Corner, it's the law! But Dog didn't seem to see the humor in that, so I said I'd catch him later, and set out again for the auditorium.

I crossed the street and paused in the shade of the marquee of the now-defunct Schine's Russell Theatre, to look back. Dog was still standing on the corner, scanning the crowded sidewalk, keeping a Bulldog Drummond eye out, I was sure, for the merest glimpse of Ellie Chadwick.

Inside the auditorium, the class of '87 or '86 or some other irrelevant year was doing its presentation, so I plunged into the large company of folks milling about outside. During the next hour, I reunited with untold numbers of old schoolmates: My great pal Ray Toncray was there with Shirley, his wife of thirty-eight years, for whose favors Ray and I had contended when she was still Shirley Collings, a sultry, smoky-voiced teen temptress; and Jannie Batchelor who, as Bernice Stonebreaker, is the Jezebel of "Great Moments in Sports," and Denyce and Joyce and Ann and June and my old sweetie Laura Lou, and dear Lucia, who failed so miserably to teach me how to trip the light fantastic; and Freddie Hamm, who beat me out for class salutatorian, the only academic honorific I was ever in the running for; and Jerry and Gera and Billy the Byrdman and Dody and Breezy and Dooner and Nancy and Tubby; and Gerry Calvert, who was, along with Como and the peerless Kenny Reeves, one of Maysville High's three immortals; and Willie Gordon Ryan, to whom (product placement alert!) *The Natural Man* is dedicated; and Bob Z., that rarest of rare birds, a loveable lawyer; and most piquant and soul-stirring of all, perhaps, my long-ago secret squeeze Yvonne (let's call her), still strikingly handsome in her mid-fifties, who had been my first genuine conquest when I was barely seventeen and she was . . . careful now . . . somewhat younger.

(Yvonne and I even managed to step away from the crowd outside the auditorium long enough to reminisce, briefly, about that all-too-brief occasion. "I'm afraid I wasn't really very good at it," I admitted ruefully. "Well, no," Yvonne acknowledged, "not very." And then she smiled and leaned closer and added, just above a whisper, what are surely the most generous words any woman has ever said to me: "But didn't we have fun!")

I caught a couple of glimpses of Dog lurking about the fringes of the gathering, alone and, as the poet has it, palely loitering. I figured I probably knew the reason for his melancholy, because so far I hadn't seen the first sign of Ellie Chadwick. After a third sighting of the crestfallen Dog, I sought out my old friend Ann Crockett, who was a principal organizer of the reunion, and asked if she knew whether Ellie planned to come down to Maysville for the celebration. Ann said she'd talked to Ellie last night on the phone—first time in years, Ann said—and that she'd promised to be here in time for the basketball game, and even to join the renascent cheerleaders as—I'm extrapolating now—they'd be strutting their vintage stuff in one last, rousing turn on the sidelines, while doddering Bulldogs lumbered up and down the hardwood trying to catch up with the elusive ghosts of their lost youth.

"She's a little nervous about . . . you-know-who," Ann confided. "She's afraid he might try to . . . start something."

Don't worry, I assured her, Dog's a good guy; once he sees it's not working, he won't do anything to embarrass himself. But Ann said she was actually thinking more along the lines of his doing something that might embarrass Ellie—and also, she reminded me pointedly, it was not for nothing that they'd named him Bulldog.

While Ann and I were talking, the reconstituted MHS band struck up a rather lame "My Old Kentucky Home" (Guy Lumbago lives!) and everybody hobbled into the auditorium as docilely as ninth graders on Assembly Day. Inside, the band labored through a few more numbers, after which the speeches resumed, with a vengeance; there were more class presentations (Class of '58, Class of '57, Class of '56 . . .), and interspersed with those were tributes—to Johnny Faris the legendary band director, to Miss Collins the legendary math teacher, to Miss Wallingford the legendary English teacher, and most especially to the legendary Coach Jones, who languished in a nursing home—and by the time the program got down to the class of '51, the basketball debacle had long since begun next door in the gymnasium, and virtually the entire audience had decamped and moved on to that more alluring venue.

Which was fine with me, except that a couple of days ago someone on the organizing committee had called me in Lexington and asked me to deliver a few remarks as a part of our presentation. So I had composed an amusing but highly edifying little address rhapsodizing that long-ago first night on the town with Gene and Johnny, featuring Wild Bill's death-defying aerobatics atop the bridge—and now I was obliged to off-load my poetic reflections upon an audience of about six restive souls in a small, once-familiar auditorium that had suddenly turned into the Hollywood Bowl.

That ordeal concluded (to a smattering of applause that barely eclipsed the sound of one hand clapping), I hurried over to the old gymnasium, where I found that there were still a few dozen fans in the stands, and that the classes of '50 and '51 had combined forces, and were challenging the classes of '52 and '53—call it the Geezers vs. the Gaffers—to a five-minute geriatric pick-up game. The band was there too, cranking out a wheezy rendition of "The MHS Fight Song" (*"It's a grand old school . . . And we follow the rule . . . And we fight for the gold and the white . . ."*). On the sidelines, far across the floor, was a gaggle of ladies in street clothes, flouncing and bouncing and capering and gamboling, chanting *"V-I-C-T-O-R-Y! Victory, Victory, Maysville High!"* In their midst—be still, my heart!—was Ellie Chadwick, looking, at least to my forgiving old eyes, as fresh and blonde and winsome and bountifully voluptuous as she had been forty years ago.

Way up in the upper left-hand corner of the grandstand, I spotted a small, roundish figure, all alone, roosting up there in the rafters like a pigeon with shiny green polyester plumage.

I took a seat on the bench and waited for one of my Geezer teammates to crap out. It didn't take long: After the doughty relics had pounded up and down the floor for two or three minutes, I.Jay Weaver, panting like a puff-erbelly—those Class of '50 guys are getting up in years, poor devils—took himself out of the lineup for a breather with the score knotted at 4-4, and into the breach strode . . . Eddie the Intimidator!

Now, as Tall Eddie takes the floor in the vast gymnasium of his imagination, a mighty roar arises, and Ellie Chadwick leads the multitudes—McClanafans all, their numbers magically swollen to the hundreds, the thousands, nay, the tens of thousands—in yet another full-throated cheer: *"He's a wonder, he's a dream! He's the captain of our team! Yay, rah rah, EDDIE!"* On the very first play, he soars like an eagle to block the great Gerry Calvert's lay-up, pulls down the rebound, drives the floor, and puts up a thirty-foot jumper! String music! *V-I-C-T-O-R-Y! Yay, rah rah, EDDIE!*

The reality, needless to say, was a little different: In that version, I distinguish myself only by getting bowled over by my old pal Ray Toncray—make that my former old pal—as he unleashes an up-yours jump shot in the final seconds that wins the game for the Gaffers, 8-6. When the buzzer sounds, concluding our allotted five minutes, I am ignominiously picking my elderly self up off the ancient and dangerously splintery hardwood. The band, meanwhile, has packed up and is already filing out of the stands, and the cheerleaders seem to have left the premises. Dog, apparently, has done likewise.

The class of '51 banquet was to be held that evening at a venerable Maysville establishment called Caproni's, down in the West End on—believe it!— Rosemary Clooney Street. There would also be an after-party at the Ramada Inn, where I and most of my out-of-town classmates were staying, the flag-ship attraction of a profoundly unlovely new strip mall up on the hill above town. So, my unaccustomed constitutional in that hothouse of a gym hav-ing left me as damp as a steamed clam, I repaired to the Ramada for a desperately needed shower and some fresh clothes and, thus improved and restored, a little before-dinner drink, in grateful celebration of the long-anticipated arrival of the cocktail hour.

I took my celebratory drink to the window of my second-floor room, where I stood gazing out upon the Ramada's asphalt parking lot and, beyond the rooftops of downtown Maysville far below, a panoramic vista of north-eastern Kentucky farmland stretching off to the distant horizon, rumpled as an unmade bed, with ridges and gullies and hollers fanning out into infinity. It was a scenic prospect that could have been duplicated from almost any eminent vantage point in that part of the state, but—I realized with a start as I stood there at the window, sipping my scotch from a motel-issue plastic cup while the air-conditioner blew frigid zephyrs up my pants legs—I'd seen this particular view before, under very different circumstances. For the Ramada Inn stands exactly athwart what was once the ridge-runner tobacco patch in which I'd labored through the dog days of 1949, performing mighty Sisipheyan deeds with my magic singing garden hoe.

And then I remembered something else: Forty-two summers ago, when I was plugging wearily along in that shadeless, sweltering tobacco patch, I was regularly sustained in my sufferings by the enduring fantasy that if and when I ever got to the end of this everlasting goddamn row—or the next one, or the next after that—I'd find there a great, spreading shade tree, and beneath it would be, yes, Ellie Chadwick, clad not in one of her usual mod-est schoolgirl frocks but in Daisy Mae's unvarying wardrobe—that skimpy, tattered skirt! that off-the-shoulder blouse! (you remember, the yellow one, with the big dark polka dots the size of chocolate chip cookies!)—my very own personal Ellie Chadwick, recumbent in the deep, cool grass, fetching as a stand of buttercups, an Ellie Chadwick blow-up doll filled to bursting with the Divine McClanafflatus, awaiting me with open arms!

I raised my plastic cup of scotch in tribute to the vision, even as it faded into the ether and left me toasting the sun-blasted Ramada parking lot, vacant now except for my blue Dakota pickup.

When I arrived at Cap's, our party was in full swing in the private dining room; there was a long banquet table all laid out for dinner, and a cash bar open for business, with many of my classmates and their assorted spouses gathered 'round it, drinking and reminiscing in approximately equal measure, as though there were no tomorrows, only yesterdays. I picked up a drink at the bar and, true to my bent, intrepidly plunged headlong into the revelry.

Once again, Dog's was the first familiar face I encountered, and as before, he was in the crowd, but not *of* it; he stood off to the side, a drink in one hand and a cigarette in the other, having a conversation of sorts with our old Bulldog teammate Willie Gordon Ryan. Dog's outer man had not been improved by the day's exertions, which had evidently required a considerable further infusion of blended whiskey. He still wore his wash-and-wear suit, but it had become rumpled and disheveled, in need of less wear and more wash; he'd unbuttoned his shirt collar and loosened his tie, to receive the evening airs, and his five o'clock shadow was asserting itself on his jowls with seven o'clock authority; and although he stood more or less upright, he seemed to list, ever so slightly, just a degree or two off the perpendicular, now to the left, now to the right, like the pendulum of a clock that needed winding.

Willie Gordon, who was usually taciturn but seemed at the moment to be in an animated conversational mode, was apparently trying to re-create a moment in some historic Bulldog game, shooting free throws with an invisible basketball, putting up imaginary shots in the old style—two-handed, from between the knees—that Coach Jones had insisted on. But Dog was so obviously not giving Willie Gordon's story his full attention that after a minute or two Willie Gordon gave it up, shrugged elaborately, and drifted off to freshen his refreshment. Dog barely noticed; his bleary but still discerning eye was drawn to the far corner of the room, beyond the banquet table, where there was a smaller table at which were assembled some half a dozen ladies—girls, if you please—Denyse and Joyce and Lucia and two or three others, Ellie Chadwick prominent among them. They were in deep confab over their drinks, taking sweet girlish counsel together, exactly as they used to do when they were talking about boys in their favorite booth at Kilgus's, back when the world was young. Judging from the wary sidelong glances that several of them—though never Ellie—darted now and then in Dog's direction, he was apparently the subject of their current speculations. Ellie herself steadfastly looked the other way, but, girls being girls, it was a pretty good bet that by now they'd brought her up to speed on the long history (as they understood it) of the grand romance in which she figured so prominently.

Ann Crockett, who happened to be standing next to me in the crowd around the bar, and who was observing this tableau as intently as I was, sighed and mused, almost to herself, "Poor fellow, he's still wild about her, isn't he." I said it looked to me like she had that about right, but that it didn't surprise me much, because so was I. "Oh, well," said Ann, with a smile and an empathetic wave of her hand that was intended to include every male in the room, "aren't you all?"

I didn't even need to concede the point, for there before me, beckoning like a shimmering beacon in the dark night of the soul, was Ellie's finely wrought profile, quite as exquisite as it had been that first morning forty-three years ago in Miss Wallingford's tenth-grade English class. As I approached her table she turned her lovely countenance full upon me—the force of it struck me like a cannonball smack to the brisket, yet somehow I managed not to stagger—and rose immediately to give me a hug, which was heartening, inasmuch as the very fact that she recognized me at all seemed, momentarily, to suggest that I was as unchanged by the years as she was—until I reminded myself that 1) she had presumably witnessed my heroics in the basketball game a few hours earlier, and 2) like everyone else in the room, I was wearing, pinned to my lapel, a name tag the size of a lawyer's shingle. Still, I was happy to be greeted so warmly by so beautiful a woman, and made doubly happy by her promise, before I moved along to say hello to someone at the next table, that we'd surely find a chance to talk later in the evening.

At dinner, I found myself seated opposite Ellie—imagine Scarlett Johansson as she'll be, if she's a very lucky girl, at 58 or 59—a circumstance so distracting that it has completely erased my recollection of who my neighbors at the table were, or of who Ellie's neighbors were, or of what was eaten, drunk, or said throughout that epic rubber-chicken repast—except for one brief but ineradicable memory, which, like those painful televised home videos of people making asses of themselves, is even now in re-run on the small screen of my memory. Here's how it goes:

After our devout classmate, the Very Rev. Lester G. Pullet, pastor of the East End Four Square Pentecostal Little Brown Kirk o' the Wildwood, has unburdened himself of pieties beyond number by way of saying Grace (while those of us who recall the obnoxiously priapic Le's Pullit of his formative years suppress the impulse to snort and snigger), the Class of '51 coughs and clears its collective throat, seats itself, takes up its knives and forks, and is just preparing to tuck into its rubber chicken, when I hear, off to my left, the tink-tink-tink of a fork against a water glass. Dog has risen unsteadily to his feet, as if to propose a toast, or—Heaven forefend, considering his condition—to make a speech. His eyes are rheumy and out of focus, and he has donned his old beseeching-mendicant mask, which must've served him well in the snack food sales game back in the day, but is now in a state of slow meltdown, like a beagle morphing into a basset hound. Everybody in the room pretty much knows what's coming, and braces for it.

Which brings us to a moment I've long dreaded—for I had hoped, when I undertook to tell this story, that all the principal characters in it (with the possible exception of myself and Wild Bill Dugan) would emerge with their dignity essentially intact. But here's this pudgy, unprepossessing sixty-year-old inebriate in rumpled polyester, determined against all odds to fulfill a fantasy he's entertained for forty years, ready and even eager to make a spectacle of himself before an audience of the oldest and most admiring friends he'll ever have, the last people on Earth who still remember him as the very best he'll ever be, the last of all those cheering multitudes in the stands at the old Armory gym in Louisville in '47 who still remember how he and Como trotted out to center court in the golden glow of the Armory spotlight, side by side in their sleek white-and-gold sateen Bulldog warm-up jackets, to claim the first two All-Sweet Sixteen trophies ever taken home by a pair of eighth graders.

(I was there too, I'll remind you, another eighth grader way up in the Armory stands somewhere, that plump little apostate Polar Bear benchwarmer who would've given several testicles—preferably other people's—for one of those Bulldog jackets.)

Dog's little speech that night at Cap's—it only lasted a couple of minutes—was eloquent, even though the miasma of blended whiskey had so befuddled his mind and befuckled his articulation that much of what he said was immediately lost to history, and even though what remained was basically just an expression of his life-long amber . . . adner . . . his ad-mi-*ray*-shun for . . . a shertain shpecial pershon (across the table, Ellie looked stricken), eloquent nonetheless for all it tried to say about love and loss and longing, about all the travails to which the human heart tremulously subjects itself.

As Dog muddled on, some at the banquet table laughed uneasily, some were aghast, a few (I'd like to think I was among them) winced, and looked pained. Ellie blushed, then paled, and tears welled briefly in her fine blue eyes—though whether they were tears of chagrin or embarrassment or even sympathy, I could not have said. Dog, meanwhile, after a sort of tipsy little wrestling match with himself while he fumbled for something inside his coat, unfurled before us, as triumphantly as though it were the Magna Carta or the Declaration of Independence or at least the Desiderata, a tiny six-by-six rice-paper scroll, upon which the entire (surviving) Class of '51 beheld at last the chimerical Treasure of the Orient, a delicate little pastel watercolor rendition of the same Skool Daze photo of Ellie Chadwick that I, too, had revered so long ago. A certifiable masterpiece; in my youth I would've sacrificed any number of other people's testicles for it.

Throughout Dog's interminable two-minute dumb-show, I entertained a competing fantasy: Any second now I just might leap to my feet and tink-tink-tink Dog into submission and seize control of this whole unseemly situation! Tall Eddie Clammerham into the breach! To spare Ellie further indignities, I would rise up and take the floor myself!

But of course once I had the floor I'd be needing something to say while I held it, so maybe I'd just reiterate those stirring but little-noted remarks I had addressed to the empty auditorium earlier that same afternoon, featuring my anecdote about Wild Bill and the bridge. Yes! If Tall Eddie's prowess on the hardwood has fallen a tad short of the expectations of those invisible legions of McClanafans worldwide—fear not, dear hearts, his wit and art and charm will save the day! Yay, rah rah, Eddie!

While Dog and I were simultaneously indulging our mutually exclusive delusions, Ellie regained her composure. Her gaze was now as grave and dignified and immutable as a marble statue of Miss Wallingford—and to Dog, seeing her through a diaphanous veil of blended whiskey, she must've seemed, suddenly, just about as unobtainable. The effect, I guess, was sobering, for whatever lugubrious nonsense Dog happened, just then, to be mouthing trailed off into an awkward silence. Without another word, he pocketed the little scroll, dropped heavily into his chair, and took refuge behind his chicken cacciatore. So Tall Eddie's intervention wouldn't be required after all. My work here was done.

Well, actually, not quite. For one thing, there was Caproni's famous rubber-chicken cacciatore to be confronted, and dealt with. For another, there was Ellie Chadwick, a scant four feet away, to be distracted by.

As I've already confessed, I have no recollection at all of who Ellie's and my dinner companions might have been, although we both assiduously carried on a conversation with all of them throughout the banquet, and hardly spoke a word to one another. Dog was seated down-table to my left, out of my line of sight, and I couldn't help noticing that while the rest of us regaled ourselves, Ellie kept glancing warily in his direction, as though he might suddenly dart under the table and reappear beside her chair, sitting up, panting, begging for scraps.

And that unfortunate image, forbearing reader, will have to be the last we'll see of Dog in these pages. But I hate to leave him like that, diminished almost to insignificance by my own metaphor, when in fact I can't help thinking that there was actually something rather fine and noble in his long, undeviating passion. That forty years of quixotic wandering in the wilderness should, in the end, go unrewarded was pretty much a foregone conclusion—failure being a pre-condition of quixotic endeavors, as windmills everywhere can attest—but at least it needn't go unremarked. So whatever else this story proves to be, consider it a tribute to Dog's devotion and perseverance and even—battered though it must have been, at that point—to his pride. Of *course* he wouldn't have wanted to waddle his portly, aging person onto the floor this afternoon for the old-timers' game, knowing Ellie would be on the sidelines; after all, the last time he'd played before her, he weighed 150 compact pounds, and was a certified All-State demigod!

Yet leave him we must, for in a matter of moments, while everyone else's attention is diverted by the arrival of dessert, Ellie will lean across the table, her face so close to mine that I can almost count her eyelashes, and murmur, in a voice as soft as a butterfly kiss, with one more wary blue-eyed sidelong glance in the direction of the fallen demigod, "Eddie, would you mind taking me up to the Country Club?"

Regrettably, this was not destined to be that long-awaited occasion when Ellie would spirit me off to some exotic clime to take advantage of me and, if all went well, use me horribly. Rather, the situation was just that he—she meant Dog—was really making her uneasy, and since her older brother Tom was up on the hill above town at the Maysville Country Club, where the class of '48 was having its own reunion party, she thought maybe I wouldn't mind . . .

Mind? Hadn't I waited forty years to bird-dog that canine interloper? To borrow the rousing call to arms of Mistopher Snuffy Smif, Li'l Abner's fellow cartoon hillbilly, "Time's a-wastin'!"

But it went without saying that we mustn't make our move until the moment was precisely right—which happened, fortuitously, just a few minutes later, when Dog left the table and staggered off in the general direction of the Gents. Tipping Ellie a surreptitious wink, I excused myself as though I were hastening to the same destination—and slipped, instead, out the front door, and within seconds Ellie was at my side in the Dakota, and we were scratchin' off in Cap's parking lot.

There's a short way and a long way to get to the Maysville Country Club from Caproni's, and you may be sure I took the latter—down West Second to the end of town, three miles up the hill to Jersey Ridge Road, then another five or six miles across Jersey Ridge to the Club. After executing that dashing teenage scratch-off, I cleverly down-shifted into geezer slo-go, and what could have been a ten-minute drive became a half-hour luxury cruise of back streets and back roads, during which Ellie and I, historically as incommunicative as a pair of oysters on a blind date, chattered like magpies at a . . . okay, at a magpie class reunion. After all, we had, between us, eight decades of sheer, unadulterated autobiography to account for—and I don't do unadulterated autobiography myself, so the time allotted me for autobiographical purposes tends to expand from within, like a hot air balloon.

(The Divine McClanafflatus never sleeps!) Moreover, although by unspoken mutual agreement Ellie and I never once mentioned Dog, we quickly found that we had a vast amount to say about all the other lapsed acquaintances we'd renewed that day, and about how well—or ill—the last forty years had served our erstwhile schoolmates. We couldn't have squoze all that prattle into those ten miles if I'd been driving a horse and buggy.

Accordingly, as we clippetty-clopped along Jersey Ridge Road in our air-conditioned 200-horse Dodge powerbuggy, it briefly crossed my calculating mind to cop a quick left on Rosemont Lane and continue our conversation out on Rosemont Point, once the premier park-and-spark spot of the known world, an eminence that overlooks the lights of Maysville, the bridge, and the great, sweeping north bend of the broad Ohio, the very spot where the captivating Yvonne, that lucky girl, had had her way with me under a butter-milk sky in 1949, in the incommodious backseat of my mom's two-door Chevy sedan. Rosemont Point! Who knows? Tonight, right out there on Rosemont Point, Ellie Chadwick just might get lucky too!

But then there was the distinct possibility—make that the overwhelm-ing likelihood—that Ellie would have, in 1991, even less enthusiasm for a second date with me than she'd had in 1948, as well as the looming certainty that Hilda, my lovely trophy-bride-to-be, would have none at all, and would surely be inclined to leave my unworthy nether person at the altar in the bargain. Then, too, Rosemont Lane had somehow become (according to the classy black-and-gilt sign that arced above the entrance, between stone gate-posts topped by rampant miniature cast-iron stallions) ROSEMONT POINT ESTATES, AN ARABIAN HORSE COMMUNITY. I breathed a small sigh of regret (with just a whisper of relief), and drove on.

At the Country Club, all the classes of the 1940s, their numbers so depleted by the years (poor devils) that they couldn't muster quorums of their own, had combined for their reunion, and had engaged Woody Wood (Class of '46) and His Swinging Woodpeckers for their after-dinner dancing pleasure. (Woodson T. Wood, Esq., Attorney at Law, had been the trombone virtuoso of the MHS Marching Band, and had never quite recovered from it.) Already, by the time Ellie and I arrived, the Woodpeckers were on the bandstand, swingin' pretty lively, and several sprightly duos of doughty old parties were fox-trotting about the dance floor as though they were eighth graders again, back at Mrs. Brown's School of the Dance.

We joined Ellie's brother Tom and his pals at the Class of '48 table, and were soon rewarded by the realization that, in this company, we were the eighth graders! From the perspective of your average sexagenarian, it seemed, persons in their late fifties are in the bloom of youth and simultaneously at the very cusp of senescence—temporarily immortal, so to speak—capable of absorbing prodigious quantities of alcohol as long as it comes mixed with veiled warnings of impending decrepitude—which is to say that everybody wanted to buy us drinks and tell us about their hip replacements.

(Ten years later, after I'd had my own hip replacement, I understood a little better where they were coming from.)

When we'd enjoyed a sufficiency (not to say a surfeit) of these attentions, I actually managed to lure Ellie onto the dance floor, hoping to resume our conversation and also to demonstrate that—having unlearned the box-step one night in 1966 under the combined influence of Owsley acid, the Grateful Dead, and the strobe lights of the Fillmore Auditorium—I was no longer the Frankenstinian toe-stomper she had known and endured. But talking-while-dancing was still beyond my powers, especially with Woody and the boys blasting away as though there were seventy-six trombones on the bandstand; so after we'd danced a couple of numbers, I ventured the suggestion that we sneak outside where we could carry on our conversation unimpeded by all these noisy old pooperoos.

The upshot of this cunning bit of strategy was that Ellie and I spent one last deliciously innocent hour sitting in my pickup in the country club parking lot, talking like teapots. For my part, I wanted her to know that she'd been my beau ideal ever since I used to write her name all over my schoolbooks in Miss Wallingford's English class (I told her about the handful of caterpillars, but didn't mention that they were *en flagrante delicto*), and how unworthy I had felt when she invited me to escort her to the Sadie Hawkins dance, how utterly inadequate to that monumental endeavor I had believed—and subsequently proved -myself to be. But I had been out of my depth, I hastened to explain, pleading my case; I was just a hapless Bracken County clod, lately and precipitately plucked from his natural churlish element (presumably a Bracken County pigpen) and plunged up to his churlish earlobes in *le grand monde de Maysville*, with no idea under Heaven how to conduct himself in polite society.

Ellie giggled charmingly at my characterization of my juvenile self, and said that personally she had always considered me a Very Nice Sort of Boy (which was generous of her, although, on balance, I believe I'd have preferred being remembered as a lout), and that, at the time, she'd probably been almost as disoriented as I was, her family having moved to Maysville in 1947, only a year before I got there myself. (This was news to me; I guess I'd always assumed she sprung forth full-blown right there on the banks of the Ohio, like Venus on the Half-Shell.) Moreover, the Chadwicks were from Louisville, meaning that if my move from Brooksville had been like hopping from a frog pond into Esther Williams's private pool, then Ellie's move from Louisville would've been (to pour on the aquatic imagery beyond all human capacity to absorb it) like netting a mermaid in the South Pacific and depositing her in a goldfish bowl.

Otherwise, we pretty much steered clear of the historio-autobiographical imperative, and applied ourselves instead to telling each other, rather excitedly, about recent developments in our vastly separate worlds—breaking news, as it were.

My breathless, this-just-in story was, of course, all about the bolt-from-the-blue advent of Hilda in what had been—and what remains even now, twenty years after she brought the light that saw me through it—the gloomiest passage of my life. And I had pictures! So there I was, sitting beside one of the two most beautiful women I'd ever known, proudly showing her, by the Dakota's feeble dome light, photos of the other one! Moments when you'd like to live forever! Anyhow, it was a pretty good story, and as (knowing me) you might suppose, it took me a while to tell it to my satisfaction. But Ellie patiently heard me out and, once again, she followed it up with a pretty good story of her own:

Back home in Massachusetts, she said, she had been involved for some time in an effort (which, by the way, would ultimately prove successful) to save a famous New England landmark of American literature from some enlightened developer who wanted to turn it into an amusement park. So a few weeks ago, her preservationist group had held a garden party fundraiser—I envisioned a dappled hilltop meadow with ancient stone walls and gnarly old apple trees and lots of ladies in white frocks and picture hats (I'm very big on picture hats)—and my then-current rising political hero, the handsome, nationally ambitious young governor of Arkansas—who regularly vacationed at nearby Martha's Vineyard, and whose eye for the ladies was already acquiring a certain notoriety—had been a celebrity presence at the occasion. And Ellie had met him! In person!

So how did you like him? I inquired eagerly.

"We-e-ell," she answered, after a long moment of moderate Republican hesitation, "I'm not too sure about his politics. But . . . he complimented my hat!"

Suddenly I saw it all exactly as the young future president of the United States himself must have seen it: Above him the blue, blue Massachusetts sky flocked with snow-white apple blossoms, before him the ravishing, going-on-sixty divorcée in her billowing white Marilyn Monroe frock, her incandescent blue-eyed smile picture-perfect in the perfect circle of the picture hat—and the courtly future president finds himself, perhaps for the first time in his eventful young life, at a loss for words. Flummoxed, he gulps and grins and bites his lower lip in that ingratiating Li'l Abner way of his and stammers, "Ma'am, Ah . . . Ah sho'ly do admire yo' hat!"

"Ellie, my dear," I said, biting my own lip to suppress an insinuating chuckle, "I hate to break this to you, but I don't think it was really your hat that he was looking at."

I had lowered the Dakota's windows to catch the evening breeze, and now from inside the clubhouse we heard, signaling the party's end, the distant strains of "Good Night, Sweetheart"—and considering that the hour was late and Woody and the Woodpeckers were, to a man, well into both their cups and their sixties, "strains" was definitely the applicable word. In any case, the time had come for Ellie and me to say our own goodnights, and our goodbyes as well, since she was to spend the night with her brother and his family in Cincinnati, and then to catch an early plane for Boston in the morning. As a parting tribute, I gave her a copy of one of my books, and even condescended, with becoming authorial modesty, to sign it for her—"for Ellie with love, xoxo, Eddie"—thereby presenting those frolicsome caterpillars with one last unseemly turn upon the stage. But Ellie didn't notice what they were up to. She just thanked me by way of a warm hug and a sweet little peck on the cheek, we said goodbye again, and she was gone.

Back at the Ramada, I found that the Class of '51 after-party was basically over too. Willie Gordon Ryan and a couple of other guys were sitting outside by the pool, enjoying a nightcap and taking the midnight air. They offered me a drink, which of course I took, and joshed me a bit about sneaking off with Ellie, which of course I denied—but not very convincingly, I'm afraid, because I couldn't stop grinning.

Dog, Willie Gordon said, had failed to reappear from Cap's men's room for quite a while, until finally someone discovered him passed out in one of the stalls and called his nephew (Vernon, Class of '63), who'd had to leave his own class party to come and haul his uncle away, peevishly vowing all the while to deliver the delightful old soak to the Lexington airport first thing tomorrow morning and pour him onto a plane bound for Florida and be done with him.

It was time to call it a day. I polished off my nightcap, said so long to my old pals, and went up to my room—where the first thing I did, rest assured, was fix myself another nightcap. Then I doused the light and took my drink to the window, as before, opened the curtains, and stood there for a long time, looking out beyond the dark brow of the hill upon the lights of Maysville far below, pondering all the momentous moments that had transpired during that momentous day . . . and all the ones that hadn't.

In the latter category were my inspiring oration in the auditorium, my game-winning last-second jump shot in the ball game, and my four-decades-late tryst with Ellie on Rosemont Point; in the former were two whispered confidences—"But didn't we have fun!" and "Eddie, would you mind taking me up to the Country Club?"—and a soft, almost evanescent kiss on the cheek whose imprint lingered like a memory.

And in an empty gym somewhere down there in the hometown of my heart, a phantom band played on—"*We're from ol' Kentuck . . . And we're full of pluck . . . Maysville's always right!*"—and phantom cheerleaders were still chanting, "He's a wonder, he's a dream! He's the captain of our team!"

FINCH'S SONG:
A SCHOOLBUS
TRAGEDY

And . . . there came a stray sparrow, and
swiftly flew through the house, entering at
one door and passing out through another.
As long as he is inside, he is not buffeted by
the winter's storm; but in the twinkling of an
eye the lull for him is over, and he speeds from
winter back to winter again, and is gone from
your sight. So this life of man appeareth for
a little time; but what cometh after, or what
went before, we know not.

The Venerable Bede

So here's Claude Craycraft standing in the doorway of
Craycraft's Billiards on the courthouse square in Needmore on a hot late-
summer afternoon in 1947, his triangle rack draped around his turkey neck
like a wooden cowl. Claude is leaning against the door frame eating cherries
from a brown paper sack, idly spitting the pits across the sidewalk at the
windshield of his half brother Clarence Fronk's '34 Plymouth coupe, when
who does he spy coming up the street but Clarence himself—"Finch," as he
is called—a loosely organized little bundle of tics and tremors and twitches
inching along like a ten-cent windup toy, attempting (the yellow-bellied,
knock-kneed, bald-headed, tongue-tied little shit-ass, Claude opines
inwardly) to look over his shoulder with his right eye to make sure nothing
sneaks up on him, while keeping his left eye fixed on the sidewalk at his feet
in case the earth suddenly decides to open up and gulp him down.

Finch Fronk is a sick old man. Nothing new in that, of course, for he's been working up to it all his life. He's been a sick infant, a sick boy, a sick youth, a sick young man, and now at last he's a sick old man of twenty-eight and getting sicker (Finch tells anyone who can spare the time to hear him out) "b-by the god d-dern m-m-m-minute!" Heart trouble, that's the problem. Finch was born as blue as a cobbler's thumb, and young Dr. Jibblet, who attended his arrival in this vale of sorrows, proffered the unhappy diagnosis manfully. "With this heart," prognosticated the youthful physician, his stethoscope still in his ears, "the poor little dinkus will never live to cast a vote." Yet the learned Dr. Jibblet has been in his grave for years, whereas the Poor Little Dinkus, although not exactly the picture of health, has already voted in four elections and is still thoroughly sensible to the pinch. If Claude Craycraft were a betting man—and in fact he does do a little bookmaking on the side—he'd lay odds that his half-brother will outlive him too.

Which really chaps Claude's ass. According to Claude's lights (those feeble glimmerings in the stygian gloom), if a person has enjoyed the benefits and advantages of being about to die all his goddamn life, he ought to have the goddamn common Christian decency to go ahead and do it. Hadn't Mommy went and bought Clarence that shiny red Electric Flyer wagon that time for Christmas, and then made Claude pull the puny little shit-ass around everywhere in it, so he wouldn't strain his little heart, till Claude got so sick and tired of it he had to leave home and go to shooting pool full time for a living? How about *Claude's* goddamn heart, he'd by god like to know!

As to that interesting mechanism, the heart of Claude Craycraft, there has never been a soft spot anywhere inside it for his half-brother Clarence Fronk—nor, for that matter, for any person whatsoever of the slightest Fronkish extraction or inclination. Claude's own father, Dude Craycraft, a farmer—albeit an indifferent one, with an abiding passion for pool halls and beer joints and a concomitant distaste for family life—was killed in 1917 when, in a moment of inebrious abandon, he attempted to go for an unauthorized joy ride in his wife Maudie's rich Uncle Elrod's Essex automobile; unfortunately, Uncle Elrod had left the Essex in gear, and when Dude cranked it up, it promptly ran over him—which, in Uncle Elrod's oft-vented judgment, was good enough for the worthless son of a bitch. Claude was just sixteen when the Essex summarily executed its would-be abductor, but he'd already inherited Dude's affection for pool, as well as his aversion to all forms of physical exertion—as Maudie discovered when she asked him to be a pallbearer at his father's funeral and he begged off on the grounds that he'd hurt his back shooting pool the night before.

In all fairness to Uncle Elrod, by the way, we must add that when he expired in 1922, he bequeathed Claude the two thousand dollars that set up the enterprising lad in a poolroom of his own and made an ostensible man of him—although there were those Needmore skeptics who held that Elrod had made the bequest in a deathbed paroxysm of belated guilt—that indeed he'd seen Dude coming and had left the Essex in gear on purpose.

In any event, less than six months after Dude's hasty exit from our story, when his widow Maudie up and married Dude's longtime farmhand, a silent, plodding elderly German immigrant named Ott Fronk, it didn't disturb young Claude at all at first. He figured that Maudie had seen the handwriting on the wall, as far as getting farmwork out of a pool shark was concerned, and had seized the opportunity to guarantee herself a free, full-time hewer of wood and drawer of water around the place. He was, in fact, pleasantly surprised that she'd shown so much initiative. And anyhow, he reasoned, the old Kraut was already pushing seventy, and he couldn't live forever, could he?

But then it turned out that the old Kraut *could* have lived forever, evidently, if he hadn't fallen from the top tier of the tobacco barn twenty-two years later in 1939, on his ninety-first birthday. And worse—far, far worse—a scant nine months after she and Ott were married, Maudie, at the unseemly age of forty-three, gave birth to the yellow-bellied, knock-kneed, bald-headed, tongue-tied little shit-ass Claude sees coming up the street this very minute.

And now Claude notices that right there in the gutter, in the shade of the automobile, slumbers his own aged but still resolutely lustful coonhound Delano—Claude is a Republican—sleeping off a long night's fruitless pursuit of a beagle bitch desperately in heat but too short for Delano to enjoy even if a dog had knees to get down on.

"WUFF!" Delano sleepily avers, as if to acknowledge his master's scrutiny. He rouses himself just long enough to administer a couple of quick slurps to his febrile, crimson member with a long, pink tongue, then drops back off to beagle dreams again—but not before Claude recalls that he saw Finch petting that very beagle in the courthouse yard not an hour ago, while she, hungry for love wherever she could find it, wrapped herself ardently around and around Finch's pants leg. Claude grins; something is beginning to occur to him.

Moreover, chugging down the street toward the Billiards from the opposite direction is old Mrs. Turngate, the two-hundred-pound wife of the one-hundred-pound Lutheran preacher, a lady of legendary piety and propriety. At their present rate of progress, Claude calculates, she and Finch will reach the patch of sidewalk in front of the poolroom at just about exactly the same time. This here, Claude promises himself happily, is gonna be a good one.

"Hey, boys," he calls softly over his shoulder to the five or six loafers at the Billiards' bar behind him, "git a loada this!" The invitation is immediately rewarded by a gratifying little rush of patrons toward the front window. Even Pismire, the Billiards' old yellow tomcat, gets up and strolls lazily up the bar to see what's going on.

Meanwhile, Finch has eased over toward the curb, to avoid getting himself run down by the fast-approaching Turngate Express. Claude pops another cherry into his mouth.

"*Say* there, baby brother," says Claude around the cherry, in tones so amiable they leave little invisible musical notes floating in the air around the words, "ain't that a dime yonder on the sidewalk?"

Finch is halted dead in his tracks by this unaccustomed display of affability. "Wh-wh-where at?" he demands, peering at his brother with unfraternal but perhaps forgivable suspicion.

"Why, right there in front of you!" Claude says sweetly. "Don't you see it, honey?"

"Wh-where?" Finch undertakes to ask again. Then avarice seizes him, and he bends way down and begins avidly searching the pavement for the illusory dime. And that's when Claude goes "Ptoo!" and sends the cherry pit whistling across Finch's bow and plinks old Delano on the beezer, hard enough to part his hair.

"WUFF!" Delano exclaims, more emphatically this time, struggling to his feet as fast as his old legs allow, with more than half a mind to deal severely with whoever perpetrated this outrage. But as he rises, Delano suddenly detects—Yes! Oh, yes!—the delectable redolence of *essence de la chienne* upon the air. Now his rheumy old eyes swim into focus, and there before him he espies not that sawed-off slut of a beagle but, tall as a French poodle, the nether portions of Finch Fronk, who is already in what must be, from a dog's point of view, the classic missionary position. With a joyous yelp and an alacrity that belies his years, Delano makes his move; in a trice he's halfway up Finch's back, humping ecstatically, with a huge grin on his chops and his tongue a-dangle out of the side of his mouth.

"JESUS CHRIST GOD ALMIGHTY!" Finch cries without a hint of a stammer, scrabbling across the pavement on all fours with Delano riding him like an incubus, the two of them scootching along at an extraordinary clip until Finch crashes, headlong but softly, into a pair of plump white columns that have inexplicably risen up right there in the middle of the sidewalk. Slowly, reluctantly, Finch's gaze travels upward over what seems to be a haystack-sized mound of monstrous purple orchids—actually Mrs. Turngate's floral-print summer frock—from the summit of which that reverend lady's stony visage glowers down as though she contemplates squashing him underfoot before he multiplies and infests the neighborhood. Even Delano is intimidated; he slides off Finch's back and slinks beneath the automobile.

"Clarence Fronk!" the old woman thunders. "What was that you said, mister?"

"Cheese 'n' crackers g-got all m-m-muddy?" Finch ventures wretchedly, in a small, stricken voice more prayerful than profane.

Mrs. Turngate is not mollified. "Of all the langwitch!" she admonishes. "Taking the Lord's name in vain right here on the public street! Have you been a-drinking?"

Finch is on his feet now, but cringing and twitching so violently that there seems a fair possibility he'll simply shake himself to pieces on the spot, in a small explosion of springs and cogwheels and tiny parts of every description.

"Oh, n-nome!" he squeaks, wringing his little hands. "I don't dr-dr-dr . . ."

"Him and that dog's been hung up like that all afternoon, sister," Claude offers indolently from his doorway, to the very vocal satisfaction of the little audience behind him. "We was just fixing to take the hose to 'em."

"Well, I for one have never seen nothing so . . . so *crewd* and . . . and *indignified* in all my borned days!" declares the aggrieved matron, circling Finch as warily as Dives must have circled the leper at the gates of the Kingdom. "And him a school bus driver!" she flings back as she steams off down the sidewalk. "What a fine example to be a-setting for our yewth!"

Delano, noting that the coast has cleared, creeps into the light again and immediately begins sniffing at Finch's pants cuffs. Finch fetches him a kick in the slats that would've done him terrible damage if Finch had been a stronger man, and sends him scurrying.

"Sa-a-a-ay, Eleanor," drawls Claude, as he turns to go back inside, "when you and Delano has them pups, you be sure and save me one, hear?"

It ends—as it always has, as it always must—with Finch standing there awash in laughter and humiliation, the unutterable words beating against the backs of his teeth like birds in a cage, mutely entreating whatever gods might happen to be listening to grant him his heart's twin desires—for release, and for revenge.

The Yonder River, as those who live along its banks are fond of saying, is so crooked it's a wonder it doesn't screw itself into the ground. In fact, they say, the crookedness is what gave the river its name: One minute it's right here, the next it's over yonder.

On an eminence with a commanding view of what is surely one of the sorriest hillside farms in the entire Yonder valley—eighty-five or ninety steep, exhausted acres, mostly haired over with briars and brush—roosts a ramshackle old farmhouse of weathered gray clapboard, staring out upon the blighted prospect before it through two blank uncurtained windows like baleful eyes. Between the windows is a screenless door from which depends, like a crooked tongue, a two-step wooden stoop, all that remains of what was once a nice front porch, before the present occupants tore it off and burned it for firewood, along with the picket fence that once enclosed the front yard. The little yard itself is a minefield of trash, garbage, slop, and offal of every description, populated by half a dozen quarrelsome gamecocks, tethered separately to various pieces of junk but nonetheless raucously disputatious amongst themselves, and a single pair of round-bodied, tiny-headed guinea hens scuttling hither and thither like a set of quotation marks trying frantically to punctuate the roosters' colloquy.

Behind the house is a lean-to henhouse, a tumbledown smokehouse, a hog pen constructed mainly of rusty corrugated iron barn roofing, a sway-backed old tobacco barn (with several missing panels of roofing, testifying to the primacy of the hogs), and a tilted privy, caught, as if by a candid camera, in the very act of lurching and reeling across the backyard from the barn to the house, drunk on its own fumes. A narrow gravel road passes close before the house, and beside the road is an equally tipsy mailbox, with the name "Skirvin" painted crooked and bleeding along its rusty flank.

This unprepossessing property, still known locally as the Old Craycraft Place despite the latter-day invasion of Fronks and Skirvins, constituted virtually the entire estate of the late Maudie Miggs Craycraft Fronk, who left this vale of tears in 1941, and her lamented husband Otto von Himmelheinz Fronkenheimer—Ott Fronk for convenience's sake—who preceded her by a matter of some eighteen months (though he'd no doubt be here still but for that one misstep in the top of the barn). Maudie left it all, lock, stock, and bedrock, to her youngest son, Clarence—"so the pitiful little thing will have somewhere to hang his hat," said Maudie tremulously, in her final days. Remembering rich Uncle Elrod's generous bequest to Claude back in 1922 and taking into account the prosperous nature, these days, of the poolroom-and-bookmaking line—of which she'd never quite approved anyhow, just as she'd never quite approved of Claude's wife Madge, a mussy little snip who'd run off with an Electrolux salesman and left Maudie's only grandchild, Claude Elrod, Jr., to be raised by a bunch of sots and souses in a derned old poolroom—she had endowed her elder son with a lovely full set of doilies crocheted by his Uncle Elrod's widow Opal, and otherwise omitted him altogether from her will. Which, we hardly need surmise, *really* chapped Claude's ass.

By late 1941, when Clarence came into the property, he had already cheated the Grim Reaper out of two years beyond his allotted span, an accomplishment he attributed to the fact that from the day of his birth, Maudie and Ott had allowed neither Dr. Jibblet nor any other physician to lay a finger on him, having apparently concluded that the principal business of the medical profession consisted of placing curses on the clientele. Claude, on the other hand, was satisfied that his half-brother's inconsiderate longevity was owed to the readiness of certain persons Claude could name if they weren't his own goddamn mommy to tamper with the laws of nature, which decreed that the eldest son got the whole goddamn works the way the good Lord intended it to be, by god.

Well, as we have seen, the Old Craycraft Place is no El Rancho Grande. But while Ott and Maudie were on the job, the fences were tight, the fence-rows were clean, the outbuildings were snug, the stock was well tended, there were flowers in the yard and curtains at the windows. And for a time after Maudie's death, the Ladies Aid Society of the Zion Evangelical Methodist Church, where she had devoutly worshiped for more than sixty years, saw to it that Clarence's larder was stocked with pies and cakes and other delicacies from their own kitchens, and they badgered their husbands (as they had done for Maudie since Ott's passing) into keeping up with the work on the little farm. That winter, despite Pearl Harbor and the sudden distant rumble of the war, Clarence's neighbors did his milking and slopped his hog; in the spring they set his tobacco and planted his corn and put in a garden for him; in the summer they chopped out his tobacco and weeded the garden; in the fall they cut the tobacco and housed it and picked the corn and ground it and killed the hog and put up the meat and stripped the tobacco and took it to market for him.

And more and more every day, they grumbled about it among themselves. The war effort was in full swing by then, their sons were getting drafted, help was hard to come by. As might be supposed, their complaints found a sympathetic ear at Craycraft's Billiards.

"Why, hell," Claude would commiserate, no doubt apostrophizing his uncooperatively durable late stepfather as well as his seemingly immortal half-brother, "if me and you was Fronks, and never done nothing but lay up in the bed till noon, we might live forever too!"

And to tell the truth, in those days, Clarence *was* enjoying himself a bit more overtly, perhaps, than was prudent, given his circumstances. Without Maudie clucking and wringing her hands over him all the time, he found that he could sometimes go for hours at a stretch without thinking about his imminent demise. He didn't sleep till noon, true, but all too often he came out of the house, yawning and stretching, at eight-thirty or nine to discover some disgruntled neighbor laboring away in his garden or his tobacco patch. A few times he went down and sat under a nearby shade tree and tried to keep that day's Good Samaritan company—it seemed to him the least that he could do—but they were usually in such a bad mood that he finally decided they were all prejudiced against people who stuttered, and anyhow, watching them work gave him nervous palpitations of the heart, so mostly he steered clear of them. He spent a lot of time down at the river, fishing—though the sight of fish guts upset his stomach, so one of the neighbors had to clean them for him. In the heat of the afternoon, he'd generally get in Ott's old Plymouth coupe and drive slowly around the countryside, to cool himself so he wouldn't get the heatstroke. Often, he'd drop by Claude's poolroom for a nice cold bottle of beer, to calm his nerves.

"We-e-e-ellll!" Claude would greet him. "If it ain't John D.! Would you keer for a cocktail, Mr. Rockyfella? I see you ain't died today, Mr. Vandybilt!"

Clarence, surprisingly, was not at all disturbed by these affronts. Indeed, his half-brother's bitterness confirmed, in a certain sort of a way, Clarence's own victory and was therefore even rather gratifying.

Yet who are we to say that Claude's case against his brother had no merit? It takes one to know one, goes the adage, and the failings Claude charged Clarence with—cowardice, self-pity, sloth, and an insufficiency of brotherly love—were certainly ones that Claude should have recognized on sight. What if Doc Jibblet had it wrong, what if all of Clarence's forebodings were unfounded? It was true, when you came right down to it, that his heart had never really *pained* him. But other men's hearts didn't go pittypat-*whup*, pittypat-*whup* inside their chests when they was laying up in the bed of a night, trying to get theirself a little sleep, other men's hearts didn't flip-flap around sometimes like a chicken with its head off, or jump into their throat every time anybody said boo to them, other men's hearts didn't leak and drip and gurgle so loud you could hear it clear across the room. ("That ain't your heart, that's your damn stummick!" Claude had hooted, the one time Clarence had ventured to call the phenomenon to his attention.) Oh, he was a sick man all right, sick as a poisoned crow. But was his ailment seated in his breast, or was it—Claude's diagnosis—all in his goddamn mind? We have nothing to fear, the president had once assured the nation, but fear itself. Clarence could have told the president, in no uncertain terms, that fear is more than enough to be afraid of.

Most evenings Clarence spent at home, listening to the radio—he started with *Lum and Abner* at five o'clock and listened straight through *Moon River,* which came on at midnight—but a couple of nights a month he'd get back in the Plymouth after his supper and drive to Limestone, twenty miles away in the next county, where, in a little shotgun house down by the railroad tracks, there lived a lady named Mrs. J. T. Mooney, whose husband, Mr. Mooney, had a bad case of the TB. After she got Mr. Mooney settled for the night, Mrs. Mooney would raise the shade in the sitting room window, as an all-clear signal, and if you pulled up out front and tooted the horn, Mrs.

Mooney would come out and, for two dollars, take a little ride with you. Clarence figured Mrs. Mooney was real good for his nerves; he even got to thinking that if he outlasted Mr. Mooney—as was beginning to seem, to his amazement, not just possible but probable—he might consider offering Mrs. Mooney the opportunity to become a citizen of Burdock County and an honest woman again.

But the bubble was about to burst. For on the day after Christmas of 1942, Clarence received a letter that began "Greetings from the President of the United States . . . " He'd been drafted!

Not that he was worried; his heart, that sore but steadfast organ that had so often stood between him and a hostile world, would certainly protect him this time. The notice did mean, though, that he'd have to take the physical and submit his delicate interior to the prying scrutiny of the U.S. Army, and he feared the army doctors might renew Doc Jibblet's ancient malediction. Then he recalled, not without a certain niggling satisfaction, that his old nemesis was already the *late* Doc Jibblet, and it occurred to him that he might possess a little maledictory power of his own. If the U.S. Army intended to win this war, he told himself darkly, maybe they'd just better not mess with Clarence F-F-Fronk.

They held the physical over in Toomes County, in the Mount Ararat High School gym, which had been designated an Official Temporary Preinduction Examination Center. To get the local draftees to their appointment with destiny, the government had hired a Burdock County school bus and its operator, who happened to be Clarence's quasi-nephew and Claude's only offspring, a rather dense young man named Claude Elrod Craycraft, Jr.— Buster, they called him—who would himself be taking the physical. Buster had volunteered for the draft, not out of patriotism (as the father of three with a fourth on the way, he was entitled to an automatic deferment) but because he was married to a fat, mean, ugly woman fifteen years his senior, who seemed bent on surrounding him with fat, mean, ugly children, from the entire lot of whom the war would be a welcome respite.

The bus ride to Mount Ararat was a rough one for Clarence—an endless hour jouncing along the back roads in the close confines of a school bus packed with thirty-five or forty other young men (Clarence, remember, is at this time only twenty-three himself, though he looks twice that and carries himself like an octogenarian), mere boys, many of them, preparing to set out on the first great adventure of their lives. Those who passed the physical would have another twenty-one days to get their affairs in order, but that meant twenty-one days of fond farewells, twenty-one days of being petted and pampered and adored. Soon they would go marching off to war; women would swoon, children would throw flowers; soon they would be heroes, lovers, killers; soon they would be men.

So they were excited—nay, they were beside themselves, half-crazed with a volatile admixture of eagerness and apprehension, anticipation and regret, fear and valor; they were *wild*, as rowdy and raucous as a pack of schoolboys.

Naturally, they took it out on Clarence; they mocked his stammer and called him "Heartaches," they grabbed his hat and tossed it around and threatened to pee in it and throw it out the window, and then they *did* pee in it and throw it out the window, and one great hulking fellow administered a stimulating Dutch rub to Clarence's downy little skull for good measure, claiming it would grow hair. And the driver, his own nephew Buster, enthusiastically encouraged their depredations. "Pants him, boys!" Buster kept calling over his shoulder. "Pants that little booger!" And they *did* pants the little booger and wouldn't give him back his trousers till they'd passed the Mount Ararat city limits sign, and by then they'd tied the pants legs together and pulled all the buttons off the fly. Clarence tried to maintain his dignity and stay above it all, but it wasn't easy. It'd serve them right, in Clarence's opinion, if he just hauled off and had a heart at-t-t-tack right then and there.

Outside the gym were parked eight or nine other school buses from adjoining and nearby counties, and inside they found perhaps as many as three hundred naked men, each with a handful of papers and a little canvas bag of personal effects around his neck, some sitting in the bleachers filling out forms, some milling aimlessly about the basketball court, some shuffling around in little squads under the hectoring commands of a score of officious corporals who seemed to be everywhere at once, like sheepdogs working a newly sheared flock. Almost immediately, Clarence was naked, with his little coin purse and his daddy's pocket watch in a bag around his neck and any number of corporals nipping at his heels.

"*Awright, ladies, take it off! Drop your jocks and show your cocks! Now milk it down, milk it down, milk them peckers down, you got a drip, the corporal wants to see it! Move it out now, move it out! Awright, bend over, bend over, spread 'em, spread 'em, you got a asshole, the corporal wants to see it!*

Now cough, c'mon, cough, goddamn it, cough for the corporal, he's doin' you a favor, who else is gonna feel yer nuts? Awright, move it, move it, don't you know there's a goddamn war on? Up on the scale, hurry it up, move it, what the hell's the matter with you people, move along, move a —Jeezis Kee-reist, corporal, wouldja look at this here little plucked dicky-bird here, a hunnert and six poundsa chicken-shit, look at 'im shake and shiver, let's feed 'im to the Japs! Awright, Shorty, move it out, move it out, don't you know there's a goddamn . . . "

At the blood-test station, the man in front of Clarence—who chanced to be his kinsman Buster—fainted dead away at the sight of his own blood. But when it was Clarence's turn, he stepped right over his prone nephew and held out his arm and shed his heart's blood like a natural man, watched it surge into a syringe the size of a water tumbler without a blink or a tremor—possibly because he'd looked ahead and seen that at the next station there was a corporal with a stethoscope, and he knew that when he got there, his ordeal would soon be over.

"'Kay, ya toids, let's check dem tickers!" This corporal apparently hailed from Brooklyn; he sounded exactly like Harrington on *Mr. District Attorney.* "Hey, cheez, lissen t' dat, dis one really *does* tick!"

"That's Daddy's w-watch."

"Oh, yeh, I got yez on yer goodies dere, din't I! 'Kay, here we go"—now the stethoscope was on Clarence's breastbone, cold as the barrel of a gun—"hey, dat's betta, dat's betta, sound as a dolla, ya got yerself a reggala Gene Kruper in dere, 'kay, next man, next man!"

"B-b-b-but—"

"C'mon, Shortcake, 'fya can't talk, shake a boosh! Move along, move along, ya got a beef, take it to da koinel, he's da doc! Move it on out now, don't you know dere's a war on?"

Dazed, Clarence stumbled on toward the next station, where they were checking for flat feet. Behind him, he heard the revivified Buster ask the Brooklyn corporal, "You mean he ain't . . . ?" But Clarence—moving it on out, as ordered—was too far away to hear the rest of the question or the corporal's answer:

"Hey, man, I ain't no fuckin' heart expoit, I'm a goddamn cloik-typist! Da reggala heart guy had da shits dis morning. Dis is da goddamn U.S. Army, man, one guy can't do it, da next guy does! 'Kay, let's hear dat ticker dere, dat's it, sound as a dolla, move along, move it on out!"

But Clarence couldn't hear the Brooklyn corporal; what he was hearing instead at that moment was the flat-feet corporal, screaming, "Fer crissakes, lookit them tootsies! What the hell are you, bub, a goddamn duck? Jeezis Kee-reist"—he grabbed Clarence's papers out of his hand, smacked them down on his table, slashed a check mark beside the "flat feet" designation, scooped up a rubber stamp and slammed an ink pad so hard with it that droplets of ink flew out as if he'd smashed some large, black-blooded insect, then slammed the stamp down on the topmost paper with even greater force, and thrust the whole stack back at Clarence with the word REJECTED emblazoned across it in inch-tall letters—"where the hell do these hayseed draft boards find these goddamn misfits? Get your clothes on and get the hell outta here, Donald Duck, go set it in the goddamn bus!"

"B-but the ker-ker-ker . . . "

"C'mon, gizzard-lips, spit it out! The colonel's a busy man, he ain't got time to waste on no goddamn 4-F, he's got twenty-five able-bodied men tryin' t' talk him into givin' 'em what you just got without even askin'! Move it out, move it out! Next man, next man, next man! Ain't you people heard there's a goddamn war on?"

"Hey, Unk!" Buster chortled after him as Clarence tottered off in search of his clothes. "Dad's gonna be *quite* tickled to hear you ain't sick!"

During the bus ride home to Needmore, the Burdock County warriors-to-be were a good deal more subdued than they had been that morning, evidently having found their initial experience of military life surprisingly humbling. All of them had passed the physical save one grossly obese young man, one half-blind young man, and Clarence; and if any one of those three unfortunates could have read the thoughts of his fellow passengers, he might have discovered that for the first time in his young life, he was more envied than pitied or despised.

But even if Clarence were entertaining any such speculations, he would have taken very little solace from them. He rode home huddled in the rear-most seat of the bus, alone with his own unhappy thoughts. If he didn't have heart trouble, then what *was* that thing beating itself to death against his rib cage? What was it that spoiled his appetite and ruined his digestion and stopped his breath in his throat and woke him up with night sweats? How come his nerves was all the time shot plumb to billy hell? If he didn't have heart trouble, then who the hell *did,* he'd by god like to know!

Yet who would ever believe him now? He longed powerfully for the sweet, consoling, costly embrace of Mrs. Mooney, but at the same time he understood that he must never know that brief ecstasy again; it was too dangerous, he had to take care of himself, because who else would? No more cold beer, either; he had to keep his wits about him now. He was in peril every minute, everything was about to change, his trials were just beginning!

And in that, at least, he was dead right. Within a very few minutes after the bus arrived in Needmore, Buster Craycraft was in deep consultation with Claude, back by the pissery in Craycraft's Billiards, and already Claude had what he liked best: a scheme. Pismire, eyeing Claude from his vantage point on the bar, knew him for a soul mate at a glance, for his master was grinning like the celebrated feline that had just swallowed the canary—beak, birdsong, and tail feathers.

Clarence was awakened the next morning by the bawling of his milk cow, Maybelle, standing in her stall in the barn, unmilked and decidedly out of sorts. According to Daddy's watch (which Clarence kept under his pillow at night, for company), it was twenty-five till nine. *What's the matter with people nowadays?* he thought irritably. Then he remembered, and despaired. The word was out.

Needless to say, Clarence was not a practiced milker; it was nearly noon by the time he got Maybelle to agree to go back to the pasture—and by then she'd already shown her displeasure by kicking over the milk bucket, unburdening herself of a cow pie on his knee, and clubbing him several times in the back of the head with her tail, which was full of burrs and dried manure and as hard as a hoe handle. Wearily, Clarence slogged back to the house and threw himself on his bed again, and fell asleep with a desperate prayer that the neighbor who'd been milking for him in the evening would show up. But when he awoke at four-thirty, Maybelle was back in the barn, bawling—and no sign of the neighbor. It was pitch-dark before she let him leave the barn this time, and he'd missed *Lum and Abner* and *Just Plain Bill* and all his other early evening favorites. And he had to fix himself a can of pork and beans for supper; the Ladies Aid Society had thrown him over too.

After three days of Clarence's inept attentions, Maybelle came down with mastitis. "You ain't been getting her stripped out," Pillbox Foxx, the veterinarian, said disgustedly after he'd looked her over. "You ort to let her go." Meaning, Clarence knew, that Pillbox regarded him as unfit to own a good milk cow. So Clarence called his neighbor, a man named Kinchlow—the very neighbor who had failed to turn up for the morning milking three days ago!—and Kinchlow came and after treating Clarence to yet another unspoken display of withering contempt, said, Yeah, he reckoned he could take her off his hands, Clarence being so busy and all—and offered him half what she'd have been worth three days ago! As they were loading Maybelle into Kinchlow's truck, Clarence couldn't stop himself from asking if Mizriz Kinchlow was making any of those good banana cream pies of hers lately. And Kinchlow said, No, by god, she wasn't, and if she was they'd be eating it theirselves, because sugar was rationed and bananas was hard to come by, and didn't he know there was a goddamn war on?

Clarence had to spend most of what he got for Maybelle to pay Pillbox's fee, and his little bank account was already running low. His dab of tobacco money was almost gone, mostly by way of certain bonuses that had been extracted from him by the blandishments of the winsome Mrs. Mooney. Moreover, that alluring creature had revealed, back at hog-killing time, an overweening passion for a bit of pork now and then, and had subsequently acquired, in the form of little gifts of hams and chops and bacon, most of Clarence's hog. Indeed, all that he had left was a jar of pickled pig's feet, which Mrs. M. didn't particularly care for.

Still, he held out for another week, subsisting principally on pork and beans and black coffee and baloney sandwiches. But on the fifth day, the weather turned malevolently colder, just as he got down to his last few sticks of firewood. He huddled in bed for two more days, under a mountain of blankets, quilts, dirty clothes, Maudie's old winter coat, Ott's old bib overalls, and Maudie's hand-hooked rag rug off the sitting room floor; he even took her lace curtains out of the front windows and piled them on. Then, on the seventh morning, a Saturday, he opened his last can of pork and beans and found the contents frozen solid. He took the jar of pickled pig's feet back to bed and ate as much of it as he could stand, to build up his strength a little, and then got up and went outside and tried, hopelessly, to start the Plymouth, as he had done yesterday and the day before. It wouldn't start, of course, so he waited there till he saw, far upriver, the mailman's car working its halting way along the river road; then he left the Plymouth and stood by the mailbox, shivering violently in the spitting snow, till the mailman got there and grudgingly agreed to give him a ride to town.

It being a blustery midwinter Saturday morning, the Billiards was already full of noise and smoke and farmers, but when Clarence came scuttling in out of the cold, it was like in the westerns when the Fastest Gun comes striding through those swingin' doors: You could've heard a pin drop.

"Why, as I live and breathe!" exclaimed Claude, as the beer drinkers at the bar grinned and nudged and snickered expectantly. "If it ain't the Duker Windsor! I figgered you was liable to show up any day now. So what brings you to town, baby brother? Your money crowd you out of the house, did it?"

"I—I need somewhere to st-st-stay, big b-brother. I ain't got no heat out at the p-p-place. I was thinkin' ab-b-b-bout that r-r-r-r- . . . "

"You was thinkin' about that nice little room I got upstairs here, I'll just bet! Why, yes indeedy, you can move right in, baby brother! Glad to have you!"

"Well, how much would you ch-ch-ch-ch- . . . ?"

"Charge you? Why, not one penny, sweetheart, not one penny! But I tell you what, I been needing me somebody to clean my spittoons and swab down the pissery of an evening, and rack balls for me when it gets busy in here of a Saturday afternoon and all. Now you take on them little chores for me, honey, and I'll let you have that room absolutely free of charge. How's *that*, by god! And don't you thank me for it, neither! Because, you know, what's a brother for?"

Clarence could only gulp and nod in acquiescence, but he was horrified. What about his weak stomach? And that thought reminded him of another, even more pressing question: "B-Big brother, where'll I eat at?"

"Well, sir," said Claude, with an air of vast magnanimity, "I been studying about that, too, and I have done come up with a leet-tle plan. Because I would hate to have to see you go to the county poorhouse—it might reflect bad on the family name, and all. But before we get into that, Waldo there"— he indicated the far end of the bar, where a notorious sot named Waldo Skirvin languished facedown in a pool of spilled beer—"Waldo there had him a little accident back in the pissery a while ago, he kinda threw up a little. So maybe you wouldn't mind . . . " Claude reached under the counter and came up with a bucket and a mop. "Now don't you rush yourself, honey. You got all the time in the world, all the time in the world."

Clarence trudged off to his work, numberless days of spittoons and little accidents before him, pickled pig's feet already roiling in his innards.

When he emerged from the pissery twenty minutes later, pale as moonlight, he was greeted with a ragged but rousingly derisive little cheer from the barflies up front, but he barely heard it. Filled with dread—what further raptures might his brother have in store for him?—he staggered forth to meet his fate.

"Now then," Claude said, leaning over the bar as if to speak to Clarence in the strictest confidence, yet talking loud enough that everyone in the place save the comatose Mr. Skirvin could hear his every word, "now then, where was we? I believe you was saying something about . . . eating?"

"N-not right now," Clarence said, with a shudder. "No time soon."

Well, anyhow, Claude went on, when it's breakfast you want, we got pickled eggs right here—he directed Clarence's attention to a gallon jar full of sallow ovals floating in a bilious yellow fluid—which ain't but fifteen cents apiece, and crackers throwed in free. And when you want your dinner, there's you a big selection of all the finest candy bars and Nabs right there, a nickel apiece. Comes to supper, it ain't a better bowl of chili anywheres in Burdock County than they got down the street at the White Manor Cafe. But it takes money, bud, it all takes money.

Clarence couldn't argue with that—and he declined to try.

So, Claude explained, here Clarence was with a farm he couldn't use, and here was Claude's son Buster with a school bus *he* couldn't use, beings as he was about to go off and win the goddamn war. But as it happened, that school bus wasn't really Buster's, it was Claude's, because it was Claude which had put up the money for it and which had went to the school board and got the boy the route and the contract in the first place. So it was by god Claude's bus to do with as he seen fit. And what he seen fit was, he would just trade Clarence even-up, one little old piddly-ass worthless scrap of a raggledy-ass farm for one good-running nearly brand-new two-year-old Reo school bus, and he would throw in, abso-by-god-lutely free of charge, whatever it had cost him under the table to buy Buster the goddamn route from the school board in the goddamn first place, and how was *that* for a goddamn deal?

B-b-but, big brother, Clarence managed to inquire, what do you *want* with the farm?

Well, said Claude, Gene Kinchlow had run old Waldo there off his place after Waldo got drunk and set Gene's tenant house afire. (Waldo raised his head just long enough to grin in modest acknowledgment of the distinction, before his forehead hit the bar again.) So, Claude went on, he thought he'd just let the Skirvins have the farm, to crop on shares. Then, too, he'd been looking around for somewheres outside the city limits where him and a few of the boys could have theirselfs a little friendly cockfight or shoot some craps now and then of a Sunday afternoon (from the barflies came a murmur of appreciation for Claude's civic-mindedness), and that old barn out there would be just the ticket.

"But here's the size of it, baby brother," Claude continued, speaking mildly at first but with growing vehemence as he drove home his point, "a thing that's mine, I just naturally want to get my hands on it, see, I mean that's just the kind of hairpin I *am,* by god! If it ain't mine I don't want nothing whatsoever to do with it, hardly. But if it's mine, I *want* it, you see! And that farm was handed down to me by my goddamn anchesters, or ort to been, by god, and it's *mine,* and I mean to *have* the son of a bitch!"

There was an assenting thunk of beer bottles all along the bar; you couldn't fool this jury, they knew justice when they saw it, yes, by god! Clarence reeled back from the bar a step or two, looking wildly from one impassive face to the next, and appealed to the room at large, "B-but what if I . . . I mean, all them little ch-children!"

"Pshaw," said Claude lightly, "it ain't a man in Burdock County as precautious of hisself as you are, baby brother. Them childring couldn't be safer if they was in their mommy's arms."

There was just one thing left for Clarence to say—part plea, part threat, part promise—and at last he forced himself to say it: "I . . . I'll *d-die!*" he cried.

Now there arose from his bar stool a tall, skinny, dour old retired barber named Geezer Wirtschaffner, who had cut Clarence's delicate little curls once a month until they'd all but disappeared when he was in his teens. For a moment, as this venerable sage approached him, Clarence supposed that here at last was the friend and defender he so desperately required. Geezer stopped before him, towering, worked an immense chew of tobacco here and there inside his mouth to clear his wise old tongue for speaking, then reached down and, with a long forefinger as rigid as an arrow, jabbed Clarence on the breastbone, hard, just above the heart, and said, "Clarence, my boy, you ain't dead *yet!*"

On the following afternoon, Sunday, Clarence and Buster and Buster's best friend Chick Greevey, who hauled dead livestock for the fertilizer company in Limestone, moved Clarence's meager belongings from the homeplace

I JUST HITCHED IN FROM THE COAST

to the room above the Billiards. It didn't take long. There was just Clarence's little bed—an iron World War I army surplus cot he'd slept on since he was five—and all those bedclothes, and a few clothes of his own, and a wooden kitchen chair, and a small, framed snapshot of Ott and Maudie on the courthouse steps on their wedding day, Maudie smiling uncertainly beneath a cloche hat scarcely bigger than a walnut shell, Ott looming and somber behind a shaggy walrus mustache the size of a pitchforkful of hay. They used Chick's malodorous truck, the dead wagon, for the move, and every night for months afterward Clarence shared his bed with the faint but inextinguishable stench of death clinging to the bedding.

Monday morning, with Buster riding shotgun to show him the route—which happened to include the river road, the crookedest, narrowest, meanest, most hellish twelve miles of unpaved perversity in Burdock County, the very road that passed before the homeplace—Clarence took his first turn at the wheel. Among the stops was Buster's own house (actually his mother-in-law's house, which Buster and his wife, Iota, and their several fat, mean, ugly children generously shared with her), where they picked up Buster's eldest, a corpulent third grader named Clayton, known to his intimates as Clabber, who climbed into the bus and, to the vast amusement of his amiable parent, immediately smacked his Great-half-uncle Clarence on the back of the head hard enough to make the poor man bite his tongue. It was the first installment of a ritual that would be unfailingly repeated every school day, morning and evening, for all the ensuing years of Clarence's life.

Clarence never had a chance. From the very first day his passengers were utterly out of control, his bus a self-contained tumult and chaos, a rolling anarchy, hell on wheels. The little lambs fought and swore like drunken sailors, they beat each other over the head with schoolbooks and lunchboxes, the older boys smoked cigarettes and chewed tobacco and spit on the floor and boldly felt up the squealing girls, the younger ones threw up in the aisles and peed out the window, they carved "Fronk You" in the leather seat cushions, and then pulled the stuffing out and piled it in the aisle and set fire to it, they pelted Clarence's hunched shoulders with whatever came to hand, spitballs and marbles and apple cores and art gum erasers—and one afternoon, in his sixth or seventh week as driver, he glanced in the rearview and saw to his horror a great brute of a boy named Harry Tom Powers creeping up the aisle behind him with what appeared to be an immense drop of some pale, viscous fluid dangling from his paw, and an instant later there came crashing down on Clarence's battered skull a Trojan filled with half a pint of buttermilk. The school bus lurched into the ditch and stalled.

"I'll *die!*" the children sitting nearest heard their driver vow, as he wiped the whey and thin, white shreds of rubber from his eyes. "I swear to god I'll d-die, I *will*, by god!"

And he just might have done it, too; he just might've clenched his jaw and gnashed his teeth and held his breath and sweated and strained until, b-by god, he *did* succeed in willing himself a heart attack. But at least for the time being, the will to live triumphed over the will to die—and so he lived, and didn't die.

It was along about this time that he acquired the trait that, in turn, brought him the nickname that was to stay with him the rest of his days. For so insistent had become his habit of glancing fearfully over his right shoulder, to see what mischief his darlings might be up to next, that the gesture had joined his nervous little repertoire of tics and twitches, a quick, mechanical, sidelong hitch of the head every ten seconds or so during all his waking hours. In the poolroom, some imaginative wag speculated that Clarence had lately been visited by an invisible little bird, which had perched on his right shoulder and was with him always, and that he turned his head time after time in order to hear its tiny song. In honor of the bird, they named him Finch, and like the bird itself, the name never went away.

But the chimerical bird brought him no more luck than it had brought companionship. Clarence—Finch, as he is now—was like that gloomy little man in the funny papers with his own personal rain cloud: Misfortune dogged him everywhere, he couldn't win for losing, he was wedded to calamity. Any time he ventured out on the streets of Needmore, keeping a wary eye on the sidewalk, a pigeon was sure to fly over and dump its sodden ballast on his hat, or some old lady to lean out an upstairs window and shake her dust mop over him. Or if, instead, he watched the sky, his foot was just as sure to find a steaming coil of Delano's unsavory business on the pavement, or he would fall off the curb, or a car would come along and splash muddy water on him.

Even aside from the twice-daily horror of the school bus, Finch's life seemed to him an endless round of abominations and persecutions, ill usage and adversity, gall and wormwood, wormwood and gall. The door of his room upstairs wouldn't stay closed, and Pismire kept sneaking in to use his bed for a cat box; and so frequent were the "little accidents" in Claude's noisome pissery—which, unhappily for Finch, doubled as his own bathroom, the only one he had—that he'd begun to suspect Claude's clientele of getting sick in there on purpose, to torment him; and he knew for a fact that they were chewing way more tobacco than they used to, just to keep the spittoons overflowing all the time; and on Saturday afternoons they shot a lot more pool than . . . than decent people ought to shoot, trying to run him ragged racking balls for them and make him have a heart attack, because . . . well, because they wouldn't believe there was anything wrong with him.

Eventually there appeared, taped to the Billiards' back-bar mirror, one of those cartoon postcards depicting a disconsolate-looking little fellow sitting shoulder-deep in a toilet bowl, puling, "GOO'BYE, CROOL WORLD!" with his upraised hand upon the lever, ready to flush himself away. Next to the drawing, the anonymous party who'd posted it had penciled in the name "Finch," to make sure no one would miss his point. The handwriting, Finch could not have failed to note, was unmistakably that of his affectionate half-brother.

When school let out for the summer, Finch hardly noticed. He didn't have to drive his bus by day, of course, but in his dreams the river road unreeled endlessly before him, all those tortured, twisting miles still undriven and the roiling muddy waters waiting far below. Before he knew it, he was back at the wheel again, and young Clabber, fatter, meaner, and uglier than ever, was walloping him convivially on the back of the head to greet him on the occasion of the opening of the new school year. Finch grimaced silently and thought of the old story Maudie used to read him about the Pied Piper, who had led the children into the sea.

And so the weeks and months rolled on, and America fought its war in places Burdock County never heard of, and now and then word came back that a son of Burdock had fallen somewhere, hurt or dead. Eventually, local patriots installed in the courthouse yard a billboard-sized Burdock County Servicemen's Honor Roll, with gold stars for the slain, red stars for the wounded, blue stars for the missing and the captured. Among the luckless heroes were several in whose company Finch had made the trip to Mount Ararat that dreadful day—including the one who'd pantsed him (red star, in the Philippines), the one who'd peed in his hat (red star, at Guadalcanal), and the one who'd thrown it out the window (gold star, felled by a mortar at Anzio). Finch was unable to suppress the apprehension that a terrible kind of justice might be at work here, yet he took no satisfaction from it—for he was himself no stranger to loss and suffering, and nowadays it sometimes seemed to him that grief was everywhere, as omnipresent as a long spell of bad weather.

One of Finch's lesser sorrows during those dark days was the slow but inexorable dismantling and befoulment of the homeplace at the hands of the irrepressibly squalid Skirvins, under the indulgent eye of Claude, their landlord, who was actually rather enjoying the process, this little bonus contribution to his brother's misery. With every passing day, Finch noted to his disheartenment, there seemed to be more Skirvins on the place, and more Skirvin residue. There were Skirvins everywhere, a dozen or more at any given moment in the house where Finch had lately dwelt in solitary splendor: Waldo and his wife Goldie and their five children and Goldie's brother Chump Slackert and Chump's wife Myrtle and their two children and a parade of old aunties and uncles and half-wit cousins wandering back and forth from the Burdock County poorhouse a few miles down the road, where all Skirvins and Slackerts seemed, eventually, to end up.

The weeds took Maudie's flower bed like a panzer unit, and the front yard was soon ankle-deep in tin cans, broken bottles, automobile parts, potato peelings, tobacco chaws, dog droppings, and other Skirvin spoor that had just as well remain undescribed. The picket fence went up the chimney their first winter on the place; the front porch followed, then the shutters, then the barn doors, then the privy door—for if there had been a Skirvin lexicon, the word "modesty" would not have been included. They would've torn the stripping room off the barn and burned that, too, except that Waldo's old one-armed daddy was living in it; they would, indeed, have burned the barn itself, but for their landlord's Sunday afternoon crapshoot and cockfight socials, on which that enterprising gent was making money by the fistful.

"If M-Mommy seen the way them Skir-kir-kirvins has done her flowers," Finch ventured to complain at last, "she would turn over in her gr-gr-gr- . . . "

"Let 'er roll, baby brother, let 'er roll!" cheerfully rejoined the rightful scion of the House of Craycraft. "She ain't got nothing else to do, has she?"

In early 1944, a blue star appeared beside the name of Pfc. Claude Elrod

Craycraft; the valiant Buster had been taken in northern Italy, doubtless after a terrific struggle, and was to sit out the remainder of the war in a German POW camp, where—according to a report that filtered back from a Burdock County lad who was imprisoned in the same camp—he attained great celebrity among his fellow prisoners for snitching on them to their captors at every opportunity.

Meanwhile, back on the home front, the fair Iota kept her knight-errant's memory alive by continuing annually to produce fat, mean little uglies just as though he weren't gone, thanks to the good offices of Buster's old pal Chick Greevey, who'd had to miss the war after inadvertently lopping off his trigger finger with a meat cleaver the day before his scheduled induction into the army and who had subsequently taken on the servicing of Iota as an alternative patriotic duty.

In the dreary depths of March in 1945, Finch came upon an ad in the local weekly announcing that a certain P. Cosmo Rexroat, Doctor of Natural Theosophy, Chiropractic Science, and Colonic Irrigation, distinguished graduate of the Universidad del Medico Diagnostico of Nuevo Laredo, Mexico, would be holding private consultations for a limited time only at the Rexroat Mobile Diagnostic Clinic in the city of Limestone, diagnosing and treating ailments of the heart, lungs, liver, kidneys, stomach, spine, joints, digestive system, nervous system, and feet, with female complaints a specialty, not to say a calling. The ad featured—but did not depict—an apparatus of the doctor's own invention, called the Electro-Magno-Static Diagnosis Machine, a modern scientific miracle that was said to possess the capability of reading the patient's inner workings like a road map, instantly directing the attending physician to the trouble spot without the subject's experiencing the slightest pain or discomfort whatsoever. Cash payments only, no appointments necessary.

Now here was a doctor a man could depend on and have a little faith in. Not one of your stick-in-the-mud backwoods hick country quacks, neither, but a fellow with some get-up-and-go about him, which had went abroad and studied up on all the latest progressive modernistic scientific advances. Early the next day, right after his morning bus run, Finch fired up the Plymouth and hied himself to Limestone.

The Rexroat Mobile Diagnostic Clinic occupied a beat-up old house trailer parked in a weedy vacant lot beside a beer joint called Charlie's

Dream Bar, and the Electro-Magno-Static Diagnosis Machine turned out to be a more or less exact replica of that grim fixture known in gangster movies as the Hot Seat, next to which was a panel mounted with a bewildering array of wires, switches, knobs, lights, bells, vacuum tubes, transformers, and other electro-magno-static what-have-you, and one large round dial labeled around its perimeter with the terms CANCER, GALLSTONES, HEART DISEASE, BRAIN TUMOR, TUBERCULOSIS, and all the other ills with which the sicklings might suppose themselves afflicted.

Dr. Rexroat's nurse and trusted laboratory assistant, a gruff, barrel-chested, oakum-haired woman of rugged aspect and raw demeanor, strapped and clamped the terrified Finch into this disconcerting article of furniture ("Christ on a crutch, hon," she muttered, as to an errant child, "stop that goddamn squirmin', will ya!"), and then, with her patient securely pinioned in the chair, said she'd just slip next door to the Dream Bar to fetch the doctor. She returned several long moments later with the great diagnostician firmly in tow, a dirty little gray gent whose entrance immediately added the heady bouquet of bay rum and blended whiskey to the already somewhat close and fulsome atmosphere inside the trailer. The doctor boozily inquired of Finch just what he thought his trouble might be, then made "a few minor adjustments" behind the instrument panel, and without further ceremony, threw the switch. Bells clanged, lights flashed, a slight shock coursed through Finch's body, and the red pointer on the big dial leaped from its post and flew like love's own arrow straight to the "D" in "HEART DISEASE."

"It *did*!" as Finch told it later in the Billiards, so excited that for the first time in his life (though not the last, as we have seen), he almost forgot to stammer. "And that doctor told me, Mr. Fronk, he says, it is a act of God you're still a-living, for you got as bad a case of 'c-cute heart disease as ever I treated! And he said I was to come back on Friday and let him irritate my c-colon for me! And he never charged me but twenty dollars, and for two dollars extry he throwed in this free book!"

The book was a slim volume entitled *Prayers for My Good Health,* by the Very Reverend P. Cosmo Rexroat. Finch pored over it, and doted on it, and pronounced the reverend doctor the savior of his life and soul.

The Billiards crowd was impressed; they'd never known a certified act of God before—or, at any rate, they hadn't known they knew one. Claude scoffed at first, of course, but when Finch showed him Dr. Rexroat's chapter entitled "A Prayer for My Enlarged Liver"—a condition with which Claude was intimately acquainted, it being an occupational hazard of his profession—and Claude observed that the doctor prescribed colonic irrigation and an occasional petition to the Almighty but didn't say a word about not drinking fifteen or twenty bottles of beer every day, even he decided there might be something to it. And so, for a couple of days, Finch's credibility was at an all-time high.

The Friday of Finch's appointment happened to be Good Friday, and school let out at noon. By early afternoon he was on the road to Limestone, thinking as he drove that he'd probably feel so invigorated by his treatment that he might just have to hang around town till evening and pay a little call on Mrs. Mooney.

Alas, it was not to be. When Finch arrived at the site of the Rexroat Mobile Diagnostic Clinic, there was in the vacant lot only vacancy, and weeds, and the three cinder blocks that had served as the clinic's doorstep. Finch went next door to the Dream Bar to find out what had happened, and Charlie, the proprietor, told him they'd left town in the dead of night after the wife of the mayor of Limestone had brought her female troubles to the doctor and had been singed bald-headed by a crossed wire in the Electro-Magno-Static Diagnosis Machine.

"And y'know," said Charlie, "I'm gonna miss that little old bastard, too. He was smart as a tack, the way he would set around in here and talk in them big words and tell you the sayings of Shakespeare and whatnot. He kinda dressed the place up, like, and I enjoyed him, know what I mean? Last time he was here, he run up a pretty good tab, and then he says, 'Charles, my boy'—he would always call me Charles—'Charles, I fear I am suffering from a temporary embarrassment of funds,' or some bull like that, and says would I perhaps accept a copy of this book which he had wrote hisself? Well, I seen he had me, because I liked the old rip, and wouldn't've called the law on him under no circumstances. So I says, 'Reverent, I will, by god. But I want you to autograft it personal for me.' And he done that, and here"—Charlie took down a copy of *Prayers for My Good Health* from the back-bar shelf and opened it to the flyleaf and passed it over the bar to Finch—"is what he put down in it. I can't make heads nor tails out of it myself, but I'm real proud to have it, just the same."

"Every man," Finch read, steeped to the lips in misery, "should have a motto, Charles, and I take mine from the Immortal Bard. To wit:

Diseases desperate grown,
By desperate appliance are relieved,
Or not at all.

Warmest personal regards, P. Cosmo Rexroat, BS, MS, PhD."

Then at last the war was over, and by ones and twos the boys—now men—came straggling home, some with medals on their chests, a few with an empty sleeve or a prosthetic leg, one with wild eyes and ruined nerves and a metal plate in his head. Then, too, of course, there were those who did not come at all, except in the form of little packets containing dog tags and personal effects. Some of the returnees went back to their jobs or their trades or the family farm as if they'd never left, some joined the 52-20 club—twenty dollars a week in government "readjustment" money for fifty-two weeks—and ran around the county like madmen for a year, drinking and carousing, some took the GI Bill and went to college and, for all practical Burdock County purposes, disappeared from the face of the earth forever. All of them, it seems safe to say, had seen more than country boys were ever meant to see, and Burdock County would never look quite the same to them again.

For a time, Finch allowed himself to hope that the end of the war would bring about some small easing of his own woes. Buster would be wanting his old bus route back, he reasoned, so Claude would just have to find Finch something else to do. Maybe, if they could somehow dislodge the Skirvins, he could even go back to the farm, or what was left of it, and learn to milk this time, and to garden a little, and to clean his own fish—his stomach was stronger now, thanks to the regular testing it had been put to in the pissery—and manage to keep himself, for whatever little dab of time was left to him.

But when Chick Greevey heard that Buster was on his way home, he took off like a scalded dog for parts unknown (Buster wasn't much of a threat, but then it didn't require much of a threat to send Chick Greevey scurrying), leaving the dead wagon without a driver—a line of work that was more to Buster's liking than the school bus had been, since the dead animals weren't on any particular schedule and didn't oblige a troop to muster his ass outta the rack at oh-five-hunnert hours (Buster hadn't been much of a soldier either, but he came home speaking Military as though it were his native tongue) to drive them here and there around the goddamn countryside, and also your dead animals would lay still and not worry the ass off a troop that was trying his level goddamn best to get them to school on time, where they could get some education and improve their goddamn selfs a little bit.

Buster scarcely deigned to notice that whereas he'd left home the father of three with a fourth on the way, he returned less than four years later the father of six with a seventh on the way. Iota's genes having held dominion over both his and Chick's, all the children looked just alike anyhow—so what the hell, Buster said philosophically, Iota wasn't no Betsy Grable he would admit, but after a troop's ass has set nineteen goddamn months in a goddamn Noxie hellhole, nookie's nookie, ain't it?

One sultry August afternoon in 1947, not many days after his contretemps with the amorous Delano, Finch sat on an iron bench in the courthouse yard through a sudden, violent thunderstorm, drenched and trembling, trusting the iron to draw the lightning down. When neither physics nor metaphysics would oblige him, he lifted his hands to the angry, fulminating heavens, silently imploring, *Why me, Lord? Why m-me?*—and was answered on the instant by a prodigious bolt of lightning that split the top out of a courthouse elm not twenty yards away and then, as Finch scurried belatedly for cover, by a peal of thunder as tremendous as God's colossal rejoinder in the old joke: "BECAUSE . . . YOU . . . PISS . . . ME . . . OFF!"

His purpose in life, Finch saw now all too clearly, was to provide, by his sufferings, for the amusement and diversion of his fellow man. By little and little, Finch's dread of his departure from this mortal coil had almost entirely given way to a deep, inchoate longing to begin the journey, a longing not so much to die as merely to be . . . elsewhere, to be *taken*, to join those shadowy legions known as The Departed.

But God's mercy is yet another commodity upon which we ought never to presume. How could Finch, in the toils of that unhappiest of summers, have dreamed that before the coming school year was as much as two weeks old, love would arrive like a late-blooming flower in the barren door-yard of his life and bring him a purer joy than any he had ever known?

For this was to be no profane, two-dollar love, no Mrs. Mooney kind of love; this was an exalted, even a godly love, the love of a father for a son, in whom he is privileged to recognize both himself and some faint intimation of a glory far beyond himself. Miraculously, the son that was born to Finch in the fall of 1947 was already nine years old. All the more remarkable, he was neither a Fronk nor yet even a Craycraft, but . . . a Skirvin!

Of Goldie Skirvin's five living babies, Brownie had been the last and certainly the least, weighing in as he did at four and a half pounds, a month early. A few days after his arrival, when the county health officer showed up to certify the birth, Goldie still hadn't thought of—indeed she hadn't even thought *about*—a name for the little sojourner, because she'd hardly dared to hope that he'd be with her long enough to need it. She'd lose this one, she warned herself, the way she'd lost the three otherns that come puny.

So when the health officer went to fill out the birth certificate, she'd snapped, "Names is gettin' skeerce these days, y'know!" to put him off for a minute, so she could think.

But then the only thing that came into her mind was the name of a little old dog she'd had one time, a mangy little old feist that wasn't no account for nothing, but had bit Waldo once when he was drunk and needed biting, and had finally went and got itself run over by the mailman and caused her to cry over it when she pitched its little body in the sinkhole, because it had the saddest, sweetest big brown eyes that had looked right back at a person even from the bottom of the sinkhole, just exactly the way this little old baby looked up at you from down there in the warsh basket where it was a-laying. So she named it Brownie, after the dog, on account of sentimental reasons.

Well, like Finch before him, Brownie had lived but he hadn't thrived; now, in his ninth year, he was a head shorter than the next tallest of his third-grade classmates, and as thin as a shitepoke, with rickety legs and bad teeth and, beneath the dirt, an inauspicious pallor. Yet his tiny, doll-like features, framed by tangled sorrel curls and graced by his namesake's big brown limpid eyes, were not without a certain shy, fragile beauty—which automatically made him the mortal enemy of Clawvern Craycraft, Buster's boy, arguably the most ill-favored of Iota's unlovely spawn.

Like his older brother and his several winsome sisters, Clawvern was distinguished by an ovoid anatomy, green-rinded teeth, a disagreeable nature, and the presence at all times of one or the other forefinger in one or the other nostril. All in all, he was as loathsome a dirty-necked, knot-headed, misbuttoned, snot-besotted, mossy-toothed, eczema-ridden little mouth-breathing article of juvenile degeneracy as ever graced the halls of Burdock County Elementary. His scholarship also distinguished him; though he was going on thirteen, he'd only made it to the fourth grade so far—incontrovertible evidence, in Clawvern's view, of the failings of the Burdock County educational establishment.

So, to balance the scales, Clawvern had lately taken upon himself the education and forming into manhood of young Brownie Skirvin, to which purpose—"to make him *smart*," Clawvern guffawed—he cuffed and pinched and tweaked and pummeled the little fellow tirelessly; he sat behind him on the bus and pulled his hair and flipped his ears; he entertained him with hotfoots and Dutch rubs or thumped his Adam's apple as though it were a cantaloupe. To teach him family values and the virtues of good breeding, he regularly made a point of reminding Brownie that his father was a souse, his mother was a scagmaw, his brothers were burglars, and his sisters were punchboards.

One day, noting that Brownie looked a little peaked, Clawvern prescribed one of his own personal slightly used tobacco chaws and saw to it that Brownie worked the delicacy until he'd derived maximum nourishment from it, as evidenced by his turning green and throwing up in the aisle. That's how you worm a pup (Clawvern assured him, all noblesse oblige), and you worm a Skirvin the same damn way.

And for all these services and considerations, the only return Clawvern exacted was the five cents Goldie somehow managed to scrounge together every day for Brownie's lunch, which would have been—if he were ever allowed to eat it—a nickel's worth of cheese and crackers at the grocery store across the street from the school yard. Instead, Clawvern now topped off his own light lunch—two baloney sandwiches and a Pepsi—with a Milky Way, courtesy of the humbler classes.

And should Brownie even think of protesting these very pleasant arrangements, Clawvern would be obliged, he warned, to report the insubordination to his venerable grandparent, who'd promptly send Waldo and Goldie and Brownie and Chump and Myrtle and Popaw and them a-hoofing it down the road to the poorhouse, where they belonged.

The end result of Clawvern's attentions, Finch had noted in his rearview, was that the smaller boy regularly left the bus with tears welling in those great brown eyes. But although Finch certainly recognized and felt for him as a fellow sufferer, he had plenty of troubles of his own, and at first it just didn't occur to him that he and Brownie had all that much in common.

In his own childhood, desolate though it was, Finch hadn't really been tormented by his schoolmates; in fact, they'd usually treated him with the most gingerly respect, because big old Ott, in his thick-tongued, menacing way, had put out the word that if anybody teased the boy and caused him to have a heart attack, he'd have *der hundsfott* charged with murder and sent to the electric chair. So they had all pussyfooted around little Clarence as if the wrong word might blow him to the winds; his weakness, his very vulnerability had been his armor. But poor Brownie had no defenses at all—and Finch sure couldn't see himself providing any, should it ever come to that.

His and Brownie's similitude was not made manifest for Finch until the day, when that school year was less than two weeks old, that Brownie's third-grade teacher, Miss Vermillion, passing among her scholars while they were assiduously at their studies, happened to glance down as she passed Brownie's desk and saw, to her horror, that his tousled curls were fairly hopping with . . . well, call them cooties, crumbs, wig rats, shag bunnies, galloping dandruff, or even, as the poet had it, "crawlin' ferlies." In a word, lice.

Miss Vermillion threw up her hands and gasped, "Chinches!" (that having been the popular designation for the species during her own girlhood), and thereby instantly apprized the entire English-speaking world—at least so far as Brownie understood its boundaries—of the wildlife that was just then so enjoying his hospitality.

On the bus that afternoon, Brownie's sympathizers outdid themselves in their zeal. No wonder he had fleas, they said, named for a dog the way he was. But they had plans for his immediate improvement.

"Let's shave off that damn bug rug for 'im!" Clayton Craycraft urged, brandishing his pocketknife.

"Nah," amended Harry Tom Powers, at fifteen a fixture for the past three years in the fifth grade, where he'd acquired so much learning that it threatened to become a burden to him. "Let's shave off *half* of it, see, and set fire to the other half! And when them graybacks runs out into the open, we'll stab 'em with an ice pick!"

Finch, eyeing the rearview mirror as though it were a little window on his memory, had the distinct feeling he'd seen all this before.

Now Clawvern labored to his feet, a squat, lumpish ogre waddling into the aisle. "I got a good idea!" he squealed, unplugging his forefinger from his nose to make a grab for Brownie's cap. "Let's pee in his hat and throw it out the winder!"

Now you know! piped the tiny muse on Finch's shoulder. *Now you know, now you know!*

And that's when Finch slammed on the brakes and sent Clawvern tumbling ass over teacups up the aisle, breaking his left arm in two places.

"I thought I seen a c-c-cat," Finch explained that evening in the poolroom to the fuming Buster, who had just plunked down forty-seven dollars to have Clawvern's arm set. "It run right a-c-c-c-cross the r-r-r- . . . "

Clawvern, tearstained and sniveling at his father's side, adorned now from his shoulder to his wrist by nine pounds of plaster, declared that *he* never seen no shitten cat—and kicked his uncle smartly in the shin for emphasis.

"Next time," Buster snarled through clenched teeth, as he dragged Clawvern off by his uninjured limb, "break the goddamn *cat's* arm, will ya!"

Finch was glad Clawvern had kicked him, because the pain in his ankle put a damper on his happiness and kept him from laughing at them right out loud.

Things are not always as they seem, and so it was with Goldie Skirvin, who for all her failings in the areas of personal hygiene and household sanitation—and they were monumental, the stuff of local legend—was, within the narrow limits of her power, a good and certainly a loving mother. Thus it was that every morning before bus time for the next several weeks, she spent half an hour combing coal oil through Brownie's curls, a remedy that had the doubly salutary effects of killing his cooties while simultaneously keeping his other persecutors at a respectful distance.

Not that Brownie was the first to reap the benefits of Goldie's nurturing. Hadn't she about brained Waldo with the frying pan that time he tried to whip Irmadene for getting herself in a family way by some of them Toomes County scallywags? And hadn't she took a whole carton of cigarettes every week of the world to Ronnie and Donnie, her two oldest boys, when they was in jail for breaking into Pincherd's feed store, summer before last? And didn't Bernice, her oldest girl, that was doing real good working in the buckle factory up in Hamilton, Ohio, send her the sweetest Mother's Day card last year and write "SWAK," for "Sealed With A Kiss," on the outside of the envelope? Goldie had even set up half the night giving a sugar-tit to that sorry Myrtle's little baby Elmo when it was colicky the other week, while Chump and Myrtle, the sorry things, was up there in the bed a-wallering to where they rattled the lid on the chamber pot. And if she did have to say so her own self, she took a whole lot better care than *he* did of Waldo's poor old one-armed daddy, Popaw Skirvin, which wasn't no baby she would admit but which was worse than one, the way he messed hisself so bad they'd had to move him out of the house into the stripping room.

But it was for little Brownie that Goldie reserved the roomiest corner of her capacious heart. Because he was so tiny and delicate—and maybe just because she'd so loved holding him, such a baby doll he was—she'd kept him on the breast till he was nearly three, all night long night after night till he'd sucked her dry as a shucky poppet, him lying there in her lap gazing up at her so solemn and grave with that brown unwavering study, as though he saw something deep inside her, something no eyes but his had ever seen. I'm old and ugly and plumb wore out, she used to tell herself sometimes, and this pretty little thing is the only one in all the world, the only one in all my life, that ever really knowed me.

So she loved Brownie best of all, and when that nice young Mr. Fronk came to the door early on a September Saturday and asked her could he take the boy f-f-fishing, she never thought a thing about it, seeing as how (she said later) he looked to her like the harmlessest thing that ever was, standing there on the front step with his little hat in his hands, just a-stuttering and a-twitching. Which all goes to show a person, don't it, that you can't depend on nothing in this day and age.

Finch came almost every Saturday after that. He and the boy would go off down to the river with their fishing poles on their shoulders, carrying the minnow bucket between them, Finch with a little breakfast of baloney sandwiches or Moon Pies or cheese and crackers for them in his pocket, and they'd be gone till up around noon, when Goldie would see them working their way slowly back up the hill through the warm late-summer sunshine, stopping under every shade tree so Finch could rest his heart.

And when they'd got close enough to see Goldie standing in the doorway of the house, watching them, they'd stop and wave, and whichever one was carrying the stringer of fish would hold it up so she could see that they'd caught some, and she'd wave back and then go to the stove and put on a frying pan of lard, to have the grease hot when they got there. She liked her fish rolled in cornmeal, and Finch said that suited him just f-f-fine (though he scarcely ever actually ate any, because, to tell the truth, his stomach still hadn't strengthened to the point that it could handle the state of Goldie's kitchen), so that was how she fixed them.

It being Saturday, Chump and Waldo would've already went to town, thank the Lord, to get drunk, but Myrtle would always say, Well, yes, she guessed she would *try* a little taste of fish, although she did *perfer* her fish rolled in *flahr* and fried in *bacon* grease—and then she would set right there and eat three or four pieces like they was going out of style.

Then Goldie would have to fry up some for Myrtle's little twins Stella Mae and Mae Stella (about the only thing Goldie and Myrtle agreed on was that names *was* getting awful skeerce nowadays), and the twins would slip bites to Baby Elmo (which they wasn't supposed to do, because Elmo was still on the titty, and milk and fish is poison, y'know, when you mix them), and Goldie's second girl Irmadene sometimes come over from Toomes County with her bosoms all pooched out of the top of her dress like half of Burdock County—half the men, anyhow—hadn't done seen more of them already than they had any business seeing. And old Aunt Nepp Slackert and her idjit boy Cousin Harold was liable to show up from down at the poorhouse in time for a little snack of fish, and Goldie would always send Brownie out to the stripping room with a piece or two for Popaw, along with a dipperful of cistern water in case he was to get a bone in his old throat.

So they would all have quite a good feast, and Goldie did love the way her little boy's eyes would shine so big and bright when, between mouthfuls of fish, he would tell his new friend Mr. Fronk about his pet black game-cock Joe Louis (whose fate, time would shortly prove, was that he'd soon be slashed to chicken salad in one of Claude's Sunday afternoon bird-lovers' convocations), or about the rusty old red wagon he'd found under the porch when they tore it off for firewood (Finch's eyes misted over at that; he was remembering Ott and Maudie and a Christmas of long ago), or about how he was teaching Cousin Harold (who was thirty-two years old but, as even Aunt Nepp admitted, "kinely back'ard") to tie his own shoelaces.

And Goldie noticed, as a mother would, that this nice Mr. Fronk fairly beamed whenever he looked upon her boy, and that he always had some little trinket for him in his pocket, a candy cane or a yo-yo or a water pistol or a pencil box, and that sometimes when he reached out to pat the boy on the cheek, his hand would tremble like a leaf. She wondered a little at all this, but at last—because she cared so deeply for the boy herself, and also, perhaps, because she enjoyed a good fish dinner now and then as much as anybody—she listened to the vibrant, thrumming chords of the mothersong within her and concluded—quite correctly, as it happens—that Finch loved her boy for the son he'd never have and that there wasn't no harm in him whatsoever, not in no way, shape, or form.

Which all goes to show a person, don't it now?

Meanwhile, on Finch's school bus things had taken, remarkably, a turn for the better. For thanks to one of those sweet little ironies by which Providence reminds us that there is some justice after all, the more vehemently Clawvern Craycraft insisted that Finch's c-c-cat had been a fiction, that there had been no c-c-cat at all, and that Finch had slammed on his brakes for the specific purpose of breaking Clawvern's arm, the higher Finch's stock rose among his passengers and the more precipitously Clawvern's plummeted. Believing Clawvern, even the surliest of his fellows revised in an upwardly direction their low opinion of their driver: any grown man, their instincts told them, who would deliberately set out to break a twelve-year-old boy's arm with a school bus was not to be taken lightly.

And, Harry Tom Powers warned, if Clawvern didn't hush his goddamn pissing and moaning about that goddamn cat, Harry Tom would personally be forced to break Clawvern's other arm for him, and then the little dipshit would have to pick his goddamn nose with his goddamn feet.

In the face of these (and many similar) civilities, Clawvern repaired, more or less permanently, to the furthermost corner of his seat to sulk and to carry on his exploratory nasal probings *in camera,* glaring at the back of Finch's head as if he hoped his very eyebeams might knock that inconsequential article off his uncle's shoulders.

Now for the first time ever, Finch found himself looking forward to the daily bus runs. To his inexpressible delight, Brownie had seemed to understand right away that he had a new friend and protector. Reeking of coal oil—for all that mattered to the doting Finch—he began the very morning after Clawvern's mishap to take the seat on the bus directly behind the driver's seat—in the rearview, his grave little face appeared to be just at

Finch's shoulder, as though the wee fabled bird itself had come at last—and from that day forward the seat was his alone.

By the return trip that afternoon, the two of them were shyly passing the time of day as they rode along, and by the following afternoon, a Friday, Finch, his heartbeat quickening almost alarmingly, heard himself inquire whether Brownie might like to do a little f-fishing one of these days. Yessirree, said the boy, he sure would, and Finch said, Well, how about t-tomorrow? And so they embarked together upon the happiest season of their lives.

For the rest of his days, Finch lived for Saturday mornings. All week long, on the school bus, he and the boy planned their next outing, earnestly considering—and reconsidering, and reconsidering—which holes they'd fish this week, what bait they'd use, what kind of snacks they'd take along, how many fish they intended to catch. On Friday night, Finch could hardly close his eyes, and on many a Saturday morn he spent the last hour before dawn sitting in the car a hundred yards up the road from the homeplace, with the headlights off and the motor running, while he eagerly scanned the eastern horizon for the first pale blessed hint of daylight, so that not a single minute of the precious morning would be wasted.

Intuitively, Finch understood that the less Claude knew about his new affection, the better would be its chances to grow and thrive and prosper. So as best he could, he kept his happiness out of harm's way, slipping out of the poolroom early each Saturday morning before Claude came in to open up and making sure he was back in time to rack balls and tend his spittoons for the Saturday afternoon crowd.

Finch tried to steer clear of Waldo Skirvin, too. Not that, ordinarily, Waldo would've cared—or even noticed—that someone had performed some small kindness for his child. But in return for a roof over his head and a sufficiency of intoxicants to keep him in a more or less continual state of oblivion, Waldo was Claude's bondsman and devoted minion, and if, in some soggy recess of his mind, he were to stumble across the notion that there was something going on that his indulgent proprietor would want to know about, or any little enormity he could perpetrate that might ingratiate him with that eminence, he would not scruple to discharge the office.

Thus did that glorious autumn slip away and the golden Saturdays go tumbling by. And sometimes it seemed to Finch, sitting there on the bank of the Yonder with the boy chattering gladsomely beside him, as their bobbers danced in the current among the drifting autumn leaves, sometimes it seemed to him that he'd lived his whole life for just these moments, that all his fear and loneliness and suffering were but a long, uneasy dream, and that his present happiness was the only reality there had ever been in all the everlasting history of the world.

Sundays—cockfight day, that fall—were the longest day of Finch's week, because on Sunday both Claude and Waldo hung around the barn at the homeplace all day long, and there was no chance at all that he and the boy could be together.

Waldo was the trainer and cornerman for Claude's stable of feathered warriors, which for all their unappeasable bellicosity when they were securely snaffled at a safe distance from one another in the front yard of the homeplace, nonetheless sometimes exhibited a singular meekness of spirit in actual combat situations. (The Sunday that poor Joe Louis went into the tank, Brownie had snuck up to the barn just in time to see his august parent scoop up the limp and bloodied bird and take its beak between his lips and seem to blow it up like a rooster-shaped balloon, to the robust cheers of a crowd of men clutching bouquets of greenbacks in their fists—all to no avail, for moments later Joe Louis's opponent deflated him again, this time for good and all.) Rumor had it that their want of pluck owed something to Waldo's practice of surreptitiously introducing, suppository style, certain soporifics, muscle relaxants, and deadweights—once, it was said, a four-ounce plumb bob—into the hindmost apertures of his paladins. And indeed, it must be owned that Claude, who, ever the considerate host, covered the little wagers by means of which the other sporting gentlemen demonstrated their support of these wholesome athletic endeavors, did seem to reveal, now and then, a remarkable clairvoyance as to their outcome, and profited accordingly.

But as busy as Claude was on Sundays with his social responsibilities, Finch knew from long experience that his half-brother's muddy yellow eye never missed a trick; and even Waldo, whose Sunday duties obliged him to maintain at least a minimal level of sobriety, would be a good deal sharper than was ordinarily his habit.

One restless Sabbath, nonetheless, Finch did allow himself to go out for a little Sunday drive, in the course of which he just sort of happened inadvertently to mosey past the homeplace, where it was his amazing happiness to catch sight of Brownie sitting on the front step, playing with the yo-yo Finch had brought him the day before. Finch tooted the horn discreetly as he passed; they waved to one another, and Finch went home to his little room, which was scarcely large enough to contain the memory of that brief joy.

Brownie wasn't alone, though, in marking Finch's passage before the homeplace that afternoon. Up in the barn lot behind the house, Claude Craycraft himself had just stepped outside, momentarily alone with his always interesting thoughts, to take a meditative leak among the parked cars and pickup trucks of his guests. He too noted the Plymouth's passing, the faint tootling of the horn, the furtive wave.

Now who's he honkin' at? Claude mused, contemplatively hosing the dust off the hubcap of somebody's spanking new '47 Chevy. It occurred to him that Finch had maybe taken a shine to Goldie Skirvin or Myrtle Slackert, but he dismissed the thought as quickly as it came when, in the little adding machine that served him for a mind, he totaled up those ladies' personal attractions and found that—unless you counted Goldie's all too natural perfume, or the single gold tooth that prominently graced Myrtle's otherwise almost toothless smile—the sum came to absolute dead zero. Nah, Claude reckoned, buttoning up; the high and mighty little shit-ass likely thinks he's way too good for Myrt and Goldie.

"You keep a eye on him," Claude instructed Buster, later that day. "We don't want some little shit-ass of a Fronk to disgrace the name of Craycraft."

Came a cold, rainy Saturday morning in November and, the fishing being less than promising, Finch put the boy in the Plymouth and took him to the Poll Parrot shoe store in Limestone and bought him a new pair of high-tops with heel and toe taps, and then to Western Auto and bought him a fish knife with a special hook-remover blade, and then to the barbershop—Goldie's coal oil treatments having finally dislodged the colony of tiny squatters from his scalp—for the first store-bought haircut of his life, and then to the Belchert's Café for two chili dogs and a Dr. Pepper.

Afterward, as they made their way back to the car along Limestone's rain-wet sidewalks, Brownie suddenly paused and tucked his little hand into Finch's only slightly larger one and piped, "Know what, Mr. Fuffronk?"—that being his innocent transliteration of the way Finch himself pronounced his name—"Them was the best chili dogs that ever I et!" They walked on, hand in hand, the new shoes ticktocking along like a dollar watch, Finch's heart filled near to bursting with paternal pride.

And so intent were they upon each other—or, if you will, so powerful was the heady reek of Florida Water rising from Brownie's slick new haircut—that as they crossed the street with the traffic light at the corner of Main and Bank, they didn't see or even catch a whiff of Buster Craycraft's dead wagon, though they passed beneath its very snout while it sat, throbbing and muttering, waiting for the light to change.

But Buster, at the wheel, saw *them,* you may be sure, and when he did he turned to his passenger—none other than Clawvern of the broken wing, who'd come to town with Buster that day to have his cast removed—and shook his head, clucked his tongue, curled his lip, seized Clawvern's knee and squeezed it affectionately enough to make him wince, and said, "Holdin' hands, ain't that cute! You keep a eye on that little shit-ass, hon. Daddy *said* he was up to somethin'!"

"Holdin' hands, who'd-a thought it!" Claude Craycraft exulted, rubbing his own hands together as gleefully as a sorcerer over a seething cauldron when Buster and Clawvern drew him back by the pissery to report their uncle's latest transgression across the bounds of human decency. "I always knew he was some kinda gizmo! But Lord, boys, ain't it a blessing, there ain't a drop of Craycraft blood in him!"

Still, Claude was a bookmaker, not a gambler; he liked short odds better than long and a sure thing best of all—and he didn't see a sure thing here, not just yet. Patience, that was the trick. Wait till the bird was in the hand, where a man could get a-holt of it by the shorthairs.

Finch, then, remained, for the time being, blissfully at large, free to perpetrate new outrages on an unsuspecting Christian citizenry. If he felt the crosshairs of official Craycraft scrutiny upon him, well, that was nothing new, and he was undaunted by it.

Indeed, if anything, he even became, in the fullness of his heart, a little bolder. When the coming of early winter drove him and Brownie from the riverbank, Finch, casting about in his mind for something to occupy their Saturday mornings, hit upon the Limestone Opera House, a crumbling, rat-infested old vaudeville theater that now showed triple-feature westerns twenty-four hours a day, a dime a ticket, for the enlightenment of a handful of snoring winos and derelicts who couldn't quite finance a thirty-five-cent bed at the Star Hotel, which was upstairs in the same building. By a few minutes after eight o'clock each Saturday morning, Finch and his little companion would be settled in their second-row seats, gnawing on three-day-old popcorn and cheering the heroics of Johnny Mack Browne or Wild Bill Elliott or Bob Steele or Lash LaRue or, on really good Saturdays, the great Gene, the great Roy.

For Finch, who'd been an old man since the day he was born, these were the Saturdays he'd been waiting for all his life. During his own boyhood—if you could call it that—Maudie, fearful that the excitement might prove too much for him, had never let him go to the picture show in Needmore, so it was all as new to him as it was to Brownie. If he was Brownie's spiritual father during all his other waking hours, while they were in the Opera House he was just another little boy, pal of his pal, his buddy's buddy. When the lights went down and their looming heroes took their turn upon the screen, Finch and Brownie hunkered low in their seats and leaned toward one another in the dark as small boys—and lovers—will, shoulders touching, heads together, hearts racing side by side to the rhythm of the pounding hooves of Wild Bill's pinto paint.

And that was the tableau on the last Saturday morning before Christmas, when down the darkened aisle sidled a squat little figure who stole like a diminutive gumshoe into the row of seats just behind them and stood for a long moment looking directly down on the oblivious pair, as if he contemplated collaring them on the spot for some nameless indecency or crime. The interloper's aspect was obscure in the flickering shadows, but an observant witness might have noted that his forefinger was firmly implanted in his nose, and that when at last he moved along, he left hanging in the stale air the faint dead-wagon fetor of putrescence.

On the afternoon of Christmas Eve, Finch went to the bank and drew twenty dollars out of his little savings account (he'd been putting away ten dollars a month ever since he moved to town—for his funeral, he supposed; not for his old age, certainly), and then he drove to Limestone, where he bought Brownie a Red Ryder model Daisy BB gun at the Western Auto store. While the clerk went off to get a box, Finch took up the little rifle and put it to his shoulder and sighted down the barrel, and imagined he was Wild Bill

Elliott in the last Red Ryder movie they had seen, and that Brownie was at his side with a feather in his curls, playing Little Beaver. Later, driving home to Needmore with the package on the seat beside him, Finch was all aglow with happiness and pride; you could've followed him through the dusky evening like the star of Bethlehem.

Alas, his happiness was even shorter-lived than usual; it went out like a light when, as he tried to creep unnoticed through the crowded poolroom to the back stairs, his sharp-eyed brother goosed him with a cue stick and hollered, "Whoops!" Finch threw up his hands, and the package slipped from beneath his coat and clattered to the floor.

"Whoa there, Goosey! I believe you dropped the set outta that diamond ring I gave you!" Elbowing Finch aside, Claude bent and picked up the package himself and squinted at the label. "Why, a BB gun, is it! You wasn't planning to shoot yourself, I hope?"

"Oh, n-no!!" Finch said, half apologetically, as though he hated to be such a wet blanket. Beyond Claude, he saw Waldo Skirvin at the bar, mercifully a-snooze, his head pillowed on his arm. "It's j-just a Ch-Christmas p-p-p-p—"

"A Christmas present!" Claude interjected, with a grin that was a hideous, leering mockery of the convivialities of the season. "Bless your heart, it's for that sweet grandboy of mine, that little Clawvern! You just leave that right here with me, baby brother," he went on, tucking the package firmly under his arm, "and I'll be old Santy for you and put it under his tree tonight!" Horrified, Finch undertook to utter a tiny peep of protest, but Claude said not to thank him, because what were brothers for? He stashed the BB gun out of sight behind the bar; then, herding Finch along before him by means of a couple of discreet pokes in the ribs with the cue stick, he steered him out of earshot of the other players, where he took the liberty of politely reminding him (waggling the cue stick under Finch's nose for emphasis) that even a Skirvin has his pride and wouldn't necessarily be overjoyed when some rich nabob with bad morals came along, throwing his goddamn inheritance around like it wasn't no tomorrow, and tried to give one of the little Skirvins things that was way too fine for him and would spoil him rotten and hurt his daddy's feelings in the bargain, beings as Waldo wasn't in no position to give the boy so much as a hatful of shit his own self, because deep down inside Waldo was as sensitive as . . . as the next man, and would sooner see the boy do without.

"And speakin' of Waldo," Claude added as he turned back to his game, "he took a smidge too much Christmas cheer and had one of his little accidents in your pissery. So you got some catchin' up to do, my lad."

"B-Bad m-m-morals?" Finch called bleakly after him, in a voice as faint as a dying breath.

Claude, chalking up, favored him with another fraternal leer. "And a Merry Christmas to *you*, baby brother!" he called back, with vast holiday bonhomie. "Yes, by god, and a Happy New Year, too!"

On New Year's Eve, Waldo Skirvin's proud but sensitive nature required him to heave a pint gin bottle—empty, of course—through the plate-glass window of Hunsicker's Home Furnishings, enabling him to reach inside and turn on the television set in the window display so that he and Chump could watch midget wrestling. Waldo was rewarded for this unprecedented exhibition of initiative with a forty-five-day, all-expenses-paid vacation in the Burdock County jail.

Chump, though he stoutly maintained that all in the world *he* had done was hand Waldo the bottle and urge him to throw it, would be sharing the accommodations for the first thirty days of Waldo's temporary respite from the liquid vortex that was his life.

So for the next several weeks a principal impediment to Finch's happiness would be in cold storage, out of the picture. Yet the development failed to cheer him. Ever since Christmas, Finch had labored under a heavy fore-boding, unable to shake the feeling that something ominous and menacing was afoot, stalking him. People were looking at him differently, he was sure, watching him out of the corners of their eyes, talking about him behind his back. Instead of teasing him the way they used to, the Billiards crowd seemed to fall silent whenever he came in, as if teasing were too good for him. Sometimes, when he was sweeping up the poolroom, he would feel their eyes on him, like the weight of an unfriendly hand.

Once, glancing up, he thought he saw—he was *positive* he'd seen—Geezer Wirtschaffner lean toward his neighbor at the bar and, still eyeing Finch in that knowing way, mouth the words *"Bad morals!"* while poor Finch stood there trembling in his shoes, he knew not why.

On the first school day after New Year's, Burdock County awoke beneath a downy five-inch blanket of un-tracked snow. No school. By the following day, the snow was a foot deep and still falling; no school. That night the temperature dropped below zero, where it was to remain, unprecedented in local memory, for the ensuing thirty-two days, while the Yonder River froze solid for the first time ever. Meanwhile, the snow kept falling until it reached the unheard-of depth of twenty-one inches. No school, no school, no school.

Finch was desolate. Some guardian instinct had advised him to keep his distance from Brownie after Christmas, so the last time they'd been together was the day Clawvern had detected them in unholy congress with Wild Bill Elliott at the Opera House.

Finch missed the boy desperately, but he had consoled himself with the thought that school would soon reopen, and then he'd see him twice a day no matter what. Now, imprisoned in the poolroom by the snow and cold, it seemed to Finch that his whole life had frozen in place, holding him suspended like the fish at the bottom of the Yonder.

The weather, having driven Needmore society indoors, straightway set about to drive it stark staring mad with cabin fever. The Billiards crowds grew larger by the day and more restive and surlier—ugly to look at, uglier to deal with. By the end of their second week in captivity, fistfights and scuffles were breaking out among them almost hourly, and billiard balls flew through the air like snowballs; the sawed-off, leaded cue stick that Claude kept behind the bar for a coldcock was regularly employed, as Claude happily rapped out a steady tattoo on the skulls of his irascible clientele. Cringing and cowering, Finch went about his work, trying desperately to remain beneath the fray, out of sight and out of mind. You could hardly see daylight through the little black cloud that fulminated above his head.

Out in the countryside, meanwhile, frozen poultry had begun dropping from the roosts like feathered coconuts, and livestock was expiring at an apocalyptic rate: cows freezing upright in the barnyard, hog wallows turning overnight into shallow gravesites as hard as concrete for half-buried pigs as stiff as alabaster statues of themselves. Buster's dead wagon, a heavy rig with dual wheels and a winch for pulling itself out of trouble, had the snowy back roads pretty much to itself. Cruising through town with a truckload of belly-up carcasses, Buster might have been mistaken for a dealer in some macabre line of four-poster beds.

Late one Saturday afternoon in the bitter dregs of January, the winter claimed its first poolroom victim when the aged Delano, having taken a bad cold, relinquished the ghost. Delano's passing was attended by a circle of mourners, most of whom, anticipating the worst, had already got a head start on the wake and were as drunk as fiddlers. As the old dog breathed his last and slipped into a state of dignity that had been resolutely denied him in his lifetime, a ragged hue and cry arose among the survivors to the general effect that Finch was now a widow . . . which prompted Buster to advance the theory that Delano had died of a broken heart, upon hearing the rumor that Finch was partial to . . . well, Buster would rather not say, due to delicate family considerations.

"I knowed this boy's daddy," Geezer Wirtschaffner reminded them all, waggling that bony forefinger at Finch so emphatically that once again, for the merest fraction of a moment, Finch thought Geezer was on his side. "Knowed him well," Geezer went on. "He had as fine a head of hair as ever I put a scissor to. You ain't half the man he was, sonny boy. It wasn't one ounce of sissy in that old man's body."

Claude, during this interval, had grieved his fill. "Junior," he snapped, "go pitch that dog in the dead wagon." He turned to Finch. "You go to your room, Petunia. I won't be needin' you this evening."

Dejectedly, Finch followed orders, trudging off through a hail of insult and disparagement, knowing full well he'd have to pay some awful price for this unwelcome night off. Upstairs, he flung himself across his little bed and fell, in time, into an uneasy sleep and a dream in which he and Brownie galloped a great white stallion across an endless western plain. He was awakened just after midnight—closing time—by a fearsome pounding on the floor beneath his bed; Claude was downstairs hammering on the ceiling with the butt of a cue stick.

"Hump your ass down here, Daisy Mae!" Claude shouted up the stairwell. "I wanna have a word or three with you!"

Finch found his brother behind the bar at the till, counting his receipts. The poolroom was in its predictably deplorable Saturday night condition—empties everywhere, spittoons overflowing, the floor carpeted with cigarette butts—and Finch knew without even looking that numerous little accidents would have transpired in the pissery.

Claude went right to the point. "I tell you what it is, bub," he said. "Some way or the other, people around here has got the notion you're up to somethin' with that little Skirvin."

"B-Big brother," Finch pleaded, "you d-don't think I . . . "

"It don't make jack-shit what *I* think. There ain't but two schools of thought you need to worry about, see. One of 'em says you oughta be tarred and feathered, and the othern is holdin' out for corncobs and turpentine."

But, he continued (while Finch clung to the bar and tried not to faint dead away), Claude Craycraft was the kind of hairpin that done his duty as he seen it, so he had just took the bull by the shorthairs and rode out to the homeplace the other day with Buster and told Goldie Skirvin just exactly how the land laid, and him and her agreed that the thing to do was to pack up her and the boy and take them over to Limestone and put them on the Greyhound and send them up to Hamilton, Ohio, to live with Bernice, which Junior done this very afternoon at Claude's own expense—set him back eleven dollars and seventy cents for the bus tickets—and now what Finch was to do was just lay low and keep his nose clean and mind his P's and Q's while Claude undertook to put the quietus on the turpentiners, and maybe by the time Finch was fifty-five or sixty years old (heh heh), all this would've blowed over.

"They've done g-gone?" Finch gulped.

"This very afternoon," Claude said. "But they say the boy has got TB and ain't long for this world anyhow. So you won't be missing much."

"T-t-t-t-tee b-b-b-b-b-b—?"

"Bee," Claude finished for him. "So"—he handed Finch his mop and bucket—"you better just get started swabbin' out your pissery, Mr. High and Mighty, and leave the dirty work to me."

Finch would've turned to go, but Claude still held the handle of the bucket.

"And lookahere, John D., they tell me you've got money in the bank" (indeed, Claude had known about Finch's little bank account from the very first, and over the years had formed the habit of mentally calculating its growth so that at any given moment he knew its value almost to the penny— and as Finch's next of kin, considered it practically his own), "they tell me you've got a wad of money in the bank, but I'd take it very personal if you was to send a goddamn nickel of it to that poor child, which won't live long enough to spend it anyhow."

Finch nodded mutely, and Claude turned him loose. Bemused, he watched him go, feeling that on the whole, it had been a very satisfying interview.

The weather broke on the following Tuesday, with a vengeance. A warm southern breeze had swept across the commonwealth in the night, and by midmorning it had brought a steady downpour with it, which continued, more or less unabated, for a solid week. The snow vanished almost overnight, but the ground beneath it was frozen so hard and so deep that it carried off the water like a tin roof; innocent freshets became instant raging torrents, dry branches roaring sluices of destruction. The ice in the Yonder broke up quickly and then formed monumental ice jams that clogged the channel and forced the burgeoning river from its banks. Flash floods abounded, and half the roads in Burdock County were soon under water. School would have to wait.

It was all the same to Finch; he was ready whenever they were. Let it happen.

Deep inside himself, Finch had changed almost as dramatically as the weather. He had peered into the shallows (there were no depths) of the Enemy's very soul and had found nothing there but obdurate, pitiless rancor. He'd never see his boy again; not in this life, he knew that. But with that grievous knowledge came a kind of grace; there being nothing left to live for, he was released at last from the fear of dying and in its stead was gripped by the savage courage of the implacable avenger. He would put his faith in a just and angry God and be ready to play his small part when the time came.

When at last the skies had wrung themselves dry and a pale, cheerless winter sun emerged, the fractious creeks crept grudgingly back inside their banks, taking with them as many outhouses and chicken coops as they could get their watery clutches on. One by one, the back roads cleared; on Valentine's Day—exactly forty-one days after that first infamous snowflake fell to earth—the school board announced that as of tomorrow morning, school was back in session.

Chump Slackert, meanwhile, having served his time and been declared a free man, had for the last two weeks been exercising his First Amendment rights by ventilating to all the world his loud assurance that the first thing his brother-in-law Waldo Skirvin planned to do when *he* got out of jail was to tear Finch Fronk a brand-new nether orifice.

On the face of it, this report needn't have troubled Finch all that much; even if Waldo—who'd have his liberty at noon tomorrow—managed to stay sober long enough to carry out Chump's threat, Finch was prepared to suffer and was eager—more than eager—to expire. But his own revenge took precedence over Waldo's, and if he intended to exact it, tomorrow morning might be the last opportunity. So that evening he slipped off to the drugstore and bought a Big Chief tablet and a number two pencil and an envelope and a stamp, and late that night, sitting on the edge of his bed with the naked light bulb dangling above him like an inspiration, he wrote a sort of valentine:

> *Last Will & Testimate I Clarence Fronk*
> *leave all my wordly goods to Mrs. J. T.*
> *Mooney on Railroad St. in Limestone.*
> *Sined Clarence M. Fronk Feb 14 1948*

Finch folded the paper carefully and put it in the envelope, along with his little bankbook showing that, with interest, there was eight hundred twenty-six dollars and thirty-four cents in the account. He sealed the envelope and addressed it to Mrs. Mooney (eight hundred and twenty smackers, he reflected, would buy a lot of pork), and as he stamped it and laid it aside, a kind of serenity descended upon him. He allowed himself a few scant moments to enjoy it, and then he turned out the light and took himself to bed, went to sleep without thought, and slept without dreams.

Promptly at six-thirty in the morning, Finch awoke refreshed, dressed himself, and went out into the foggy, bone-chilling dark of the morning, dropping the envelope in the mailbox as he passed the post office. ("He left it all to that old two-dollar flat-back, the little pansy!" Claude would be heard to howl a few days later. "And never done jack-shit for his own goddamn loved ones!") Finch felt light-headed and strangely elated, as though some great and wonderful occasion were impending—the way he used to feel when he was on his way to Brownie's of a Saturday morning. He noted a faint intimation of pressure blooming in his breast, but there was more in it of vengeful exultation than there was of pain or dread.

Finch's bus was always the first out on the morning run, because he had a nine-mile drive up the county highway before he turned off onto the river road and picked up Harry Tom Powers, his first passenger—the same Harry

Tom who'd administered Finch's baptism by buttermilk, five dismal years ago. After Harry Tom were the two Barley boys, who shared a congenital predisposition for motion sickness and regularly left Finch a token of their esteem between the seats. Then came, in rapid succession, untold numbers of Brattons, Creeches, Patmores, and Foosneckers, the girls all screechy little harpies, the boys pint-sized assassins, spitball terrorists.

Finch hated them each and every one, equally and unequivocally.

Or so he assures himself as he pilots the bus through the darkened streets of Needmore. At the city limits, shifting into high, he feels the pressure tighten its grip around his heart and the first sharp stitch of pain, an ice pick between the ribs. Finch welcomes it and pushes on steadfastly into the darkest hour before the dawn.

After the Foosneckers, the next pickup will be the Kinchlow girl, a blue-eyed blonde whose sweet-sixteen beauty has sometimes set off a certain stirring of the blood even in Finch's own meager loins—but whose misfortune it is to be the daughter of the very Kinchlow who'd robbed Finch of his milk cow, back when the world was young. And so of course she has to go—as do the Pennister boys, who come next, and the Gibbses, and Geezer Wirtschaffner's grandson Johnnie Buckles and some others, and, finally, Buster's nasty little brood. Then will come the long downgrade, and the river.

The county highway snakes along the piney ridges north of town, now and then breaking into the open to reveal the eastern horizon limned by the first pale hint of daybreak. At the Zion Crossroads, where Maudie's old church stands lonely sentinel, Finch takes inventory of his symptoms and determines that his condition is progressing satisfactorily: there's an aching, iron band of pressure around his upper body, like a bruise so deep it goes clear through; he's sick at his stomach, sick as a poisoned crow; his breath is coming hard and fast and short; his puny little arms weigh forty pounds apiece and ache right to the fingertips. And although it's brutally cold inside the bus, his long-handle underwear is drenched with sweat; he's ablaze with fever, yet he's shivering violently, as though someone were walking on his grave.

When you need mercy, importunes a small, familiar voice at his right ear, *be merciful! Take pity! Take pity!*

Finch presses on, clinging grimly to the wheel like a sea captain in a heavy gale, as though he were trying to out-distance his tiny counselor's exhortations. But when he swings off onto the river road, the admonition is still with him, a faint hope striving desperately to make itself come true: *When you need mercy . . .*

The old Powers place, a huge, dilapidated frame farmhouse at the top of the first rise, immediately looms into view above the fog. Finch can see the yellow light of a coal oil lamp in the kitchen window and, as he urges his bus on up the grade, the shadowy, hulking shape of Harry Tom lumbering across the front yard toward the roadside. By the time the bus tops the rise, Harry Tom is standing by the mailbox, yawning hugely in the headlights. Finch downshifts for the stop, and his foot is already poised above the brake, when—*Be merciful!* implores the voice. *Take pity!*

Suddenly—he couldn't say why for all the Mrs. Mooneys in the history of the world—Finch pops the clutch and floors the accelerator; the bus slews crazily, spewing mud and gravel; fighting the wheel, he somehow finds the strength to keep it on the road; it rights itself and roars past Harry Tom, his yawn now a gaping oval of astonishment.

Take pity! Take pity!

Finch rushes on into the darkness, the gathering dawn at his back. A few hundred yards down the road, the bus plunges headlong into a pocket of fog so dense that he can only steer by memory and instinct, but he doesn't falter; moments later he breaks into the clear again, his foot still mashing the accelerator to the floorboard. Amazingly, even in that brief interval the night has been lifted just a little by the advancing wedge of daylight. The Barley boys float swiftly past the windshield, their faces twin balloons wearing identical stunned expressions. Finch's heart labors mightily, and the pain in his little bosom is colossal, yet Finch himself seems to hover just above it, weightless as a jockey on a sprinting racehorse. The old bus gains speed, slipping and slewing, floundering perilously through the curves. Other faces flash by as fast as fence posts, Brattons and Creeches and Patmores and Foosneckers all slack-jawed and agog, the angel Kinchlow like a roadside statue of the Saint of the Wayfaring Stranger, indiscriminately blessing whoever happens by.

And with each passing face, Finch feels his burden of bitterness and melancholy lifting from him, giving way to something that almost partakes of joy, just as the night gives way to dawn.

There go the Pennisters—four gangling scarecrow silhouettes loping across the front yard, vainly waving their skinny arms—there go the Gibbses, there goes Little Johnny Buckles, bug-eyed as a tree frog.

Meanwhile, three-quarters of a mile down the road from the onrushing bus, Buster Craycraft, having survived yet another night of connubial bliss in the arms of the divine Iota, groggily climbs behind the wheel of the dead wagon, pursuant to an early-morning engagement with a none-too-recently deceased mule over in Toomes County. Iota has succeeded in driving his children—his and Chick Greevey's children—out of the house to meet the bus; they're assembled in a restless little knot beside the road, entertaining themselves by bashing one another over the head with lunch boxes and schoolbooks. The two boys, Clabber and Clawvern, have already reduced all three girls—Claudia, Claudette, and Claudine—to tears of pain and outrage; Clawvern is evidently attempting to make a croquet post of Baby Claudine by hammering her into the front yard with his geography text.

Buster, lowering his window, maneuvers the dead wagon out of the barn lot onto the roadway. "Hey, shit-heel!" he yells at Clawvern as he passes before the house. "If you don't cut that out, I'm gonna peel your ass when I get home!"

And if Buster hadn't glanced up the road at just that moment, those could've been the last words he ever spoke. Because here comes Uncle Finch's school bus careering round the curve below the house, headlights like owl's eyes in the morning gloom, highballing right straight up the middle of the road as though Buster and the dead wagon aren't there. Buster instinctively slam-shifts into bulldog and stomps on the accelerator, and takes the dead wagon directly to the ditch, as the school bus barrels past it on the left.

For a fraction of a fraction of a second, Buster and Finch look full into each other's face, no more than a yard apart. ("He was white as a onion!" Buster will testify later at the coroner's inquest. "And you coulda knocked his eyeballs off with a broomstick!") Then the unpeopled windows of the bus flick past like empty picture frames, the dead wagon comes to rest in the ditch, and Buster leans out his window and looks back in time to see the rear end of the school bus fishtail crazily in the road, scattering Clawvern and the rest of Iota's flock like barnyard fowl.

But Finch's wheels somehow find the graveled ruts again all by themselves—for the ghastly face that Buster saw was already the face of a corpse, and there is a dead hand at the tiller, and a dead man's foot still jamming the accelerator to the floorboards—and in the blink of an eye the bus has dropped over the brow of the hill and disappeared down the long grade toward the river, even as Finch—*our* Finch, not that poor dead thing at the wheel—is borne aloft by a cloud of tiny golden birds crying, in a thousand thousand sweet discordant little voices, *Per-chick-o-ree! Per-chick-o-reeee! Take pity! Take pity!*

From the hilltop, the Yonder valley spreads itself tremendously, bathed in wan, pellucid light; the swollen river, clotted with black, undulating mats of drift, waits below, shreds of fog rising ghostlike from its gloomy waters. Finch watches from a great height as the bus, freewheeling now, riding the ruts, galumphs almost joyously down the slope toward its destiny, comically waggling its plump behind as it waddles along from shoulder to shoulder, a jolly cartoon jelly bean of a school bus, like something he and Brownie might have seen one Saturday in the selected short subjects at the Opera House. Entering the curve at the bottom of the hill, with one last boomp-sadaisy flounce the bus parts company with the road and tumbles end over end down the brushy riverbank and plunges with a mighty cartoon splash into the river. In a heartbeat the murky yellow waters have closed over it, as though it had never been.

Per-chick-o-ree! Per-chick-o-reeee!

Exulting gloriously, our hero soars up and up into the breaking day. He'll be meeting Brownie soon, on some far distant shore. They're going fishing.

Printed in the United States
by Baker & Taylor Publisher Services